Mary Balogh was born in Swansea, South Wales. She now lives in Saskatchewan, where she taught for twenty years. She won the *Romantic Times* Award for Best New Regency Writer in 1985 and has since become the genre's most popular and bestselling author. Recently she has begun to write historicals, which have received critical acclaim as well. Her most recent Regency is *Lord Carew's Bride* (Signet), and *Longing* (Topaz) is her latest historical.

Jo Beverley is the author of the acclaimed Regencies *Lord Wraybourne's Betrothed* and *The Stanforth Secrets*. She has been critically hailed as an "extraordinary talent." Ms. Beverley, who lives with her family in Ottawa, Canada, now writes historical romance and is also the author of award-winning science fiction.

Sandra Heath, the daughter of an officer in the Royal Air Force, spent most of her life traveling to various European posts. She now resides in Gloucester, England, together with her husband and daughter. Her most recent Regency is *Magic at Midnight* (Signet).

Edith Layton, historical romance author, is the winner of numerous awards, including the first *Romantic Times* Award granted for Best Short Story Author in 1992.

Laura Matthews was born and raised in Pittsburgh, Pennsylvania. But after attending Brown University, she moved to San Francisco, where she lives with her architect husband, Paul. Ms. Matthews' favorite pursuits are traveling and scrounging in old bookstores for research material.

A Regency Christmas

FIVE STORIES BY

Mary Balogh

•

Jo Beverley

•

Sandra Heath

•

Edith Layton

•

Laura Matthews

A SIGNET BOOK

SIGNET
Published by the Penguin Group
Penguin Books USA Inc., 375 Hudson Street,
New York, New York 10014, U.S.A.
Penguin Books Ltd, 27 Wrights Lane,
London W8 5TZ, England
Penguin Books Australia Ltd, Ringwood,
Victoria, Australia
Penguin Books Canada Ltd, 10 Alcorn Avenue,
Toronto, Ontario, Canada M4V 3B2
Penguin Books (N.Z.) Ltd, 182–190 Wairau Road,
Auckland 10, New Zealand

Penguin Books Ltd, Registered Offices:
Harmondsworth, Middlesex, England

First published by Signet, an imprint of Dutton Signet,
a division of Penguin Books USA Inc.

First Printing, November, 1995
10 9 8 7 6 5 4 3 2 1

Contents

The Christmas Ghost
by Sandra Heath

It was on a wet and windy morning three days before Christmas that Rebecca Winterbourne first felt the frightening grip of the ghostly hand. She was alone at her brother Clifford's writing desk in the library at Abbotlea Manor, about to commence a letter, when someone seized her shoulder and shook her so roughly she dropped her quill and almost knocked the inkwell over.

Alarmed, she leapt to her feet. Her brown eyes were wide as she glanced swiftly around the deserted room. Firelight flickered over the Christmas garlands along the mantelshelf, and beyond her own reflection in the chimney breast mirror she could see the windswept gardens and grounds, but she was quite alone in the room. After a while her alarm subsided, and she sat down again, telling herself she'd imagined it.

But her concentration was too rattled for her to get on with the letter, and her attention wandered to her reflection. Her gaze became critical. She was thirty now, with long, almost black hair that of late had shown a tendency to be flecked with gray at the temples. It was a family trait, as she'd noticed from the portrait of her mother, who'd died giving birth to her. The pale complexion was also inherited, although right now the pallor was perhaps a little exaggerated. Sleepless nights had that effect. But at least she could be proud of her figure, which was still slender and enviably small-waisted, in spite of having borne two children.

She gazed at the wine velvet gown she wore. Edward had always loved to see her in warm shades of dark red, which he said brought out her brunette coloring to perfection. Tears suddenly stung her eyes. Oh, how she missed him, missed his warmth and laughter, his touch, his lovemaking. When she awoke at night and he wasn't there, the pain of loss was so great she almost couldn't bear it. But on those occasions grief sometimes turned to anger about all those wasted nights when the gaming table had more claim upon him than she did. They'd only had six years together before his death, so all those squandered hours seemed more poignant than they otherwise might. Instead of sitting in his club, he could have been with her. They could have lain naked together, making love, and sharing precious seconds; instead he lingered over the turn of another losing card. But even now she still forgave him his weakness, still adored the memory of his roguish charm and irresistible smile. He'd left her penniless, without a roof over her head, but she didn't for a moment doubt the depth of his love for her and his sons.

More tears shone in her eyes. Edward had been gone two years now, but was still so fresh in her mind that it seemed wrong to have discarded widow's weeds. But black was hardly appropriate for a woman who'd just decided to marry again. Since receiving Sir Oliver's unexpected proposal three days ago, she'd lain awake at night trying to think what to do, but at last her mind was made up.

She lowered her glance to the sheet of paper on which her letter of acceptance would soon be written.

This second marriage was hardly set to be the heavenly match her first had been. Sir Oliver Willoughby was too elderly to be the dashing hero of romance, and she wasn't a foolish young girl who'd been swept off her feet, nor would her heart ever miss a beat at the thought of the rather vain, attention-seeking man who was a friend and contemporary of her late father's. But Sir Oliver was kindly enough, which counted a great deal in her decision to accept his proposal. For the two years of her widowhood she'd been a burden on her brother's finances, and it was time to do what she could to provide for herself and her sons, especially now that her sister-in-law, Margaret, was at last expecting the child she and Clifford had longed for throughout their fourteen-year marriage. Rebecca sighed. They didn't yet know about the proposal, let alone her decision to accept, and their reaction was bound to be mixed.

Dipping the quill in the ink, she prepared to start the letter, but almost immediately the invisible hand grabbed her again, shaking her so violently that this time the inkwell would definitely have spilled if she hadn't somehow managed to rescue it.

She glanced around uneasily. "Who—who's there?" she whispered. Her heart was pounding so much she couldn't count the beats, and she was so conscious of an unseen presence that when the door opened suddenly to admit her sister-in-law, she gave a frightened scream.

But as Margaret entered, so did a great gust of wind. Rushing and whirling, it seized the neatly piled documents on Clifford's desk, tossing them around the room like a snowstorm. It was as if the gale outside had somehow become trapped in the house, and was roaring through rooms and passages, trying to find its way out again.

Rebecca pressed her hands fearfully to her mouth as the papers fluttered wildly around her head, and Margaret, who was only six weeks from being brought to bed, was so taken by surprise she could only cling to the door handle with her skirts flapping around her legs and the lace tippets of her day bonnet streaming across her face.

At last Rebecca found her tongue. "For heaven's sake close the door!" she cried.

Margaret managed to obey, and the wind stopped as suddenly as it had begun. As the papers sank in profusion all over the floor and furniture, she gave an uneasy half-laugh. "I—I've never known a draft as fierce as that before. There must be a window open somewhere."

"Yes, I suppose there must." Rebecca placed her hands on the desk to hide how much they were trembling. She felt unnerved. First there had been the hands, and then this. . . . She pulled herself together sharply. There had to be a logical explanation; indeed there was *always* a logical explanation!

Margaret surveyed the scattered documents in dismay. "Clifford will be furious—you know how fastidious he is," she said.

Rebecca got up to gather them. "He'll only be furious if he finds out," she said briskly, determined not to let events of the past few minutes cause her imagination to run riot.

Margaret helped, her voluminous chestnut dimity robe rustling as she bent. She was thirty-four, a petite, pretty redhead, with green eyes and freckles, and when the last paper had been collected, she straightened and looked hesitantly at Rebecca.

"I'm sorry I startled you. I should have knocked, I know, but I was so excited. . . ."

"Excited?"

"About something that came for you in the post. Rebecca, I don't know for sure, of course, but I'm almost certain you've been invited to the Almondsbury Park ball the day after tomorrow." Margaret placed an impressively sealed letter on the desk.

Rebecca stared at it. "It can't possibly be an invitation. I think the duchess would rather die than receive me. Unless . . ." A thought struck her. Was this Sir Oliver's doing? He was always welcome at Almondsbury Castle, and might have made a point of asking for her to be invited. Yes, the more she thought about it, the more convinced she became. He'd expect her answer before then, and if it was favorable, he'd make certain they were the center of attention at the ball, a state of affairs that would be joy to his vanity.

Margaret grew impatient. "Oh, do open it and see! I can't bear the suspense."

Splinters of ducal sealing wax fell on the desk, and then the costly vellum crackled as Rebecca began to read aloud. "December twenty-first, 1812. The Duke and Duchess of Almondsbury request the company of Mrs. Edward Winterbourne at their Christmas Eve ball at Almondsbury Park."

Margaret clapped her hands. "You're to be allowed in from the cold at last! I didn't think you could be excluded forever, not when you're a Winterbourne, and your sons are Winterbournes, too!"

Rebecca put the invitation down. "Margaret, I don't think this has anything to do with who I am now, but everything to do with who I'm about to become," she said quietly, thinking that now was as good a time as any to break the news of her impending betrothal.

Margaret was puzzled. "With who you're *about* to become? I don't understand."

"I'm going to marry Sir Oliver."

Margaret's jaw dropped. "You're what?" she said faintly.

"He's proposed to me, and I've decided to accept. I was about to write to him when you came in. I believe he's mentioned his proposal to the duke and duchess, and that's why I've suddenly appeared on the guest list."

Margaret was shaken, and had to sit down. "You and Sir *Oliver*? Oh, Rebecca, you can't! He's old enough to be your father!"

"It's best all around if I marry him. He'll provide for Matthew and Frederick, and I'll be off your hands at last."

Margaret looked earnestly at her. "Rebecca, Clifford and I don't want you 'off our hands,' as you put it, and certainly not if it means you marrying a shameless old rake who doesn't give tuppence for your children, but just wants to get you between the sheets!"

"Margaret!"

"Well, it's true. He's been giving you the glad eye ever since I can remember."

"My mind is made up."

Margaret got up. "Your father was Sir Oliver's friend, but he certainly wouldn't approve of your decision. He called him 'Lothario' Willoughby, and once described him as good-natured but totally unreliable. It was an accurate assessment, for if it came to a choice between an appointment with his Bond Street tailor and a problem concerning Matthew or Frederick, you may be certain the tailor would take precedence."

"You're wrong," Rebecca insisted, but she looked away. She wasn't approaching this match with her eyes blinkered. In return for conjugal rights, her new husband would provide her with a title, a luxurious home, and more than sufficient allowance to properly take care of her children's upbringing. It was a marriage of convenience, and Margaret was right, her father wouldn't approve at all. In fact, he'd probably have disapproved of her marriage to Edward as well, for he'd have foreseen not only the opposition and trouble it would inevitably cause, but also the penury that would ensue from Edward's addiction to gambling.

Margaret pressed her. "Please think again, Rebecca. You won't be at all happy with Sir Oliver."

"I've done little else but think about it, Margaret, and I've concluded that this marriage is right. Clifford has been supporting me ever since Edward died, and I know from when Father was alive that Abbotlea Manor isn't the most productive of estates. You're having a child of your own, so it's unthinkable of me to remain a burden. Then there's the small matter of Clifford's desire to enter politics. . . ."

"Clifford has long since given that up, Rebecca."

"Through force of circumstance, not choice."

"Don't marry Sir Oliver," Margaret pleaded.

"Look, I realize it won't be like Edward all over again."

Margaret turned away. "Forgive me for saying this, Rebecca, but Edward Winterbourne wasn't perfect either. If he'd thought more of you and his children, and less of gambling every night, he wouldn't have left you financially straitened."

"Please don't disparage him, Margaret."

"I know you loved him, and I'd like to think you'd be happy again this time, but you won't."

Beset by a mixture of indignation and acknowledgement of the truth, Rebecca looked earnestly at Margaret. "We'll quarrel if you persist, so please let's change the subject."

"Very well." Margaret picked up the invitation again. "Which gown will you wear? The strawberry silk? Or the aquamarine taffeta?"

"Neither. I'm not going to the ball," Rebecca replied firmly.

Margaret was appalled. "But you must go!"

"The duchess has only invited me in order to please Sir Oliver. I'm sure she'd rather I stayed away, and I'd certainly prefer to remain here rather than give her false smiles."

"Rebecca Winterbourne, I'll never forgive you if you show Abbotlea up by refusing to go. Society may have treated you very badly because of Edward, but that's no reason for you to sink to their level now."

Rebecca was silent for a moment, and then gave her a rueful smile. "I suppose I'll wear the strawberry silk," she said.

Margaret smiled too. "I agree, for it suits you best. At least, it used to, but you're so pale these days. . . ."

"A little rouge will rectify matters."

"True." Margaret moved to the fire, and held her hands out to the flames. "There's something I haven't mentioned. Piers Winterbourne will be at the ball as well. Or should I say, Lord Winterbourne?"

Rebecca stared at her in fresh dismay. Piers was Edward's cousin, and had much to answer for concerning her unhappiness, past and present. She found her tongue. "But he's in London, isn't he?"

"The rest of the Winterbournes are, but he's back at the castle for Christmas. Actually, it's rumored there's soon to be a Lady Winterbourne again."

Rebecca was shaken. "Piers is to marry?"

"I gather so. An heiress from Westmorland. Or is it Northumberland? Somewhere in the north, anyway, and fabulously rich."

Rebecca had to turn away. Piers was marrying? She had to say something, but could only think of being disparaging. "The lady would be best advised to remain safely in the north."

Margaret glanced at her. "You're being unfair."

"Am I?"

"Yes."

Rebecca's eyes flashed. "You surely don't expect me to be pleasant about a snake like Piers Winterbourne!"

"You may call him a snake, but he's always been more than polite to me."

"You weren't the one who presumed to marry his cousin!" Rebecca replied shortly.

"Yes, but—"

"Oh, don't be so taken in by his winning smiles and dashing charm, Margaret. Outwardly he's all that's attractive, but beneath it all he's as odious as his horrid father before him."

"Has it ever occurred to you that you might be wrong?"

"No, because I'm not," Rebecca replied crushingly. "Piers was pleasant to me while I remained plain Rebecca Newton, but he became positively savage when I reached up above my station in life to become a Winterbourne."

Margaret sighed. "I suppose this means you've changed your mind about going to the ball?"

"No, I'll still go."

"And you'll be polite to Piers if you meet him?"

"I'm not the one who was ever *im*polite."

"Have it that way if you choose, just promise me you'll be civil to him."

"Of course I will, Margaret, why are you in such a stew about it? What does it matter if I'm amiable or not?"

"I'm not in a stew," Margaret replied.

"Yes, you are, and—"

"Goodness, is that the time? I've such a lot to do!" Margaret cried, gathering her skirts to hurry from the library.

"Margaret!"

But the door had already closed.

Rebecca turned to go to the window and look out at the windswept December scene. Abbotlea Manor stood at the edge of the village of the same name, and had been the home of the Newton family for two hundred years. The house itself was a rambling red-brick Tudor building, gabled and mullioned, with floors that had become very uneven as the house settled over the years. It was set in gardens that in summer were a riot of roses, but which now looked gray and uninviting as the relentless wet weather gusted dismally across the countryside.

To the west, behind the village, rose the forested hill that separated Newton land from the thousands of acres belonging to the Duke of Almondsbury, while to the north, above a winding river valley that carved through the lower slopes of Dartmoor, was the vast tract owned by Edward's aristocratic family. The high moor was swathed in cloud, and she could only just make out the battlemented towers of Winterbourne Castle, nestling in the lee of the bleak crag known as High Tor.

Oh, how she loathed that great house, and the people who lived in it, not only for excluding Edward after his marriage to her, but for denying his children as well.

She lowered her gaze to the rain-spattered Christmas roses trembling in the flower bed below the window. She'd planted them the Christmas she and Edward met eight years ago. What a festive season that had been. It had turned everyone's world upside down, and nothing had been the same since.

It began with the annual Almondsbury Park ball, to which the Newtons wouldn't have been invited if the duchess hadn't required to make up numbers. Clifford's political association with the duke had made him, his wife, and sister seem acceptable, and, just as had happened to her again now, they received a last-minute invitation. Edward had nearly not attended, either, for he'd only been visiting his family at Winterbourne Castle, but the duke had invited him in person when they'd met at the local stag hunt.

So chance brought them both to Almondsbury Castle that Christmas Eve, but when he'd asked her to dance a ländler with him, it was as if they'd known each other forever. From that incredible moment on, the famous ball, an occasion steeped in snobbery and etiquette, had become a place to throw caution and propriety to the winds. He'd held her too close, and they'd soon attracted shocked attention as they moved around the floor with their arms entwined. Shock had turned to outrage when, at the end of the dance, he'd taken her beneath one of the mistletoe bunches suspended from the ballroom ceiling and kissed her lingeringly on the lips.

When she accepted his proposal only days later, she hadn't realized he was defying other betrothal arrangements being painstakingly made for him by his tyrannical uncle, Lord Winterbourne, whose fury had known few bounds. Such was the offense taken by his lordship, that Edward had been immediately forbidden to set foot in the castle again, and had been completely cut out of the will. Lord Winterbourne let it be widely known that he considered his nephew's union with a young woman from the lower ranks of Devon gentry to be a misalliance of monstrous proportions. Society took its cue, and the old man must have been gratified by the extent of his success when his nephew and his nephew's new bride were shunned by everyone of note. The one thing that pinched Lord Winterbourne to the quick was the fact that Edward wasn't financially dependent upon him, but had sufficient income from his late mother's estate to thumb his nose at the spiteful old despot.

Rebecca continued to gaze at the Christmas roses. She and Edward hadn't been the ones to suffer because of Lord Winterbourne's wrath. Clifford had suffered too, seeing his hopes of becoming a member of parliament dashed beyond redemption. Until the fateful Christmas ball, he'd been in favor with the duke, who had a constituency in his gift. But after the ball, the duke withdrew his support, and Clifford had seen someone else receive the patronage that had hitherto been his.

She drew a long breath. Clifford's relegation to the political wilderness would soon be over, for Sir Oliver had influence at Westminster, and had intimated to her that if she became Lady Willoughby, he'd put her brother's name forward where it mattered. So, not only would her second marriage take care of her and her children, it would go some way toward repaying the immense debt she felt she owed to Clifford and Margaret for the blows they'd received because of their loyalty to her.

Her thoughts moved to the Winterbourne family. How cruel and heartless they were, never forgiving or forgetting. They'd ignored Edward's wedding, the births of his sons, and almost his funeral as well. Almost, but not quite. Edward's cousin, Piers, the new Lord Winterbourne, had arrived disgracefully late, and left insultingly early. It would have been better—and less hypocritical—if he hadn't bothered to come at all.

A sad light entered her eyes as she thought of Piers, whose opposition to her had been as vehement as his odious father's. She'd found his antagonism as hurtful as it was unexpected, for until he'd learned of her closeness to Edward, he'd been very different. There had never been a great deal of contact between Abbotlea Manor and Winterbourne Castle, just the average communication between two such unequal but neighboring estates. She'd been sixteen before she even met Piers, but unlike his supercilious father, he'd always been civil and agreeable. Her encounters with him had become increasingly frequent whenever he was in residence at the castle, and each meeting had served to make her like him more. Which was why, when her name became linked with his cousin, his sudden hostility had cut so very deep.

She glanced a little guiltily at her wedding ring, which shone palely in the gray morning light. Then she put her hand crossly behind her. She wouldn't dwell on the past, she *wouldn't*! The future was what mattered now, and Piers Winterbourne could rot for all she cared. She was glad he found the hothouse life of London's *haut ton* so much to his liking, for it meant he rarely graced Devon with his presence. But when he did come here, his penchant for long rides in the surrounding countryside frequently took him through Abbotlea village, where from time to time they'd come uncomfortably face to face.

Oh, the devil take him! Turning, she went back to the desk to resume her attempts at letter writing, but almost immediately she was interrupted again, although this time not by the invisible hand. Instead there was the whirlwind arrival of her sons, Matthew and Frederick. Aged seven and six respectively, and dark-haired and dark-eyed like her, they rushed in, arguing noisily over ownership of a toy soldier.

She had no option but to abandon Sir Oliver's letter in order to mediate. But as she put the quill down once and for all that day, she was sure she heard someone give a low laugh. A cold finger ran down her spine, and again she looked uneasily around the room. But there was just the boisterous and increasingly tearful arguing of two small boys.

It was to be the following afternoon before she at last wrote and dispatched the letter of acceptance to Sir Oliver, who she soon learned hadn't been in the least discreet about his proposal, or about his conviction that she'd become Lady Willoughby. As far as he was concerned, it was a fait accompli, and all that remained was to enjoy the physical pleasures of actual union!

She was right too about his being behind her invitation to the ball, and about his reveling in the stir caused by news of the impending betrothal. He told everyone he met, so that word had spread all over Dartmoor by the time her letter arrived at Willoughby Castle. One place it didn't reach because of Sir Oliver's indiscretion was Winterbourne Castle, for no one was keen to be the bearer of such tidings concerning Edward Winterbourne's widow.

But within an hour of Rebecca's conversation with Margaret, someone in Abbotlea Manor itself dispatched a note to Piers at the castle. The note contained news of both Rebecca's invitation to the ball and her imminent betrothal, and arrived just as he was about to take luncheon in the castle's lofty, beamed dining room. The news robbed him of any appetite.

His blue eyes darkened as he read the hastily written

lines. He sat back in his richly carved Jacobean arm-chair, his fingers beginning to drum loudly on the table. He was tall, lean, and muscular, with the thick blond hair and rugged good looks of all the Winter-bourne men. Aristocratic in bearing and graceful in manner, he wore a superbly tailored sky-blue coat and cream breeches that were set off to perfection by a blue-striped neckcloth and sapphire pin.

He suddenly felt the need to escape from the castle confines, and glanced up at the footman who'd brought the note on a silver salver. "Have my horse saddled. I've decided to spend the afternoon riding."

"My lord."

As the man hastened away, Piers got up and ripped the note into tiny pieces, but as he threw them on the fire, they seemed to hover willfully away from the heat. For seconds on end they danced in the air like tiny butterflies, apparently self-supporting.

Startled, he drew back, but as he watched they sank onto the logs, where they caught flame. All except one, which lay among the ashes in the hearth. The single word written clearly upon it seemed to command his attention in the moments before it too succumbed to the heat. *Rebecca.*

While Piers was out on his ride, Rebecca and her sons emerged from Abbotlea Manor to gather holly and mistletoe to decorate the house. It was an annual expedition to a particular tree along the riverbank just outside the village, where the ancient trees of an adjacent cider-apple orchard bore masses of mistletoe.

The weather was still appalling, but the wind and rain seemed to suit the boys' exuberance as they dashed ahead of their mother and then came racing back again with squeals of laughter. They wore matching clothes, dark blue coats and gray tasseled caps, and glowed with health and energy as they played peeka-boo among the bushes along the riverside path.

Rebecca's mulberry wool cloak flapped wildly around her, and the wind tugged so fiercely she had difficulty keeping the fur-trimmed hood over her dark curls. She smiled as Matthew at last spotted the holly tree, and grabbed his little brother's hand to run toward it. They'd already picked armsful of holly by the time she reached them. Then, leaving the sprays on the wet grass, they dashed off again, this time scrambling over a stile into the orchard.

She'd been watching them for a few minutes when something, she didn't know what, made her turn suddenly to look across the river. A cloaked man was standing on the other bank. She could tell by his general demeanor that he was elderly, but didn't know who he was because his face was in shadow from his top hat. His long cloak billowed in the wind, and he was absolutely motionless. She knew he was staring at her, because she could almost feel his unwavering gaze, but he didn't raise a hand in greeting, or doff his hat.

As he continued to stand there, a feeling of unease began to seep through her, and she was so intent, she didn't hear the horse approaching. She knew nothing until Piers suddenly greeted her. "Good afternoon, Mrs. Winterbourne."

The moment he spoke, the cloaked man disappeared. She was looking directly at him, but he just vanished. Startled, she cast around, half-expecting to see him striding away toward the village. But the meadows opposite were empty.

Collecting her wits, she made herself turn to Piers. "Good afternoon, Lord Winterbourne." He was mounted on a restive bay thoroughbred, which he controlled with almost casual ease, and instinct told her he hadn't seen anyone on the other riverbank. Perhaps the cloaked man had just been a trick of the light. Yes, that was it.

Piers removed his top hat, and his blond hair was bright, even on such a gray, overcast day. She was suddenly reminded so forcefully of Edward—and of her own deeply buried secrets—that she had to glance away.

The silence grew heavy. "I trust I find you well?" he asked at last.

She gave a faint smile at that. "Do you?" she murmured. Why hadn't he simply ridden around the other side of the orchard? Why hadn't he stayed in London!

"Yes, I do."

"Please don't attempt to indulge in small talk, my lord, for it rests exceedingly uneasily between us."

"Very well, I'll come straight to the point. Among other things, I'm given to understand you've been invited to the Almondsbury Castle ball. Is this correct?"

"It is."

"Do you intend to be there?"

Her dark eyes were quizzical. "Why? Will it embarrass you if I am?" she inquired.

"No, I merely wish to know."

"Then, yes, sir, I intend to be there, and if that offends you, I make no apology."

"Did I say it offended me?"

"You didn't need to."

"Clearly I've made a grave error in trying to smooth things over with you," he observed coolly.

"Is that what you're doing?" Her dark eyes were full of disbelief.

"I didn't *have* to make a point of speaking to you."

"That's very true, so I wonder why you took the trouble."

"Perhaps I'm tired of the ill feeling."

She raised a scornful eyebrow. "Indeed? Well, may I remind you that you, your father, and your entire family were the cause of that ill feeling?"

"True, but your own family wasn't exactly ecstatic," he reminded her.

"Edward and I proved you all wrong," she replied defiantly.

"Neither of you proved anything I didn't know already," he observed enigmatically.

"What's that suppose to mean?" she demanded, wishing again that he'd go away. Nothing changed. He'd always had the unerring ability to affect her, and always would.

He didn't answer, but looked away toward the boys in the orchard. She couldn't help studying him. She supposed he must be thirty-five now, in his prime, some might say, and they'd be right, for he seemed more handsome and lithely masculine than ever. London life hadn't made a fop of him; he was every inch the man, every inch the aristocrat. Why did he always have to look so superb? Why couldn't he have mud on his boots for once? Who else but Piers Winterbourne could ride for miles in weather like this without looking like something dragged through a hedge?

He spoke, but on a change of subject. "Your sons are a credit to you, Mrs. Winterbourne."

"I'm surprised you recognize them, sir," she observed dryly.

Irritation flashed through his gaze as it swung back to her. "How bitter you are, to be sure."

"Justifiably so."

"Indeed?"

She looked away again. "I believe congratulations are in order," she said then.

"Congratulations?"

"I understand you are soon to be married."

"There's nothing definite." He toyed with his reins. "Since marriage is the subject of the day, I gather I should be congratulating you too."

His knowledge caught her off guard, for she hadn't yet discovered the extent of Sir Oliver's premature tongue-wagging. "How did you hear?"

He ignored the question. "So it's true?"

"Yes."

"A very unwise move, Mrs. Winterbourne. Willoughby isn't for you."

"Nor was Edward, it seems. Just who, in your considered opinion, *would* be for me, my lord?" she asked icily.

He gave the thinnest of smiles. "Someone younger than Willoughby, and without Edward's fecklessness," he said.

"You aren't fit to criticize Edward, sirrah!" she replied sharply.

"Possibly, but I'm certainly entitled."

She didn't reply.

He smiled. "The point goes to me, I think," he murmured.

"I wish you'd go away, sir, for you and I have nothing worthwhile to say to each other. I intend to avoid you at the ball, and trust you'll do the same for me."

"Madam, on this occasion your wish is most definitely my command. You have my word upon it. Good day to you." Tugging his top hat back on his head, he turned his impatient horse away, urging it to a reckless gallop along the riverbank.

Tears stung her eyes as she watched him. He was the bane of her life, and always would be. The only road that mattered led back to him, and she resented it with all her heart. She turned away. He could only be the bane of her life if she allowed him to be! No one knew what went on in the depths of her soul, no one, except her, and that was how it would remain. Forever.

Suddenly the hand was placed on her shoulder again, shaking her urgently for a moment before releasing her. Terrified, she cried out and whirled around to see if anyone was there. But, of course, there wasn't. She tried to tell herself she was still imagining it all, but in her heart knew better. Someone, or something, kept seizing her shoulder, and right now she could actually feel the imprint of those ghostly fingers. Ghostly? Yes, for what other word could describe it?

She remembered the cloaked man, and her gaze flew across the river, but the other bank remained deserted. In her mind's eye she could still see him, though, and with hindsight, he seemed somehow familiar. No, that was foolish, for he'd been swathed in a long cloak, with his face completely in shadow. And yet . . .

Matthew and Frederick shouted as they climbed back over the stile with armsful of mistletoe. Somehow she managed a bright smile as they raced toward her.

Piers had reined his horse in again while still in view of the holly tree. He watched the boys run to their mother, and saw how tenderly she put her arms around them both. Then they gathered the holly that still lay scattered on the ground, and carried it and the mistletoe back toward the manor house. He could just hear the boys' laughter, and from time to time Rebecca's laughter too.

A wry light passed through his blue eyes as he pondered the marked contrast in her now. It was almost like watching a different person. The cold, antagonistic Rebecca had gone, and in her place was the softer, warmer creature he remembered from the past. The too-distant past, it seemed now. How old had she been when they'd first met? Sixteen? Seventeen, maybe? He'd been a few years older, and susceptible to her fresh, unspoiled beauty.

It had been at the midsummer fair, and he'd rescued her from the rather importunate attention of an inebriated lawyer from Plymouth. She'd been so sweetly grateful, and so delightfully overawed by his grand birthright, that he'd been flattered beyond belief. She may not have been part of the exalted circle in which his family moved, but there'd been a sparkle in her eyes and a glow on her cheeks that set her completely apart.

Piers gazed at the three figures disappearing into the distance. Yes, there had been something that set Rebecca Newton apart, something that eventually elevated her into the Winterbourne family itself. Much good it had done her.

His lips twisted savagely as he kicked his heels to urge his horse on again.

The night of Christmas Eve arrived, and the weather was still atrocious. Clouds scudded endlessly across the dark sky, and the gale could be heard whining around the eaves as Rebecca emerged reluctantly from her room to go to the ball. She held a lighted candlestick because the passage was dark and uneven, and beneath her gray velvet evening cloak she wore the strawberry silk gown. Her dark hair was pinned up into an elaborate knot trimmed with ribbons to match the gown, and she carried the same fan and silver sequin reticule as the night she and Edward met.

Too late, now the moment of actual departure was upon her, she realized how many deep memories were bound to be stirred by attending the ball again. She'd now learned how much Sir Oliver had done to spread news of the betrothal over the county, and so was only too aware of the interest she'd attract from the moment she arrived at Almondsbury Park.

Feeling daunted, she paused with a hand shielding the candle flame. Truth to tell, she was beginning to feel intimidated by the whole business. She'd hated the unfair notoriety she'd gained because of Edward, and shrank from the same thing happening all over again. She wanted to hide away, but instead must face practically the whole of Devon society, to say nothing of Sir Oliver in particular. He made no secret of his delight with the stir his marital affairs were creating, and had done his utmost to try to escort her tonight, but she'd managed to fend him off. She wanted the freedom to leave when she felt like it, and so was determined to use Clifford's carriage.

Piers was another reason for wanting to be able to come home when she wished. She was bound to see him, and even if they didn't speak, his mere presence would still affect her. Their meeting on the riverbank had left her feeling confused and vulnerable. But that was how he always left her. . . .

Clifford had heard her door from the hall, and came impatiently to the foot of the staircase. "Do hurry, sis, for it won't do to be unnecessarily late!"

The light of the candle wavered as she walked on. Ghostly hands and strange cloaked men couldn't have been further from her mind in that moment, but as she approached the head of the staircase she had the oddest feeling someone was watching from the bedroom doorway behind her. She turned sharply, and the candlelight shivered, but the shadows were empty. Her hand trembled a little as she protected the flame again. Gradually the sensation of being watched began to subside, and after a moment she continued down to the hall, where her brother and sister-in-law waited.

Clifford was nine years older than his sister, and shared her dark coloring. Tall, and rather heavily built, he possessed the sort of imposing articulate presence that was ideal for the hurly-burly of parliament. Rebecca thought he was certainly wasted as just the master of Abbotlea, for he had much to offer.

His glance raked her, and came to rest approvingly upon her intricately pinned hair. "You look excellent, sis."

"Thank you."

"You can be sure the future Lady Willoughby will be a success tonight," he observed levelly, his shrewd gaze making note of the reluctance in her eyes.

"I hope so," she replied resignedly.

"You don't *have* to marry him, you know."

"I think I do."

"Why? Because of my political ambitions?"

"That, and the need to spare your purse now you're to be a father," she replied.

"My purse can manage, and as to my desire to grace Westminster with my Devon common sense and wit, I can do that without Sir Oliver."

Rebecca looked at him in surprise. "What do you mean?"

"Simply that if I choose, I can turn to another sponsor." He glanced briefly at Margaret, whose gaze was carefully averted.

"And who, pray, is this other sponsor?" Rebecca inquired.

He fell silent.

She smiled a little. "A valiant attempt, sir, but patently transparent. So my reasons for marrying Sir Oliver remain. It may not be a love match, but it will do."

"Your first venture into marriage left you penniless, so if you imagine marrying for money will bring happiness, I fear you're sadly mistaken."

"It's my decision."

"Rebecca—"

But Margaret put a warning hand on his sleeve. "Leave it, my dear, for there's nothing to be gained from arguing."

He drew a long breath. "As you wish, my dear, but you and I both know things that—"

"Clifford!"

His lips clamped shut, and he looked away.

Rebecca looked curiously at them both. "I'm missing something here, am I not?" she said. "What's going on that I haven't been told?"

"Nothing," Margaret replied with a disarming smile.

"I don't believe you."

Margaret gave a tinkle of nervous laughter, but then became serious as she changed the subject. "Rebecca, you *will* be courteous to Piers tonight, won't you?" she said suddenly.

"I'll do my best."

Clifford cleared his throat. "We'll hold you to that, sis."

"Yes, I'm sure you will." Why were they so concerned she should be civil to Piers? It was almost as if it were a matter of considerable importance! But as she was about to put the question into words, Margaret spoke again.

"I do trust you'll enjoy the ball, Rebecca."

"I just hope I'm not too much the center of attention."

Clifford gave a grunt. "It's a vain hope." At that moment the carriage arrived at the door, and he offered her his arm to escort her outside.

The wind gusted and rain stung her face. She shivered as he assisted her into the vehicle, which a moment later drew away toward the wrought iron gates into the village street. Rain shone in the arc of light from the lamps as the coachman tooled the team up to a trot. The wheels splashed through puddles, and the vehicle was buffeted by the gale. Few people were out and about, and the lighted cottage windows looked cozy and inviting. Ribboned Christmas wreaths were fixed to doors, and the parish church was dimly lit from within as the village women put up the seasonal decorations of holly, ivy, and fir.

Rebecca glanced at the open church doorway as the carriage passed. An elderly man in a long cloak was standing there, his figure a mere silhouette against the candlelight within, but she could feel his gaze upon her. It was the man from the riverbank! With a gasp she turned to look back, but he'd vanished. One moment he was there, the next he might never have been.

She drew nervously away from the window. Her heartbeats had quickened and she felt both hot and cold at once. To calm herself she counted to ten, and then exhaled slowly, telling herself there hadn't been anyone there, just shadows.

She looked out at the dark night again. At least one puzzle had been solved now, and she knew why the cloaked man seemed familiar. His stocky build and the tilt of his head put her strongly in mind of her father.

The carriage began the long climb over the forested

hill toward Almondsbury Park. The wind soughed through the trees, and the vehicle jolted over deep ruts. They heard the roar of water as they neared the rocks where the rain drained from the saturated hilltop into a steep gully and began its descent to the river valley below. A humpbacked stone bridge carried the road over the torrent, and then at the summit just beyond was the fork with the road from Winterbourne Castle.

Low clouds swirled mistily through the trees, but if she'd glanced to the right along that other road, she might just have been able to make out the lamps of a stationary carriage. At last the long descent toward Almondsbury Park commenced, and as the road swooped down below the cloud again, the coachman brought the team up to as smart a pace as he dared.

Piers had set out from Winterbourne Castle intending to drive straight to the ball, but as his carriage left open land to negotiate the forested hill, he began to doubt the wisdom of attending at all. He looked out at the shadowy trees swaying in the storm, and saw the first tendrils of cloud coiling swiftly between the crowding branches. Soon everything began to turn gray and indistinct, until at last he could only just make out the trees at the side of the road.

His doubts increased. This damned Willoughby business had already caused sufficient stir. Too many old embers had been fanned, and his presence beneath the same roof as Rebecca after all this time was bound to make it a damned sight worse. He leaned his head back against the carriage's green leather upholstery. God-damn it, what was he to do? Should he go, or would it be more politic to turn around and go back to the castle?

He needed time to think. Leaning forward, he lowered the rain-spattered window glass and told the coachman to halt. Then he raised the glass once more and sat back. The thought of watching that elderly peacock Willoughby basking in his betrothal glory was too much to stomach. The fellow would be brandishing his success like a battle honor, and smugly boasting to the world about his good fortune in securing such a beautiful and desirable bride. And when alone with male acquaintances, he'd be constantly winking and grinning as he stirred their envy over the physical delights that would soon be his alone to enjoy.

The wind moaned through the trees outside as Piers sighed. Yes, indeed, the prospect of Willoughby's triumph was far from uplifting. But almost as bad would be the sight of Rebecca's smiling compliance. She didn't want to marry the odious fellow. Plague take Clifford Newton for getting his wife with child after all this time!

The uncharitable sentiment aroused his guilt. God, this was getting him nowhere. The fact was that Rebecca intended to go ahead with this cursed match, and there was nothing he could do about it. The best thing all round was for him to attend this damned Christmas ball, behave as if he didn't give a damn who his cousin's widow married, and then leave as soon as he could. Yes, that was the only real choice, for to stay away might draw even more unwelcome attention to the past.

His decision made, he lowered the window again to instruct the coachman to drive on, but as he leaned out into the wind and rain, a movement caught his eye. He was sure there was someone about ten yards away, next to an ivy-draped tree.

He peered through the swirling cloud. "Who's there?" he called above the noise of the night.

There was no reply, but still he was certain someone was there. "Who's there?" he demanded more authoritatively.

No response was forthcoming, but he felt sure he could just make out a shadowy silhouette. It looked like a man in a cloak. Whoever it was clearly had no intention of revealing himself, which left the obvious conclusion that he was a poacher. Well, good luck to him on a night like this.

He heard another carriage pass over the bridge by the fork just ahead. It was Rebecca's, but he didn't realize it as he returned his attention to the figure by the tree. But it had melted away into the cloud, leaving only shivering ivy sprays. He called to the coachman, "Drive on!"

"My lord."

The whip cracked, and the carriage jolted forward. Piers glanced back toward the tree as he began to raise the window glass again. The cloaked man was there, and for a moment was clearly visible, although his features were concealed by the low set of his hat. Piers was in two minds whether to order the coachman to halt again, but then decided against it. The carriage drove on.

The lights of Almondsbury Park appeared ahead. Rebecca gazed out unhappily, and as her carriage turned through the impressive wrought iron gates, it was difficult to resist the impulse to turn around and return to Abbotlea. But she knew the gauntlet of society had to be run sooner or later, and it was best to get it over and done with.

Every tree in the grounds had been hung with lanterns. A long line of elegant vehicles was drawn up along the drive, and as hers neared the main door, she heard music drifting out into the stormy night. She looked up at the great house. The windows were illuminated, and the rooms behind them were lavishly adorned with Christmas greenery. It was all very seasonal and exciting, but now she was here, she was more prey than ever to nerves.

The carriage door was opened by a liveried footman, and she alighted hesitantly, her hair ribbons fluttering in the wind. But as she stepped down, she was dismayed to see Piers emerge from the carriage behind. He didn't see her as he paused to adjust the froth of lace at his tight-fitting cuff.

Few men could have appeared to more advantage in the close-cut black velvet coat and white silk breeches that were de rigueur for occasions like tonight's. Again he brought Edward strongly to mind, and yet at the same time he managed to be totally unlike him. One couldn't imagine Piers becoming addicted to the turn of a card, or accepting wild challenges such as the horse race that led to Edward's premature death. Not for Piers the folly of a patently unfair ten-mile gallop through a summer downpour against the best horse in the south of England. But her foolish Edward had accepted, inevitably lost the race, and paid the ultimate price by contracting a fatal fever.

An ironic smile played briefly upon her lips, for Piers differed from Edward in another even more significant way: he would never have made a monumental misalliance with an inconsequential nonentity from Abbotlea Manor! No, *his* bride was an heiress who would bring even more wealth into his already overflowing coffers.

Piers suddenly realized she was there, for Sir Oliver, ever watchful for her arrival, emerged noisily from the house to claim her. "Ah, my dear! My dear!" he cried, taking her hand and drawing it palm uppermost to his lips.

He was of slight build, with receding gray hair that had once been a mane of rich brown curls. His mouth was wide and his hazel eyes were bright in the lamplight as he lingered over her hand. He wore the same formal evening wear as Piers, but whereas on Piers the tight coat and breeches emphasized his well-formed masculine shape, on Sir Oliver they served only to draw attention to his narrowness and lack of height.

His loud greeting saw to it that Piers wasn't alone in becoming aware of her arrival. She felt other nearby guests all turn to stare at her, and from the corner of her eye she saw fans raised to whispering lips.

Sir Oliver clasped her hand in both his, and gazed ardently into her eyes. "I'm flattered that because of you I'm the center of attention tonight. It does my vanity good," he said frankly.

She managed a weak smile, but her heart sank apace. *He* might revel in being the center of attention, but she certainly didn't.

He didn't notice her reserve. "Come inside, my dear, and let us brave them all together." He ushered her into the glittering vestibule, where Christmas decorations were festooned around the gilded walls, and small boys in eastern costume handed out ribboned favors for the ladies to wear on their wrists.

As a footman relieved Rebecca of her cloak, she glanced back to where Piers still stood. His blue eyes were upon her, their expression hard to read. She turned hastily to the front again, and allowed Sir Oliver to tie the favor to her left wrist before he escorted her toward the ballroom staircase.

Piers watched her. Willoughby could justifiably boast about winning her hand, for she was without a doubt one of the most beautiful women in Devon. Probably in the whole of England. There was still something about her, something fresh and sparkling, like the best champagne. But for Piers Winterbourne, the champagne was little more than vinegar.

With a wry smile, he entered the house.

Rebecca and Sir Oliver paused at the head of the ballroom steps. The great blue-and-gold chamber was magnificently illuminated and mirrored so that lights and guests seemed to be repeated over and over again on all sides. The orchestra played from an apse high on one wall, and the Duke and Duchess of Almondsbury received each new arrival at the foot of the grand steps. Refined laughter and conversation vied with the music of the polonaise that was in progress, and plumes trembled and jewels flashed as the ladies danced.

There were Christmas decorations everywhere, including the gilded ceiling, where huge mistletoe kissing boughs were suspended, their gold satin ribbons trembling in the rising heat. Rebecca glanced up at them, remembering the first kiss she and Edward had shared so publicly in this very ballroom, but then her brow drew together in puzzlement as she saw what appeared to be a huge nest fixed to the center of the ceiling. It was filled with something white; she couldn't make out what. Then her attention was drawn down to more immediate matters as the master of ceremonies rapped the floor with his staff and announced their names.

"Sir Oliver Willoughby and Mrs. Edward Winterbourne."

A great stir went around the gathering, and all eyes swung toward them. Rebecca felt dull color staining her cheeks, and kept her gaze lowered as Sir Oliver conducted her down to be greeted by their hosts, whose expressionless visages made it clear she'd been invited only for the sake of her husband-to-be, not for herself.

She curtsied, reflecting on how amazing it was that she still had such an effect. And all because she and Edward fell in love and married eight long years ago! It wasn't even as if one or the other of them hadn't been free, just that he came from prideful aristocratic stock, and she from mere gentry. If she'd been the heiress daughter of a wealthy mill owner, or if, through judicious dealing, her father had risen from the position of mere clerk in the East India Company to become a nabob, all would have been well, for that was the double standard that ruled this stifled society. It wasn't really one's breeding that counted in the end, just the plumpness of one's purse!

She rose from the curtsey, and gave the duke and duchess a false smile, which they duly returned. The duchess allowed her glance to wander witheringly over the strawberry silk gown. It was a glance Rebecca found provoking in the extreme. How dared such a tasteless creature presume to criticize, when her own gown, a gaudy confection of vermilion satin, made her look like a varnished orange! And as for the towering plume in her hair, on anyone taller it might have dusted the chandeliers! For all her blue blood and title, the Duchess of Almondsbury was a person of atrocious taste, and yet had the front to register contempt for others.

Piers watched from the head of the staircase behind them. His sharp glance took everything in, and he read Rebecca's expression like a book. He silently applauded her dignified hauteur. However poor relations might be between them, he couldn't help but admire her spirit. There were times when he had to concede she conducted herself with more style than many a more blue-blooded lady. It was a pity there were also times when she displayed a mulishness that was decidedly unbecoming!

He waited until Sir Oliver had led her further into the ballroom, and then nodded at the waiting master of ceremonies, who immediately commanded attention by announcing his name.

There was another ripple of whispering, but Rebecca didn't turn to look. For her the ordeal of the evening had now begun in earnest, and each passing moment served only to verify her worst fears. She hated being the object of such interest, but Sir Oliver was positively wallowing in it. Watching how he preened and basked, she was forced to wonder if marrying him would indeed prove a disastrous move. If he didn't care a fig for her discomfort now, he clearly wouldn't after she'd become his wife. And if she felt as ill at ease in his company now, how much worse would it be when they were married?

But there was no time to consider her doubts. Being the cause célèbre of the moment, she was very much in demand, and required to dance a succession of measures, from polonaises, cotillions, and minuets, to allemandes, gavottes, and contredanses, each one with a different partner. It was exhausting physically as well as mentally, but as midnight approached she at last managed to slip away on her own. The hour was to prove opportune, for an appropriate diversion had been planned to usher in Christmas Day itself.

But the entertainment had yet to commence as she made her way around the ballroom to a quiet corner by a greenery-entwined column. She paused thankfully, finding the scent of the evergreens pleasantly refreshing after the exertion of so much dancing. High above the dance floor, the mistletoe bunches turned gently in the heat, and the mysterious net with its white contents still defied her powers of conjecture.

The last dance before the Christmas diversion was in progress, and by cruel fate it happened to be the very ländler that had brought Edward and her together. The remembered tune drifted achingly over her, and she had to close her eyes. Memories engulfed her then. In his arms she'd allowed the spell of the dance to carry her away. How improperly they'd behaved, gazing ardently into each other's eyes, and holding each other so close their bodies touched. But she hadn't cared, for there had been something unbelievably magical about that night. Her senses had stirred so strongly that just to meet his gaze had made her breasts tighten with desire. Physical attraction had devoured them both, and she'd been oblivious to everyone and everything, except him.

She knew he felt the same way too, when for a moment he'd held her even closer, so she could feel his maleness pressing to her. She should have been shocked by such a very forward action, but already things had gone too far between them for her to play the coquette. One touch of his hand, and she'd known he was the one for her. And when the dance was over, and they stood beneath the mistletoe, she'd gone more than willingly into the reprehensibly overt kiss that had brought the ball to a stunned halt.

Rebecca opened her eyes unhappily. That was how she'd tried to convince herself it had been; the truth was very different. Oh, she'd danced with Edward, she'd done nothing to spurn his advances, and at the end she'd consented to the kiss that had eventually led to a happy marriage and two wonderful children, but there was an important aspect of it all that she'd striven to obliterate from her memory ever since. It was an aspect that lay at the heart of so much, and the pain didn't lessen with the passing years. Tonight it was like a fresh wound, because nearly everything was the same as it had been then. Edward was no longer here, but Piers was, and he felt as little for her as ever.

She exhaled slowly and tremulously as she confronted the truth about herself. It was because of Piers's indifference that she'd danced with Edward that night and relinquished her reputation. She'd been young, inexperienced, and wretched with unrequited love for Piers, whose lack of the right sort of interest hurt her so much she turned instead to the cousin who looked so like him.

That was why she'd stepped onto the floor with Edward, and allowed the headiness of the ländler to sweep her along. But if it was with Piers that she'd mentally stepped out to dance, it was with Edward that she finished the measure. His bold smiles and engaging charm had captivated her, and in spite of all his faults, she'd never regretted marrying him or bearing his sons. But at moments like the present, when events conspired to recreate that long-past evening, she knew that her love for Piers had always marched alongside her love for Edward, and probably always would.

Remorse rushed hotly over her. "Oh, go away, go away," she breathed, addressing the feelings she wished so much did not exist. She wanted freedom from Piers Winterbourne, not the endless sentence of being affected by everything he said or did.

As tears of frustration filled her eyes, her glance fell suddenly upon Piers himself. He was laughing as he stood with a group of gentlemen beneath the orchestra apse, and it seemed she could single out his laugh from that of all the others. The perfection of his profile cut through her, and the curve of his lips seemed to taunt with the invisible kisses she would always be denied. What would have happened during that other ländler if he'd been the one she'd danced with? Would caution have been tossed aside then too? Would he have made her as physically conscious of his virility as Edward had done? Would he have kissed her beneath the mistletoe with the same passionate abandon as his cousin? She furiously blinked the tears away. No, of course he wouldn't, for Rebecca Newton was too lowly for him!

To her relief, the Christmas diversion commenced. As the final note of the ländler died away, the floor was cleared and a murmur of interest ran around the gathering as footmen on tall stepladders carefully extinguished most of the chandeliers. Then, when the ballroom was in semidarkness, carolers were heard approaching. They were singing "Deck the Halls With Boughs of Holly," and carried lanterns which swung to and fro as they descended the ballroom staircase and formed a circle in the center of the floor. There was great applause as they finished, and then silence fell again as they began another carol, this time "I Saw Three Ships."

The carol singing went on for about half an hour, ending with "Good King Wenceslas," when at last the mystery of the ceiling net was explained. Ropes were attached to it, and several footmen began to pull on them, slowly opening a small hole in the net through which the contents began to fall. Illuminated by the carolers' lanterns, thousands of tiny pieces of white paper and cloth fluttered gently down like snow. It was so simple, and yet the perfect Christmas touch, and the duchess smiled with elegant satisfaction as her guests gasped and clapped with admiration.

Rebecca clapped too. Gazing at the "snow," she was

suddenly reminded of the strange draft that had blown Clifford's papers around the Abbotlea library. But it was only a fleeting thought, for her attention returned once more to Piers. He was gazing up at the artificial snowstorm, and the expression on his face suggested that he too might have been reminded of something.

Suddenly a disapproving face among his group seemed to leap out at her, and her heart almost stopped with shock as she stared into her late father's eyes! The artificial snowflakes fluttered silently all around him as he continued to hold her gaze, and his visage was so darkly reproachful that she felt like a disobedient child again. "Father?" she whispered.

As she watched, he raised a hand to wag a scolding finger at her. What had she done to make him angry? Her bewilderment was replaced by confusion. This was foolish. He couldn't be angry with her, because she couldn't possibly really be seeing him. She was imagining it. But as the chiding gaze remained upon her across the ballroom, she knew she *was* seeing him. She also knew beyond all doubt she'd seen him on the riverbank *and* at Abbotlea church.

She remained motionless with shock as the carol singers left the floor and the chandeliers were relit. It wasn't until the master of ceremonies announced a minuet, and sets began to form, that the strange paralysis left her. She had to go to her father!

Leaving the shelter of the column, she hurried blindly onto the crowded floor, but as she pushed through the crush of dancers, she momentarily lost sight of the group beneath the apse. The last of the artificial snow still fell, clinging to her face and gown as at last she reached Piers and his friends, but there was no sign of anyone who looked even remotely like her father.

She seized Piers's sleeve agitatedly. "My lord?"

Startled, he turned. "Madam?"

His companions were taken aback, but she ignored them as she held his gaze. "My lord, the gentleman who was with you a moment ago . . ."

"Gentleman?"

"He was elderly, with a wig. He was with you, but has gone now."

"There was no elderly gentleman, madam."

"But I saw him," she insisted.

"There was no such gentleman," he repeated.

She felt the others' quizzical eyes upon her, and knew she was making a scene. Dull color rushed into her cheeks, and she hastily removed her hand from his sleeve. "Forgive me, sir—evidently I was mistaken."

"Evidently."

Gathering her skirts once more, she hurried away, threading her path along the edge of the floor until she reached the supper room. Her heart was now pounding so much she felt dizzy and unwell.

She didn't realize Piers had followed her, until suddenly he took her arm to steady her. He steered her through the supper room into an unoccupied antechamber, where he ushered her to a sofa and made her sit down. "You appear more than a little overwrought," he said, reaching out to brush off some of the tiny fragments of white paper and cloth that still clung to her hair, but then thinking better of making such a gesture. "Shall I, er, bring you something cool to drink? Some lime cup, perhaps?"

She shook her head. "I'll be all right in a moment or so."

He knew there was more to it than merely feeling unwell. "Tell me what's wrong," he said gently.

She hesitated. "I—I thought I saw my father." Fresh

tears sprang to her eyes, and she searched her reticule for a handkerchief.

He pressed his own into her hand. "Your father? But that can't possibly be so, madam. As I recall, he passed away from influenza at least ten years ago."

"You think I don't know that?" she replied a little edgily, twisting the handkerchief agitatedly in her hands. "But he was there beside you; I saw him as plain as day."

"There was no one such as you describe in my group," he insisted as he sat down next to her.

"So I gather."

"You make it sound as if you don't believe me, but I'm telling the truth, and, with due respect, you were not only on the other side of the ballroom, but that damned snow was between us as well." He glanced away, for the snow had reminded him of the odd incident with the ripped note he'd tossed on the fire at the castle.

"I know what I saw," she whispered, twisting the handkerchief in hands that still shook.

"You know what you *think* you saw," he corrected gently.

"It hasn't just been tonight," she said suddenly.

"What do you mean?"

She looked away. "If I tell you, you'll think I'm losing my wits."

"Try me."

Drawing a shaking breath, she told him about the ghostly hands, and about the mysterious cloaked man. When she'd finished, she looked at him. "I realized tonight that the man in the church door reminded me of my father, and then, just now, I definitely saw my father standing with your group. He was angry with me about something."

For a moment Piers didn't say anything. A cloaked man? Wasn't that just what he himself had seen on the way here?

She searched his face. "Have you no comment to make? No crushing observation upon my diminishing mental faculties?" she asked at last.

"I merely think the strain of this ill-judged betrothal is showing," he replied, deciding against mentioning his own cloaked man. She was upset enough already, without that as well.

She colored. "Now I wish I hadn't told you; indeed I don't know what possessed me to confide in you of all people."

"Nor I, but you did." He looked at her. "There was a time when you and I were much in each other's confidence."

"I thought so too, sir, but I swiftly learned how poor a friend you really were. The truth is you always looked down on me, but didn't show your true colors until I was presumptuous enough to welcome Edward's attentions."

"You clearly have a very low opinion of me," he observed dryly.

"Under the circumstances, you surely don't expect anything else?"

"Maybe I do. Maybe I expect you to be more reasonable after all this time," he replied.

"I was never *un*reasonable," she answered.

"As you wish." He rose to his feet again. "But I swear upon my honor that there was no one such as you describe among my party a moment or so ago, and I respectfully suggest you're in no condition to remain at a crowded, overheated function such as this. Home, and a restorative medicinal draft would seem advisa-

ble. I'm sure Sir Oliver would be only too glad to see
you safely back to Abbotlea."

"I can see myself safely home, sir."

With a stiff bow, he turned and walked away.

She closed her eyes and struggled to regain her shattered equilibrium. It was several minutes before she'd
recovered sufficiently to return to the ball, and when
she did she was immediately snapped up again by Sir
Oliver, who'd been searching all over for her. It was
her intention to tell him she was going home, but a cotillion was announced, and instead she found herself
being ushered into one of the sets, which, to her consternation, also contained Piers and the duchess.

The dance commenced, and she avoided Piers's
eyes, even when they were face-to-face because of the
measure. In the heat of the moment she forgot that the
sequence of this particular cotillion included a kissing
forfeit, nor did she realize that it would be Piers to
whom she had to pay it. Not until he actually took her
hands and drew her toward him did she remember, and
by then it was too late.

She moved as if spellbound, allowing him to pull
her into his arms and kiss her on the lips. It meant
nothing to him, he was merely going through the motions of the dance, but for a wonderful moment she
could surrender to the sorcery of her secret. Her lips
softened and parted beneath his, and her eyes closed as
she savored the brief intimacy she'd always longed for.
It was all she could do not to give in completely to the
emotions that coursed through her veins like fire. She
wanted to link her arms around his neck, to draw his
tongue deep into her mouth, and know the exquisite
pleasure of feeling his dormant masculinity begin to
stir against her. It was Piers she wanted, Piers she'd al-

ways wanted. . . . Oh, forgive me, Edward, please forgive me.

In all too few seconds the forfeit was over, and Piers released her as the dance continued. Fresh color warmed her cheeks, and she couldn't meet his eyes when next they faced each other. How much had she given herself away? Had he realized the truth? Please don't let that be so, for she couldn't bear it. But when she glanced at his face, it was expressionless. She could read nothing of his thoughts.

More and more guilt tumbled through her. It had been a terrible mistake to have come here tonight. She'd tried for so long to deny the way she felt about Piers, and usually succeeded in fooling herself, but not now, not here. Suddenly she couldn't bear to stay a moment more, and as the cotillion ended, she told Sir Oliver she had a dreadful headache and intended to go home.

At first he insisted on seeing her safely back to Abbotlea, but she was equally insistent that he should remain at the ball. She was polite but firm, and to her relief he at last gave up trying to persuade her of anything. She slipped away from the ballroom just as the clock struck one.

The night was still wet and galeswept as her carriage commenced the long climb over the hill. But Piers had also decided to leave the ball early, and as his carriage passed hers, the weather fled from her mind as she saw her father gazing sternly at her in the light of the lamps. This time he was so close she knew there was no mistake. It wasn't simply someone who resembled him, it *was* him!

A daunting chill struck through her at the reproachful stare of those beloved eyes, but then the other carriage drew ahead, and the spell was broken. Quickly she lowered the window glass and leaned out to call to her coachman.

"Drive after that carriage!"

"But, madam, it's Lord Winterbourne's carriage!" he cried back, raising his voice above the racket of the wind and rain.

"Just catch up with it!"

"As you wish, madam."

The whip cracked, and the carriage sprang forward.

Rebecca clung to the leather handgrip as the vehicle swayed alarmingly through the darkness. She was filled with a tumult of emotion that matched the wildness of the night. The wind shook the carriage, and lashed the rain against the glass. She heard the coachman's whip again as he urged the horses to greater effort toward the summit, where the lamps of Piers's vehicle swung away to the left toward Winterbourne Castle.

Rebecca's coachman followed. Clouds suddenly obscured the road directly ahead. He heard someone shouting, and just in time saw a light being waved through the murk. The other carriage had halted and was blocking the way. With a cry of alarm he applied the brakes and reined his team in with all his might, bringing them to a standstill with only a few feet to spare.

Piers's carriage had struck a large stone in the road, and he and his coachman had removed one of the lamps to see how much damage there was. Hearing the oncoming vehicle, they'd called out a warning. The lamp shone on Piers's startled face as the lead horses loomed out of the swirling clouds. "What in God's name—?" he cried, astonished that another carriage should take the Winterbourne road at this hour.

Rebecca lowered the window to see what was happening, and as she saw Piers, she flung open the door to alight.

Startled still more, Piers thrust the lamp into his coachman's hand. "Mrs. Winterbourne?"

She hardly heard him as she ran to look into his carriage, but it was empty. Tears stung her eyes as she whirled about to face him. "Where is he?" she demanded, her voice catching on a sob.

"Where is who?"

"My father!"

Irritation visibly swept through him in the lamplight. "Not again! Mrs. Winterbourne, I don't profess to know what all this is about, but I *do* know your father died some time ago, so will you please—!"

"But I saw him! I *saw* him!" The tears welled helplessly from her eyes, and she hid her face in her hands. She must be losing her mind! What other explanation was there?

He saw she was at the end of her tether, and went to take her hands and lower them gently so he could look into her distraught eyes. "I left the ball alone, I swear," he said reasonably, his voice only just audible above the storm.

Her face was wet with both tears and rain. "But he was there," she insisted. "I had a clear view of him looking out at me as you passed me on the hill, and he was angry with me. So angry. I *know* I wasn't imagining it; he was seated right there!" Her finger trembled as she pointed into his carriage.

"Mrs. Winterbourne—Rebecca—it's clear you're most unwell, and I think I should see you straight home to Abbotlea. I'll explain to your family about—"

He didn't finish, for there was a sudden gust of wind so strong that it almost blew them from their feet. The coachman had to cling to one of the horses, and dropped the lamp, which immediately went out. There was an ominous splintering sound, followed by a huge groan and a crash as one of the trees behind the carriages fell across the road, completely blocking the way back to the fork.

A gale-whipped debris of twigs and bark scattered through the air, and Piers instinctively pulled Rebecca close to shield her. He stared at the fallen tree, realizing that it was the very one by which he'd earlier seen the cloaked man. Unease washed stealthily through him. There was something strange abroad tonight, something a little beyond his comprehension. . . . What was that old countryman's prayer his nurse used to say? *From ghoulies, and ghosties, and long-leggedy beasties, Good Lord deliver us.* . . .

The moment the superstitious thought came to him, he cast it angrily aside. Pull yourself together, man! The tree is pure coincidence, and Rebecca keeps seeing her father because she's ill! But still he couldn't help staring at the tree. With hindsight it seemed to him it had fallen almost as if on cue, and now it obstructed the road as surely as any locked gate. There was no turning back; the only way was straight ahead. To Winterbourne Castle.

He spoke gently to Rebecca. "It's all right; we've come to no harm."

For a fleeting second she felt his fingers move softly in the hair at the nape of her neck.

He turned to the two coachmen. "We've no choice but to go on to the castle now, and since my carriage is damaged, I'll take Mrs. Winterbourne in hers." He nodded at his own man. "Come along as best you can. The wheel should hold, but I'll send help as soon as possible."

"My lord."

Rebecca was alarmed. Go to the castle? She couldn't! She shook her head defiantly. "No! Not the castle. I won't go there—"

He interrupted. "You aren't being given the choice. I'll send a rider to Abbotlea to let them know what's happened, then in the morning I'll have the tree hauled aside so you can go home. For the moment, however, you're accompanying me to the castle, and that's the end of it."

Determined to brook no further objection, he ushered her toward her carriage. She glanced agitatedly over her shoulder at the open door of his vehicle. For a moment she was again sure there was a shadowy figure inside, but as she continued to look, she knew no one was there.

Piers helped her into the carriage, and then climbed in with her. A moment later the Abbotlea coachman maneuvered around the damaged vehicle and drove carefully on down the hillside, bracing himself for the buffeting of the wind where the road emerged from the shelter of the trees onto more exposed land.

The other coachman prepared to follow as best he could. He climbed back onto his seat and took up the reins, but as he moved the team gingerly forward, he was watched by a shadowy figure near the fallen tree. The cloaked man's garments flapped in the wind, and there was a smile on his spectral face.

Rebecca stared at the rain on the window as she was conveyed toward the castle where she'd sworn to never again set foot. Her hands clasped and unclasped in her lap, and several minutes passed before she spoke to Piers.

"I vowed never to enter Winterbourne Castle again."

"Needs must when the devil drives, and I'm afraid he has the reins right now. Or would you have preferred me to leave you at the roadside?"

"Maybe."

"Oh. Would that be because such neglect would provide you with yet another reason to point an accusing finger at me? I can't believe that even you would rather be stranded in weather like this than be beholden to me."

"The Winterbournes have given me precious little reason to wish to have anything to do with them," she replied.

He caught her gaze and held it. "You're always so sure of your facts, aren't you? So quick to form opinions and cling to them as if they're something precious. Well, it may interest you to know that whereas you're right in everything you think about my father, who was all the unpleasant things you say, you're most certainly wrong in virtually everything where I'm concerned. There are uncomfortable facts of which you know nothing, madam."

"What do you mean?"

"Home truths, madam. Home truths." He looked away from her, and the ensuing silence was broken only by the noise of the storm. The wind howled dismally down from the craggy heights of High Tor, and dark clouds raced across the night sky. He gazed out. It might be Christmas, but this was indeed a night for ghoulies, and ghosties, and long-leggedy beasties. . . .

A quarter of an hour later the carriage turned through the griffin-flanked gates of the castle and drove along the wide drive with its avenue of beech trees. Rebecca looked up at the trees. The last time she'd been here it had been high summer, and leaves had cast dappled shadows across the way. Now bare branches swung to and fro overhead as the wind whistled through them.

The lights of the castle were reflected in the unsettled water of the moat, and then the carriage wheels rattled on the wooden drawbridge that gave into the shelter of the courtyard.

The moment the coachman reined in, Piers alighted and held out a hand to Rebecca. "Welcome to Winterbourne Castle, Rebecca," he said, his voice quite clear because the walls of the castle rose protectively all around, shutting out the full rage of the night.

He'd used her first name a moment before the tree fell. She didn't notice then, and she didn't notice now as she hesitantly accepted his assistance to alight. Rain fell coldly on her face as she glanced around. How odd it was to be standing here again after all this time, and with Piers instead of Edward. The storm raged beyond the great stone walls, and she shivered as for a moment she thought she heard someone calling her name on the wind. *Rebecca . . . Rebecca. . . .*

Piers took her arm. "Come inside, for the sooner you're in the warm, the better."

A wall lantern swayed by the arched doorway as they left the night behind to enter the great hall. The vast medieval chamber was brightly lit by heavy wheelrim chandeliers suspended from a hammerbeam roof, and by free-standing candlesticks by the walls. Suits of armor glinted in the glow from the Yule logs that burned brightly against the andirons of the two great stone fireplaces, and priceless displays of weapons and shields shone on the stonework above the dark oak wall paneling. Christmas garlands were festooned all around, and the smell of spiced wine drifted from the large jug keeping warm by the nearest hearth.

Piers beckoned a waiting footman. "Have some men

ride back along the road to assist with my damaged carriage, and see that a message is sent to Abbotlea Manor to inform Mrs. Winterbourne's household she will be unable to return there tonight because the road is blocked by a fallen tree. A rider won't have difficulty getting through."

"My lord."

"And I want the principal guest chamber prepared immediately for Mrs. Winterbourne. Select one of the maids to attend her. Kitty would seem the wisest choice."

"Very well, my lord." The footman bowed and hurried away.

Piers waited until he'd gone before speaking to Rebecca. "I'm afraid propriety is a little at risk, for this year my sisters and aunts prefer to spend Christmas in London, but the castle is large enough for us to keep well apart." He poured a glass of the spiced wine, and pressed it into her cold fingers. "Sip this—it will help restore you."

She cupped the warm glass in her hands. "How determined you are to be the attentive host," she murmured.

Swift anger lit his eyes. "And how determined *you* are to be the injured party," he replied. "Very well, madam, the time has come to set the record straight. I warned you there were home truths you had yet to hear, and now I'm about to tell you some of them. To begin with, I have *never* disapproved of you; in fact, the opposite has always been the case. But I did disapprove of your marriage to my cousin. Not because I thought you weren't good enough for him, but because I knew *he* wasn't good enough for you."

She lowered her glass incredulously.

He continued. "I'm tired of the reproach and accusation I see in your eyes every time we meet. You charge me with treating you and your children shabbily, but I've been leaving you alone because that was what I thought you wanted. If anyone treated you shabbily, it was my cousin. Edward was a charming wastrel, a disarming rake who was completely incapable of putting anyone before himself."

"How dare you!"

He continued as if she hadn't spoken. "Edward had more than sufficient income to support a wife and children in comfort, but instead chose to gamble it all away. Not content with that, he indulged in wild escapades like the race that eventually led to his death. Time and time again he put his own selfish pleasures first, and in the end he left you without a penny, just as I always knew he would."

"How can you say such dreadful things?" she whispered, trembling so much she had to put her glass down.

"Don't delude yourself anymore, Rebecca. Edward Winterbourne wasn't worthy of the love you lavished on him, and that's why I was against the match."

"Oh, how noble of you, to be sure! Well, let me remind you that everyone here at Winterbourne Castle—including you, sirrah!—was implacably and vengefully—"

He broke in again. "Rebecca, I make no excuses for my father, whose prejudices were renowned, or for the rest of my family, who meekly went along with his wishes, but you've wronged me all along!"

"I think not!"

"I admit I mishandled matters when you and Edward first came together," he conceded.

"Mishandled? You changed overnight from friend to enemy!"

"I've never been your enemy."

"Your attitude toward me altered the moment Edward and I stepped out for that ländler, and you've remained hostile ever since," she accused.

He drew a long breath. "Hostile isn't the word I'd choose."

"I'm sure it isn't, but it's the appropriate one."

"No, Rebecca, it isn't remotely appropriate. What would you have had me do? Pretend to approve of a match I thought was wrong? You made it only too clear that Edward was the be-all and end-all of your existence, and since his death you've continued in the same vein. Rather than be confrontational, I decided to observe my res—" He broke off.

"Observe your what?" she asked.

"Nothing. Shall we say I simply felt it was preferable all around if I stayed well away from you. I thought that was how you wished it to be, or are you now about to say I've been wrong?"

She couldn't answer.

He searched her face. "Rebecca, I—"

At last she realized he was using her first name all the time. "I gave you no leave to address me so familiarly," she interrupted.

His anger flashed into life again. "Damn it, I've known you since you were sixteen, so I'm taking that leave anyway! I've had enough of your stubbornness and unfair accusations, Rebecca. I concede that things went lamentably wrong between us when you and Edward announced your betrothal, but I didn't mean to give the impression I did. Put it down to my callow youth; after all, youth is no doubt the excuse you use for your own behavior at that time."

She colored.

He gave a dry laugh. "I see I'm right!" Then he became more serious. "Rebecca, I'm more sorry than you'll ever know that I permitted things to deteriorate between us. I've never looked down on you, and right now there's nothing I'd like more than to put all mis-understandings behind us. I'll begin by telling you that the doors of this castle have never been closed to you since I've been master here. You and your children are even more than welcome to reside beneath my roof if you so wish."

Her lips parted. "Reside here?" she repeated.

"It's your sons' birthright, Rebecca. My father may have excluded them for what he perceived as Edward's misalliance, but I restored them to their rightful place the moment I succeeded to the title. In fact, right now your eldest son is my heir."

Shaken, she stared at him. "Your—your heir?" she whispered.

"The title and inheritance must pass through the male line, and although I have sisters, aunts, female cousins, and *indirect* male family in plenty, Edward was my only direct male relative. Unless and until I'm blessed with a son of my own, who else would I name but his sons? Oh, but please don't fear that residence here is a prerequisite for your son's inheritance, for I quite understand Sir Oliver wouldn't view such a course with any favor." His blue eyes were piercing. "So much for your dearly held misconceptions about me, Rebecca. There's much more I could tell you, but perhaps it's better I don't."

She was so stunned to learn that Matthew was his heir that she didn't know what to say.

He gave her an almost mocking smile. "I appear to have given you food for thought, Rebecca, so I'll leave you now. A maid will attend you shortly. Good night, madam." Inclining his head coldly, he turned to walk away toward the dark oak staircase that rose from the far end of the hall.

She had no time to think, for just as he disappeared from view on the floor above, fresh footsteps swiftly echoed across the hall as a maid hurried toward her. "I'm Kitty, madam, and I'm to wait upon you," she said, bobbing a curtsey. She was small and tidy, with short dark hair, and wore a neat blue woolen dress and starched apron. "If you'll come this way . . . ?"

Rebecca's mind was still in a whirl as she followed the maid to the principal guest chamber, which was as sumptuous as its name suggested, with dark paneled walls, rich red-and-gold velvet hangings, and a specially built bed of such splendor it was almost regal.

As Kitty helped her change into a silk nightgown belonging to one of Piers's sisters, the only sound in the room was the crackling of the fresh logs on the fire. Soon pins tinkled into a dish, and strawberry satin ribbons slithered in a little pile on the dressing table as Rebecca sat for her hair to be brushed. She removed the favor from her wrist, and toyed thoughtfully with it as the hairbrush crackled through her dark tresses. Going to the ball tonight had been a huge mistake.

When Kitty had finished, she bobbed another curtsey. "Is there anything else you require, madam?"

"No. Thank you."

"As you wish, madam. Good night."

"Good night, Kitty."

"Oh, and a happy Christmas to you."

Rebecca managed a wry smile. "And to you, Kitty," she murmured. There was nothing happy about this Christmas, nothing at all.

As soon as the maid had gone, she climbed swiftly into the huge bed, curled up into a tight ball, and pulled the bedclothes over her head. But in the cocoon of darkness, she could still hear Piers's voice, and still see his face.

She hid her face in her hands. He'd said there were other things she didn't yet know, but there were things *he* didn't know either. Such as how much she loved him. And that although she was alone in this great bed, she wished more than anything that he were with her. If only he were, if only his arms were around her now, his lips soft against hers, his body urgent with the same desire that coursed so needfully through hers. This night she wanted to surrender to the feelings that had ruled her for so long, but she knew the dawn would come and nothing would have changed. She'd still be enslaved by secret passion, and he would neither know nor care.

But the night hadn't finished yet. The cloaked man was already striding through the stormy darkness toward the castle, and would soon be within its walls to continue making fate—and Rebecca Winterbourne—bow to his wishes.

She was still awake a little later when slow, echoing footsteps approached her door. She sat up with a frightened gasp as a single imperative knock reverberated through the entire castle.

Holding the bedclothes to her chin, she gazed nervously toward the sound. "Who—who is it?"

The only reply was a second firm knock, then whoever it was walked slowly away, and again the steps echoed loudly.

Trembling, she flung the bedclothes aside and went to press her ear to the door. As the steps grew more faint, she opened the door to look out into the dark passage. Candlelight flickered at the far end as someone turned the corner and passed out of sight. She just caught a glimpse of a dark hem, and then the candle-light faded.

The cloaked man! Her father? Gathering her flimsy nightgown, she hurried barefoot after him. The cold of the night didn't seem to touch her as she ran, and as she reached the corner, she was in time to see the man disappearing down the staircase.

"Stop!" she called desperately. "Please stop!"

She reached the top of the stairs, and paused with her hand on the greenery-swathed newel post to watch the shadowy figure walking slowly across the firelit hall toward the arched door of the library Suddenly he turned to look back at her, and his candle shivered, sending wild shadows leaping over the floor. Its uncertain light shone momentarily upon his face.

"Father? It *is* you, isn't it?" she cried.

He didn't reply, but made a beckoning gesture with his arm, and then continued toward the library.

She hesitated, then gathered her skirts again to follow; but as she reached the foot of the staircase, the library door closed resoundingly behind him. Her bare feet were almost silent on the stone floor as she ran across the hall, but suddenly Piers's call halted her.

"Rebecca?"

She turned and saw him standing at the top of the staircase where she'd been a moment before. He was still wearing his evening clothes, and had been smoking a Spanish cigar in his room when he'd heard her cries.

Her voice shook. "My father has just gone into the library."

"Please stop this, Rebecca," he replied, coming down toward her.

"But it's true! Didn't you just hear the door close? He's in there now, and he wants me to follow him."

Turning, she continued toward the library, but as she flung the door open, what she saw inside brought her to an astonished standstill.

The room was in darkness, except for a soft glow from the hearth, but by that light she saw a blizzard of airborne documents. Every private paper in the castle seemed to be eddying around the room. Her father's ghostly figure was by the fire, dark and mysterious against the flames, and as she stared, he pointed at one of the papers, which gradually floated to the carpet at her feet. As she bent to retrieve it, her father immediately disappeared, and the flying documents tumbled to the floor like a huge pack of cards.

Piers ran up behind her just in time to see the figure vanish and the papers fall, and he gave a startled gasp. "Great God above!"

She clutched the paper she'd picked up, crumpling it slightly as she gazed around nervously. What did it all mean? Why was her father appearing to her like this?

Piers took her arm and drew her protectively toward him. "It's all right, it's stopped now," he said gently, but there was a slight tremor in his voice.

"He *was* there, wasn't he? My father? You saw him too?" she asked anxiously. "Please say you did."

"Yes, I saw him."

Tears sprang to her eyes, and she turned to look up at him. "Why, Piers? Why is it happening?"

"I don't know." He glanced uneasily at the paper she held.

She saw his glance, and looked down at the paper too. Then her lips parted with fresh shock as she read the first legal sentences written in beautiful copperplate. *This day, being the first of March in the Year of Grace eighteen hundred and ten, has an agreement been made for the monthly allowance shown below to be paid to Mr. Clifford Newton of Abbotlea Manor in the County of Devon, by Piers Winterbourne, Tenth Lord Winterbourne, of Winterbourne Castle in the County of Devon, for the maintenance and well-being of Mrs. Edward Winterbourne and her sons, Matthew Edward Henry and Frederick William James. . . .*

She stared at the writing for a long moment. Suddenly so much became clear, not least being how Clifford and Margaret had managed to stretch their finances to provide for three extra mouths! And she understood why they felt she'd been wronging Piers. Of course they'd think that, for they knew Piers was her benefactor. That was why they were always so anxious when she told them how badly her latest confrontation with him had gone, and why they'd been so at pains to gain her promise of good behavior at the ball. How doubly deceived she'd been! By him, and by her own family!

Piers looked uneasily at her. "I didn't want you to find out like this, Rebecca."

She quivered with anger. "No, I'll warrant you didn't. So this is what you declined to elaborate upon earlier! You almost blurted it out, didn't you? You began to say that rather than be confrontational, you decided to observe your responsibilities by paying my brother a suitable sum! That's correct, isn't it?"

"Yes," he admitted unwillingly.

"Have you any idea how this makes me feel?" she cried. "I thought I was dependent upon my brother's charity, but all the time *you* were keeping me!"

"Keeping you?" He laughed a little. "My God, if *that's* what I've been doing, I've reaped scant reward from the arrangement! Oh, Rebecca, is it so demeaning to receive help from me? Do you hate me so much you'd rather your sons went without than accept anything I offer? Damn it, I'd have paid much much more if Clifford thought he'd be able to fool you into thinking the money came from him."

"I'll never forgive Clifford for this, or Margaret!"

"Unlike you, they've been putting your children's welfare first," he said coldly. "That's why your brother sent word to me as soon as he heard of your intention to marry Willoughby. He doesn't think Sir Oliver is a suitable person to be your sons' father, nor do I! But you, as always it seems, are incapable of making a sensible choice of husband!"

"I find you deeply offensive, sirrah!" she breathed.

"That, madam, is your prerogative."

She struck him, and her fingers left angry marks on his cheek. Bitterness and resentment flooded so strongly through her she couldn't help herself, and she'd have struck him a second time if he hadn't seized her wrist.

"Once is more than enough!" he said softly, and then flung her wrist aside to walk away. Suddenly he halted and came back, seizing her by both arms and shaking her slightly. "You're the most provoking and stubborn woman I have ever known. Believe me, if you were being kept by me in the fullest sense of the word, I'd see you were always too busy between the sheets to indulge your propensity for carefully nurtured grievances!" His eyes were like blue ice.

"There speaks the true gentleman!"

"More of a gentleman than the spendthrift you married, and certainly more than the vain old featherbrain you're about to wed! You're so fond of telling me how *you* feel, aren't you? Well, have you ever paused for a single second to wonder how *I* feel? Has it ever crossed your mind to think for a moment *why* I behaved as I did when you took up so very publicly with my cousin? Well, has it?" He shook her again.

"I—I don't understand!"

"No, you *never* understand! You merely judge and condemn out of hand!"

"Piers—"

"If you had any idea of the pain and heartbreak I felt when you danced with Edward and then allowed him to kiss you in front of the entire ball ... Rebecca, I wanted it to be me! *I* wanted to kiss you like that, *I* wanted to hold you close and show the world how much I loved and needed you. But in the space of a few short minutes, suddenly you were Edward's. And now we've come to this—hating each other so much we can't be civil for more than a few seconds."

She was so thunderstruck she could only stare at him. He'd *loved* her all those years ago? Oh, Piers, Piers ... But as her lips parted to confess that she'd not only loved him then, but loved him still, he spoke again.

"Well, Rebecca, we may not have just finished a ländler, and there may not be mistletoe or a host of on-lookers, but I'm damned well going to take that kiss I wanted all those years ago!"

Before she knew it, he'd pulled her close and put his lips over hers. He held her tight with one arm, while his other hand slid richly over the warmth of her body through the thin stuff of her nightgown. He pressed her against him so that she could feel the arousal at his loins, and all the time his lips taunted her remorselessly. It was the skilled kiss of a man who'd made an art of lovemaking, and knew how to give as much pleasure as he took.

But then, as abruptly as he'd taken her in the embrace, he released her again, and without a word turned on his heel to walk away, leaving her standing in the library doorway with the crumpled paper still in her hand.

She called after him "Piers?"

He didn't look back.

"Piers!" she cried.

But he walked on, ascending the staircase and passing out of sight as if he hadn't heard her. After a moment she heard his door close softly.

Suddenly the ghostly hand seized her shoulder again. Its grasp was cold through her nightgown, and its strength fierce as it shook her angrily. She stumbled forward as it let go, and this time when she whirled about, her father stood there, his face grim in the uncertain light.

Tears sprang to her eyes. "Why are you doing this, Father? Why have you come back? What have I done?"

In reply he walked past her, stepping so close she felt the sweeping draft of his cloak. His steps rang on the floor as he crossed to the staircase, where he turned to beckon before going slowly up.

She obeyed the silent command, her feet making no sound as she went after him. At the top of the staircase she paused, for he'd disappeared. She looked all around, but there were only shadows. She didn't know what to do. Where was she supposed to go?

Walking on, she paused again at Piers's door, trying to summon the courage to tell him the truth. But when she remembered the cynical way he'd kissed her, and how he'd refused to even look back when she'd called after him, she couldn't go in.

Gathering her nightgown, she cravenly began to hurry on toward her own room, but suddenly her father's reproachful figure barred the way. He shook his head, and wagged his finger, then he pointed at Piers's door.

"I—I can't," she whispered.

He pointed again, more commandingly this time.

She searched his face. "You want me to go to Piers?"

He nodded, and suddenly she could hear his voice, even though his lips didn't move. "You can find complete happiness with Piers Winterbourne. Seize your chance, Rebecca, for there will not be another one."

As the last word was uttered, Piers's door opened of its own accord, as if inviting her to enter. She hesitated, but her father's gaze was still upon her, commanding and determined. She lowered her eyes submissively and stepped into the anteroom between the passage and the main apartment. As soon as she was inside, the door closed behind her.

Leaving the anteroom, she went into the apartment beyond. It was quiet, and the Jacobean furnishings were elegant in the mixed glow of candles and firelight. Piers stood looking into the fire, with one foot resting on the polished fender. He had a glass of cognac, and his golden hair was burnished as he stared into the flames without realizing she was there.

She gazed at him. Events beyond her control had brought her here, but she was in control now. She knew that if she said his name and went toward him, she'd expose forever the close-guarded secret she'd kept safely hidden for so long.

Suddenly he sensed her presence and turned. "Rebecca?" He placed his glass on the mantelshelf. "Why have you come here? If it's to demand an apology for my monstrous conduct a few minutes ago, then I apologize."

"If—if anyone should apologize, it's me, Piers."

"You bear a share of the blame, I'll grant you that."

"I deserve your anger. And my father's," she added.

"Your father's?" He looked at her and then smiled a little. "If I hadn't seen what I did in the library, I'd still think you were imagining it all. No, that's not strictly true, for there have been other things." He told her about trying to burn Clifford's note, and about the shadowy figure he'd seen by the tree on his way to the ball.

She swallowed. "I—I wish you'd told me, instead of leaving me to think I was suffering from hallucinations. I kept seeing my father everywhere—by the river, in the church doorway, at the ball, in your carriage, and then here in the castle too. And there were the invisible hands on my shoulder, to say nothing of apparently winged documents taking to the air both here and in the library of Abbotlea." She lowered her eyes for a moment, and then summoned her courage. "Piers, there's something I have to confess."

He searched her face. "A confession? I can't imagine what sin you've committed."

"It's not a sin exactly."

"Whatever it is, I hardly think I'm the one who should play confessor, do you? Surely Sir Oliver now has first claim upon that role?" He said this last with heavy irony.

"Sir Oliver hasn't got first claim on anything. I—I'm not going to marry him." Until the words came to her lips, she didn't realize she'd even made the decision, let alone made it so firmly and irrevocably.

"Wisdom at last, belated maybe, but better late than never. It was an appalling idea from the outset. You have no need to marry again, unless for love of course. If you'll only permit me to do what's right, I'll gladly make a generous allowance to support you and your sons. It's my duty to do it, Rebecca, and it's a duty I'd undertake only too willingly."

"Is that what I've become? A duty?" she asked then.

He didn't reply.

She seized all the courage she could find. "Piers, by the library a few minutes ago, you said . . . You said you once loved me."

"Anger brings forth rash disclosures," he murmured.

"And contrition is about to bring forth the same from me," she said quietly.

"Indeed? And what have you to be contrite about?"

"My obstinacy."

Humor lightened his eyes. "Which quality you have in plenty."

"I know."

He searched her face. "Although some may call it splendid spirit," he said softly.

"There's nothing splendid or spirited about my faint-heartedness at this moment."

"I don't understand."

Somehow she managed to meet his gaze. "Piers, the feelings you once had for me . . . I—I share them. I mean, I still have them, although I know they're very much in the past for you."

"I'm not sure I follow your meaning, but I certainly hope I do." His blue eyes were quizzical in the fire-light. "Would it help if I said those feelings have never become past for me? They're as strong for me now as they always were."

Her lips parted as hope leapt into her heart. "They are?"

He smiled. "Well, I think so. Provided we're talking about the same thing. We *are* talking about the same thing, aren't we?"

She stared at him. "I—I don't know."

"Then we may be here for some time, both timidly tiptoeing around the issue without being bold enough to say it outright."

Suddenly she found the strength she needed. "I'll say it outright, Piers. I love you, and I always have." A huge weight seemed to be lifted from her, and she closed her eyes with relief. She'd said it. After all these years, she'd told him what she'd kept hidden for so long!

He didn't say anything, and at last she opened her eyes to look anxiously at him. But he was smiling. "Oh, my darling, darling Rebecca, we were indeed talking of the same thing," he said softly, holding out his hand to her.

She gazed incredulously at him. "We were? We truly were?"

"How can you ever doubt it? Come here."

With an overjoyed sob she ran to him. He caught her fingers tightly to pull her gladly into his arms, then his lips found hers in a kiss so filled with released longing it seemed to turn their flesh to fire.

Then for a long moment they stood in a passionate embrace. Her forehead rested against his shoulder, and her eyes were closed as she made the other confession that had tormented her for so long. "Piers, it was you I wanted at the ball when I danced with Edward, but I thought you weren't interested."

His fingers coiled the hair at the nape of her neck. "But I *was* interested," he whispered. "I wanted you more than anything, but suddenly it was too late, and I'd lost you to him."

She drew back slightly to look at him. "I did love him, you know."

"I know."

"I just couldn't stop loving you as well."

"You've been hiding it very well," he murmured, pushing a stray lock of her dark hair back from her face.

"It was self-defense," she replied.

He smiled a little. "So was my brief dalliance with that northern heiress. I was trying to put you from my mind. It didn't work. That's why I came back here this Christmas. I couldn't stay away, I had to at least *see* you."

She moved away a little awkwardly. "There'll be talk, you know. When it gets out that not only have I broken the match with Sir Oliver, but did so after spending the night alone here with you . . ." She glanced at him. "I became notorious enough when I married Edward, but at the ball tonight it was clear I've become positively infamous. I dread to think what will be said when the latest chatter spreads. There won't be a teacup in Devon that doesn't rattle."

"Let them rattle until they shatter; it doesn't matter to me. Nor should it matter to you, for you've never done anything wrong."

"Maybe not wrong, just foolish."

He smiled. "Possibly."

She went back into his arms, holding him tightly around the waist. "Whether or not I was foolish in the past, I'm my own woman now—a woman, not a shrinking virgin," she whispered.

"I loved the shrinking virgin of sixteen, and I adore the woman," he breathed, bending to press his lips to the pulse at her throat.

She closed her eyes. It seemed she'd wanted this man forever, as if she'd lived two lives: one the reality of Edward, the other the exquisite dream of Piers. The dream was flesh and blood now. Oh, such exciting flesh and blood.

He cupped her face in his hands. "Love urges me to go on now, to make you mine in every way. If that is what you wish too, you only have to say. But if you wish to stop now . . ."

Her eyes were warm and dark. "I never want you to stop," she said softly.

His hand moved to enclose her breast through her nightgown. She moved seductively against him, welcoming kisses that became more and more passionate. Oh, how long she had waited for this moment, yearned for it so much that it keened through her like a persistent echo.

He unbuttoned her nightgown so it slid to the floor, then he gathered her into his arms and carried her to the great damask-hung bed. She lay there with her hair spilling in dark confusion over the rich tapestry coverlet, watching as he slowly undressed. His body was pale and lithe, but firm and muscular, and his virility was now a pounding erection that pressed hotly into her flesh when he lay with her on the bed.

He leaned over her, his blue eyes dark with desire. "I love you, Rebecca," he whispered.

She closed her eyes as his lips sought hers again. Kiss followed kiss, caress succeeded caress. They explored each other's bodies, exulted in the intimacy they'd both secretly craved for so very long. Even with Edward she'd never known such delight and satisfaction from mere kisses.

But these weren't mere kisses; they meant everything in the world to two people whose own blindness had kept them apart.

When at last he entered her, tears of joy welled from her eyes. She shivered with ecstasy, and her breath caught on a cry as he withdrew in order to push in once more. It was the sweetest rapture, and she wanted it to go on forever. She knew she'd never tire of him, never secretly wish he were someone else. He was the one, the only one.

His strokes quickened as emotion overwhelmed him. Then at last the moment was there, bewildering in its intensity. Shuddering surges of pleasure made them both weightless, ethereal beings, entirely fulfilled.

She clung to him, still silently crying. He kissed her, and tasted her tears.

They lay in each other's arms, their passion sated, and after a while she spoke. "I'm so happy, Piers."

He hesitated. "Well, I would be too, but . . ." He deliberately allowed the sentence to trail away unfinished.

"But?" She sat up anxiously in order to search his face.

"But I can only be truly happy if you're here with me all the time. This castle needs a chatelaine, and you seem to be the only possible woman for the role."

She stared at him. "You—you're asking me to marry you?"

"I should have done it years ago, at that other damned ball, but I didn't. I don't intend to make the same mistake again. So will you marry me, Rebecca?"

"Do you really mean it?"

"I've never meant anything more in my life."

"Then I accept," she whispered.

"I almost wish Christmas Day would forget to dawn, for I want to lie here with you like this forever," he said softly, pulling her down into his arms again.

But Christmas Day did dawn, and as the sky lightened, the wind and rain seemed to die away. The sound of Abbotlea church bells drifted distantly on the still air as Rebecca opened her eyes.

She was warm and loved in Piers's arms, and her only regret was that so much time had been lost in foolish misunderstanding.

Another sound attracted her attention. Someone was calling her name outside. Her lips parted, for it was her father.

She slipped naked from the bed, and put on her nightgown to go to the window, which looked out along the moorland road toward the wooded hill where the tree had fallen.

It was snowing, large flakes that skimmed through the air in a way that reminded her of the papers in the libraries, and the Christmas diversion at the ball. Then, just as at the ball, she gazed through the snow and saw her father's face.

The familiar cloaked figure stood on the moor, and as she looked, he removed his hat to wave. At last his face was happy and smiling, not angry or reproachful, and she distinctly heard his voice.

"Good-bye, Rebecca."

"Good-bye, Father," she answered.

Then he turned and began to walk away. His silhouette gradually became more indistinct, until the snow obscured him altogether.

Piers stirred behind her. "What are you looking at?" he asked curiously, leaning up on one elbow.

"My father." She turned. "I won't see him again."

"Can you be sure of that?"

She nodded. "I know now that he only came back to make me face the truth about myself. I've done that, so his task is complete."

Piers smiled. "No more cloaked man?"

"No more cloaked man."

He held out his hand. "Come back to bed," he said softly.

She went to him, and he drew her down into the warmth, before pulling the bedclothes over them both. Then he leaned to look down into her eyes. "This is the most wonderful Christmas of my life," he whispered.

"And of mine."

She closed her eyes in delight as he kissed her once more, and she was sure that in the far distance, carried on the Christmas snow, she heard her father's farewell call.

"Be happy now, Rebecca."

The Rake's Christmas

by Edith Layton

He sat outside the glow of candlelight, sprawled at his ease in a chair at a table, looking every inch the hard, reckless, heartless young man about town. He was well and expensively dressed, his dark hair was slightly mussed, his neckcloth slightly loosened. But he was otherwise scrupulously neat, even though he'd been drinking all night. Although his pose was relaxed, it was clear he wasn't. His dark eyes glittered with restless energy, his long hand was tight and white-knuckled on his glass; nothing that happened before him went unnoticed, but he took no part in anything that did. All he did was drink and watch, though he'd been invited to much more. He was a man of action, obviously waiting, but no one in the room could say for what. He was also clearly troubled, and clearly trouble, too, and so even the bravest wenches eventually left the room on other men's arms, though they left him with their lingering, longing looks as they did.

It was hard to say if he sensed their interest. He definitely didn't seem to care. Which was odd, because he sat in a luxurious brothel, and the men that came there seldom came only for the wine, superior though it was.

He was dark in every aspect of the word: appearance and mood. His lean body was fashionably dressed in dark evening attire, but his skin was unfashionably deeply tanned, and his cropped hair was black as his mood was dangerous. He sat straight as the soldier he had lately been, and his brooding face showed no emotion but impatience. His features were regular, his face fine-boned, he was almost handsome—that is, if one could ignore the long, deep, dark scar that cleft one lean cheek from beneath his dark eye to his tightly knotted jaw. And yet, even so, that harsh face was attractive—in the way that deep black water and stormy midnights held their own dark fascination. The women who gazed at him as they slowly left the room with other men seemed to think so. But then, they were the sort of women who had already ruined their lives, and so could hardly be expected to care about what further damage they did themselves.

The hour grew later, the room slowly emptied, until only one other man remained. That one, a middle-aged gentleman, seemed content enough with the conversation he was having with the proprietress of the establishment. That was odd, too, because the gentleman was a famous rake, and Madam Felice was no longer appealing to any of her customers. Even if she were, it was well known that her only interest in her business was in the business of it now. The dark young man didn't seem to notice that either. He merely tossed off the last in his glass, which was the last of the bottle he'd just had, rose from his chair and strode toward the door, signaling to a footman for his greatcoat.

"But my lord!" Madam Felice cried when she saw him. She cut off her conversation midsentence and hurried after him. "Leaving so soon?"

The young man grew very still. He looked down at the agitated madam of the house, and his harsh face grew colder. "I am," he said in a chill voice.

"But how have we offended?" she asked.

"I was not aware," he said in distant tones, "that it was necessary to apologize. Things must have changed since I was last in London. Must a man now remain in a whorehouse once he enters it?"

She winced, and it might have been that she paled beneath all the makeup she'd painted on her face. Like so many of her kind, she had little heart, less pride, and fewer emotions, but they all were invested in her trade.

"We prefer to think of ourselves as a house of accommodation," she said in a strained voice, "but of course you don't have to stay on. It's only that we pride ourselves on our—accommodations. Where have we failed you?"

Now he smiled. It was not a pleasant smile. And when he spoke it was more to himself than to her. "You have not," he said. Sketching her a mocking bow, he added, "My expectations didn't meet your reality—or rather, your reality overcame my expectations. Whatever. I find I am not in the mood for reality tonight. Good night, madam."

He shrugged into his coat, clapped on his hat, and left her.

She turned to find the last gentleman in the room putting on his coat as well.

"My Lord Shelton! Now I have offended you!" she cried in dismay, because this gentleman was a renowned rake and his trade meant more trade to her establishment.

"Not in the least," he said. "It is only that my business here is done for the night. I only stopped by to drop off a pourboire for you and the ladies, in the spirit of the holiday to come. I'll be out of town for Christmas and didn't want you to think I'd forgotten."

She grimaced; it was ridiculous and they both knew it. He could have sent a footman if that was all he'd

wanted. "Ah! I apologize; it's all my fault," she said
unhappily. "It was getting late and I no longer thought
you were coming tonight. That's the only reason I told
dear Louisa to go off with another gentleman instead
of waiting for you. But I should have listened to her!
For of course she hesitated—she prefers you. Forgive
me, my lord, I should have told her to wait; I know
she's a favorite of yours."

"Not your fault, or hers," he said amiably, drawing
on his gloves. "My only favorite is diversity, which
means I can have no other. By your leave, madam, I go
to seek it now."

He didn't have to explain himself to her. But Lord
Shelton was a gentleman as well as a rake, and could
no more help his good manners than he could his carelessness, about whom he used them with. She had no
course but to smile and bid him good night. She went
to the door and saw him out and was so angry with
herself she didn't notice that he seemed to be following her last customer down the street and into the
night. That might have interested her. It might have reminded her that while she and Lord Shelton had chatted, that particular young man's name had come up
early, and often. Not that she had much to tell about
him, even though he had patronized her house. Only
what everyone else seemed to know: Ian Laurent Hunt,
the newly named Viscount Hunt, just home from the
wars, was thoroughly a rake, and though a lover of
mellow wine and tender women, as cold and dangerous
as a man could be. But her girls liked him as much as
he seemed to like them. And that was considerably.

The women at the theater Viscount Hunt went to
next liked him too. Not only the common prostitutes
who prowled the aisles, or the uncommon ones who sat
with their protectors in the boxes. But also the ladies

who stole surreptitious glances at him when their fathers or husbands weren't looking. As did the actresses and dancers who had performed tonight and now thronged the Green Room backstage, looking for more applause from their admirers—or more tangible forms of appreciation for further performances of a more intimate nature, to be arranged.

Some of the men who had made their way backstage carried flowers, others bore small packages that clearly contained expensive trinkets, still others fawned on the women they met, and some could not stop posturing for them. Viscount Hunt merely had to take off his coat to call attention to himself. His darkness and stillness, that one harsh face in the midst of so much gaiety, set him apart as surely as if he had shouted. That, and the strong, virile body his tight-fitted evening clothes displayed. The wry smile that grew on his well-shaped mouth as he looked at the company twisted his terrible scar, but he approached no one. He didn't have to. Every female in the place was looking at him. He was high drama, and there was nothing ladies of the theater liked more than that—except for money, which he was rumored to have in plenty, and a certain masculine magnetism, which needed no rumor to confirm. He smiled more wryly at the stir he caused, until he heard a man's voice at his side.

"I wish you might tell me what sort of cologne you use," the middle-aged gentleman who had come up to him said pensively. "Here I am, ready to be taken advantage of by any of these charming young things, and you appear and take their minds off simple commerce."

The viscount looked at his new companion, and though his face didn't change, his voice carried a hint of amusement in it. "Simple commerce, my lord? I think not. You are said to be generous."

"My reputation reached all the way to Spain?" Lord Shelton asked in surprise. "Oh, dear."

"I've been in England for over two months."

"Then there's hope for me. You relieve my mind," Lord Shelton said.

"You trouble mine," the viscount said. "I know about you for good reason. You are in your way a famous man, at least in the *ton.* I am not. Yet you know of me. Is there any particular reason for this?"

"My word, but you're a blunt fellow!"

The viscount didn't deny it. He stood patiently, waiting for Lord Shelton to say more. It wasn't a restful waiting. So he must have stood waiting for orders to go into battle. He radiated tension; he seemed capable of any sudden violent emotion. A lesser man might have made a weak jest and skulked away at this point. Lord Shelton laughed heartily instead.

"Put down your lance, Corporal," he said, "and don't slay me for my impudence or my puns. I know of you because of a certain opera dancer you met the other week. A pretty little creature all curls and giggles. At Sadler's Wells? Lord, the arrogance of youth—does the name Melissa Careaux strike a chord in your recent memory? Ah. The penny drops. Yes. She who was mine—in the loosest sense of the word, you understand—do forgive me my puns, they are the last refuge of an aging intellect. As I was saying, she was under my protection, but when she met you she also sought yours. And received it, and more, I understand. A few weeks past. *That* is how I know of you."

Something like weariness, something like boredom, something very like disgust showed in the younger man's dark eyes. "I see," he said. "Is it to be swords or pistols? Name your seconds and the time and place. I am at your convenience."

"A duel?" Lord Shelton said, aghast. "Did you think I would duel for a doxy's honor? It was, as you said, merely a matter of commerce for me. Although I flatter myself to think that in my youth I would not have needed that much money," he added sadly. "But then, in my youth, she would not have strayed, I don't think."

Now Ian Hunt, the newly named Viscount Hunt, studied his companion more carefully. Lord Shelton was a renowned rake, but he didn't appear to be dissipated or jaded. He looked clean and well maintained and was handsome enough for his years, of medium height with a stocky but strong, sturdy frame. He had all his brown hair, and it was cropped neatly. In short, a pleasant but unexceptional looking man, in spite of his reputation. But then, Ian realized he wasn't sure what a fellow who spent his life pursuing females *should* look like, after all.

He'd never thought about it before, but now realized he'd expected a man with the reputation of a rake and seducer to be slender and effete, oily and unctuous. Or else, grossly fat and coarse. He didn't know why. Now that he thought about it, he remembered that a man's behavior seldom wrote itself on his face or form. He himself had known men who could kill without compunction if ordered to, yet who would weep over a stray dog. He'd seen women with the faces of angelic children who had slit men's throats with no hesitation because their cause required it. He'd seen children who . . . The viscount blinked, aware too much time had passed since he'd last spoken, and that he'd been staring at Lord Shelton for too long without seeing him.

The war was over, he reminded himself. He redirected his thoughts.

"I see," he said abruptly. "I was not aware of your prior claim. I am newly returned to London, and as you seem to also know, was a soldier for many years before that. I was not aware of the rules."

"There are no rules." Lord Shelton laughed. "Or rather, it's a game where we constantly reinvent the rules. It's just that I wondered if you had a new game in mind. Because, you see, it was not only charming Melissa. Just the other week there was also Annabelle, my favorite little minx at Madam Felice's. Before that, the beautiful La Starr herself, and then that notoriously delicious Turner woman just last month. She still can't stop talking about you, by the by. It has her husband looking like thunder—not to mention what it has done to my poor self-esteem. I was wondering if you were concentrating on my particular familiars for any reason. Revenge for my dalliances with a friend or favorite of your own, perhaps? Or some other reason I should know of?"

But now the harsh face before him showed something other than impatience; the viscount was clearly stunned.

"I have no quarrel with you," he said stiffly, "nor had I any idea I was dallying with any of your . . . That is to say, I had no idea. I bear you no ill will, either, I promise you. Nor do I like the idea of consorting with women who . . ." He paused, realizing it was stupid to say he didn't like sleeping with women who had other men. What did he think opera dancers, actresses, and women who lived in bawdy houses did when he wasn't with them? His dark face grew darker with embarrassment. "My apologies," he said gruffly. "I'll be more circumspect in the future."

But now Lord Shelton roared with laughter. It was a rich, hearty sound that caused many in the room to smile with him. "My dear boy," Lord Shelton finally managed to say, "why should you be? It is the nature of men such as we to go after the most delicious females on the town. If we were to mind stepping on each other's toes, why, we'd be sitting home each night with our tabbies and nice cups of tea. Not our sort of fun at all. Nor fun for the dear ladies of our nights, either. Where would they be without us? No—so long as I know you've no intent other than the pursuit of pleasure, why, then, let the best man win. It may be," he said slyly, "that I can take one from you one day, you know. Youth and appeal are not everything; experience counts, too."

The viscount's dark eyes showed a flash of sudden pain. Those luminous eyes of his spoke volumes when he forgot to keep his thoughts from them—which was probably why the man kept himself under such tight control, Lord Shelton thought. Because even as he watched, he could no longer be sure of what he'd seen; the viscount's harsh and dour expression was back in place, his eyes cold again.

"The field is yours. I have no wish to compete. I am not a rake," Ian said in a tight voice. "Nor do I wish to become one. It's merely that it was a long war for me, and I find myself in need—of diversion."

"Ah, yes. I see," Lord Shelton said thoughtfully.

"I don't wish to return to the countryside as yet," Ian said, as though the words were forced from him. "I only recently came into the succession. My brother died when I was in Spain. It took months for me to hear of it. I returned to England to find that his wife still needs time before I take over her house and home. So I remain in London, and while I do, I ..."

"No need to explain, my lord," Lord Shelton said quickly. "I quite understand. More than you know. After all, I inquired about you when I believed you bore me a grudge. And I did know your father. Yes, we were at University at the same time, different years of course, but there was an overlap." That was all there'd been. Lord Shelton had been sent down from school so many times his term overlapped many others'. He only vaguely remembered Viscount Hunt. They'd had nothing in common. But the remembrance served to calm his son down now, and that was all he wanted.

"But as for being a rake?" Lord Shelton continued blandly. "I don't recall exactly vying for the title, either. It was awarded to me without my knowledge because that's how it is acquired, like honors for work done. One day I was just a young rogue looking for an accommodating female to pass a night with—and when I turned round a few years later, why, I was a full-fledged rake.

"You seem discomforted," he said, seeing the viscount's unease. "Please don't be. Just think of the other roles a fellow of title and fortune can play in our weary world and you'll see being a rake is not such a bad thing. It's certainly more interesting than being a dandy. Clothes are important, but those fellows make haberdashery their religion and their tailors, high priests. And being a rake is far less exhausting than being a Corinthian. All that sport wears one out before one's time. Not like my sort of sport, which is amazingly revitalizing. We rakes do tend to get a measure of healthful, restorative sleep as a natural result of our accomplishments, you know."

The harsh face before him grew a slight grin, which softened it.

"Nor is it like being a 'Peep o' Day' boy, either,"

Lord Shelton went on, encouraged, "which is only a jolly name for a nasty fellow who enjoys roughing up old men trying to eke out existences as watchmen, or tipping over barrow monger's carts, when they're only attempting to make a living as well, or bullying women they find defenseless, or forcing them . . . No, no. *That's* not in our line at all. Rakes *like* females. Nor do they dally with underage girls—that's for men who are afraid of grown women. No, rakes want full-blown willing females. And in order to succeed with them— for a rake is not a man who always buys his pleasure, that's a hedonist—why, then, he must have manners, charm, and intelligence. The dance is just as important to a true rake as what happens when the music stops, you see. The rake's ideal is to make the acquisition of a female as interesting and pleasurable an experience as the having of her is.

"Or so it used to be. But those were different days, when I shared the honors with the likes of Torquay and Bessacarr, Kidd, Austell and North—men of wit and title whose quirkish personalities were distinctly rakish. True rakes, to a man, in that they enjoyed women, sequentially. Alas, they've all fallen to matrimony, and all that changed. They're as constant as they were inconstant before, and that is to say considerably. While they're still excellent fellows, they're staid as standing stones now. I like them very well until they begin to talk about their families. I have none, you see—except for some tedious relatives who are beginning to wonder what I'll leave them besides a bad reputation. Perhaps that's why I was so quick to claim you as one of my diminishing fraternity. You remind me of myself in my salad days, you see."

The viscount's smile slipped.

"At any event, no hard feelings, eh?" Lord Shelton

asked. "I hope we meet again at some more opportune time. But I find myself quite unable to concentrate just now," he said, pointedly staring at a pretty little dancer who was smiling at him from across the room, "so if you'll excuse me?"

The viscount bowed. Lord Shelton stuck out his hand. "Courtesy is all very well, but I'd feel much more assured of your goodwill if we shook hands on it."

"Gladly done," the viscount said, and they shook hands.

The hand Lord Shelton took was a hard one, the clasp strong, but tempered. As he'd expected. He'd seen that hand many times during this past week as he'd watched the viscount from afar: seen it holding cards and wineglasses, as well as a woman's waist as he'd steered her across a room. It had told him more about the viscount than rumor could. Because the way a man touched a woman could show another man much about him. Ian Hunt didn't grab, or grasp a woman greedily or roughly. That lean, tanned, long-fingered hand held a woman carefully but firmly, with possession yet consideration, with grace and manners, no matter what her station.

Yes, this was the man he needed, Lord Shelton thought, pleased and reassured. He smiled, bowed, and then wandered off into the crowd.

Alone again, Ian stood deep in thought. He'd left Madam Felice's because he had been waiting to see the girl he'd enjoyed last time, and finally had—but as she was returning from a trip upstairs with another man. It shouldn't have bothered him. That was her business. He was no boy; he knew the popular jest about her sort: they were the luckiest tradespeople in the world because they could keep selling what they had and still have it to sell. But he'd never seen himself as one in a line before, as a man buying the same goods someone else just had. At least he'd never let himself see it. Tonight he had. And so he'd left, to see if he could meet a woman at the theater, perhaps one who wanted a person instead of a patron.

Because tonight he wanted more than a willing body. He'd had enough of that in London. It hadn't been what he'd needed. But instead of finding a merry, yielding woman, he'd met a man who considered him a rake. Maybe he was becoming one. Maybe it was time to leave London.

After all, Christmas was coming. He couldn't escape knowing that here. Every shop window proclaimed it. From jewels to jellies, every item in the merchants' windows was displayed with holly, every bakeshop bore Christmas on its brandied breath, street vendors cried wares for the coming holiday, street musicians caroled it, and every beggar whined its name. Even Madam Felice's had been draped in evergreens, and as a rare old jest, slung with mistletoe. When he'd been soldiering in Spain, he'd missed Christmas at home. But so had all the Englishmen there, and he hadn't felt so alone. Here, home at last, the coming of Christmas made him homesick for a home he dared not return to.

That might have been what sent him into the arms of so many women. He wanted to believe that, and not that he'd become a rake like Shelton. Because whatever else a rake might be, Ian was sure he couldn't be a man of honor. And that was what he tried to be.

A second son, junior to his brother by more than a decade, by the time he'd come along his brother and his father had become more than father and son, they were fast friends. They'd tolerated him, but never let him into their magic circle, and had only grown closer to each other after his mother died. He regretted that but reckoned they taught him a valuable lesson, one that had saved his life many times in Spain: to never be sure of his welcome.

His brother was the heir, and like his father, of robust health. Ian had never thought to inherit, and there were traditional careers open to a younger son he thought he could be happy with. The church wasn't for him, so he'd bought his colors. He'd thrived in the army. For the first time in his life he'd felt he belonged, and found the uniform and regulations easy to endure in exchange for the pleasure of feeling he was in the right place doing the right thing. He hadn't been a harsh man then. But then he'd gone to war.

He found he hated killing, whatever the cause. But he'd also found he had to kill in order to live. The man who had split his face for him had died on his sword as retaliation, and he didn't need the scar to remind him of it. He understood the necessity but regretted that death—and all the others he'd dealt the foe. It wasn't only the enemy he could see. A mistress of his in Spain had turned out to be a spy. He'd left before she was hanged, and had grieved for the thought of what she'd done more than for her. He'd helped a starving child once, in a ruined village in the mountains of Spain. He rode away feeling that maybe he'd done one good thing in that ravaged land, and turned his head to wave good-bye—just in time to see the boy fire at his back and run when he saw he'd missed. It turned out the boy had wanted his horse, not his charity.

Ian Hunt had come to realize he couldn't trust anyone, except his own men. And yet now when they invited him to their homes, he found he couldn't bear to go. He'd had enough of war; he didn't even want to reminisce about it.

When he'd heard that his brother had died in a hunting accident, he'd been stricken. Since he was sole heir, he was ordered to leave the army and take up his responsibilities. He was amazed to find himself relieved, and glad to go home. But he soon saw he couldn't stay. His brother's wife was not much older than himself, and mother to a baby girl. She wanted another husband, and silly, shallow creature that she was, she badly needed one. And though he'd tried to disbelieve it, it seemed she considered him her likeliest candidate. His father had died some years past, which meant that if he remained at home there was no way he could escape her constant company. Ian was an abrupt, plainspoken man, and he knew it. He didn't want to hurt her, but neither did he wish to so literally fill his brother's shoes. Home was not possible for him now—at least not until she found another man, or removed to the dower house.

By default, it was London for Christmas for him. But he reckoned it didn't have to be unpleasant. London had many thousand souls in it; surely he could find someone he could enjoy the holiday with, someone to be close to, have a good time with—without using money, or false charm. Someone he was not trying to use solely for his own pleasure—so that he wouldn't become a man like the one he'd just spoken with. Who was, he realized in alarm, possibly the only person he'd talked to since he'd returned from the war who really amused him, and who made any sense.

Ian Hunt, Viscount Hunt, pulled on his greatcoat, clapped on his hat, and left the Green Room as precipitously as he'd arrived in it. Leaving behind several

disappointed young women. And one very thoughtful
older gentleman.

"Hunt! My dear fellow, how delightful a surprise to
find you here!"

Ian looked up from his plate at the sound of the
merry voice to see Lord Shelton beaming down at him.
"Indeed?" he asked the older man harshly, his knife
and fork lowered but held in clenched hands. "But this
is my hotel, and it is breakfast time. I, however, am
surprised to find you here. It is not your hotel. And
only army men rise this early."

Lord Shelton laughed. "By your leave?" he asked, as
a footman pulled out a chair for him.

The viscount nodded abruptly and turned his attention back to his plate. Another man might have taken
umbrage at such curtness. It was just this side of inci-
vility. But it *was* just this side of it, so Lord Shelton
seated himself, requested coffee and toast before he
sent the footman away, and then sat smiling, as though
he'd been greeted with open arms. At least the viscount wasn't reading his paper, he thought. It would
do. He wondered if he was right when his companion
lowered his knife and fork and looked at him steadily
from eyes the color of pistol barrels.

"What is it?" Ian asked in a dangerously soft voice.
"Cut line, Shelton. You may be the world's most suc-
cessful seducer, but if so, it only points out the frailty
of women to me. I don't want flowers, smiles, or
charm. You've sought me out once too often. Why?"

"I need a favor," Lord Shelton said calmly.

"Ah. Well, then," the viscount replied, nodded, and
went back to eating his beefsteak and eggs. He looked
up after a minute to see a bemused expression on his

companion's face. "Fire away," he said, putting down
his cutlery and sitting back to listen.

"Indeed, one is tempted," the older man murmured.
And was rewarded with a harsh laugh.

"Yes. To be sure," Ian said ruefully, "and you're not
the first to say it, either. Your pardon, my lord. I have
manners. Sometimes, I forget. Please, do the same for
me. What can I do for you?"

Such a turnabout! But of course, Lord Shelton
thought with satisfaction, further proof this man was
more comfortable doing for others than himself. "I
need a friend," he said without preamble, and was gratified to see the puzzlement and concern that temporar-
ily appeared in the viscount's eyes. It's as well that he
guards that face of his, the older man mused. Those
emotions are deep as the man himself is. Good.

"You see, as I said the other night," Lord Shelton
went on, "most of the men I know and trust have wives
and families now, and so much as they might be willing to help me, they're not able or willing to go haring
off on an adventure with me, especially now. They're
snug at their hearths at this Yuletide season. I should
know—they've all invited me to share in the pleasure
of it with them. But I've managed to restrain myself
from the rapture of romping with their sticky children
and beaming at their adoring wives whilst lifting a cup
of wassail with them." He paused to let a footman pour
his coffee and waited for his companion to stop chuck-
ling before he continued.

"I have my own interests to pursue at this joyous
season, you see," he went on. "I've been invited to
many house parties, but there is one, in particular, that
I wish to go to. It's to be given at Moon Manor, to the
north of here, in Buckinghamshire. The problem
is . . ." He gave an embarrassed cough. ". . . that I am

what I am. You see, my name entitles me to many honors, but being at a respectable gathering is, alas, not one of them. In other words, I might be welcome at the home of a former rake like Torquay because although he's a righteous family man now, he was never a sanctimonious prig. Moreover, he knows he can trust me to behave, if behave I must. Similarly, I'm welcome at my Lord Talwin's gala gatherings right here in London because he's still a rake—his daughters are safely married and out of the house, and his wife, wise to his ways, manages to be otherwise occupied at their home in the countryside.

"Ah, but Squire Moleswirth!" He sighed. "He's a very distant relative, squire of Moon Manor, and a most *respectable* man. I know I say it as though it were a rare disease, but in his case it might as well be. It's almost as if he suffers from it. Well at least *I* do. He has moderate wealth, adequate learning, but certain expectations. He wants to climb into the highest society. He has daughters he's wishful of marrying off, brilliantly. He also has sons he wants to see in high places. He dimly perceives that despite my gamy reputation I am much more likely to gain admittance to such places than he, or else he'd never let me set foot in his house."

"Why should you want to?" Ian asked curiously.

But now Lord Shelton's candid blue eyes shifted, he cleared his throat and said evasively, "Normally I should not. Normally I'm thrilled, should I even chance to think of him, to realize that we only have to meet when senior members of the family toddle off this mortal coil and we literally bump into each other at a funeral. But I have my reasons for wishing to be at this house party, this Christmas. So I thought that if I brought along a vastly eligible young man my welcome would be assured. And thus eclipsed by my brilliant guest, my subsequent activities would be—shall we say—ignored?"

"There's someone you want to seduce and you want me to divert them so you can," Ian said baldly.

Lord Shelton looked offended. "'Pon my word, Hunt! Barking out orders on a battlefield has made you very brusque indeed. You must see to trimming your tongue, my dear fellow. Warfare is one thing, social life another. Shouting a command may save a man's life, but such bluntness can lose a man his friends. Some matters are best spoken of in a circumlocutory manner, with finesse, with nuance ..." He looked at the stern face of his companion and his own face fell. He shrugged, and looked down at his hands. "In a word, then: I have my own reasons."

"In a word, indeed," Ian said. He was silent for a moment, and there was no warmth in his voice as he asked, "But why ask me? If I'm known as your friend, why should I be unsuspected—or welcome at all, for that matter? After all, you yourself thought I was grazing in your pastures. So I must have a certain reputation of my own now."

"My dear boy, you do. But what of it? A reputation is only disastrous for a female; they themselves love rakes—*young* rakes, that is. All females believe in their powers for redemption. It's their greatest weakness, did they but know it," he added on a small smile. "But as for *old* rakes, few females, however devout, actually believe in miracles." He laughed—but stopped when he saw that the viscount did not.

"Wait! Before you say no," Lord Shelton said quickly, "hear me out. I'll do no harm by what I do, *that* I promise you. Only great good. No, really. I don't seduce, I—convince. And I've never left anyone worse off than when I met them. That, too, I can promise you in this instance." He paused to think over what else he had to say. Then he spoke with such unusual seriousness that the viscount listened closely, despite his reluctance to be drawn into any schemes.

"This young person I am thinking of has no future without my interference," Lord Shelton said carefully. "By which I mean to say that she has only a bleak one, with little joy and less reward. She is, of course, lovely, with masses of brown hair, eyes like honey in the comb, peaches aglow in her cheeks, and the merest dusting of freckles on the bridge of her little nose that saves her from the dullness of perfection. Needless to say, she has a delightful figure as well."

"Needless to say," the viscount echoed wryly.

"She's also intelligent, graceful, and charming," Lord Shelton went on. "In short: eminently desirable. But she suffers from a dreadful affliction for which there is only one cure, and it is one I am unable to provide her. I'm merely trying to do what I can to help."

Now the harsh-faced viscount looked surprised. "You—dealing with a wench with a fatal illness?" he scoffed. "Cut line."

"I didn't say fatal," Lord Shelton said testily. "I said dreadful, and so it is. It's poverty. Or as near as makes no difference. She's a poor relation, with no prospects at all. Related on Moleswirth's wife's side, and distantly at that. She appears at his house for holidays and disappears when the Season comes and they remove to London. Because although Moleswirth's not a bad man, he has his own daughters to marry off and would be a fool to present them with such competition. Her own family can't present her. There's good blood there, but that's all. Her father's a scholar, poor as a church mouse and proud as a prince, and though her mother comes from a fine family, she came *from* it. The marriage was a misalliance; they were neighbors—the poor scholar and the fine lady, that sort of thing. Very romantic, but it doesn't help the girl at all. They live next to nowhere, up North, too grand for the local folk, too poor for the gentry. She's near to being on the shelf. Four and twenty, and ready to put her glorious hair under a spinster's cap. I want to offer her much more.

"I can't offer her anything at her home, of course. Nor can a man with a reputation like mine invite her anywhere, or ask anyone else to do so, lest word of it leak out. But she'll be at Moon Manor for Christmas. And so, then, shall I be."

"Why all the plotting? Why don't you simply offer her marriage?"

It took a long time for Lord Shelton to stop laughing. When the viscount started to get up from the table, the laughter stopped abruptly.

"It is not a possibility," Lord Shelton said quickly.

"Yes, I see. Then thank you for the invitation," Ian said just as quickly, "but I . . ."

"Wait! Sit, please. I've only told you the reason I wanted you there. I haven't told you why you might want to come. I think you would."

The viscount slowly sat down.

"A Christmas house party at Moon Manor is the perfect place for a gentleman newly home from the wars," Lord Shelton said earnestly. "Moleswirth isn't a bad fellow, only respectable. The manor is beautiful, the countryside pristine; there'll be guests of all ages, but a great many young ones because of all the sons and daughters. It's a splendid place to pass Christmas. Idyllic, in fact. I've seen the festivities in past years; they're a delight. There'll be a Yule log, caroling, sledding and sleighing, dancing and pantomimes, wassail and a grand feast among normal, good, and well-intentioned people who will be delighted to meet you. You might even find yourself a wife, if you're so enamored of the married state."

The viscount shook his head and began to rise from his chair again.

"Good Lord, Hunt, do this favor for me," Lord Shelton cried, "and do one for yourself. I need a friend; you need a diversion. Why not?"

"Perhaps because you need a diversion more than a friend."

"As a favor, then. I really am in need. And you'll thank me for it, one day. But I won't plead," Lord Shelton said with a wave of his hand, suddenly shifting emotions, looking as bored as he had seemed impassioned a moment before. "What's the point? If you want to remain in London pursuing your usual pleasures, I quite understand. Who better? Christmas in London is likely more to your taste. Madam Felice's will be open, as will her girls' arms. As will be the public masquerades, the theater, and several gaming houses. How foolish of me to forget. After all, now I come to think of it: a quiet rural manor house at Christmas, among decent young people, I agree—a most unlikely place for a rake to be."

The viscount took a long deep breath and gazed at Lord Shelton with an unreadable expression. "When would you like to leave?" he finally asked.

They rode alongside Lord Shelton's carriage, which was heaped with their luggage. Lord Shelton's valet rode alone in it. The viscount's manservant, who had tended to him in Spain, had been told to go home to his own people for the holiday. After token protest, he'd done so. After all, his master said, a man about town needed a valet in London, but a man who knew his way about the world didn't need one for a brief visit to the countryside. Most men of fashion might shudder at this assessment, but the viscount was a man after his own fashion. He took care to be neat and clean but didn't spend more time on his appearance than was absolutely necessary; as an old army man, he knew how to make short of it, unassisted.

It was a cold, dry day, and the roads were frozen hard. The horses made good time. At noon Lord Shelton consulted his watch.

"We're so far ahead of schedule we've time for a leisurely lunch at that inn just ahead," he told the viscount. "Such places often have the best home brews, and a guest ought to arrive sated so as not to put his hostess in a dither. What say you?"

They gave their horses to the ostler and went into the inn. They acted like common men but fooled no one. Both men were simply but elegantly dressed, and stood out so much in that country place that the landlord himself hurried to serve them. He seated them at a table near enough to the door to show any casual observers what quality of customer he had, but far enough from it to ensure them privacy.

"Excellent," Lord Shelton sighed with satisfaction when he finally put down his tankard after taking a long quaff. "Why can't they brew like this in London?"

"They probably do. It's the country air," Ian commented. "The same reason the roughest wine in Spain tasted better than the finest French one in London."

"Such a cynic! I believe the answer is that they are both superior brews, the air and the ale . . . but what's this? Is there to be no peace for me?"

Ian looked toward the doorway to the inn, where an anxious, travel-weary footman was standing, peering inside, squinting against the brightness of the day, trying to see into the relative gloom of the taproom. When he spied Lord Shelton, he looked relieved and hurried to his side. He handed him a paper, saying breathlessly. "This come for you this mornin', soon's you left, Lord. Beekins said as to how you'd want to 'ave a look at it right off, so I set out after you. I caught up, and seen yer coach, and here I be."

"Bedamned and blast!" Lord Shelton muttered, frowning as he rapidly scanned the paper. He folded it, thrust it into an inner pocket, and rose from the table. "I'll return with you; see to my horse," he told the footman, who went hurrying out again. "A personal matter," he told Ian, "that cannot, unfortunately, wait. Not a matter of life and death, only of finance, which can lead to the same. I must return to London."

"Very well," Ian said, as he got to his feet. Nothing in his face showed his disappointment, but only because he had mastered his emotions long since. Because against all odds, he'd actually found himself looking forward to this impromptu holiday. The clean, fresh air, the countryside, the bright day, the brighter prospects of new people and a welcoming home for Christmas—even if it wasn't his home—had appealed to him. But he was used to disappointment. He flung some coins on the table.

"Where are you going?" Lord Shelton said in surprise. "Stay, finish that excellent beef."

"I'm going with you, of course; there's excellent beef in London, too."

"London? What are you talking about?" Lord Shelton said in surprise. "You must go on to Moon Manor. They're expecting you."

"Without you? I think not."

"But I'll be joining you in a day or so. You must go. This will suit my purposes even better, come to think on it. They'll be so full of the glory of you that they'll scarcely pay any mind to me when I arrive."

Ian considered the matter. He was a man who was used to instant decision-making, and so he was bemused to discover that he very much wanted to be persuaded to go on to the manor. "But I hardly think they want a stranger arriving on their doorstep. . . ." he said.

"No such thing! I sent word that I'd be bringing a guest with me. You'll be no stranger to them. Even if you were, they'd want such a stranger: young, eligible, rich, and noble—you can be sure of that."

"Yes. But . . . ," Ian said, some imp of perversity making him want to deny himself the treat he'd been promised. ". . . what if I find your—'special interest'—to my own taste? You won't be there to challenge me."

Lord Shelton hesitated. Then he smiled to himself. "What of it?" he finally asked flippantly. "I'll be there, sooner or later. Life's been dull of late. I love a challenge. Anyway, she's not your sort. She's the type to appeal to an older rake, like me. Because she doesn't glitter—she glows. And she's highly moral and very clever. In short: a challenge to a jaded taste like mine, not a lure to a man such as yourself. Younger men like their pleasure simple and straightforward, and are attracted to diamonds of the first water who know their way around. And who shall blame them? A man with healthy hungers seeks a wholesome meal; a fellow who is sated seeks only something to titillate a weary appetite. Go along to the manor. If you don't fix an interest with her, you're sure to find another there—it's an interesting place."

"Very well," Ian said, surprising himself, and liking

the feeling. It was holiday time, and he hadn't had a holiday in such a long time. "I will. But you'd better hurry. Because I mean to have a good time."

"As I do. I'll see you there—soon as I can," the older man said.

They left the inn, mounted their horses, and rode off in opposite directions.

It was a pleasant ride for the first part of the day, but as the brief afternoon drew to a close, the wind began to bite. Ian was glad when he saw the gate to Moon Manor, even though he wasn't sure of his reception there. He was gladder still when he rounded the turn of the drive and finally saw the manor in all its glory. It was everything Shelton had promised. Christmas seemed to sit upon the manor's ancient brow like a benediction. Set in a pleasant park, the manor was made of red stone that the centuries had mellowed to a dusky rose hue. Warm golden light glowed out from every frosted window of the old house, and the front portico was swagged with fresh-cut fir, holly, and ivy. Ian gave his horse to the smiling stable boy who came running to greet him. Then he went to the front door, feeling as though he were coming home, although he knew too well he was only going among strangers again.

The great oaken front door opened on a rush of warmth and color and laughter. The scent of a delicious dinner cooking as well as pungent wood smoke from many hearth fires greeted him, even as a bowing butler did. There was a brightness of candles and a brilliance of smiles from the servants as they ushered him in, took his coat and hat, and showed him into a huge salon off the great hall he'd entered.

"The Viscount Hunt," the butler announced.

There were a number of laughing people in the

room. They turned to stare at him, and then they all smiled. One came forward with hands outstretched.

"My lord," a portly, balding, jovial older man said heartily, as he sketched a bow, "I bid you welcome to Moon Manor. Our good friend, Lord Shelton, sent word that you'd be coming with him. I am Jasper Moleswirth, and here is my good wife, Belinda. I'll introduce you to my family and friends in a moment—but where is my wife's relative?" he asked, peering into the empty hall behind the viscount.

"A message arrived when we were halfway here," Ian said stiffly. "He had to hurry back to London to take care of some business, but asked me to tell you that he'll be here as soon as possible. He insisted I go on without him. But if it is too much trouble, I . . ."

"Trouble? My dear lord, how could it be? It's Christmas. Come, let me introduce you round."

Everyone seemed delighted to meet the viscount. He was introduced to people of all ages. And just as Lord Shelton had said, to many, many lovely young ladies as well. Several were beautiful, and some winsome, too. But instead of being overwhelmed by them, Ian found himself wondering which was the object of Lord Shelton's personal attentions.

It was not the most stunning dark-haired beauty, he decided. No, Miss Merryman was a toast of the Season, and a more perfect example of cosseted, pampered young womanhood would be hard to find. She was magnificent, and knew it, and even though she flirted, only a very foolish man would take her seriously—unless he was willing to do just that.

Nor was it the most bewitching blond lovely there, either, he thought. Because of the color of her hair. Lord Shelton had specified brown. But neither could it be the best-looking brown-haired beauty, because of

her aplomb. In Ian's experience, poor relations might
be many things, but never self-confident. Still, there
was a redheaded chit who was amusing, and a petite
dark-haired one he found charming. . . . And then there
was such a crush of laughing young charmers crowding around him, asking him teasing questions about
London, that he began to forget Lord Shelton's devious
mission. He'd almost forgotten it entirely, deciding that
the poor relation the old rake had set his sights on must
literally be sitting in the cinders somewhere in the
kitchens, when he looked up—and saw her coming
into the room.

It could be no other.

It wasn't because of what she wore. She was dressed
as well as any young woman there, in a simple ice-blue
gown. Nor was it because of the color of her hair. He
couldn't tell that it was brown. From where he stood
those loose ringlets coiling about her lovely face
looked to be the color of smoke and evening shadows.
Nor could he see that her long eyes were the hue of
honey in the comb, as Lord Shelton claimed. All he
could see was that she was lovely, and that she hesitated to come into the room. She paused at the doorway, looking in. A confident girl would come sailing
right into the company expecting a warm reception, no
matter what she looked like. And this girl was bewitching.

But she stood in the doorway surveying the merry
crowd for a moment before she ventured into the room.
She would have caught his eye even if he hadn't been
waiting for her. Slender, with a graceful neck and a
well-shaped head—and a correspondingly well-shaped
body—she was the sort of female he always noticed.
Although she was in no way waiflike—as the Grecian
fashion of her gown displayed to perfection—she

seemed to him to be fragile and vulnerable as she hesitantly entered the room. Yes. The tentativeness. That settled it. He nodded to himself. That was exactly how a poor relation would come to the feast: as though she were afraid she'd be told to leave it. His heart went out to her—until he realized that it might be in his eyes.

He turned his eyes from her as he pretended to listen to all the nonsense being said to him. But he didn't stop watching her. She had his complete attention. He was a seasoned hunter, and so no one could know it—especially not she.

Eve came into the room, and stopped near the hearth and held her hands up to the roaring fire. Her hands were cold, but not because her room had been. The squire always had a fine fire lit in its hearth, the same way he kept them ablaze in all the hearths in his home. She wasn't cold, except in her heart, and her hands were chilled by fear. As she waited for inspiration—or someone to notice her and call for her to join them, or introduce her to the gentleman whose gaze had stopped her in her tracks—she covered her embarrassment by counting. There were twelve days of Christmas. If she added the two before Christmas that she'd yet to get through, and then the one after when she could leave, that left only fifteen more days. Only a fortnight and a day. It could be done, Eve thought. It could even be done with ease—if she could only manage to forget who she was, and why she was better off forgetting it.

Because objects of charity were meant to be given at Christmas—and in her case, being an object of charity herself, to be given a Christmas, too. Squire and his wife were ruthlessly charitable, and there was nothing she could do but smile and bear with their kindness until the new year freed her. If she insisted on remember-

ing that she was their favorite philanthropy, she'd
suffer instead of having a good time. She'd resolved to
forget about it this year. And had tried, and almost succeeded . . .

. . . until the stunningly attractive man who had just
arrived reminded her just now. Because he didn't know
her, or about her, and so had looked at her as though he
thought she was fascinating, eligible, *possible.* At least
he had in that instant when she'd first seen him and
they'd traded astonished stare for stare—as though
they'd recognized each other after years apart—in that
transcendent second before his face turned cold and
harsh again. Which was exactly how it would look
once he was told who she was. And they'd certainly
tell him, of course.

*Oh, that's our Eve. Poor relation. Charming girl. So
sweet. Our Caroline just dotes on her. That's one of
our Caro's gowns on her; isn't it lovely? Trust Caro to
do the right thing by poor Eve. Not a penny to bless
herself with, poor chit. She seldom gets a chance to
meet people. Lives in the back of beyond, and looks
forward to coming here each year, you know. Just
wouldn't be Christmas without her.*

Next year, Eve told herself fiercely, she'd finally be
able to stay home. At five and twenty, they have to
agree when you say you're entirely on the shelf and
content to remain there. Because then she would be.
She'd be free to stay home at Christmas—and dream
of what might have been if she'd come here again. Oh,
bother, bother, bother! she thought, staring down into
the fire and biting her lip in vexation. If they'd only
not invite such gentlemen as to give a girl dreams of
what might have been if she'd been born otherwise . . .
or if she *was* otherwise, she thought, remembering
Lord Shelton, who had not come with his friend after

all, thank heavens. *That* would just be too embarrassing—although she found herself thinking that she would love to see him anyway, since he was the only man in the world who seemed to understand her.

"Eve, my dear, come and meet the Viscount Hunt," Squire said merrily. She looked up to see the harsh-faced gentleman standing next to her host, looking at her with no expression, his eyes cold as his face.

"Here's our little Eve, my lord," Squire said. "Eve Thompkins—my Lord Hunt. She's quiet as a mouse," Squire confided loudly as Eve curtsied to Ian's brief bow, "but don't let that pious little face fool you; she's clever as one, too—who knows what sort of rumbunction's going on in that wise little noggin? Father's a noted scholar, don't you know?"

Trust Squire to damn her even as he praised her, Eve thought sadly. Three times damned: "Clever," "pious," and "wise" all in the same sentence describing her? It was code for "spinster." Incurable spinster at that. Because an eligible girl was a "clever puss," if she was supposed to be witty, never "pious," and certainly not "wise."

"Miss Thompkins," Ian said.

His voice was dark as his visage, and abrupt. It warned away sympathy for the terrible scar on his cheek. But it lured her as well, because it was rich as it was dark, and she seemed to hear it in her very bones.

"Ah! Here's my Caro!" Squire said before Eve could answer and stammer some polite foolishness. "*Now* the party begins! Watch yourself, my lord; she's a clever little puss, too. Not one for books, mind, but how could she be with an old dunderhead like me as her papa? But no one's sharper, I promise you, for all she's a beauty! Caroline, my love, here's the Viscount Hunt, all the way from London town."

But Caroline already knew that, Eve thought sadly as her cousin dimpled up at the bemused viscount. Caro had seen him arrive, seen him being shown around, and had waited until her father had introduced him to all the rest of the company before approaching him. That way she could take his arm, as she did now, and steer him into the party as his companion, and not have to worry about anyone else he might meet taking him away from her.

And why not? It was her home, her house party, and all the eligible men in it were at her disposal. She was looking for a husband. He wouldn't be hard to find; she had everything a gentleman could want. She was young and pretty and had a good family and a neat dowry. She was comely in the most fashionable way: slender, but just rounded enough so that even her elbows were dimpled. Her hair was dark and it curled, her eyes were fashionably blue, and her smile frequent and radiant. The worst part of it, Eve thought sadly, as she trailed along in the backwash of her cousin's bright laughter, was that she was a thoroughly nice girl, too. So it was impossible to dislike her for taking what was rightfully hers.

But it *was* possible to envy her from the bottom of her heart. And to her disgust, Eve found that for the first time in her life she did envy her fortunate cousin. Not for the manor or the dowry or the fashionable clothing, or any of the things her cousin had and she did not. But only for the one dark man she now proudly displayed like a new trinket on her dimpled arm.

They knew how to make Christmas at Moon Manor. Ian was glad he had come. It was better than being at his own home. Because although it was clear that Christmas was a tradition here, replete with many warm memories, they weren't his memories. His own wouldn't have made for a very glad holiday. And so he was pleased to share in those at the manor.

His room was comfortable. Dinner was delicious; the company sparkled. He hadn't been in "proper" mixed company in a long while, and found he'd missed it. He was seated next to Caro, the squire's eldest daughter. She was so charming he almost forgot the poor girl Shelton had designs upon. But not quite. Not that it mattered. She sat so far down the table from him he couldn't keep his eye on her without being obvious about it, and whatever he was, he was never obvious. He would bide his time. It was easy to do.

Caro Moleswirth either thought he was a great catch or had heard of his reputation and thought that it would be fun to play with fire. Because she set out to snare his interest with a vengeance. She did it with such a complete misunderstanding of what it was a rake wanted in a woman that he couldn't remember when he'd been so entertained. He almost regretted it when the ladies left the gentlemen to their port.

The girls crowded together in a salon that had been designated the ladies' withdrawing room for the night. It was supplied with chamber pots and lined with looking glasses, and all the women crowded in before going into the grand salon where they would rejoin the gentlemen. The older women simply relieved themselves, repaired their maquillage if they wore any, tended to their hair, and chatted briefly. But the girls fussed over their clothes and hair, and jested and gossiped with each other excitedly, sounding like a treeful of cheerful birds.

"You've got yourself a beau, Carol!" one of them teased her host's daughter.

"And, mmm, what a handsome one he is, too," another chirped. "Such lowering black looks. Byron would be *madly* jealous."

"A lot you know of Byron," another girl said laughingly. "Your mama would wash your mouth out with soap for merely mentioning his name, much less knowing him. But I agree. Hunt is so madly attractive. So . . . daunting. How I envy you."

"Oh, *Hunt*?" Caro asked with an air of unconcern as she studied herself in the glass. "Lud! What a gloomy Gus it is! He never smiles."

"He doesn't have to," another girl sighed. "Such madly attractive eyes; I vow you can actually *feel* them on you," she said with a delicious shudder. "Black and hot . . . or are they brown?"

"I don't know," Caro said carelessly, as if she hadn't been trying to stare into them all evening and only stopped because they were always more intent on his dinner than on herself. She wasn't a vain girl, but had too much pride to continue to try to compete with a goose and a side of beef. ". . . dark brown, I suppose."

No, Eve thought, *gray*. They were gray. She knew because she'd seen the sides of his eyes in the candlelight as he'd gone into dinner. They caught the light and refracted it as brown would not. They were gray as dark ice. Gray as gun metal, and just as merry.

"Perhaps he doesn't smile because he was so lately at war," Eve said softly.

"Pooh!" Caro said, tossing back her head and smiling at how her curls bounced. "Latimer was in the wars, and so was Johnny Stevens and Philip Connors, and a merrier crew I've never seen."

"Latimer patrolled the regent's palace at Brighton,

and Johnny never takes anything seriously, and Philip is a man of the world," one of the girls said.

"Whereas Hunt's a man of the boudoir," one of the girls whispered with a sidelong look to be sure her mother wasn't listening. "Or so I've heard."

"Yes, he's got a dreadful reputation," her friend reported. "But the wonder is that he's still welcome everywhere."

"He's young enough to change, or so my mother says," another said.

" 'With his income, title, and that estate, my dear,' " her friend said with mock haughtiness, imitating her own mother, " 'it scarcely matters.' And with that face, that manly form, and his outrageous reputation," she added on her own giggle, "who cares?"

"Well, I suppose he is a bit fascinating," Caro said lightly, "and so whatever else, I shall get him to laugh tonight—you'll see!"

But it was hard for her to get near enough to him to get the chance. Because when the gentlemen joined them at last in the grand salon, the viscount was surrounded by men, from the youngest blades to their hoariest elders. They hung on his every infrequent word.

"He don't talk much, but when he does, Lud!" young Latimer confided to Caro and Eve when he finally left the crowd around the viscount and joined the ladies. "He makes sense. The man's been to Spain, fought valiantly—and has got some dashed fine ideas on how to end the conflict. Even m'father says he's got a head on his shoulders."

Eve looked at the head that sat so proudly on those wide shoulders. The viscount's face was handsome, starkly attractive, but cold. And the scar he bore seemed to go deeper than his skin. She saw no lust in his eyes, not exactly—he only looked at a girl as though he were evaluating things about her that she didn't know she had, but soon found herself wishing she did. When he did laugh, those strong features only rearranged themselves; it was hard to imagine him ever looking lighthearted. Surely a rake would be all cozening sweetness, all compliance and smiles? If physiognomy was destiny, as some men of science said, then it made no sense that the man was a rake.

A rake was a fellow who lived for the pleasures of the flesh. A rake was a man who made his way through life with flattery and cunning. Eve knew rakes—well, at least one rake. He was charming, in no way like the viscount. Because Hunt did not try to charm; in fact it almost seemed as though he tried not to.

But then that head turned as though she had called his name, not just thought it. He looked across the room and straight at her, the hard gray eyes cool and assessing. Eve turned away, flustered. *Perfect,* she told herself bitterly as she caught her breath and studied her shaking hands with rapt attention. *Now you're turning into a true spinster, all sighs and glances and romantic fantasies. When shall you start looking for handsome strangers under your bed each night?* she asked herself angrily. She turned her attention to her cousin, praying she hadn't been seen goggling at the grim viscount. She needn't have worried. Caro was too busy whispering with her mother to have noticed anything.

The squire's wife nodded, and left her daughter in order to have a word with some of her lady guests. Within moments one of them struck up a merry tune on the piano, another approached her spouse and elbowed him hard, yet another crossed the room and breathed some harsh, pertinent words in her husband's ear.

Slowly the group of gentlemen around the viscount parted, and they rejoined the ladies.

There were tables set up for cards, and those inveterate gamblers among them soon settled down at their favorite games. Matrons gossiped, trading recipes and stories about children, husbands, and servants. Their husbands chatted about hunts, races, mills, and property. There was a devilish hot game of charades being played by the younger folk in one corner of the room, and a riotous game of snap going forth in another. Consecutive players kept the piano thumping, there was singing, and before long someone moved a chair and someone else called for a footman to help move a table and there was some jolly impromptu dancing— with Squire shouting, "No polkas, now! Here—have a care for the furniture. We'll have a ball another night," as everyone laughed.

Eve had her admirers, but both she and they knew that was all they could be. So she smiled at them and let them go on to more promising girls. She'd met most of them before at these holiday affairs. If she had not, Caro had kindly explained their situations to her, so she'd have no illusions. None of them could afford a pauper wife. They either needed a fortune, wanted one, or had a parent who insisted. Even if they didn't, Eve didn't encourage any of them—she'd lived in a marriage that was a misalliance and would not wish it on anyone. Not that her parents weren't happy, and didn't love each other. They were, and they did. But her mother had known better before her marriage, and her father knew it, and it shadowed their lives. And absolutely limited their daughter's.

So she passed the evening by smiling and watching and counting the hours and pretending to have a jolly time. As Caro clung to the viscount's arm like lint.

"Now, listen!" Caro finally cried to the company as the candles began to gutter and the first guests started to move toward the stairs. "This is very important. Christmas Eve is fast approaching and we have things to do! We have traditions here at the manor. Tell them, Father!"

"You tell them, my love!" he laughed, as amidst much laughter, he put his hands round her waist and lifted her to a chair so she could lecture to the company.

But in truth, only the viscount didn't know the traditions, and the fact that this lecture was one of them, and had been since Caro had been able to lisp directions.

"Since tomorrow bids to be fair, and we cannot say what Christmas Eve shall be, tomorrow is the day we'll need help from *everyone* to bring in the mistletoe. The servants will cut the holly and the ivy," she said, shaking a finger at her guests, "but we girls must bring in the mistletoe—and mind, not a sprig in the house until evening or it's bad luck. You gentlemen can help my father find the Yule log, no matter how long it takes," she said, as all the men pretended to groan, as if they didn't know that Squire had found it weeks ago and guarded it jealously since. "For you know it must be *found,* not taken." The men smiled, because that meant Squire intended to lead them on a merry hunt, a good long ride to shake the cobwebs out. "And when we're done—I propose we skate on the pond till we're dizzy!"

There was a ragged cheer, much laughter, and the company began to make their good nights. Caro stood at the foot of the stair, flushed with pleasure at being the center of attention. Eve stood watching. In that moment, she felt as though she were standing in some distant audience, seeing all the brightness and laughter being played out before her, and that it was already receding into some enchanted memory she'd never really been part of. It made her homesick for a home she'd never had. It made her realize this was her last Christmas as a girl. If she ever did return here it would be in her caps, as a certified spinster, with not even the fantasy of a match before her. The only way she could meet a dark, brooding, fascinating stranger at home would be if he got lost on the moors. A lump rose in her throat; she was appalled to find tears in her eyes. She looked away, trying to collect herself. And saw him looking straight at her—with sympathy, with understanding, with an echo of her own sorrow instead of the usual coldness she saw on that harsh face.

Ian had been watching her all night. He didn't know why. Maybe it was because he knew her future better than she did, and felt in some way responsible. She was one with all the other girls here tonight, but if Shelton had his way, she would be in the business of providing pleasure for the gentlemen by the time another Christmas came. It bothered him.

He hadn't had a chance to speak with her. Maybe she didn't deserve his sympathy. But he knew too well that though she stood in this respectable company tonight and was part of the festivities, if rake Shelton had his way, by next year her name would be a scandal and her presence an anathema to them. He felt like a man who saw a pretty little fish swimming in a pond, all unaware of the hook she was about to be impaled upon. Because he saw how lonely she was now, and so surely when an experienced man like Shelton cast his lure, she would bite.

Ian was not a moralist, certainly. But somehow the thought of rakish matters seemed wrong in this cozy

country setting. The contrast between lustful longings
and the sweet innocence of Christmas was so stark as
to be appalling to him. What should he do? Save her?
From herself? Or for himself? Graceful and shapely,
she was certainly lovely enough—and sad enough to
tempt him. He was always drawn to sorrow, because he
knew he could never disappoint a woman who was
already unhappy.

As he looked at her now, while the rest of the company laughed, he saw tears glittering in those remarkable eyes Shelton had praised. They made him catch
his breath. Because in that moment when he should
have been merry, he realized he felt like an outsider,
too. It wasn't only because he was privy to Shelton's
plans. He had his own dark secrets. He bore the stench
of war about himself, and his body held the recent
memory of soulless lust. Where did he fit into this
sweet Christmas celebration? What did he have in
common with all these charming, foolish young girls?

There was only one female here who stood in
danger of being cast into the darkness he knew in the
new year. And when he'd glanced up in spite of
himself—as he had all night—he'd seen tears and realized she was the only one here who was as out of place
as he was.

But he didn't know her. She might be just another
greedy young chit who would only profit from Shelton's patronage. Hadn't Shelton himself claimed
that?

Eve saw the viscount's face turn grim again as he
stared at her, and she felt as though he'd struck her.
She turned away, furious with herself. The sympathy
she'd seen had probably been a trick of the light. Why
should he have any fellow feeling for her? They'd
never exchanged a word. She'd been fantasizing again.

He was probably nothing more than a rake. Maybe some rakes did draw women with vinegar, not honey. How should she know?

And so as the company climbed the stair, singing snatches of carols and laughing about Christmas to come, Eve dreamed of Christmas long gone, and prayed for it to go faster. She counted the days again, like her own personal rosary. Fourteen. Now it was only fourteen. She cheered herself by that thought— and one more—hadn't Lord Shelton said he was coming?

The morning came cold and bright.

The men prepared to go out with Squire on his wild ride, searching for the biggest log they could find.

"Mind, like my gel said, can't cut it—got to find the biggest log you ever saw for *our* Yule log. And it must already be on the forest floor, you know," Squire cautioned his crew, his words turning to smoke in the wintry air in the courtyard as they prepared to ride out.

"We must gather *baskets and baskets* of mistletoe," Caro instructed her group of young girls. "You know why," she said as they giggled. "And mind, don't let any of it touch the ground—that's very bad luck!"

They looked like a legion of nuns from some very odd order, all caped and hooded as they were. For few nuns wore fur, or cloaks of scarlet and peacock hues. They called jests to the men, and then each group set off in a different direction, the girls crowding together as they walked down the path to the forest, the men riding out in a group after Squire.

Eve found the gathering of mistletoe a pleasure. Although there was giggling and teasing, finding and snagging the mistletoe was essentially solitary work. The crisp air and brightness of the day made her spirits

soar. She was almost sorry to get back to the man-
or and surrender her basket to a servant. But it was
time to hurry down to the pond with the other girls for
the proposed skating.

Squire had everything there in readiness for the
party. Fires were lit at the side of the pond, and chairs
ringed round them so that the chaperones could keep
their toes and fingers toasty while they kept their eyes
peeled. A few comfortable seats had been mounted on
barrel staves so that some of the more enterprising old-
sters could be pushed round the pond as well. And everywhere, servants waited with steaming urns of hot
tea and cider.

Eve saw Caro step onto the ice and skate round and
round in lazy rings as she looked up toward the manor,
waiting for the menfolk to return from the great Yule
log hunt. Eve sat down to put on her own skates, but
stopped when she heard the first hearty "Hallo!" from
one of the returning men. They were coming down the
slope from the manor to the pond. She slowly put
down her skates when she saw them. Soon, they'd pair
off together with the girls, just as though it were a
dance. Some would skate in a line, but most would not,
and she suddenly knew she couldn't bear to see the
bright lads and lovely ladies single each other out and
skate away, leaving her to watch and pretend to be
having fun again.

Eve waited on the sidelines, far from the fires and
the skaters, heedless of the growing cold, wishing she
were with them, glad she was not, and so she was startled to hear a voice addressing her.

"You don't skate?" he asked.

She knew who it was before she turned her head to
see him looming up beside her. Who else would be so
abrupt? Who else would cast such a long shadow on

the snowy ground, and strike such fear and excitement in her heart just by being there?

"I do skate," she said, calmly as she could, "only I don't feel like it just now." *Not an inspired answer; what a doltish reply; no wonder no one talks to you,* she berated herself. *Couldn't you have said something clever?* Only she didn't know what else she could have said, given the question. She told herself it didn't matter anyway.

It didn't. He dropped the subject, and gazed out to the skating pond. "Our host has turned the outdoors into the indoors," he said.

Well, she thought, that wasn't a question or a comment she could add anything to because it was so obvious. So she only nodded.

Her face was turned from him. If he didn't see her breath occasionally puffing out a cloud before her he'd think he was talking to an empty hood, Ian thought, and frowned. He was not aware of how terrible that looked.

"Did you get enough mistletoe?" he asked abruptly.

The hood went up and down. "Yes, lots," a small voice finally said, and then she fell still. What else could she say? But there was so much more she wanted to tell him. She stole a glance at his face and lost her breath. She could bear being ignored. But she was not used to being sneered at.

Well, then, good luck to Shelton, and good riddance, Ian thought disgustedly, with a mixture of relief and disappointment. *It might as well be an empty hood; the girl had no brain. And while high, full breasts and a sweet little bottom had their allure, the rake was welcome to them if they came with an empty head. No fortune and no brains. She was likely far better off under Shelton's protection after all.*

"Only I don't know why we gather mistletoe," Eve said in a rush, the words escaping from her lips like steam from a boiling teapot. "The vicar won't even let it into the church because it's part of the old religion and belongs to the High Church of Druid, not England. I don't know why you hunted the Yule log, either. You know the reason you couldn't cut one is because people used to believe you'd be punished by the fairy folk for taking one from the living forest. It had nothing to do with Christmas. They just kept the tradition in order to convert the people of Britain, who didn't want to give up everything when they took on a new religion. Well, they gave up the human sacrifices and such, but they had to let them keep *some* things to keep them happy. Because even the mistletoe used to be used for *far* more than kissing. . . ."

Her cheeks flamed. But although she diverted from the dangerous topic of Druid fertility rites, she went on doggedly, not knowing how to stop. "But Christmas happened in the Holy Land, where they have neither mistletoe, holly, nor Yule logs, for that matter . . . or so I read," she finally murmured, her voice dwindling, aware that he had blinked. She lifted her chin. Better to be thought a bluestocking than an idiot.

He stood still. "I was aware of that," he finally said. "At least, that Christmas took place in the Holy Land. I didn't know the bits about the Druids. I knew they had human sacrifices—but, ah, what exactly did they do with the mistletoe?"

She dared look up because of the odd note in his voice. He was smiling. Now she lost her breath altogether. It was a real smile. Rather than twisting his awful scar, it lightened it and gave luster and light to his whole face. She'd found him magnetically attractive in his bleak mode. She was dazzled now. White teeth gleamed in that dark face, and his gray eyes shone like sunlight on the ice under the snow on the pond. He looked not only younger but transformed. He was twice as attractive, which was so much so she found she couldn't look away from him.

And he thought her eyes were indeed like molten honey; they glowed. Her lips were full and soft and parted, and red from the cold—but so was her nose, he thought with tender amusement. There was a light dusting of golden freckles on the bridge of it. He idly wondered if he'd ever desired a woman with freckles before ... before he realized he was just standing and gaping at her like a besotted boy. His brows drew together.

"No, don't!" she cried, before she heard herself and her gloved hand flew to her mouth as her cheeks grew pink—but not from the cold. "I mean," she said, "don't scowl again, please. It frightens me."

"Does it?" he asked, charmed by the notion as well as by her candor. Dozens of women had told him they were going to be the one to erase his dark scowls. None had ever said it frightened them.

"Well, I suppose not really," she admitted. "At least, I'm not going to run screaming. But I like it much better when you don't frown. Unless, of course, brooding is what you prefer. I know some women must find it most attractive, and so if it is your mode, so to speak, then forgive me and go right ahead."

He threw back his head and gave a shout of laughter. It was so unexpected Eve stared. As did several ladies who had been watching him from afar.

"Miss Thompkins, I have never given thought to my mode, and God forbid that I should," he said, sobering. "But I do know my aim. It is to please you. So if you prefer a smiling fellow, I'll try. I can't promise anything, though, being unaccustomed to levity."

But now she sobered, too, and looked regretful. So, of course, would a rake say, since all they ever wanted was to please the ladies. But why should he need to please her? There were prettier girls here, and far richer ones. . . . But of course. She knew how rakes' minds worked. Didn't she know Lord Shelton? The fascinating viscount was interested in her, because—of all the girls at Moon Manor this Christmastide—she was the only one he could possibly trifle with without fear of retribution. She had no parent present, no lordly family, and no money at all.

She contemplated him, cocking her head to the side and looking full at him, carefully noting the darkly handsome face, the intelligence in those gray eyes, even looking her fill at the terrible scar, which gave him a dimension few men possessed.

He waited patiently. He'd been stared at before, if never so openly. His lips quirked at her candid inspection, and he wished he knew what she was thinking. Whatever it was, it was soon decided.

"All right, then," she said, nodding her head. "I mean yes, I would like to see you smile more often."

"Fine. Then you should change your mind about skating. It's difficult to laugh when your mouth is frozen shut. Shall we skate? It warms the blood. I promise to try to laugh—if you'll be so kind as to remind me every so often?"

Now she laughed, and taking his proffered arm, walked down to the pondside with him. Because she had decided. If it was true that she was only a poor lass to be trifled with, then she'd make the most of it. She'd laugh and flirt and be outrageous. Why not? This was her last Christmas as a girl. She'd throw her bonnet over the windmill once before she put on a spinster's cap for life. She'd have a memory or two to take with her to light all her dark Christmases to come.

And if a little voice warned that it might be more than her cap that she'd lose, she turned a deaf ear to it. One last fling was all she wanted, and if she wasn't sure what that entailed, so be it. She knew one rake very well, and knew what he wanted of her. But this rake was an entirely different story—if only because it was one she hadn't heard yet.

They skated together, and she found it an oddly peaceful, companionable thing to do. If she didn't look at him, that was. Because when she did, she stumbled. Then she'd feel his strong hands holding her steady, and feel the tensile strength of his whole long body beside hers. Then all sense of companionship vanished and she was left more than a little shaken. So she didn't look at him as they went round and round the pond. They skated well together. Or so she thought, because it didn't feel as though her skates actually touched the ice.

They spoke about the skating, the weather, and how the other skaters were doing. Or so she guessed they did. She was too busy feeling wonderful to pay too much attention. Because for the first time she could remember, other girls were looking at her, and envying her. Because for once she was actually doing what the others were doing, and not only because she thought she ought to. And because she was feeling all this— and something else that was much more. She was with him, and he was neither curt nor abrupt nor cold. He seemed instead exactly the man she'd always wanted to be with. She didn't know what he was really thinking. She didn't want to, either.

Well, if this was what a rake was, she thought, it was a great pity the world wasn't filled with them.

"Enough?" he finally asked.

"I don't know," she said dreamily as she sailed along on his arm, the world and everything in it but him forgotten.

"I only ask because it is growing dark," he said, his voice low and amused, "and the others are leaving."

"Oh!" she said, stumbling as she looked up and around and saw it was true. He held her firmly, for just long enough to steady her, and quite long enough to get her heartbeat cantering, before he let her go again. "I'm sorry," she blurted. "I didn't think—you must be frozen to the bone! I—I just love skating," she concluded weakly.

"As do I," he answered. "I only ask because I think if we go round one more time, we'll go through our tracks in the ice, and end up in the water."

"Oh, of course," she said, hardly knowing what she said as they skated to the pondside.

He got to one knee and helped her off with her skates, and though her legs were frozen as the ice she'd skated on, and she wore woolen stockings besides, she swore she could feel the warmth of his touch. It wasn't so warm as the look in his eyes.

But then, she told herself as he led her back to the house with the others, it was getting dark after all, and anyone could imagine they saw anything in someone's eyes. And yet . . . When they arrived at the manor, he insisted on helping her off with her cape. And when she dared look up at him, she swore she saw the same look in his eyes again. Until Caro interrupted.

"Lud! You two are late! You'd best scurry and dress for dinner, my lord," Caro teased him. "If you don't shake a leg I'm afraid it will be crackers and milk in the kitchen for you."

He looked down at her, his face cool and unreadable.

"Then I'll be brief," he said. He bowed to them both and went up the stairs, leaving Caro unsmiling, and Eve to wonder if she'd only imagined the warm, smiling man she thought she'd seen.

She didn't see that man again at dinner. But then, she couldn't have seen the old one, either. Because her hostess had seated her so far down the table from him that it was almost as if they were in different rooms. And she supposed that was only fair—after all, they were in different worlds. Being ineligible had been uncomfortable before, but it was nothing to what she felt now. Then at least she could dream. Now she knew what it was to long for something she could never have. Something she never, ever should have imagined she could have, she told herself fiercely.

She made poor work of her dinner. When the ladies went to the drawing room to wait for the men to join them, she sat on a small settee at the side of the room by herself. She'd go to her room as soon as the men arrived, she promised herself. That way no one would notice her leaving. The only thing worse than being ignored by a man who had seemed to take such pleasure in her company before would be everyone else seeing her being slighted.

"You really are the privileged sex," the viscount complained.

Eve startled. She stared up to see him standing beside her.

"I don't know why we men are supposed to keep sitting after dinner and you're allowed to get up and stretch your legs," he went on. "You're supposed to be the weaker sex. If social graces made any sense, you'd be the ones forced to languish over brandy and port."

Her delight at seeing him was so profound she was speechless for a moment. But only for a moment. She recovered quickly. "Yes, I suppose," she said, with a glowing smile, "but you'd never get us to smoke those nasty cigars the way you gentlemen do. And I doubt you'd get us to sit and swill down even more alcohol after such a feast."

"*Swill,* is it?" he asked with a quirked smile that made her heart turn over. No female had ever used such a word to describe his behavior—to his face, that was—he thought with amusement. "May I sit down and defend myself?" he asked. She nodded, afraid to speak lest she say what she was thinking: which was that he could sit down, and say anything.

But that was exactly what he did. He started by teasing her about her choice of words, and then got to talking about the different way men and women used words.

"But you are so short-spoken," she said, greatly daring because he seemed to invite and appreciate her candor. "Why, you hardly use words at all, my lord."

"*I?*" he asked, one eyebrow rising.

Which reduced her to giggles. Which seemed to please him even more. He watched her with a bemused expression, so near to sorrow that it finally topped her laughter. Then he said simply, "No. Don't. I mean to say, don't let my grim face upset you. Keep laughing; it's a good sound. I'm a plainspoken fellow, more used to the company of other men than to a lady. Remember that, and forgive me my blunt ways, will you?"

She nodded. His "blunt ways" held more charm than other men's easy smiles. If this was how this rake made his name and reputation, then she was helpless against him. But she chose to believe that this was the real man she spoke with, and not the man who had made such a name for himself.

They sat and talked, and laughed, and the rest of the company sang carols, played charades and cards, and gossiped—mostly about them, it turned out. Because after the company parted for the night, after he'd bowed over her hand and left her at the door to her room, and Eve was about to float inside it, her cousin called her.

"Eve . . . dear," Caro said.

Eve turned, a bemused half-smile still on her lips.

"Are you having a good time, dear?" Caro asked. Before Eve could answer, Caro went on, "*Such* a lot of things to do at Christmastime that one doesn't get the chance for a good long coze with one's dearest friends, does one? At least I haven't had the time—but neither have you—Eve, dear," she said quickly. "I would be much remiss if I didn't—oh, this is so difficult, but mother and I were talking—as are all the girls and their mothers, actually—and as yours isn't here with us, not that we don't invite her every year, but . . . the short of it is, Eve—everyone's remarking how much time you're wasting with Hunt."

"Wasting?" Eve asked, because that was all she could think to say.

"Well, yes," Caro said, "since he is a rake, after all. What else could you call passing time with such a fellow? It's such a mistake; we have so many eligible young men here—take Anderson, for example. He stammers a bit, and it's true he's shy as a dormouse, but he comes from a good family, and . . ."

"I don't consider it a waste to talk with the viscount," Eve said quietly, but with enough emphasis to cut off her cousin's spate of words.

"Eve, dear," Caro said impatiently, "he *is* charming, and so attractive—in a glowery sort of way, of course—that we can quite understand. No one blames you! But do be sensible. Do think. He cannot have a serious intention in his head. At least not toward you. So far as we know, he is not hanging out for a wife. And if he were—oh, how difficult, but it must be said—it would be a lady of similar place and condition to his own."

Eve's face grew hot. There were a dozen things she wanted to say. She couldn't. Her cousin had only voiced what she'd thought, but it hurt to hear it. She could only face it squarely. "So you think he wants me for a mistress?" she asked defiantly.

"My heavens, you've grown frank, haven't you?" Caro said, fanning herself, her own cheeks flaming.

"Well, then, why not?" she muttered, raising her head. "Think on, my dear," she said. "What else would he want of you?"

"I don't know," Eve answered, "but I intend to find out."

"Oh!" Caro said.

"Yes. Indeed," Eve said.

Since neither of them could think of another thing to say, because so much that was unsaid was understood, to their mutual anger and dismay, they merely nodded at each other. Caro took her skirt in one hand and swept away, and Eve, head high, went into her room and pulled the door shut behind her. Then she closed her eyes and rested against it, weak as though she'd been running a long way.

She was so insulted her head and body ached from it. She vowed she'd never come here again—never! But she couldn't leave just yet, either. There were thirteen days left of Christmas. They were suddenly very precious to her. The flirtation might not last the duration. Her courage might fail, or he might grow bored with her. But she was determined to see it through. Because she knew there would be little left for her after, one way or another.

"A spotted hound, too high-spirited for hunting, too charming to give away. He fell to me. He had no nose, and less sense. But he had a very warm belly. A dog of little use, except he was better than a hot brick when winter came. He was worth a dozen of my father's finest scent hounds—at least to me. My father didn't believe in coddling his sons, so the fire in my hearth was always meager. Thank heavens my dog was not." Ian laughed, remembering.

Eve laughed with him. He thought the sound was gayer than the bells jingling on the sleigh as they glided over the snow. Other guests had gone skating or riding, some visited the little village nearby. Some stayed in the warmth of the manor, playing cards and parlor games. But he had begged and bribed a horse sleigh from the stables, and they'd been riding down country lanes all through the brief winter afternoon. Where else could a man of his reputation take a girl of hers, to speak privately? It was an open sleigh and the temperature hovered below freezing. If he stayed to the open roads, even the most evil-minded houseguests couldn't gossip. Even they wouldn't believe he was a determined enough rake to risk frostbite on his more tender parts, no matter how much he might want to seduce her.

Seduce her? he thought quizzically, seeing her glance at him and away again, as if his image burned her eyes. Would holding her, petting her, protecting her, and assuring her that he wouldn't let her come to harm be called seduction? Yes, he answered himself. In her case. Because he knew he'd never stop at an embrace.

It was so cold their breath no longer made white puffs, so cold she was sure the tip of her nose was cherry red, so cold her teeth hurt when she smiled at what he said. But she couldn't stop smiling, because he said so many clever things. They'd been chattering without letup since they'd gotten into the sleigh—since breakfast—since they'd caught sight of each other in the morning, she realized.

They spoke about his past—the parts he could tell her about. They talked about her past, what little she had of it. He told her he'd been brought up as any other well-born lad was, except she heard the loneliness of it in his voice. She said she'd been brought up as no less than any richer girl was—and maybe more— because her parents had taught her to think. She said it proudly. And he realized her parents were too out of society to know thinking wasn't a fashionable thing for a girl to do. They discovered they both loved hounds, and chocolate and mince, and detested turnips, treacle pie, and lap dogs. They acted as though this were a revelation.

He told her about the war, and she knew how to listen and sigh in the right places. In fact, she was as easy to talk with as any man of good sense he'd ever met, and so he had to keep reminding himself that she was a lady. She had to keep reminding herself Christmas was almost upon them, so she'd better store up every word he spoke, every gesture he made. Which was difficult, because she hardly dared look at him lest she forget herself and keep staring, drinking in her fill of him.

So she looked at the sky, at the snowy landscape, at

the lap robe over her knees, as the sleigh carried them down the lane. And even so, saw only him.

He smiled. She was staring at her gloves again. A moment before it was at the horse's rump. Anywhere but at him. He saw more of her profile than her eyes, and that both tickled and irritated him. Because he was as charmed as he was touched by her inexperience. Damn Shelton, he thought suddenly. How was he to broach the subject of what lay ahead for her? It was why he took her out in the sleigh today, to get her alone to speak of it. Time was running as quickly as the runners slid over the snow, and he hadn't been able to bring up the subject yet. Hadn't been able, he corrected himself, or hadn't wanted to?

"What is it? What's happened?" she exclaimed in consternation, turning her head all the way toward him and staring.

"Nothing—what's the matter?" he asked, pulling back on the reins and bringing the horse to a sliding stand, alarmed at her concern.

"You were frowning again. I mean," she said, embarrassed by her outburst; "you suddenly looked as you did when I first saw you."

"That bad, eh?" he laughed.

That bad—and yet that good, she thought on a secret sigh. For while the sight of his dark face laughing did her heart good, his brooding look did something altogether different to regions a little lower down. "I meant—well, yes," she said, greatly daring, "that bad. Was it something I said?"

Now he did frown. "No," he said, turning in his seat to look at her. "Something that I have to say. Look—Eve—I . . . Blast! Do you know Lord Shelton?" he asked abruptly.

She blinked. "Lord Shelton? Why, yes. I do. Why?

Oh, no!" she cried, her face growing pale, her hand flying to her mouth. "Has anything happened to him?"

His brows drew together. "No, nothing I know of," he said. "Why are you so stricken? Is he important to you?"

"Important? Why, yes—he is," she said thoughtfully. "But why are you scowling? I thought you were friends."

"Acquaintances," he snapped. He stared at her, trying to phrase the thing smoothly, knowing there was no easy way. "Then you are aware of his interest in you," he finally said.

"Yes," she said, lowering her gaze. "I could scarcely not be."

"And?"

"And what?" she asked in confusion, her eyes wide as she gazed at him. Molten fire, he thought dazedly, liquid amber shining. He had to drag his attention back to what she was saying. When he did, he forgot her glorious eyes. "He has a dreadful reputation; is it that you think I don't know it?" she was asking him. "I do. But I also know he is much maligned. For he has always been kind to me."

"Kind?" he asked, astonished. He didn't say it angrily. But she heard the insinuation.

"I cannot say I approve of the way he has lived his life. But I can say," she said, her chin coming up, "that he has harmed no one—and nothing but his own reputation."

"Indeed? He has done no harm?" he asked, as angry at her defense of the rake as he was troubled by it. "And so I may presume that your superior but unconventional upbringing gave you Latin and world history, watercolors and maths, but stinted on the Bible? And you never went to church of a Sunday morning?"

Her nostrils pinched, and she sucked in her breath. He was right, of course. She hadn't thought. But she was a proud girl and hated to look foolish. "Oh! And you are a Methodist, I presume?" she asked haughtily.

"Hardly," he said. "But at least I know what a rake is. Do you?"

"Of course" was what was on her lips, but when she opened her mouth, she found his lips on it instead. He just reached over and pulled her up against his chest and kissed her hard. They'd been riding in the frosty air for hours. Their mouths were cold. It should have been like kissing ice. It was. For a moment.

But then she felt the sweet, treacherous fire of his mouth, and his lips softened as he felt the incredibly sweet warmth of hers. And they both forgot the ice and the hour, the day and the moment. She was shocked, and then astonished, and then overwhelmed. The kiss led to a second's breathing space, and then to another kiss. And another. She gave herself up to his embrace.

He was the one to come to his senses first. Not because he was less moved. But only because he knew what to do with such an outpouring of passion and discovered he could not do it. His body craved more, his hands sought more—the silk of her cheek, the curve of her neck, the contours of her breast—and found only frustrated desire. Because as he reached to caress her, he became aware that he was wearing gloves, and she, a heavy woolen cloak. When he realized that their kisses, stupefyingly sweet as they were, could actually lead nowhere that he wanted to go—at least not in the open air, with the temperature freezing—he reluctantly raised his head. And so freed her. She gasped, and scuttled back to her end of the seat, staring at him.

He didn't know what to say.

She thought she did.

She bit her bottom lip, still rosy pink from the kisses, and asked fearfully, "Is it—were you trying to show me what a rake is?"

"God, no," he breathed. "But I suppose I did, didn't I?"

They stared at each other. They both knew what a gentleman's kiss meant to people of their station. It could be tantamount to a proposal—if . . . *if,* she thought, he regarded her a social equal. On one level she knew it wasn't really always so. Many girls kissed and were kissed, and thoroughly, too, without having to marry the poor fellow who dared. Many a fellow dared and didn't have to take a wife for it. But today her feelings were raw as the day, and she wondered if he thought her too poor, too insignificant, undesirable for anything but what a rake found women good for.

A kiss was as good as a declaration, he thought. *If* a girl was a high stickler—which he was sure she was not. But such a kiss could be considered a declaration of intent if a gentleman chose it to be. But that was madness. He didn't really know her or what her feelings were toward him. She might just have a weakness for rakes. Just think of her defense of Shelton . . . no—he didn't want to think about that. Instead, he realized that he had kissed her, and so he might actually have to propose marriage to her. He was shocked by the thought—more so when he realized he wouldn't mind as much as he ought. Still, that was a powerfully big step to take in return for a few minutes of madness—delicious madness, he remembered with renewed interest.

He collected his thoughts with difficulty. He had to know what she thought. The more fool he if he actually declared himself if he didn't have to—or if she didn't want him to. He was no coward. Nevertheless he didn't look at her when he spoke.

He cleared his throat, and took up the reins. "Forgive me, will you? In the spirit of Christmas?" he asked. "I mean, can you simply pretend we were under some mistletoe?" He laughed, and never meant it less.

She smiled, though she felt like weeping. But her tone was no less light than his.

"Consider it done," she said, and paused, and then said too brightly, "my goodness! Just look. The sun is starting to sink and I'm afraid my reputation will, too, if we stay out much longer. . . ." She stopped, flustered by her missaying, but went on valiantly, "I mean, we ought to be getting back, don't you think?"

"Eve," he said seriously, "I meant nothing by it— damnation! I mean to say I meant no harm to you, believe that. And I give you my word that no harm will come to you because of it, come what may."

She muttered something excusing him, he nodded, snapped the reins, and they sped back to the manor. They didn't speak, but they were both too busy thinking to realize that they weren't.

No harm did come to her because of what he did—at least, not exactly, Eve thought later that evening. But she was sure people were looking at her differently. The girls her age seemed cooler toward her, their mothers and chaperones definitely colder. And the gentlemen seemed to be eyeing her differently. Shy young Mr. Kensington, who had been one of her most persistent friends, stole sad glances at her but didn't approach. And that portly bachelor Lord Fellowes, with his red face, big belly, and roving eye, who had never spoken directly to her before, was now seeking every opportunity to talk with her, even though she only replied in monosyllables.

She chided herself for having an overactive imagination, coupled with a guilty conscience—and a new understanding of men and what they could make a girl feel. If they were the right man. Which none of them were but the one who hadn't shown up in the salon yet. She didn't know how she should react to him when he did arrive. She wished he would ignore her when he came—equally as much as she yearned for him to come directly up to her, sweep her into his arms, and kiss her before all the company and the immediate world.

He did neither. He only came into the room, saw her, and walked to her side, as though she'd been waiting for him by prearrangement.

"Tonight's the lighting of the log, and the caroling, isn't it?" he asked her after a moment.

It wasn't a loverlike comment, but she smiled at him as though he'd just offered her the most flowery compliment on her gown and hair.

"Yes," she said shyly. And he looked at her as though she'd just offered to rush up the stairs and hurry into his bed with him.

"Well, then," he said, offering her his arm, "shall we?"

He took her into dinner as though he were taking her to that bed. And she went with him like a bride.

But their hosts had sat them so far apart they might as well have been in different houses, not just rooms.

Ian couldn't even catch sight of her down the long table. After a while he gave up trying. He ate his dinner in stony silence, in spite of the conversational efforts of the married lady on his left and the single one on his right. It didn't discourage them. His glowering looks only fascinated them more. His reserve didn't bother the men they sat with, either. They took his taciturnity as interest, and kept boring on about their opinions of the war he'd just fought. He was so glad when the meal was over that he shocked the company by rising, without comment, and leaving the table when the ladies did.

Eve didn't notice. She was trying too hard to keep her head up as she left the room. Because no one had talked with her at all.

He stopped her in the hall. "This is nonsense," he said.

She nodded.

"Come with me," he said, and led her into the drawing room, where the Yule log—a stout half of a goodly sized tree—lay in the hearth, awaiting Squire's ceremonial lighting.

The other guests followed soon after, eyeing the pair avidly all the while. But before long they were forgotten; the possible scandal unfolding before the guests' eyes couldn't compete with Christmas at Moon Manor.

When all the guests were assembled, Squire strode to the great hearth, raised a charred stick, and showed it to the assembled company.

"The last bit of last year's Yule log," he announced, waving it in front of them. A servant brought him an old-fashioned tarry torch, and Squire solemnly used it to ignite the stick.

"Thus, Christmas to Christmas we go at Moon Manor, wishing you all the joy of the season, and all the peace, goodness, and luck of it, too. The log shall burn through the holiday, but no brighter than our hopes and hearts," Squire intoned, holding the flaming stick high before he touched it to the massive log in the fireplace. He laid that bit of the old log atop the new one (and

the tarry torch, too, though that was supposed to go unnoticed), and the bed of dry brush and tinder under the
great log began to chuckle and spit. Soon the log was
surrounded by a filmy wall of dancing flames, and the
company cheered.

"Wassail!" commanded Squire.

"Caroling first," one of the guests cried.

"Not at Moon Manor," Squire retorted, and the
company laughed as bowls of hot punch, redolent of
ale, cinnamon, and nutmeg, with roasted crab apples
bobbing in them, were borne in by smiling servants.

"Now," Squire called, raising a steaming cup to his
guests, "the caroling. Caro, if you please?"

Caro, her face aglow, swept her father a deep curtsy.
Then she beckoned the company to follow her to the
great hall. When they were all there, cups in hand, she
signaled to the footmen—who flung open the front
door. Music blew in on an icy draft, because there were
carolers on the doorstep. The guests cheered and then
joined in.

Before long, the carolers, who were neighboring
landowners, tenants, and villagers, were in the man-
or, cups in hand. That was when the musicians, who
had been cleverly concealed behind a holly-and-ivy-
covered screen, began to play. There was impromptu
dancing, much singing, and more laughter. And not a
few guests took advantage of the kissing boughs of
mistletoe above the doorways and hanging from the
chandeliers.

Ian wouldn't let Eve out of his sight, nor would he
share her with any other man. He danced her beneath
the mistletoe many times. But each time he kissed her,
it was the sort of kiss a gentleman might give any lady
in public—brief and charming, a salute rather than a
pledge or a promise or a deep, dark, and disturbing

hint of what might be, like the kisses he'd given her when they'd been alone.

Eve knew she'd never forget this Christmas. So she forced herself to forget to worry about all the barren Christmases to come, when her dark and dashing rake was gone somewhere else to dazzle some other lucky girl. She knew she was an amusement of the moment for him and she was determined to seize that moment and ignore what would come. Because she could no more see a future with him than she could see one without him now. She couldn't be his mistress; he'd never want her for his wife. But he would be her dearest memory, so she was resolved to live every moment of her time with him while she could.

She didn't stop smiling until Caro appeared at their side, grave-faced and uncomfortable as she gazed from one of them to the other.

"We've had a message," Caro said, looking from Ian to Eve, and back again. "Lord Shelton sent word that he is delayed, but that all's well with him. He said to tell you not to worry, he'll be here as soon as he can."

Before they could ask a question, she turned and walked back to the thick of the company with one of her many admirers.

"Are you desolated?" Ian asked Eve. He stood very still, looking down at her, waiting for her answer.

"Are you joking?" she asked him, her eyes wide.

"I thought . . . as you were so quick to defend him . . ."

"I've known him a long time," she said carefully. "We're old friends."

Ian's mouth twisted, and the scar on his face made it an ugly sneer. Her back stiffened.

"Whatever you think, nevertheless, we are friends," she said briskly. "I care for his welfare as he cares for mine. I always look forward to seeing him for many reasons, but especially here, at holiday time, because he always treats me with respect, and more. . . ." She cocked her head to the side, considering. "Though he wants nothing more than my friendship, and knows my state, he always treats me as though I *mattered*."

"And I do not?"

She colored. "Yes, you do, but . . ."

He nodded. "But that's what rakes do—is that what you were going to say?"

"Do they?" she asked seriously, instead of answering him.

He stared down at her. She was wearing a gown of amber velvet, the color of her eyes. She looked very lovely, very vulnerable. The way the soft velvet caressed her lovely form almost made him forget how vulnerable he was to her. But not quite. He was a cautious man. He knew rake Shelton had this girl almost in his clutches, and he yearned to save her—but he was still not sure how much in need of saving she was. Or he himself was. He decided words weren't adequate for what he felt or what he yearned to feel. And so he offered her his arm instead of answering her question.

"I'm not a man for capering, standing on my toes, and showing off my winsome self," he said, motioning to the antics of some of the gentlemen dancing around them, "but they've struck up a waltz. I can do a slow and steady version of one. If you dance with me, no one will notice how bad I am at it. Will you?"

She stared into his harsh face, willing herself to see more than impatience for her answer there. She ducked her head in a little nod, and took his arm. He was with her tonight. She'd dance with him, and the devil take tomorrow. Because, she thought as they swept into the dance, she had only a handful of tomorrows left with him. She settled into his embrace and sighed. This was enough for now. And now was all she had.

Ian danced with her, and breathed in the soft summer scent of her perfume, and felt her lithesome body move with his. He wanted to think of nothing else but the unexpected pleasure of holding her thus, holding her close without fear of commitment or censure from the polite world. She felt so good in his arms, so absolutely right, that he no more wanted to think about tomorrow than she did. But he couldn't stop thinking about the message that had been delivered to them both this evening—because he couldn't stop wondering which of them rake Shelton had sent the message to.

Christmas came bright, and sleighfuls of guests were sped through the crisp morning to the old church at the edge of town. The old church wasn't as grand or spacious as some of the stately cathedrals that stood near more famous noble homes. But it was older than the manor itself and said to be as old as any on the entire island. And so, tilted and bearded with lichens as it was, it was magnificent because of it.

Sunlight streamed in through stained windows so warped with age that no one but historians knew which saints they depicted. The congregation's breath showed in the air. Eve stood next to Ian, and disregarded the looks she got from Caro and her mother for it. She wouldn't compound matters by staring up at him as she wanted to. But she never forgot the tall, straight, silent man she stood beside.

He looked down at the good book he held in his gloved hands. That made it easy for him to slide his eyes to the side to gaze at her. The sight made him take in his breath. A ray of sunlight, capricious as the magic of the day, ringed round her head and gilded her face, and turned her eyes and hair to the hue of honey in the comb. She looked very beautiful, but very young. *But I am not so old, either,* he thought, for the first time since he had gone off to war. She was smiling as she sang, and he wondered how much she would be smiling next Christmas—after Shelton arrived. Or more to the point, after he eventually left her, as he doubtless would.

But Lord Shelton didn't come, and Christmas did—and went. Christmas Day was marked by a huge dinner, and more singing, wassailing, dancing, and merriment. There was a pantomime on Christmas night. Villagers had got it together and came to the hall to perform it. It was wonderfully amusing for the guests because it was so well done by amateurs, and because it was so badly done for people used to seeing England's finest perform on London stages. But it was more than wonderful for Eve, because Ian sat beside her and his laughter was rich and warm. And Ian couldn't remember having laughed so much, and for so long.

But it didn't last that long. Because the next morning, on Boxing Day, his hostess stopped him in the hall.

"Good morning, my lord," Caro said flirtatiously. "How are you? More to the point—how have you been? Because Christmas has come and gone, and I haven't had much chance to talk with you, have I?"

"Because you've been so busy with your admirers," Ian said gallantly, although his voice was cool.

"And you," she said sweetly, "with yours."

"No," he said abruptly, the old harsh expression erasing his slight smile. "I've been busy with those I admire."

"Indeed?" she asked in acid accents, because she

was a girl who was used to compliments even when she didn't deserve them. "So I expect we may breathlessly await an announcement?"

He was still. "It is early days," he began to say, but she cut him off by laughing. She tapped his shoulder lightly with one little gloved hand.

"Or will it be something *accomplished* rather than announced?" she asked sweetly. "Fie! And if it is, I shall never know, shall I? This is Eve's last Christmas here—or so she keeps insisting. Now I suppose I know why. Lud! Look at the time. Everyone will wonder where I am, and Father has the most wonderful surprise for me, he says. Good morning, my lord," she said as she hurried away. Because even if her father had nothing for her, it was better than what the viscount's dark and glowering eyes promised her.

He was strangely silent with Eve when he met her. She noticed, but didn't worry. She was so happy to find him her companion again that she ignored his darkening mood. Then, too, Squire's having given foolish presents to his guests in the spirit of Boxing Day lifted everyone's spirits.

So Eve didn't worry. Until that night. Because then there was more dancing, and Ian danced with her. But then he danced with other ladies, too, without a backward look to her. Or so she thought. But he was a wily campaigner, and a good soldier never loses sight of his objective. So even though he danced with many others, he never once lost sight of her. Then, or later.

The days seemed to fly by for both Eve and Ian, and they were both relieved and upset by it. Because while they had ample time to jest together and confide in each other, it seemed they never had time to seriously discuss anything—especially the future. They had neither the time nor place because Squire kept them so busy with planned entertainments. It might have been their own reluctance to face the facts that kept their conversations safely to what had been, rather than what might be. But one thing was certain: their hosts kept them in sight at all times. And so while they kept almost constant company, they were never alone . . . until the last day of the year, when they managed to slip away for a walk in a deserted garden.

"Imagine! In just one day, we shall have a whole new year," Eve sighed as they picked their way down the paths of the manor's frozen knot garden. "It makes me feel very old."

He gazed down at her without speaking, but his expression was quizzical. It cheered her, because he had been so lost in thought she wondered if he remembered where he was, and who he was with. The weather had thawed only a jot, only long enough for this short walk. It was a brief respite in late afternoon, and she knew the night and the cold and the last of her holiday were coming as quickly and surely as the new year was. She wanted to remember him smiling, so she smiled up at his bemused expression.

"Yes, you are very old," he agreed, on a slight smile.

She was heartened. "Well, I was born in the last century, you know," she said brightly. "Late in it, to be sure. But, nevertheless, a different century. Tonight will bring in yet another year. You can't help but feel ancient when you're older than the century you live in."

He nodded, but his face grew grave again. He knew a new year was coming, the holiday was ending. Yet nothing was resolved. He decided that it was time for something to be. In fact, he'd resolved it sometime between midnight and dawn, in the long hours he'd passed pacing in his room.

"Eve," he said suddenly, turning to look at her, and stopping her in her tracks. He took her hand in both of his. "I'm a man of few words. But the words I speak are considered ones. I've been thinking about this, about us. About you. And about your friend Shelton. I worry for you. You think you know what he is, but you don't. Not really. You couldn't."

"I do," she said haughtily. "You don't know everything; I haven't told you everything. . . ."

"Nor can you," Ian argued. "And I'm not saying you shouldn't like him . . ."

"You couldn't," she said.

"Nor am I saying I'm better than he," Ian persisted, his heart sinking at her defense of the older man. But then, Shelton was a practiced rake and she, an inexperienced girl. He couldn't blame her for her opinion. Had he himself acted any better than Shelton would? He'd known she was without protection of her family here, and he had not only monopolized her time, but kissed her shamelessly, without ever stating any intentions. And hadn't his intentions been . . . mixed, at first? Wasn't that a rake's actions? Wasn't that what he had been—until he met her? Until he'd realized she was clear as a mountain stream, kind and good, warm and beautiful, and everything he'd ever wanted and needed?

Now he had to put his own best case forward to show her that for all he seemed the same as rake Shelton, he was different. He had to be, for her sake as well as his own. He wasn't sure he knew how to convince her, but he knew he had to. He persevered.

"Indeed, I may not be better," he went on, "but I'm sure I feel more for you—I don't think I could feel more. I've had a wonderful time these last days. Christmas at Moon Manor turned out to be as spectacular as your friend Shelton promised. More so. Because I met you here. I am loath to leave it at that."

He fell still, marshaling his thoughts, trying to say the thing right, and finding it hard to do while that sober little face stared up at him with fear and sorrow clear to see in her honey-colored eyes. He didn't know why she should be afraid or concerned, and couldn't think about it. All he really wanted to do was to clasp her to him and kiss the consternation from her expression. But she was brought up as a lady, and he as a gentleman, so he knew he had to say the thing first. He was a brave man, but found himself reluctant to put his luck to the test. But he had no choice.

Time would have been his best ally, but he had no time. Christmas was already gone, a new year was coming—and rake Shelton, too. Ian didn't know what had kept him so long, but he did know he couldn't count on him being delayed much longer. He had to speak, and quickly. Because lately every time he heard a carriage rumbling over the cobbles in the front drive, he was afraid it was Shelton arriving. He'd laughed at the thought of competing with the old rake before he'd come to Moon Manor. Now he didn't find it humorous at all.

She cast her gaze down to the frozen ground, and bit her lip. Her heart sank even as it soared and her pulse pounded heavily in her ears. It was coming. A proposal. She knew what kind. She realized she'd always known. She was too clever to play with fire and not know what would happen.

And now? she asked herself. *Now after he makes his offer to keep you as his mistress, you squeak and cry, "How dare you, sir? A girl of my class and caliber?" But you knew he was said to be a rake. You knew you had nothing to offer him but yourself, and a viscount*

*would want more from a wife and less from a mistress.
And still you led him on. Worse, you led yourself on,
my girl,* she told herself. *And so, now?*

"I'm not a flowery-spoken man," Ian said bluntly,
and then frowned, because he'd said that, hadn't he?
"and I have many faults. My face, for example, is
ruined."

She gasped and began to deny it, but he went on
roughly, "Be that as it may, I'm not precisely a monster, either, and you are used to it, I suppose. But even
if my face doesn't dismay you, I have other shortcom-
ings. I'm curt to the point of arrogance and I know it."
He paused. *Go on,* he told himself angrily, *tell her all
your faults; that's how to woo a lady, isn't it, idiot?*

"But I mean nothing by it," he added hastily. "I'm
just plainspoken. That doesn't mean I have no feelings." He paused—*better, that was better*—then went
on. "Or that I don't need people—persons—you.
Damn it, Eve—pardon my damned profanity—but I'm
only making a mull of it and an ass of myself, aren't
I? I lack a mother's influence; I've lived too long
among men, that's the problem."

He sighed. He had to tell her all the reasons he
wanted her. If that didn't work, he would try to win her
over by telling her everything he could offer her. But
he was only able to state the bare facts. Because he
was, as he said, a plainspoken man.

"I've had a wonderful time with you," he said
abruptly, "as I think you have had with me. I don't
want that to stop. Why should it? We can make it last.
I have money and position and will use both to bring
you comfort. Much comfort, much pleasure, I promise.
Eve, I want you. What say you?"

She gaped at him. What could she say? She wanted
him, too. Christmas was over, her holiday was ending,

and if she left him she had a terrible feeling she'd
never be the same and her future would be just a constant replaying of these past days with him. She'd
vowed to throw her bonnet over the windmill, but now
that the time was come, she trembled. She thought of
what her mother and father would say, and couldn't
speak. She squeezed her eyes shut, trying to see her
way clear to answer what she yearned to.

"I'm not so bad," he said a little desperately, "nor
lost to propriety. I know it's early days, but I know my
own heart and mind. More time won't change them.
Neither of us are children; I'd hoped you felt the same.
It's true I'd have liked to ask your father first, but
there's no time. . . ." Her eyes flew wide.

"He's miles from here," Ian went on, "and if I
waited to ask him, Shelton will come. Damn it, Eve—
pardon, I mean, the one thing I can offer that I know
he can't is my name. I'll try to be a good husband; I'll
be a constant one because that's my nature. What more
can I say? Tell me what you want me to say, and I
shall . . ."

"Husband?" she asked in astonishment.

Now he looked astonished. He paused, and then
said, "You thought I meant . . ."

She could only stand and stare at him, wide-eyed,
her hand at her mouth.

"I see," he said slowly. "I see," he said with more
energy. "What sort of a fellow do you take me for?" he
asked angrily. "Just because Shelton invited me . . .
You think my reputation . . . You think that I
would . . . ? I see," he said again, glowering at her.

"You want to *marry* me?" she squeaked.

"No, I'm a cad, a rake, a rogue, like your beloved
Shelton," he growled. "Of course I want to marry you.
Wanted to marry you," he said, stepping back and fold-

ing his arms in front of his wide chest as he scowled at her. "Of course, with your estimate of me . . ."

She continued to stare at him speechlessly. He frowned at her. And then he started to grin, just a tiny uplifting of his stern mouth. A tic, no more. But she saw it. And her own mouth stopped trembling, and curled slightly at the corners. No more. But he saw it.

"You were thinking about it, though. Weren't you?" he asked curiously. "You were really thinking of accepting carte blanche from me?"

"I didn't want you to leave me—ever," she said. "I don't know that I could have," she confessed, "but, oh, Ian, I so wanted to!"

"Ah. I see," he said. "And here I proposed marriage, and I didn't have to."

She stopped smiling. Until she saw his face.

But she didn't see it very long, because he pulled her into his arms and kissed her ruthlessly, and then tenderly, and then as though he would never let her go. She kissed him back, and held fast to his hard shoulders, because she knew she never had to let him go.

A footman glanced out the window and saw them, and gaped. A guest saw the direction of his openmouthed stare. Soon all the guests at Moon Manor were hanging at the windows, looking out at the rake and his lady. The men grinned as the ladies sighed. Because they knew how their world worked. And knew no rake of good breeding would let the polite world see him taking his latest mistress so blatantly. But only a dark and dashing rake such as Hunt would let the world see him choosing his wife that way.

Lord Shelton arrived the next day. He stepped out of his carriage in the drive and stood looking at Moon Manor. The first thing he saw after his host was the couple holding hands as they came out of the house to greet him. He smiled. The footman he'd paid to contact him had told no less than the truth he could see with his own eyes.

Eve broke from her beloved's side and ran lightly to him.

"Uncle!" she cried as he received her in his arms, and hugged her hard.

"Not really," Shelton said over her head to her sardonically smiling fiancé. "As she's likely told you by now, it's merely a courtesy title, my dear boy. She should have been mine—but not in the way the polite world imagined. Her mother was the lady I wanted to wive, you see. But my best friend wed her and I was left to roam the world searching for a substitute— who—I have never found."

"Fudge!" Eve exclaimed as she extricated herself from his fond embrace. "A tidy excuse, and so everyone knows, Mother and Father most of all. It's good to see you, sir. What kept you so long?"

"Plots and plans," Ian said as he came forward to take the older man's hand in his, "strategies and stratagems. Am I right?"

"Who am I to contradict an army man?" Lord Shelton shrugged. "But I never lied, did I? I said I had my reasons for wanting to be here, didn't I? And so I did. I described my girl as lovingly as I think of her, as well. Fortunately, you jumped to all the wrong conclusions. Well, so then, lad," he said in a soft voice, "how do you like your Christmas gift?"

Ian laughed, and Lord Shelton was interested to see how young he looked, and how merry.

"It was her Christmas gift, as well," Lord Shelton commented. "I studied you before I set my plans. Other men might look to the cream of society to find a suitor for a girl he holds dear. I know men too well for that. A fair name often covers a bad man. But I know my rakes, and there's no husband more relentlessly dependable and ruthlessly constant than a reformed rake. You were young enough, wealthy enough, and just possibly clever enough for Eve. Nothing less than the best for my girl.

"And how else could I bring you together? Not at her house, nor mine, to be sure. Not with my reputation. But it's not only that. You see, her father's too proud to take anything from me, always was, and always shall be. Then, too, I suspect he still thinks I mean to take his lady away; he discourages my visits— and he may well be right to. That's why I usually only see this little dear at other people's homes." He laughed. "I shall love to see his face when he sees I've given his daughter something he cannot refuse."

"Can he not?" Ian asked, suddenly grave again.

"Never fear," the older man answered. "He cannot. He will not. He dare not. Just look at her. And know that like myself, his only aim is to see her happy— stiff-necked though he is. He will be very well pleased with you, as what sane father would not be? Once he gets over his chagrin at my having been matchmaker."

"I think you only introduced us to ruffle his feathers, Uncle," Eve said on a giggle. He smiled at her, because she glowed.

"Just so," he said lightly. "And so, have you had a merry old Christmas, Eve?"

"Yes, thank you," she said.

"But not so good as next year's," Ian promised.

"Good," Lord Shelton said.

"Thank you, sir," Ian said sincerely.

"No," the older man answered. "Thank *you* for clearing the field, and leaving it to me. You were bid-ding fair to being formidable competition before you found your own lady. The best Christmas gift is one that suits the giver as much as the recipient," he added merrily.

"Father's right—what a rascal you are," Eve teased, laughing, and Ian joined in.

The rake watched as Eve looked up into her dark viscount's face, and he sighed before he tore his gaze away from them. Because as a rake, he knew very well what they were saying wordlessly to each other, and knew it was a very private matter. And because in that moment she looked so much like her mother that his heart twisted. She was the only other woman on earth who resembled her so vividly. He knew, because he passed his whole life looking.

"Merry Christmas, children," he murmured softly. "And now, if you will, let us get on to a whole new year," he said, smoothing his hair as he prepared to enter the salon. "Now, for my gift, just kindly tell me: just who is that shockingly lovely lady over there—the one with the welcoming smile, those magnetic eyes, and all that dark hair?"

"Some things never change," Ian murmured to Eve. She smiled in acknowledgment.

But, having overheard them, so too did the last rake at Moon Manor.

Lady Bountiful

by Laura Matthews

Enacting her version of a young lady fainting, the irrepressible Drucilla Carruthers fell back against her chair, her listless hand allowing the distressing letter to flutter to the floor amidst the feathers. Her companion and former governess, Miss Script, shook her graying head with vigorous disapproval.

"It is no laughing matter, Drucilla," she protested. "You know very well why Lord Meacham is coming, despite his sweetly couched phrases of concern for your father. He's heard what's going forward here, no doubt from Sir Lawrence's attorney."

"Yes, he must have been severely provoked if he's willing to travel two hundred miles this close to Christmas," Drucilla said thoughtfully as she retrieved the boldly penned missive from the worn Axminster carpet and tucked it carelessly into the second volume of the novel she was currently reading.

"He can bring the matter up before a magistrate," Miss Script warned, her thin hands nervously gripping the pillowcase in her lap.

Drucilla's smile made her blue eyes dance. "Fortunately, it is Sir Edward who would have to act, and I believe him gone to visit his son in Somerset for the Christmas holidays. I should be very surprised if Lord Meacham were able to accomplish much before the next assizes. But really, it was too bad of Mr. Wicker to have told him."

Miss Script, however, could not agree, since she was well aware of the tactics Drucilla had used to divert the elderly solicitor. From the time Drucilla was a small child, fair and angelic looking with her blond curls and wide azure eyes, she had been perfectly capable of disturbing Miss Script's nice sense of propriety.

"I'm sure Mr. Wicker only saw it as his duty, Drucilla. He has, after all, like his father before him, been the solicitor for the baronets of Tarnlea for close to fifty years. My understanding of solicitors is that they are constitutionally suspicious men. Mr. Wicker has been urging you for three years to make plain the situation here, and you've managed to avoid every query. You must have known he would eventually relate everything to Lord Meacham."

"Certainly I did. I only hoped that I would be able to prevent him doing so until the work was completely finished. Still, we've accomplished a great deal these last years, May, haven't we?"

Her companion stretched the muslin pillowcase she was stuffing from a sack of clean goose down and feathers. "I worry that you've taken too much upon yourself. Not that your father's tenants don't deserve it!" she hastened to add. "But you have surely invited trouble upon yourself. Lord Meacham will hardly be complaisant about the expense."

"It did turn out to cost considerably more than I'd anticipated," Drucilla admitted. "But the necessity was surely there. My father . . ." With a sigh she shrugged and said only, "I won't have anyone disrupting his peace, or making him a byword in the neighborhood."

"Lord Meacham may have some legitimate complaints, though, since he is heir to Tarnlea."

Drucilla's nose wrinkled in distaste. "I daresay. I remember meeting him once as a child. It was just after my mother's death, so I must have been five and he couldn't have been less than twelve at the time. What does that make him now—twenty-eight? He was already a very stuffy fellow."

"When a boy must take over his father's dignities at a young age, I believe he usually has a tendency to be stiff and overresponsible. You know it was true of Lady Nibthwaite's son."

"Heavens, yes," Drucilla agreed, her dimples peeking out. None of her acquaintance was more officious than Lord Nibthwaite. "I recall thinking Lord Meacham was full of his own consequence. Odious boy. It would serve him right if I bankrupted Tarnlea. He has sufficient property of his own."

Miss Script, though the most amiable of companions, was not just at present prepared to hear her former charge discourse on the inequities of fate with particular regard to the inheritance practices of the British Isles. "I'm sure you are very well provided for under your dear mama's will, though it will indeed mean wrenching yourself from the only home you've known when the time comes. But pray recall that young ladies who marry do so all the time."

"Which just proves what milk-and-water misses they are!"

"Never mind that now," Miss Script admonished. "We must consider how best to prepare for Lord Meacham's arrival. When does he come?"

Drucilla did not need to consult the short letter. "He should be here in a matter of hours. He seemed to think the letter would reach us yesterday."

"Hours!" squeaked the poor woman opposite, hastily rising from her chair. "Today? He's coming today?"

"So he says." Drucilla staunchly retained her seat. "We are to make no preparation for him, he insists. He was very clear about that, May. Let him find us exactly as we are every day. That is precisely what he wishes."

"Well, he may wish it, but we most certainly cannot allow it. To find us here stuffing feathers into pillow-cases as though we were pinched for pennies. And look at what you're wearing! Quickly. Upstairs! Change into the blue muslin with the golden ribbons. It's very attractive and just the sort of thing you might have been wearing, if, for instance, we'd been expecting Lady Nibthwaite to tea."

"But we weren't expecting Lady Nibthwaite to tea and I have no intention of changing," retorted the recalcitrant young lady.

"But, my dear, the only reason you're wearing that washed-out sprig muslin is because we were working with the feathers. It's not what you would ordinarily wear."

Drucilla dismissed her companion's patient reasoning. "What does it matter? Come, May, let's not make a fuss. People probably fawn over his lordship all the time; we will be a refreshing change, treating him as just another member of the family."

"You're purposely being contrary, Drucilla. There is also the matter of showing the proper respect for one of his position."

"Oh, very well. But not the blue gown. Lady Nibthwaite is coming to tea tomorrow and I plan to wear it then. Lord Meacham can wait a day to see my very best day dress."

As Drucilla rose to follow Miss Script out of the room, there was the sound of horses drawing a light vehicle on the gravel outside the parlor window.

Drucilla grinned at her companion. "Too late. His lordship has obviously made very good time."

Curious, she moved quickly to a slight gap in the heavy winter draperies where she could not be seen by their visitor. The two horses, astonishingly well matched grays, were being deftly pulled to a plunging stop. Gravel flew from under their hooves and the gleaming black curricle with its red trim and gold crest slid to an abrupt halt. Drucilla might have faulted his lordship's driving, except for her witnessing the cause of the emergency stoppage—a loose goat had wandered across the courtyard.

Chagrined, she turned to Miss Script to say, "Teddy's managed to get loose again and nearly had herself run over. It's probably frightened the wits out of her and now the milk will be curdled and Papa will take one of his pets."

"Oh, dear, how awkward. Perhaps we should say that your father is indisposed and can't be visited until tomorrow."

"I doubt his lordship would accept such a rebuff, since he has clearly come this distance to ascertain my father's condition. A curse on all solicitors. We could have used another few weeks."

A peremptory knocking on the entry door reminded Drucilla that she hadn't actually prepared the staff for Lord Meacham's visit. Not that he'd given her the time. She hurried to the parlor door and hastily peeped out into the hall, hissing to the venerable Hastings that he should put on his very best face, for it would be Lord Meacham come for a visit.

The butler Hastings regarded her with astonishment, but only for a moment. There had, after all, been any number of surprises for him during his tenure at Tarnlea, and he had grown accustomed to them. With a stolid dignity he said, "Yes, miss. I will direct that a bedchamber be prepared for him."

Drucilla drew back into the room and shook her head at Miss Script's attempts to tidy the disorganized scene. Perhaps stuffing pillows in the winter parlor had not, after all, been such a fine idea. Though the pillowcases which had already been filled looked plump and inviting, the feathers for the remainder had gotten a bit out of hand. White bits of fluff decorated the carpet, the furniture, and even the clothing of the two women.

Drucilla shrugged and regained her seat. "Let it be, May," she urged. "There's not a thing we can do that will make the place look presentable. It's his own fault for giving so little notice."

Miss Script's lips tightened, as they did when she was distressed, but she did as she was bid. She said gloomily, "The whole was bound to be discovered eventually. I'm sure I should have given you more guidance these two years past."

Drucilla heard the sounds of voices in the hall, and the stamp of booted feet. "Pooh! We've done no more nor less than our duty. And you would not have been able to dissuade me from my course, no matter how persuasive you might have been."

"I am well aware of it," her companion sighed.

There was a discreet tap on the door and Hastings entered to say, "Lord Meacham has arrived, Miss Carruthers."

"Please show him in, Hastings."

The man who strode through the meager portal seemed to dwarf it, and Drucilla could scarcely connect him with the skinny twelve-year-old she'd had in her mind for sixteen years. Though he had been driving an open carriage, his many-caped driving coat had been removed to display a flawless appearance, as though he had just left the hands of his valet. His thick black hair curled close to his head in an elegant if unfashionable cut; his cravat fell in pristine white folds; his boots gleamed with a high polish; his coat and pantaloons fit superbly. But the feature that most struck Drucilla was his eyes. From a distance they appeared almost black, so dark were their indecipherable depths. They suggested a keen intelligence, which she had not expected.

"Miss Carruthers? I'm your cousin Julian Winslow. I doubt you remember me from our one short encounter so long ago. I must beg your pardon for only a day's warning, but my time is constrained. I am due within a sennight at Meacham Court."

Drucilla made a gentle curtsy to him, which caused Miss Script to stare at her in astonishment. "We're honored to have you here. Your room has not as yet been prepared, because your letter reached us scarce half an hour ago."

Lord Meacham's brows rose. "How is this? It should have been here yesterday. You've hardly had time to accustom yourselves to the idea of my visit. I do apologize."

"There's no necessity," she assured him. "Please let me make you known to my companion, Miss Script."

"How do you do, ma'am?" He offered a polite bow in Miss Script's direction, but he seemed slightly taken aback by the condition of the room around her. "I'm afraid I've interrupted some . . . domestic chore."

Drucilla laughed. "Just the stuffing of some pillows for Boxing Day gifts to various needy parishioners. Miss Script and I do it every year at this time, don't we, May?"

"Why, yes, but never before in the winter parlor. His lordship must think us a ramshackle lot with feathers floating about in this distracting way." One had just landed on Meacham's hair, but he had yet to realize it. "Why don't I see to a fire being laid in the salon? We can sit there in great comfort."

As Miss Script rose, Drucilla said, "And perhaps you would bespeak us a luncheon as well, my dear. I imagine my cousin must be famished after his long drive."

Miss Script hurried from the room and his lordship was left facing his cousin in her worn muslin gown dotted with feathers. He wore an expression of interest and perhaps the shadow of amusement in his eyes.

"Please, have a seat," she urged. "Though I'm afraid you'll get feathers on your clothing."

"I have brought my valet, Fallot, who will be vastly diverted. He was not at all certain we had missed that goat and fully expected to be cleaning goat hair from my driving coat." Without inspecting his chair for escaped feathers, he calmly seated himself opposite her and said kindly, "I trust I find you well, Miss Carruthers."

"Perfectly well, thank you."

"And your father? I understand he is somewhat indisposed."

"Physically, there is nothing so very much the matter with him. It's his mind that suffers. He's not able to concentrate, and often his memory is very poor."

"I am distressed to hear it. He is not well enough, then, to welcome visitors?"

Drucilla bit her lip. "No, I fear not. He spends all his time in his room, with an attendant to care for his needs. He's entirely comfortable, you understand, when his routine is not interrupted."

"I should like very much to see him, to speak with him."

"Certainly. Directly after luncheon I will take you to him, but you must not expect him to recognize you."

"I could hardly expect him to do so after sixteen years."

"Well," she said hesitantly, "that is not precisely what I meant. If he had been introduced to you this morning, he would not likely recall who you were."

The viscount regarded her curiously. "You are describing a very distressed man, Miss Carruthers. I don't perfectly understand how he has been able to manage Tarnlea, suffering under such a handicap."

"He has excellent assistance in our estate manager, John Thomas. And I myself understand Papa's wishes on most matters."

"Do you? That *is* fortunate."

Drucilla's pointed chin came up a little. "Yes, I believe it is."

"But it must be very difficult for you."

"Not at all. I have John Thomas's guidance, and the encouragement of our local vicar, and the affection and cooperation of our Tarnlea staff."

The viscount nodded, but said, "I don't doubt you've risen to the challenge of your father's illness most admirably, Miss Carruthers. I am all admiration." Lord Meacham actually offered a lazy smile, and shifted one long leg over the other. "However, according to his note, Sir Lawrence's solicitor has not been consulted. Perhaps you had some reason for not including Mr. Wicker in your circle of advisors?"

Drucilla dusted a feather from the skirt of her old muslin gown. "Mr. Wicker's advice was not sought because I felt it would put him in an awkward situation. His responsibility regarding the entailment of the estate, and to you as heir, might have caused him to recommend ignoring matters that would have been an expense to the estate. And yet, as you will see, those expenses were very necessary. My other advisors had no such conflict of interest."

"Sometimes, however," he said diffidently, "we are not given the best advice when we are faced with difficult choices. Others often have a different and, shall we say, more self-interested agenda."

"Lord Meacham, I can assure you that everyone who surrounds my father has his very best interests, and those of Tarnlea, at heart. Perhaps you have been misled."

The viscount was pensive for a moment, toying with a quizzing glass he had removed from his pocket. "It is remotely possible, I suppose. Mr. Wicker sent me an account of the situation as he understands it, begging for my intervention on behalf of the estate. I am, as you have said, you father's heir."

"Oh, yes, I have always known. You told me yourself when I was five."

"I did? How very impertinent of me. And it cannot have been quite true, either. Your father might yet have produced a male heir."

Drucilla regarded him with almost ingenuous eyes. "Well, you did mention at the time that he might marry again."

"When your mother had just died? I do beg your pardon, Miss Carruthers. I was, I fear, a bit of a prig when I was that age. I trust you can find it in your heart to forgive me."

There was something whimsically hopeful in the depths of his dark eyes as he framed his apology. Drucilla was not proof against the viscount's abashed charm. "Of course, my lord. If you wish it."

"I do wish it. I wish, in fact, that I had visited Tarnlea quite some time ago. I have been most remiss."

"Not at all. We had no expectation of your concerning yourself with our affairs."

Lord Meacham watched his quizzing glass spin at the end of its black ribbon. "Though your father is alive, he is apparently unable to fulfill his position as head of the family. As his nearest male relative, I must certainly concern myself. I regret that I am, because we are so distantly related, a virtual stranger to you, but believe me that I have come to offer any assistance in my power."

"Did Mr. Wicker suggest that my father should be legally declared incompetent?"

Lord Meacham said dryly, "Mr. Wicker is not satisfied that matters are being handled appropriately in the absence of Sir Lawrence's hands on the reins. He feels there is some urgency, though he did just mention that this state of affairs had existed for 'quite some time.' "

"Much he knows," Drucilla muttered darkly, not meeting the viscount's lifted gaze.

"He seemed to think that you, ma'am, had been attempting to conceal from him the extent of your father's mental deterioration. I believe he has not actually visited your father for some little time—put off with excuses and distractions."

Drucilla could not resist, with a decided sparkle in her eyes, admitting that this was true. "For two years."

"Two years? My dear girl, you must be extraordinarily inventive."

At that moment Miss Script hastened into the room, clasping her hands tightly together at her spare bosom. "The fire has been laid in the salon and Hastings informs me that Lord Meacham's chamber is ready. Perhaps, sir, you would prefer to be shown to your room before luncheon."

Having risen when Miss Script entered, Meacham

bowed in acknowledgment of her offer. Brushing a feather from the sleeve of his coat, he said, "Yes, I think that would be wise. I've been on the road for several hours." He bent on Drucilla a decidedly rueful look. "I trust there will be nothing to keep us from visiting your father directly after our meal."

"I'll let his man know that we're coming."

"Does your father always know you?"

"So far he has."

Drucilla watched as he strode unhurriedly from the room. With a *tsk* of annoyance, more at herself for being disarmed by the viscount's diverting manners than at the inconvenience of his unexpected visit, she said to Miss Script, "I am very much afraid his lordship is not going to be so easily managed as Mr. Wicker."

"No, my dear, I think not. For all his pleasant address, he strikes me as a determined young man who expects affairs to be conducted very much as he wishes them. I shall be surprised if he doesn't press for an immediate competency hearing, and place himself in charge of your father's estate."

Drucilla pursed her lips in a thoughtful grimace. "And yet there is something about him that is not what I expected. He's a handsome devil, isn't he?"

"The Winslows are said to be uncommonly handsome."

"Perhaps I could cozen him just a bit."

"I'm not at all sure it would be wise to do so, even if you could, which I doubt. He surely has a greater knowledge of the world than you, my dear."

"Well, I shall flirt just a trifle with him, as the London ladies must do." Drucilla fluttered her eyelashes in what she considered an imitation of a practiced debutante. At Miss Script's disapproving frown, she said, "I am quite sure that is how Caroline Russell does it."

"But Miss Russell is sixteen and not out of the schoolroom, Drucilla. You are one-and-twenty and have taken it upon yourself to rectify an injustice. Which is all very well, but you have placed yourself in an awkward position. Lord Meacham may hold you very much at fault."

Drucilla found this somehow a lowering thought. She rose from her chair and said bracingly, "Never mind. I shall change into something more appropriate before luncheon, and you will speak to him with your usual good sense. We cannot fail to convince him that we are totally unexceptionable."

Lord Meacham came away from their light repast with the impression that his distant cousin was something of an original. No doubt it could be laid to the fact that she had spent her entire life tucked away in the country. For all its beauty, the Lake District did not necessarily expose her to a great deal of society. Surely there had been money enough, and the right connections, for her to be presented in polite London circles at the proper age. He wondered why she had not been.

In fact, as Meacham followed his hostess up the branching main stairway of Tarnlea, he found a variety of inconsistencies surrounding him. Although the house was clean and the servants well trained, there was no exhibit of the wealth to which Sir Lawrence could surely lay claim. The furnishings were well kept, but hardly new, and had it been his own home, the viscount would have considered a deal of remodeling in store, to say nothing of the replacement of aging carpets and draperies.

Meacham understood that the baronet's passion had been hunting, even in this indifferent country, and he directed a question to his guide. "Are there still hunters in the stables, and kennels with hounds?"

Drucilla shook her head sadly. "No. Most of them have been sold. It's been years since Papa was able to hunt."

She led the way down a long corridor untouched by the day's wintry sun, to a room far removed from the main body of the house.

"This is surely not the master suite," Meacham commented in surprise.

"No, but it is the suite of rooms my father prefers because of its view of Buttermere Lake."

Meacham was mulling the possibility that Sir Lawrence had prematurely been stripped of his dignities when the door was opened before him into a large space that could have been a schoolroom, except for the grand four-poster bed in a far corner. There were toys scattered about the room, and several tables and chairs in various states of disorder.

Sir Lawrence himself was seated in a large chair, rocking back and forth, his gaze on the rugged hills and the rippled gray lake in the distant view. He was chortling to himself and pounding one fist on the arm of his chair in a rhythmical way that Meacham found rather discomposing.

His companion walked over to the chair and laid a hand gently on the old man's shoulder. "Papa, I have brought you a visitor, Julian Winslow, Lord Meacham."

Meacham stepped forward, making a bow to the baronet. "Sir Lawrence, I'm pleased to see you again."

The baronet, who had looked up but not spoken when his daughter addressed him, turned a frowning gaze on Meacham. "Julian, bouillon, cotillion, vermilion," he said.

Meacham regarded him gravely. "Sir? Can you understand me?"

Sir Lawrence turned agitated eyes to his daughter. "Where's Nelson?" he demanded in a querulous voice.

"He'll be back in a minute, Papa," she promised.

Meacham studied the lined face and the alarmed eyes, which were a lighter blue than his daughter's. "Can I get you something, sir. Perhaps a blanket?"

"Blanket? Blanket? Is it winter, then?"

"Yes, it's December, and quite cold out, sir. Do you see the snow on the hills around Buttermere? This room is a little chilly. Shall I ring to have the fire built up, or bring you the blanket from the bottom of the bed?"

Sir Lawrence merely looked confused. "Fire. Dangerous. I used to have a pipe," he said hopefully. "Is my pipe there?"

Drucilla shook her head at Meacham while she straightened her father's disordered hair with capable fingers.

"I'm afraid there's no pipe, Sir Lawrence."

Sir Lawrence had already forgotten the pipe, but he frowned at Meacham. "I don't approve of servants wearing starched collar points of that height," he said sternly.

Drucilla flushed. "You must forgive my father. He is often confused."

Sir Lawrence had turned his attention to the view once again, and Meacham said, "Is he ever perfectly lucid?"

"He always recognizes me and often calls me by name, but sometimes he thinks I'm my mother, or even his own mother."

"So your father is not capable of making any real decisions with regard to the estate."

Drucilla continued to stroke her father's head, which seemed to calm his agitation. "No," she admitted.

Miss Carruthers, Meacham realized, had been responsible for Tarnlea, the house and the estate, for her father and herself, for the staff, for everything, for a very long time. What could a girl of her age and situation know of estate management? It seemed perfectly plausible to the viscount that one of the people on whom she relied for advice was taking advantage of her. The estate agent might be lining his pockets, or the local vicar urging excessive good works on her. Mr. Wicker had certainly hinted at an alarming outgo of capital.

"I think we needn't trouble your father any further this afternoon," Meacham said. "But you and I should talk."

Mutely, Drucilla nodded. She kissed the top of her father's head and he awkwardly patted her hand. "I shall come again later, Papa."

As she closed the door behind them, she said, "If you would give me an hour to see to some household matters, I would be grateful. Everything is a bit topsy-turvy because of your arrival."

"Of course."

Drucilla took care of her more pressing concerns before joining her companion, who was comfortably ensconced in the salon, a fire blazing on the grate. Miss Script was doing her fine filigree needlework, but she looked up at her former charge's entrance to ask, "Has Lord Meacham been to see your father?"

Drucilla seated herself at the small cherrywood desk by the window. "Yes, and I believe he now has a good grasp of my father's mental condition. There is nothing amiss with the viscount's understanding."

"Was he distressed by Sir Lawrence's condition?"

"Distressed? It was hard to tell. He was gentle with Papa, and merely said he and I must talk." Drucilla looked worried, but set herself to ordering the menus for the viscount's stay. She quickly decided to replace the simple boiled neck of mutton and vegetables with a crimped cod in oyster sauce as well as a fricasseed chicken.

"Do you suppose Lord Meacham would like a cabinet pudding?" she asked Miss Script.

Her companion looked up from her needlework and pondered the question. "I believe gentlemen generally prefer mince pies or apple tarts. And of course plum pudding at this time of year. Mrs. Kamidge will have several plum puddings soaked with Sir Lawrence's good brandy."

"Yes, it has been a real joy to dip into the best of his cellar," Drucilla admitted with sparkling eyes.

The door from the hall was behind her and she had not heard it open to admit the viscount. "Whose cellar?" Meacham inquired in a lazy drawl.

"My father's," she responded readily enough. "He laid down a remarkable collection of spirits and wines. You shall of course sample some of them during your stay, Lord Meacham. My father is no longer much interested in such refreshment, and the doctor does not believe it is beneficial for him, in any case. His pipe has been taken away because he tends to burn holes in his clothes."

Miss Script, seeing the determination in Meacham's eyes, immediately excused herself. His lordship moved to stand by the fire, leaning his broad shoulders against the high mantel and bending a quizzical look upon Drucilla. "Your father is in much worse case than I had suspected. Since he is not capable of even the least decision regarding his own fate or that of his estate, I assume the full burden has fallen to you."

"I have had help, and we contrive as best we can," Drucilla replied, setting down her quill. "My father is still the baronet, after all, and his responsibilities must be carried out."

"How long has he been as bad as this?"

"About two years."

Meacham shook his head in wonder. "That is quite a lengthy period, Miss Carruthers."

"Well," Drucilla confessed, "he hasn't been perfectly all right for five years, but at first it was merely gaps in his memory. Now he is . . ." She shrugged her shoulders eloquently. ". . . as you see."

"But in these last few years, according to Mr. Wicker, there have been very large expenses to the estate. I wonder if perhaps your agent has not taken advantage of you, Miss Carruthers."

Drucilla looked amused. "John Thomas? Oh, no, I don't think so, Lord Meacham."

"I shall just have a word with him."

"As you please, of course."

As the estate agent was not on the premises, Meacham sent word that he would meet with John Thomas the next day. He enjoyed a sociable dinner and evening with Miss Carruthers and her companion. They played a few hands of cards and sang Christmas carols, accompanied by the young lady on her pianoforte.

Miss Carruthers, her fair curls framing an animated face, made a charming hostess, full of questions about his home and family, open in her answers to his questions. She directed their conversation in a lively fashion, discussing their neighbors ("You will meet Lady Nibthwaite, the most delightful woman. She once asked Miss Script if she had ever stolen anything.") and staff ("Nelson was formerly a blacksmith's assistant and, though I cannot at all fathom why, has suited the position of attendant to my father admirably.") in such a delightful way that he could not resist its humor.

After the ladies had retired for the night, he sampled the baronet's mellow old brandy and relaxed into an almost soporific state before the blazing fire, watching snowflakes drift down outside the window. There was a peacefulness at Tarnlea that lulled him into perfect charity with the world. And if his mind drifted from time to time to the memory of Miss Carruthers seated on the sofa, that wicked gleam of laughter in her vivid blue eyes, well, who could blame him?

But early the next morning he made himself known to John Thomas, a much younger man than he had expected, and sat down with the estate books for the last five years. He was not actually in the habit of going over his own estate books, having several individuals, including a young man just down from Oxford as his secretary, whose business it was to just bring the salient points to his attention.

Indicating a chair beside the desk, he said apologetically, "If you would go over these with me, I would be most grateful, Mr. Thomas. You must excuse my ignorance of the proper columns for income and outgo. I fear it will be necessary for you to explain the expenses in some detail as we work our way through."

"Certainly, my lord." John Thomas tapped a finger on the second of the ledgers. "Four years ago is when I began, but I'm familiar with the books for some period before that."

"Was Sir Lawrence perfectly rational when you began work here?"

"Not perfectly, but much better than he is today. Or so I understand. He hasn't actually visited the estate office for a couple of years."

The viscount regarded him with keen interest. "From whom do you take your direction, then? Mr. Wicker?"

John Thomas looked perplexed. "No, sir. Miss Carruthers gives me my instructions. She's very knowledgeable about the estate."

"And if Sir Lawrence's signature should be required on some document?"

"She is always able to procure it."

"I see. And has she run the estate in the way Sir Lawrence did when you first began?"

The estate agent looked uncomfortable, inserting a finger between his neckcloth and his neck. "Perhaps I could show you, my lord?"

"Please do."

It was an instructive two hours. Meacham would have given a great deal to have had William, his admirable secretary, there to alleviate the tedium of the work, but John Thomas, if more earnest and painstaking than Meacham's own estate manager, was more than capable of clarifying any issue that remained obscure to him. The long and short of it was that John Thomas was not lining his pockets. But it became quite clear that the previous estate manager had most certainly done so.

John Thomas would point to an expense—a new roof for a barn, for instance—and say with a frown, "You will recall that this particular roof was supposed to have been repaired five years ago. Nevertheless, last year it was found to be leaking badly and there was nothing for it but to replace it again."

Time and again they were forced to search in even

older ledgers, and there could be no doubt that the cost of repairs then had undoubtedly been false entries. Though this was just as obviously the work of Mr. Thomas's predecessor, Meacham's expression became grim.

"You will forgive my conjecture, Mr. Thomas, but it seems clear to me that this drain from the estate was going on long before Sir Lawrence's illness. In fact, it is so obvious that I fail to understand how the baronet, even with the smallest oversight of these books, could have neglected to discover it."

The young man rubbed a hand vigorously across his face in an attempt to sharpen his wits. Picking his words carefully, John Thomas said, "Sir Lawrence was not in the habit, apparently, of taking particular interest in the estate. I believe he trusted his estate manager and allowed him full discretion in the matter of outlay. It was not until Sir Lawrence's illness became obvious and Miss Carruthers began to involve herself with these matters that she discovered the problem."

"How long had this been going on?"

John Thomas was not deceived by the placid tone of the viscount's voice. He had watched Lord Meacham over the past two hours and knew precisely how quickly his companion had discovered the carefully hidden fraud. "For quite some time, my lord," he admitted.

Meacham was disturbed by the picture this gave him of Sir Lawrence, but there were other matters of just as pressing concern. Especially in recent years, the ledgers showed expenses to have risen in an alarming fashion. The amounts spent on repairs of tenant farms and cottages were startling.

But Lord Meacham seldom allowed his concern to taint his air of calm acceptance. "I wish you would make these expenses clear to me, Mr. Thomas. They seem, shall we say, excessive."

"Because of the length of time no repairs had actually taken place to the cottages and farms, they were little more than hovels, with inadequate water supplies and unsanitary conditions. As the baronet became sicker and Miss Carruthers took over the reins of management, she deemed it necessary to correct these conditions. In the last two years we have done a great deal of work that should have been accomplished over a long period of time. Unfortunately, it's expensive work."

"As you say. And I feel certain that you do not make any profit from the construction."

John Thomas looked shocked. "Certainly not. Miss Carruthers has involved herself in the choosing of the laborers and the overseer. They're neighborhood people, much in need of the occupation and the income. I would find it difficult to believe that anyone has so much as overcharged us a guinea."

"I think perhaps I should like to see these repaired cottages. Could you take me this afternoon?"

Mr. Thomas bowed slightly. "Of course, Lord Meacham."

But at luncheon, when John Thomas remarked that he would be taking the viscount on a tour of the newly reconstructed cottages, Drucilla protested. "Really, Lord Meacham, John Thomas has more than enough to do this afternoon after spending the morning closeted with you. And we are expecting Lady Nibthwaite to tea. I particularly wish to present you to her. If you would be good enough to join us, I promise to show you the improvements tomorrow myself. I am thoroughly knowledgeable about them, am I not, John Thomas?"

"Indeed you are, ma'am," the agent agreed with a rueful smile.

The viscount was pleased to be offered the opportunity to spend time with Miss Carruthers. He would be able to assess for himself whether her knowledge of estate matter was adequate, or exaggerated by her well-wishers, which seemed to him the more likely possibility. She was, after all, only one-and-twenty, and had been deeply involved in managing Tarnlea for several years already.

"Very well, ma'am. I shall look forward to it."

Lady Nibthwaite was a thriving dowager of fifty-odd years whose more than ordinary interest in Tarnlea and its occupants had long been accepted by them. Since she had stood as second mother to Drucilla, she was well aware of the circumstances that had led to the present situation there, and though given to outrageous speech when in high flight was not likely to bruit about anything that Miss Carruthers would rather not have known by the viscount.

Her son, Lord Nibthwaite, had recently married, and the Dowager Lady Nibthwaite had retired to the dower house, a pretty little manor two miles from his estate. This move had not distressed the elder Lady Nibthwaite in the least. "For there will be children," she had explained to Drucilla, "and if there is one thing I cannot bear in my advancing years, it is the clutter and noise of very small children."

And indeed she seemed perfectly content with her new home. She had a handsome jointure and particularly devoted servants, so that her days were given over to her first love—minding the business of all the county, and especially the happenings at Tarnlea. If she had not already been invited to tea before the advent of Lord Meacham, she would surely have managed a morning call as soon as she was informed of his arrival. Mere gossip was not her intent, for she was a shrewd woman not at all reticent in passing along her very bracing advice and original wisdom.

She found it unconscionable that such a delightful young lady as Drucilla—so fashionably fair and pretty!—should be relegated to the country without hope of discovering an eligible match. Lady Nibthwaite had done her best to introduce to Drucilla's notice any eligible gentleman who happened to wander through the Lake District for business, pleasure, or family obligations. She could not, however, blame that young lady for her lack of interest in anyone presented thus far.

Lady Nibthwaite's first impression of the viscount was favorable. Her astute gaze took him in all at a glance, and she judged him to be quite an eligible parti for her dear Drucilla. She could not tell from the way they behaved toward each other whether this possibility had occurred to either of them, and she considered it her duty to make certain that it did. She set about acquiring the necessary information.

"Have you left your wife at Meacham Court?" she asked as she helped herself to one of the macaroons for which Mrs. Kamidge was famous.

He answered politely, if with a trace of dryness, "I am not married, ma'am."

"At your age? The girls in your district must be backward indeed! And do you never go to London?"

"Several times a year, Lady Nibthwaite. And in my younger days, I lived there for long periods. You must excuse me if I mistake the issue, but I do not believe I have had the pleasure of meeting you there."

"As to that, I never go. Though I would have done," she said, turning her gaze toward Drucilla, "had my wishes been given due consideration."

"It was not to be, ma'am, as you well know." Drucilla poured tea into a fragile cup and passed it to Lord Meacham. "Besides, it would have been the blind leading the blind. You knew nothing of London society."

"We would have managed."

Meacham, realizing that doubtless this discussion had occurred before, asked, "Is your home nearby, Lady Nibthwaite?"

"No more than three miles. In winter it can be a difficult drive, with the snow so very likely to make a hazard of the roads, but I will most always venture forth to see my dear Miss Carruthers and Miss Script."

Drucilla passed the biscuits to Miss Script, saying, "And we're obliged to you, ma'am. We would become quite secluded here in December were it not for seeing neighbors such as yourself. Do you go to your son for Christmas?"

"Yes, for Caroline has just made a very interesting announcement." There was a sly twinkle in Lady Nibthwaite's eyes. "By next Christmas we are to have a new member of the family. Did I not tell you that children would come soon? How very forward-thinking of me to have settled into the dower house in good time, was it not?"

"Indeed it was," Drucilla agreed.

Lady Nibthwaite, pursuing another avenue that had been traversed any number of times, expostulated, "The nonsensical boy *would* look for a wife amongst the Russells—you must understand, Lord Meacham, that their land marches with his—and Caroline is undoubtedly the finest of the five girls. I have nothing to say against her, but when he could have aligned himself with Miss Carruthers! I could scarcely bear to see the direction of his affections. As if Caroline Russell could hold a candle to Drucilla!"

"Really, ma'am, you put me to the blush," Drucilla protested. "I can think of no couple better suited to each other than your son and his bride."

The dowager laughed with real amusement. "You have the right of it, of course. Such a very dull man as he has become! I don't *think* he inherited it from *my* side of the family, but there, who is to comprehend these matters? Have you brothers and sisters, Lord Meacham?"

"Two sisters, ma'am, both married and settled in Gloucester."

"That is fortunate for you, if you like them."

He acknowledged this truth with a whimsical smile. "I do. And I am in rather a push to return to Gloucester to spend the holidays with them and their families."

Drucilla said, "You must not let us hold you here, Lord Meacham. Once you have seen the cottages and satisfied yourself as to their appropriateness, I believe you may feel perfectly safe in driving off again."

Meacham regarded her with pensive eyes. "You wouldn't be trying to hasten my departure, would you, Miss Carruthers?"

"Certainly not! But we do very little in the way of Christmas celebration here, you must understand, because of my father's condition and the exp—, the thinness of company at this time of year. The longer you stay here, the more danger you court of being outflanked by the weather. We very often have storms at this time of year that make the roads impassable."

Lady Nibthwaite regarded her with astonishment.

"But, my dear, that has only happened once in the last score of years! I feel certain we have no fear of heavier weather in the next week. His lordship will surely find no difficulty in returning to his home after he has spent a decent amount of time making your acquaintance. And as to the thinness of company at this time of year, you know you are always included in our plans for Christmas dinner if you would but come."

"I do know," Drucilla said sincerely, pressing the dowager's hand. "You are all kindness, ma'am. Perhaps this year Miss Script and I will allow ourselves to be persuaded."

But there was a hesitancy in her voice that made this seem unlikely. Whether it was because she wished to remain at home with her father, or not to intrude on another's family circle, or for some other reason entirely, was unclear to Meacham.

When Lady Nibthwaite rose to leave, he accompanied her to her carriage, an older but comfortable-looking conveyance that had been brought round by her coachman. Miss Carruthers and Miss Script had said their good-byes in the warm salon, so Meacham stood alone with her on the front stairs, even though he was dressed only for indoors in coat and pantaloons.

"I recognize your partiality to Miss Carruthers, Lady Nibthwaite, so I think you may be the very person to answer a question for me. Do you not think the running of Tarnlea, both the house and the lands, along with the management of her father's health, too great a burden for such a young person?"

"Too great a burden?" that august woman ejaculated. "My dear fellow, Drucilla is the most capable woman I know to be doing precisely what she is."

"Oh, I don't doubt that. But she has been to a deal

of trouble over the state of the farms and cottages these last few years."

"So I should think, the condition they were in! Quite shameful it was. Not that I wish to speak ill of those who can no longer defend themselves, but there it is."

Lady Nibthwaite had moved toward her carriage as she spoke. The door was being held open for her by a servant, and as she appeared ready to be handed in, Meacham elegantly provided this service, but could not restrain himself from asking, before the door was closed upon her, "Would you be able to advise me as to why Sir Lawrence neglected his tenants even before he became ill?"

The dowager settled a blanket over her legs. "The past no longer concerns me, sir. It is the future— Drucilla's future—that is of the utmost importance."

"I am not here to make Miss Carruthers's life more difficult, ma'am. It seems to me that I may very well be able to alleviate some its . . . tedium."

"I believe you could." Lady Nibthwaite regarded him with keen eyes. "Understand that though I believe Drucilla perfectly capable of the tasks she has undertaken, the onerous charge has severely limited her life, and will continue to do so if changes are not made. But any rearrangement of the situation at Tarnlea must take into account her sincere affection for her father and her need to see past neglect corrected."

Meacham bowed in acknowledgment of her assessment and stepped back. She gave an imperious tap on the ceiling of her carriage, and the coachman urged the horses forward. The viscount, frowning slightly, watched until the vehicle had disappeared around the bend in the carriage drive.

Coming back into the warmth of the house, he could not help but picture the two Tarnlea ladies alone in the large dining room on Christmas, with no outward sign of its being a day different from any other. A distinct melancholy gripped his mind. Miss Carruthers, Meacham felt, was not meant to dwindle away in obscurity in the country. Without a doubt she was meant to be the laughing, delightful hostess of some large family party of her own.

Meacham wondered briefly if perhaps one of his sisters could present Miss Carruthers in London, even at this late date, but his common sense acknowledged the impossibility of the scheme. Miss Carruthers was not likely to leave Tarnlea, with her father mentally deranged and the burden of both the household and estate management on her shoulders. There was a great deal more to be set right at Tarnlea than he had suspected when he began the two-hundred-mile drive there, and very little time in which to do it.

The following afternoon Drucilla took the precaution of donning her most fetching riding habit and bonnet, which were a deep shade of blue she knew to be flattering to her fair looks. The viscount had been gone for the entire morning and had arrived back at Tarnlea only in time for lunch. There had been a number of parcels in his curricle, the disposal of which he had arranged for with Hastings in a murmured discussion in the entry hall. Drucilla was extremely curious as to what Lord Meacham might have bought, but she could not feel it would be polite to ask him straight out, and her efforts to be circumspect at luncheon had failed entirely to produce the slightest clue.

Lord Meacham smiled appreciatively at her riding costume, and handed her up onto her mare with a grave gallantry. This was in every way the opposite of that gauche twelve-year-old she'd met so many years ago. As was his capability with a horse. He had chosen to ride her father's favorite horse, a large roan stallion that only the most competent of the stable boys even attempted to exercise.

Sir Lawrence, by some quirk of mind, had continued to ask after the horse, Standish, and Drucilla liked having him exercised where her father could watch from his window. She looked up now to see the baronet's white head pressed against the glass, and she waved a cheerful hand at him as she said, "I trust the lads have warned you about Standish, Lord Meacham. He's a bit of a handful."

"So I'm told."

Drucilla's own horse, a small gray mare, was well behaved and wonderfully smooth gaited. Since Meacham held back his horse so that she could lead the way over the lightly snow-covered ground, she had a chance to witness his superb control of his animal. Standish did not like following other horses and champed at the bit to be off with his rider. Meacham handled his prancing and sidling with a firm hand and neither annoyance nor alarm.

Once in the pasture, Drucilla allowed Glory to stretch out into a canter and then, with an encouraging look from Meacham, into a gallop. Standish could have outdistanced the little mare easily, but Meacham held him in check, side by side with the gray mare.

"Oh, let him out," Drucilla urged. "My father will love to see him run for all he's worth. I'll meet you at the home wood."

Following at a distance, Drucilla acknowledged that Meacham and Standish were a magnificent sight. Sir Lawrence had been a masterful rider, but without any of the viscount's grace. When Meacham rode, there was an air of excitement, even exhilaration, about him that Drucilla had not previously detected. Standish seemed to sense it as well, and lengthened his stride until he almost appeared to be flying. Even the gray mare flicked her ears at the sight of them.

When at last she came up with them, Meacham's face wore a wry grin. "Lord, I'd love to own this horse," he said.

"In time you will," she reminded him, her dimples peeking out.

"That was not my meaning, Miss Carruthers. I should like to purchase him from Sir Lawrence."

"My father still has an affection for Standish. He continues to ask about him and he loves to see him ridden. It would be wrong to take that pleasure away from him.

"Besides, how would we manage such a sale? You don't believe my father capable of any business dealings, and you don't approve of my conducting them."

Meacham raised his brows. "Surely I haven't been so rude as to say any such thing."

She shrugged her narrow shoulders. "No, but you have thought it. And I have no doubt that you have resolved on having my father declared incompetent at the next quarter sessions. Which would place you in charge of Tarnlea."

"Your conclusions are somewhat premature, my dear. Shall we just take one step at a time?"

Drucilla could only nod and bite her lip.

Within ten minutes they had reached the first of the tenant cottages. Smoke drifted from each of the chimneys, giving a snug aspect to the snowy scene. There were three groups of them on the estate, of five cottages each, and it had taken her the last two years to bring all of them into acceptable condition.

A number of tasks remained to be accomplished, but Drucilla was grateful that at least the major work had been completed. As the solicitor, Mr. Wicker, had become more and more uncomfortable with the estate expenses, she had attempted to push the renovation schedule forward, but winter was not a time when a great deal of construction could take place.

"Two years ago these were ramshackle buildings with open fires in them that blackened everything in sight," Drucilla explained as Meacham helped her down from the gray mare. "There was no water within easy reach and no privies for proper sanitation. Each cottage had only one large room, no matter how numerous a family occupied it. Now there are several divisions in each building, and often a loft above. And there is a pump for water indoors."

The viscount was contemplating the neat cottages with interest. "Not everyone would have thought a pump necessary for the cottagers, Miss Carruthers," he remarked, though with no disapproval in his tone.

"It was a simple enough matter to arrange when we were doing such extensive work. These poor people had suffered for many years with inadequate facilities. I cannot think it will spoil them to have a decent living space."

"Why was it that their quarters were so deficient even before Sir Lawrence became so ill?" he inquired as he tied their horses to a railing, giving Standish an encouraging pat.

Miss Carruthers, no more than John Thomas or Lady Nibthwaite, vouchsafed him an answer to this query. "Shall we go in?" Drucilla suggested. "I've brought some treats for the children, which will provide an excuse. And, of course, the Brewsters will be pleased to meet you."

The family seemed less pleased than curious, perhaps, but held wide their door to Miss Carruthers. Mrs. Brewster curtsied to Meacham and bid him welcome, while her husband asked after Sir Lawrence's health. Two children peeked shyly from behind a doorway.

While the couple toured his lordship over their small kingdom, Drucilla beckoned to the children. When they came hesitantly to join her by the fire, she handed each a foil-wrapped confection that she had brought with her. The little girl dropped a sweet curtsy and the younger boy said, "Thank you, miss," with an adorable lisp that made Drucilla want to hug them.

Before they left, she promised that she and Miss Script would be bringing pillows for the children's cots for Boxing Day. "We've had goose down and goose feathers all over the winter parlor," she admitted, laughing. "But we're almost finished."

As Meacham handed her up onto her horse, Drucilla noted his puzzled frown. "You make a very gracious Lady Bountiful," he said, not unkindly, "but I cannot think that is the motivation behind all this renovation."

"I have explained that the cottages were not fit to be occupied, sir."

"Yes, but neither you nor anyone else has explained to me why you have taken such a demanding task upon yourself," he persisted as he swung himself onto Standish.

"It is my firm belief that the cottagers and their children will be healthier and happier because of their improved living conditions. And if they are healthier and happier, they will be more productive."

Meacham regarded her with a reproachful gaze. "What is it you are so afraid of telling me, Miss Carruthers? Do you think I will be censorious? John

Thomas has already shown me that the previous estate manager defrauded the estate. Come, is there something worse?"

"You cannot like it that your inheritance has been depleted."

"My dear lady, I have more than enough property for any man. I'm not so concerned with the expenses as with the condition of the estate. I would have done no less than you have, had I found the tenant conditions at Tarnlea so deplorable as you say. And I certainly don't hold you responsible for the previous situation. Are you trying to protect your father?"

"He's a good man."

"I don't doubt that he is. Yet you are obviously embarrassed by the deterioration he allowed even before his illness."

"It was not his fault."

The viscount's brows rose. "If not his, then whose?"

Drucilla nudged Glory forward, and the viscount fell in beside her. "He should have paid more attention to the estate, but he trusted his estate manager," she said, not looking at him. "That was imprudent of him, of course. Would that I had been older at the time and more aware of what was going on!"

"You had more than enough responsibility at such a young age, taking care of household matters. How could you be expected to recognize that problems were developing with the estate?"

This view held little consolation for Drucilla. "How could I not have noticed such misery as the cottagers suffered? The children were forever sick. I brought them soups and gruels from our kitchen, but I considered it not at all out of the ordinary. And yet I was never sick as a child, living in that big house with a fire any time I wanted one, and more than enough food to sustain me."

"We are all guilty of being blind to the suffering of others from time to time, dear lady. You have done more than most to remedy any unconscious fault."

"You're good to say so, but I have sat for years at church listening to our vicar, Mr. Sampson, urge those of us who can well afford it to do our duty by those less fortunate, and yet I did nothing for so very long. I believe we have an obligation to the people who depend on us, don't you, Lord Meacham?"

There was something she could not identify in the viscount's indecipherable eyes, but he merely nodded. Drucilla continued, "I don't come into my inheritance from my mother for another six months, so I have been forced to use funds from Tarnlea. But Miss Script and I have lived in a frugal fashion in order to do our part."

"I wish you had not," he protested. "The burden has always rested with the estate. I beg you won't give another thought to any such claim on your own resources."

Drucilla sighed and urged her mare to a faster pace. "Do you wish to see another set of cottages or the tenant farms?"

"Another day, perhaps. Let's head back to Tarnlea."

"Then let Standish out again, Lord Meacham, if you would. He needs the exercise." And, Drucilla realized, she would very much enjoy watching the viscount's expert horsemanship again.

His horsemanship, however, was not the only thing she was aware of as man and beast swept across the barren fields. Meacham's handsome profile, the solid set of his shoulders, the athletic firmness of his legs— Drucilla could not remember feeling this odd sensation about any man of her acquaintance, and she was not at all sure she wished to feel it about Julian Winslow, Viscount Meacham.

Meacham's valet helped him into a new coat of blue superfine that fit so exquisitely his services were definitely required in the donning of it. Meacham's pale buff pantaloons were unexceptionable and his neckcloth tied in a restrained but fashionable style. He regarded himself critically in the cheval glass, then turned away.

The viscount was, in the ordinary course of affairs, indifferent to what he wore and allowed Fallot to discuss such matters only under duress. Certainly here in the country, dining only with Miss Carruthers and her companion, there could be no particular reason to pay heed to his appearance. And yet he brushed off a speck of dust from one sleeve and adjusted his solitary fob before he left his bedchamber.

The two ladies were already awaiting him in the salon, Miss Script in a discreet pastel gown, her former charge in something quite out of the ordinary. Miss Carruthers looked perfectly charming in a gown of such a deliciously rich shade of green that it made her blue eyes startlingly bright.

Meacham reminded himself that he was at Tarnlea to accomplish a specific purpose that had nothing to do with being attracted to an intriguing young woman. He would be wise to pay no heed to the artless curls that framed her face, or the sparkling animation that constantly lit her eyes. If her figure was both elegant and captivating, surely it could be nothing to him. They were to be reacquainted but briefly.

But Meacham could not resist complimenting her on her gown. "I would have no doubt of its origins, but you have not, I believe, ever been to London."

"Never."

He studied her thoughtfully. "But your father would not have completely succumbed to his illness by the time you were seventeen. I'm surprised he didn't insist upon a Season for you. He could have applied to my mother to act as your chaperone and introduction to society. She was familiar with the routine," he said, a rueful smile curving his lips, "having successfully launched two daughters of her own."

Miss Carruthers said placidly, "London is not to everyone's taste, Lord Meacham. Do you keep a house there?"

Meacham suspected that Miss Carruthers would have enjoyed London very much indeed, with her lively disposition and her quick understanding, but he refrained from saying so. "Yes, I have a house in Grosvenor Square, though it has not been much used these two years since my mother died. Occasionally I let it for the Season to a suitable family."

Without at all meaning to, he added, "I would be more than pleased for you to make use of it if, for instance, Lady Nibthwaite were to bundle you off there for a few weeks' entertainment. I think you would like London—once you grew accustomed to the noise and the bustle. There are wonderful shops, and delightful entertainments, and fascinating people."

"I'm needed at Tarnlea," she said somewhat defiantly. Then with a more conciliating air, she added, "I have only country manners, sir, and am used to a freedom not allowed a young lady in the city. I can scarce imagine not being able to ride where I wish, or not walking alone along the pavements."

"For every disadvantage, there is a compensating advantage."

"Well, as it is unlikely I shall go there, it cannot

matter." Her abstracted gaze became wistful and she admitted, "Though I should dearly love to see a play at Drury Lane, or watch the equestrian events at Astley's Amphitheater. Miss Script and I have read of them in books and journals, and sometimes I can almost picture myself there."

With very little effort, Meacham, too, could picture her there, all eagerness and ingenuous delight. Her open manners would attract the sort of people she would like, though certainly there would be those who frowned on them. What could it matter that the highest of sticklers would find her too unpolished and forward? She would not care for them at all.

If Hastings had not arrived then to announce dinner, Meacham might have described some of London's more intriguing pastimes. But the butler nodded conspiratorially at him as the ladies gathered up their skirts and rose. Meacham offered an arm to each lady, his eyes full of a surprising playfulness that made Drucilla cock her head at him and ask, "What is it? Have I said something I ought not?"

"Not at all. It is I who have taken a liberty with your home for which I beg you will forgive me. In the spirit of the season, however, I found I could not resist."

A beaming Hastings threw open the door to the dining room, and Drucilla gasped at the sight. The room was aglow with candlelight, wax tapers marched the length of the table and perched in the windows and on the side tables. Boughs of greenery were hung along the walls, decorated with red bows and gold ribbon and silver bells. The silver shone, the glass globes twinkled, the crystal chandelier above the table reflected light merrily over all. The chamber was redolent of evergreens and roast goose, with a hint of mince pies to come.

Miss Script, her eyes moist with nostalgia, said, "Oh, it's just like Christmas used to be, Drucilla. Look, they have found the bells and the wonderful Italian angel your mama brought from her home when she came here as a bride. It's like a fairyland."

At first sight of the room Drucilla had felt close to tears herself. It was impossible not to remember the many years she and her companion had tried to recreate the festive holiday atmosphere her mother had once lavished on the whole of Tarnlea. But it was some time now since they had attempted even a minimal effort at celebrating the season, what with her father ill and their attempt to trim household expenses.

Drucilla raised glowing eyes to Meacham. "It's magical. I've never seen it look more beautiful. You have indeed invaded my territory, sir, but how could I not forgive you? It was incredibly kind of you! And you have gotten all the servants in on it as well, I see."

Hastings stood beaming at the door, the housekeeper beside him with her hands folded in obvious satisfaction. Behind them were others, their faces wreathed with pleasure. "Thank you," she said. "Thank you all."

When Drucilla returned her gaze to Meacham, she found him observing her in a way that made her feel a little breathless. He was a man who held her future and that of everyone at Tarnlea in his hands, and yet by degrees she was coming to trust him. Maybe more than trust him.

The viscount raised her hand to his lips and kissed it. "A trifle early, perhaps, but no matter. Happy Christmas, cousin."

"Happy Christmas, my lord."

After Meacham and the two ladies had visited Sir Lawrence to share with him some sweetmeats Mrs.

Kamidge had made especially for him and a kaleido-
scope the viscount had purchased in the village, they
retired to the salon, still basking in the pleasure of their
meal and the delightful surprise he had arranged for
them.

The knowledge had grown on Drucilla all evening
that she was developing strong feelings for Lord
Meacham. Previously, she had been so busy trying to
direct the course of their interchanges, needing to hide
certain thing and explain others, that she had not acknowledged the full force of his character. She had
been aware during dinner that the viscount had set
himself to amuse her and make her forget her many
concerns for one evening. And she admired the way he
showed respect to her father, even when Sir Lawrence
was acting his most bizarre.

In the salon Drucilla found herself almost shy. Suddenly Meacham seemed far too sophisticated and elegant for their little family circle. This man undoubtedly
had a place in London society, where people would listen to him and respect his opinions. Until tonight she
had thought of him as one of the family, a country gentleman good-humoredly carrying out his duty.

"Is something the matter?" he asked, taking a seat
opposite her on the sofa.

"Oh, no! You've given us such a memorable evening. Shall I play something on the pianoforte?"

"Oh, do," said Miss Script sleepily. "Something
very soft and melodic, Drucilla. Nothing vigorous, if
you please. Unless Lord Meacham should object."

"Music is the very thing we need to crown our evening." He rose as Drucilla did and moved to stand by
her stool. "If you will let me turn the music for you, I
promise to pay attention."

"Which is more than May shall be able to do," she

whispered, aware that Miss Script had already closed her eyes. Within minutes her companion was gently snoring, her head fallen down against the chair's projecting wing. Drucilla played the song to its end, but looked up then to Meacham, a fragile smile on her lips. "May I ask you something?"

"By all means."

"Have you always done the right thing? I mean, is there nothing in your own life to look back on with regret?"

Meacham's momentary puzzlement was quickly replaced by an understanding of the significance of the question. "Oh, my dear, you're quite wide of the mark if you're envisioning me as some paragon of virtue. Come, I'll tell you an instructive Christmas story."

He caught her hand and drew her to her feet. For a moment they stood remarkably close, gazes locked on one another, a strangely powerful emotion drawing them together. Alarmed, Drucilla dropped her eyes and moved unsteadily to the sofa, where Meacham seated himself only slightly apart, close enough to retain possession of her hand.

"You remember me when I was twelve—all stiff and righteous and unbending. Doesn't that seem to you something to look back on with regret?"

"But you were a boy. You had too many responsibilities for your age."

Meacham nodded reminiscently. "I took it all very seriously, even when I was away at Eton. And then when I was nineteen I came to town, to London, with a friend of mine. And simply ran mad!"

Drucilla looked doubtful. "I find that hard to believe."

"Nevertheless, it was true. I had never experienced that degree of freedom, that heady realization that I had the resources to do whatever I wished. We were up to every lark—boxing with Gentleman Jackson, betting on which raindrop would slide down the glass fastest at White's, off to every prizefight and horse race, gambling in games that were far too rich for our blood, even though he, too, came from a well-heeled family."

"Did you not go to any of the balls and ridottos?" she asked wistfully.

"Most assuredly we did, but they were pretty tame for us. Standing up with our sisters, and doing the pretty to the girls one's mother introduced to one. William and I were ripe for trouble, not for something so subtle as flirtation or social pleasantries. Eventually we were taken in by a very clever gamester who was introduced by William's cousin."

"What happened?"

"Less than we deserved," he admitted ruefully. "You see, William's father is a remarkably clever fellow. Though he gave William plenty of rein, he always had his eye on his son from a distance and he allowed things to go only so far before he stepped in."

"Didn't William consider that interfering?"

"I suppose he would have, if he had not already realized that we were about to disgrace ourselves. In the most gracious manner possible, the earl showed us how to set things right. More than that, he and his wife rather adopted me into their already large family. Spending time with them had a very beneficial effect on me."

"Do you think so?" she teased.

Meacham met her quizzing with a placid smile. "So I believe. It was comforting to know that an older, wiser head was concerned with my progress in the world. With my father dead and my mother of a singularly retiring disposition, I had felt very much adrift. As you do, I think."

"And are you to be my older, wiser head?"

"I would very much like to help you, cousin. I'm older, certainly, and more knowledgeable about certain matters, but I won't claim to be wiser. Still, I think there are things you are reluctant to discuss. I wish you could learn to trust me."

Drucilla's hand squirmed under his, but he steadily retained hold. Her eyes did not meet his when she said, "You are very kind, sir. There is nothing, I think, that you need to know which is being withheld."

"Perhaps not," he agreed, giving the hand a light squeeze and allowing her to withdraw it. "And there is no reason that you should place such dependence upon me. However, I would be honored if you did."

Drucilla's lips trembled, but she forced herself to say, "It is late and I really ought to see Miss Script up to her room. Thank you so much for your delightful Christmas surprise."

Meacham regarded her with calm acceptance. "It was a great pleasure for me to arrange it, my dear. Sleep well."

It was not, in fact, very late at all, and after Miss Carruthers's withdrawal from the salon, Meacham decided that there was no reason why he should sit before the cozy fire, drinking exceptional brandy, when he could ride out on a coldly bitter night to the only inn he had discovered in the closest village. Off the main road, it was not a coaching inn, but its attractions for the local residents were surely enough to lure someone out on a moonlit night.

When he had given over Standish to a lad who promised him a warm stall for the next hour, Meacham entered the inn, brushing flakes of snow from his coat and stomping his boots. There was a festive air to the taproom, with a fire blazing in the hearth and greenery hung over the windows and doors, tied with large red bows.

Meacham requested a tankard of ale from the ruddy-faced landlord and sat down at a rough wooden table. Stretching his long legs out toward the burning logs, he discreetly surveyed the thinly populated room. In the opposite corner were two rough country men, to whom he nodded cordially. Nearer at hand sat two elegantly dressed gentlemen, younger than himself and obviously aspiring to a higher standard of fashion than generally prevailed in the country. Instead of the informal neckerchiefs he had seen sported on his earlier visit to the town, this pair wore neckcloths of pristine whiteness, carefully shaped into what Meacham guessed to be a tortured version of the Waterfall.

The viscount was aware that there was some interest piqued by his appearance in the room, both the youths and the older men covertly stealing glances at him. When one of the younger gentlemen came over to toss another log on the fire, he said to Meacham, "I've not seen you here before, sir. Are you staying in the area?"

"At Tarnlea, for a few days," he answered willingly enough.

"If that don't beat all! My family has known the Carruthers family forever. Allow me to introduce myself—James Slocum, sir, at your service." The young man swept him an impressive bow and indicated his companion. "That's Charles Gladham, who has lived here all his life as well."

"Julian Winslow," Meacham said. "Please join me."

The two youngsters, whom he judged to be about twenty years of age, took seats opposite him, and

Meacham ordered another round of ales from the land-lord. "So you've known Sir Lawrence and Miss Carruthers for many years."

"Oh, lord, yes," James Slocum assured him. "Drucilla is only a year older than I am. Known each other since we were in leading strings. Sir Lawrence was used to . . ." But he stopped abruptly and asked, "You've seen Sir Lawrence, haven't you, sir?"

"Yes. I was much shocked by his condition. Until recently I was not aware of how badly his mind . . . wanders."

Gladham nodded energetically. "So we hear, but the old gentleman hasn't been out of the house in . . . oh, years, I should think."

"My mother visits Drucilla and her companion, of course," Slocum explained. "Not that she sees Sir Lawrence on her calls. Well, I daresay she wouldn't wish to, would she? Mad as a hatter, the poor devil. But it's the sort of thing one might have expected."

"Is it?" Meacham asked, surprised.

"Not at all!" protested Gladham. "There's not a drop of madness in the family that *I* know of."

"Of course there's not," Slocum retorted. "But, lord, the way the man drank! Might have driven a lesser man crazy years ago."

Gladham could not accept this and stated, "Never knew a man to go mad of drink, Jimmy. Not like Sir Lawrence, at all events. It was his wife's dying that pushed him over the top."

"Hardly!" returned his friend. "That happened eons ago. Everyone knows that."

"Yes, but my father says it was her dying that drove him to drink," Gladham reminded him. He turned to the viscount and explained, "Made him a bit unbalanced, don't you know? Everyone says so."

Slocum glared at him. "Well, I don't know about that. The fellow was a bruising rider to hounds long after Lady Carruthers died. Had some of the finest hunters in the county."

Gladham took a long draw on his ale and appeared to consider this. "Thing is, that's *all* he cared for, demme."

"By God, it isn't," rejoined young Slocum. "Can't say he didn't care for Drucilla, Charles. Not an unnatural father, Sir Lawrence."

Much struck by this, Gladham relented. "So he did, so he did. Took her riding, didn't he? I could almost have felt sorry for her, though, little bitty thing up on one of those great hunters. Don't know as I could have done it at that age. She had the stoutest heart of any of us. Never cried craven about the biggest, wildest horse he put her on. She could ride anything."

"She don't anymore," said Slocum. "Saw her on that gray mare the other day. Nice bit of blood, of course, but no high flyer."

"Treated her more like a boy than a girl," mused Gladham.

Slocum nodded sapiently. "No heir," he said succinctly. "Some distant cousin gets the place when he dies."

Meacham coughed apologetically and said, "I'm the cousin, I'm afraid."

The two youthful gentlemen stared at him in something of a bosky haze and exchanged embarrassed glances. Slocum straightened his slender body. "No offense meant, I'm sure, sir."

"None taken," Meacham assured him. "Another round?"

"Don't mind if I do," Gladham agreed. "Have you seen Standish?"

"Yes, and ridden him. I wouldn't bet a guinea that I've ridden a more promising animal."

"Finest piece of horseflesh this county has seen in a dozen years," Slocum informed him, and proceeded to bicker with his friend as to whether his own Rufus or Gladham's Mars ranked first of the hunters originally owned by the baronet.

When Meacham eventually made his way back to Tarnlea on Standish, he had much to think about. The sharp clarity of the night seemed in keeping with his thoughts, which were centered, as they had been so often lately, on his cousin. It was obvious now that all Drucilla's efforts had been to prevent his learning of her father's careless and unbecoming behavior, both with regard to the estate and to herself. What astonishing loyalty from someone who had not been treated with even ordinary consideration!

As he rode down the lane that skirted the Tarnlea property, he imagined a young Drucilla mounted on one of her father's enormous hunters, frightened but determined not to admit it. Meacham thought that perhaps she'd been forced all her life to accept responsibilities that were only with astonishing courage within her grasp. Not many women in similar circumstances could have turned into the delightful creature he had spent so much time with these last few days.

The avenue of oak trees leading up to Tarnlea looked ghostly in the pale moonlight, but the building itself seemed grandly solid and enduring. Meacham had developed an affection for this ancient property, something he would not have expected on that morning of his arrival. Tarnlea then had seemed merely another problem in search of a solution, and one he had taken on only out of a stringent sense of duty. He had considered sending his secretary, a very capable young man, who would have surveyed the situation and brought him an admirable report. The thought distressed Meacham inordinately.

He would not have been reacquainted with Drucilla, would not have seen with his own eyes her courage and her capabilities. His secretary could not possibly have conveyed her mischievous-angel face, or the resolute sincerity of her eyes. No secondhand account of Drucilla could capture the innate liveliness or the subtle innocence of this remarkable lady.

Meacham knew that, from a distance, he might have ordained a resolution to the Tarnlea situation that would have shown his cousin very little more consideration than her father had done. The prospect appalled him. And yet, on the scene and faced with all the necessary evidence himself, he was no closer to knowing what he should do.

How could he walk away from Tarnlea? Oh, it would be simple enough to put someone in charge of the estate. That wasn't the problem at all. Nor was Sir Lawrence the problem. Drucilla was the problem.

As Meacham swung down from Standish at the Tarnlea stables, he ruefully admitted to himself that his time spent here had changed his life. Drucilla had become a necessary part of it and he would not willingly leave her behind. But he hadn't the faintest notion if she returned his regard. She had given no more indication than perhaps he had himself.

Well, there was nothing for it but to put it to the touch, he thought as he relinquished Standish to the sleepy waiting groom. An alarming prospect, the viscount acknowledged, when all one's happiness depended on the outcome.

* * *

Though Meacham was up early the following morning, he was not able to catch Miss Carruthers at the breakfast table. When he noticed that her place had already been removed, he turned a questioning gaze on Hastings, who said apologetically, "Miss Carruthers has gone to look for Teddy."

"Teddy?" the viscount repeated.

"The goat, milord."

"Of course. What else would she be doing than searching for the lost sheep?" Meacham inquired rhetorically.

Hastings gave a discreet cough. "Actually, it is a goat, milord. Sir Lawrence is excessively fond of goat's milk in his tea."

Meacham thought this sounded positively disgusting but asked, "Where would Miss Carruthers be likely to look for the ... er ... Teddy?"

"It's difficult to say. Once she was found at the home wood, another time beyond the spinney."

"Would Miss Carruthers have ridden?"

"Oh, yes, sir. The goat has roamed far afield at times."

Meacham made a hasty repast and headed toward the stables. He was already dressed for riding, as he had hoped to induce his cousin to take some exercise with him. Glory was gone from her box, and Meacham tapped his whip against his top-booted foot as Standish was saddled.

The stallion was restive, tossing his head and stamping his hooves. The groom grinned at Meacham and said, "He's going to be a wicked one to handle this morning, my lord. Seen him this way before. He'll try to unload you in the first pasture."

"Thank you for the warning. Do you know which way Miss Carruthers headed?"

"Toward the spinney, but more'n half an hour gone."

Meacham swung himself onto the horse, who was attempting to sidle toward a railing. Not wishing to have his leg crushed, the viscount spoke firmly to his mount and held the reins in a powerful grip. Standish obeyed, but Meacham knew he only awaited an opportunity to unseat his rider.

Clear of the stable yard, Meacham gave him his head across the first pasture, bearing in mind the groom's caution. Standish shied wildly at a rabbit leaping in front of him, a perfectly normal occurrence in the country. Meacham had no difficulty in retaining his perch, but Standish was far from finished with his antics. Amused, the viscount endured the bucking, twisting, and bolting with no more than a sharp dig of his heels or a tightening grip on the reins. At length the horse tired of his tricks and settled into a headlong gallop that would have outpaced many of the racehorses Meacham had backed in his younger days.

He scanned the spinney, and beyond it a tenant farm, to more pasture land. To the east there was an avenue of oak trees that led up to Tarnlea, to the south a glimpse of water. Meacham had not as yet ridden toward the tarn for which he assumed Tarnlea was named, and with a frown turned Standish in that direction. Buttermere Lake was much further away, out of the present range of his vision. But in the vicinity of the tarn he detected movement that looked very much like a riderless horse.

Distance was deceptive on the hazy December morning, and it took him ten minutes to arrive at the scene. He could easily identify Glory when he was still some little way from the mare, but she was indeed without her rider. Glory was not tied to any bush or tree, though there were plenty surrounding her.

Meacham saw no evidence of his cousin, but the mare was in a little depression nearer him than the water. A shale-covered hillock behind the mare shielded much from his view.

"Drucilla!" he called, grasping Glory's reins. "Are you here?"

A faint response reached his ears, but he could not be certain of its direction. He swung down from Standish and tied his mount to a nearby tree, trusting that Glory would stay nearby. On foot he scrambled up the steep slope toward the water, fearing that his cousin had attempted to ride Glory up it and been thrown. As he crested the hill he saw that it was far otherwise. His cousin was down on her knees, wrapping a bleating white and brown goat in her own cloak.

"Drucilla," he said quietly, so as not to startle her.

Drucilla looked up at him with surprise. "Meacham! I thought it would be Rall. He's out looking for Teddy, too. Have you seen him?"

Meacham shook his head. "Perhaps he searched in the opposite direction. Are you perfectly all right?"

"Yes," she said with a wry smile, "but this stupid goat has done herself an injury. I found her in the water with her foot caught between two rocks, and though I have managed to release it, she does not seem to be able to walk."

"I don't see how she could with your coat wrapped around her that way," he said, placing his own upon her shoulders. When Drucilla moved to protest, he said, "You'll catch your death."

"Well, if one of us has to freeze," she said, with a pert smile, "I'm certainly glad it's you. I cannot tolerate cold weather." Which was true enough, but mainly because she knew that her nose got red and her eyes watered unbecomingly when she was chilled. His coat felt heavy and warm, and she'd been out in the cold longer than she'd planned.

Meacham was regarding her with a look that was not at all indecipherable in his eyes. Drucilla felt somewhat abashed at his decidedly tender gaze and busied herself slipping her arms into his coat and wrapping it tightly about her. After a moment he reached over to lift the collar against her neck before saying brusquely, "I'll carry the goat. Let's get you back to Tarnlea where you can put on dry clothes and warm yourself before a fire."

Teddy bleated pathetically as she was picked up, but she allowed herself to settle into the viscount's arms without a struggle. Her long legs made her an exceedingly awkward burden. Meacham remarked caustically that he planned to remove goat carrying from the list of things he was willing to do for his cousin. Drucilla preceded him, grinning appreciatively as he maneuvered his way over the slippery shale and down to the solid ground below.

"I was afraid you had suffered a fall when I found Glory without her rider." Meacham set the goat down on the ground and Teddy scrambled to stand up, only to subside again when she could not bear her own weight.

Drucilla placed her foot in the hands Meacham held out for her, and he tossed her neatly up onto her horse. "She'll stay where I tell her to, if I drop the reins over her head. Why don't you hand Teddy up to me? I would dearly love to see you try to mount with her in your arms, or holding her on Standish while you swing into the saddle, but I'm afraid she would be the worse for it."

The viscount, who had been wondering how to best accomplish this feat, said, "I trust Glory will be more tolerant of Teddy than I fear Standish would. How were you planning to manage if you'd been on your own?"

"I daresay I would have been forced to leave Teddy here while I went for help." Catching the amused gleam in his eyes, she admitted, "Yes, I'm very grateful you came along, Lord Meacham. That goes without saying."

"You called me Meacham a while ago. I liked it."

"Did you? And I believe I heard you call me Drucilla, rather than your depressingly correct *Miss Carruthers*. Shall we agree to a more cousinly form of address?"

"Cousinly?" He eyed her speculatively. "By all means. You might even call me Julian."

She laughed. "Oh, I don't think I could go so far as that, sir. Come, hand Teddy up to me."

Meacham bore the goat, protesting with its knobby-kneed legs, up onto Glory's back. The mare calmly accepted the wriggling bundle, and Meacham wrapped Drucilla's cloak more securely about Teddy to keep her still. When he stood back, frowning, he said, "I don't see how you're going to hold her on and manage the horse as well."

"Glory is a very obedient creature, Meacham. Lead the way on Standish and she'll follow."

Standish was not as easily convinced that he wished to walk abreast of a struggling goat, but Meacham had no difficulty in keeping him in line. As they rode slowly back toward Tarnlea, he said, "Did you have to go yourself to look for her?"

Surprised, she turned her face toward his. "And why shouldn't I?"

He shrugged. "You have a sufficiently resourceful staff to trust them with such a task. You seem to me to feel a personal responsibility for even the smallest matter at Tarnlea."

Drucilla studied him rather sharply, uncertain as to his meaning. "I'm fond of Teddy. She's rather like one of the dogs here, a member of the family."

"Yes, but you could have stayed home in comfort. Rall would no doubt have found her eventually."

"I see what it is. You think me a *managing* female, but that is only because I have had to become one. Who was there but me to take the management of Tarnlea in hand?"

"You could have asked for my help."

Drucilla's brows rose in surprise. "Well, to be honest, that thought never occurred to me."

"I wish it had. Not that I mean to say you have not done a fine job, but it was a large burden for one of your years. I don't perfectly understand why you didn't wish Wicker's help. Perhaps you could explain that to me."

But she dismissed his question, saying only, "Mr. Wicker is far too cautious for my taste."

"In other words, you could not trust him to do precisely as you wished."

She responded to the teasing in his tone with a decided grin. "True. He might have called you in."

"I wish that one of you had. Under the circumstances Tarnlea is my responsibility."

"I have everything in hand."

"Mr. Wicker, however, no longer appears to agree with you."

"Mr. Wicker has been badgered by a younger partner into laying the whole matter before you in the hopes that a competency hearing will not only bring them in fees, but that you will choose their partnership to oversee matters here on the estate."

"I am more likely," he assured her, "to think them very lax in their duties for having taken so long to inform me of the situation."

"You mustn't blame that on poor Mr. Wicker!"

"No? Who shall I blame it on, then? A certain young lady who managed to cozen an elderly solicitor for the better part of two years with her charm and her earnestness? Did the poor man ever see your father during that time?"

"Never," she admitted. "But Mr. Wicker could see that the estate was given our every attention. And it was he who sent John Thomas to me originally."

"Probably expecting Mr. Thomas to keep him informed of what went forward here. But Mr. Thomas soon switched his allegiance to you."

Drucilla laid a calming hand on the goat's butting head. "You make it sound for all the world like a devious plot, Meacham. All we wished to do was set things to rights."

"And to get it done before I knew of your efforts."

"Well, yes, because we had no way of knowing whether you would approve of the expenditure. It has all been shockingly dear."

"And you've tried to compensate by making household economies." Meacham regarded her with amusement. "Now *that* I could not have approved of."

"Why ever not?"

"Because there was not the least need. In the first place, they could hardly make a dent in your overall outlay, and in the second, there is no reason you should not live at Tarnlea in perfect comfort."

"Oh, you are thinking we have deprived ourselves, which is not at all true. But you are quite right that our economies served little to the purpose. Meacham, do you really not *mind* what I've done?"

"I think it was probably very necessary."

She was surprised by the knowledgeable tone of his voice. For a moment she thought perhaps he had discovered her father's culpability in the disintegration of his own property, and a touch of color crept up into her cold cheeks.

The blandness of Meacham's expression reassured her. No one at Tarnlea was going to point a finger at the baronet. And if Meacham had met any local people, they would have been much too impressed with his rank and family connection to gossip about Sir Lawrence.

Drucilla was gratified that they had reached the stable yard by this time. Meacham was instantly on the ground and allowing a stable lad to lead off Standish. Teddy bleated hopefully as the viscount reached up to remove her from Glory's back. While a groom studied the goat's injury, Meacham helped Drucilla down from her horse, keeping hold of her hand a moment longer than necessary.

"We need to talk further," he said.

Drucilla looked around for some means to escape from his penetrating gaze. "Yes, certainly we shall. But now, my dear sir, I must change my clothes. I am also hopelessly behind on my daily tasks because of this wretched goat. Will you see that they take proper care of her leg? Here, you will need your coat and I must hurry into the house so that I don't freeze."

Meacham, the corner of his mouth twitching slightly, watched her hasty retreat with a mixture of frustration and amusement.

Drucilla couldn't help but wonder what the viscount might have discovered. Heaven knew she had done her best to protect her father's name and reputation in

Meacham's eyes. After all, this was her only family and she did not wish an outsider—even if he was distantly related to her—to despise her father for his lack of attention to his holdings. Sir Lawrence had been shattered by his wife's death, and embittered by his lack of an heir. If he had taken to drink, who could blame him?

Meacham could, of course. Tarnlea was his to inherit, and he could not have failed to assess when the damage to the estate had taken place. It was possible that the viscount might assume Sir Lawrence had been mentally distressed long before he indeed was, and lay his disinterest to that cause. In many ways, that was precisely what Drucilla hoped would happen, and had been at some pains to insinuate. Meacham's own youthful indiscretions, though a hopeful sign, hardly meant he would regard an adult's irresponsibility as something readily tolerated.

Putting aside her concerns, she busied herself with the task of conferring with the housekeeper about linens, and the cook about the meals for the next few days, until Meacham was safely away from Tarnlea. But her mind would not stay on these tasks. Much to her distress, an image of the viscount, usually with a laughing light in his eyes, continually disturbed her thoughts. She could interpret this light as mocking, or as humorous, but she could not interpret the way she felt each time it arose as anything but a breathless sort of excitement.

If it had been a warm and sunny day, she would have taken off across the park on a long, exhausting hike, forcing all thought of Meacham from her mind. As it was, she paced about the small library which doubled as her household office, pausing now and again at the window to stare unseeing at the shrubbery.

Thoughts of him refused to be vanquished. He had treated her with consideration, generosity, humor, and any number of other virtuous behaviors. Which did not mean that he cared for her in the slightest. It was merely the kind of man he was.

Besides, nothing could come of any attachment between the two of them, even if he should happen to return her regard. There was her father to be thought of, and May Script, and a dozen other matters large and small that she needed to attend to at Tarnlea. At times her burden seemed heavy indeed. For a brief moment she allowed herself a glimpse of a shared responsibility, and the vision was heavenly.

Drucilla considered the possibility that her desire for relief was the whole of her attraction to Lord Meacham, but she knew better. For the very first time in her life she had met a man who had caused her to succumb to love. When he went away again, she would have the delicious memory to hold in her heart and her mind.

And he would go away soon now. From the moment of his arrival he had made it clear that he must return to Meacham Court in time for the holidays. There was less than a week; at any time he would announce that he was leaving on the morrow. Probably the next time she heard from him would be a boldly penned letter announcing his plan to install a new administration for the estate.

A firm tap at the door startled her. No one ever bothered her in the small library unless she requested their presence, and today especially she had wished to be alone. Very much afraid of whom her visitor could be, she nevertheless granted permission to enter. Before she could so much as smooth down her skirts, the door opened and Meacham strolled in.

"I had the devil of a time getting anyone to tell me where you were," he said. "You're not hiding from me, are you, Drucilla?"

"Certainly not! This is my office and I come here almost every day, though I am not in the habit of receiving visitors here."

"Let's not consider me a visitor. Not only am I one of the family, but I have business with you."

Drucilla waved him to the solitary straight-backed chair and took her seat behind the desk. "Before you begin, do tell me if Teddy is going to be all right."

"Rall seems to think so. They've wrapped her leg tightly and she's able to hobble around on it. There will even," he informed her with the amused gleam in his eyes, "be goat's milk for your father's tea."

"I daresay you find it humorous, sir, but people in my father's condition can become quite agitated if their routine is disrupted."

He leaned back in his chair, very much at ease. "Does that worry you, my dear? My experience of your father is that the agitation of the moment quickly passes, which is perhaps one of the greatest advantages of having such a very short memory."

He seemed to give some underlying meaning to this pronouncement, but Drucilla was unable to determine what it was. "Perhaps," she agreed. "But what business has brought you to my office?"

"A matter of the utmost importance to me. I feel I have learned a sufficient amount about the situation here to conclude my stay, and I want to advise you of my decisions."

With a sinking heart, Drucilla said, "Please do."

"I won't object to the expenditures over the last two years, because they were obviously necessary. I do feel that it would be appropriate for me to press for a competency hearing for Sir Lawrence, so that I might be given complete control over the estate."

"But if you don't object to the way I've handled matters, I don't understand why you can't just leave things as they are."

"Because, my dear, you are not the appropriate person to set matters to rights here. That's my responsibility."

"But I don't mind! And there is very little left to be accomplished. As to the day-to-day running of the estate, John Thomas is an excellent estate manager. He would not lead me astray."

"Drucilla, I want you to listen very carefully to me. You are not responsible for your father's mismanagement of the estate. No, no, don't try to bamboozle me any further, my dear. Though it took me a great deal more effort than I would have thought necessary—your servants and neighbors being so very loyal—I have found the truth of the matter."

"But it was our previous estate manager who defrauded the estate. You saw that for yourself in the books."

Meacham regarded her with sympathy. "I am aware of that, my dear, but you must allow me my own prejudice, which is that a gentleman who allows himself to be defrauded on such a gross scale is certainly guilty of negligence at the very least."

"But . . . but there were extenuating circumstances."

"Only recently has it been impressed upon me how deeply a man might be devastated by the death of a beloved wife, Drucilla. I suppose I assumed that in a year or two, the grief would abate and life would return to normal. I'm not at all sure any longer that that's true."

A flush rose in her cheeks at the meaningful intensity of his gaze. "I believe my father was inordinately fond of my mother."

"So I understand, and that he took to drinking and hunting as his major distractions after her death."

Drucilla frowned prodigiously. "I should very much like to know who told you that."

"Yes, but I have no intention of informing you, for it was done quite unsuspectingly. And though I can understand your father's despair and his desire to escape from an unpleasant reality, I find it more difficult to pardon him for what he did to you."

"To me?" she cried in astonishment. "Why, he did nothing to me."

"Except ignore you or terrify you by putting you on his great hunters."

She waved aside such insignificant matters. "You mustn't think I suffered from his odd starts. He managed to make me into a creditable rider, and he was not an abusive man when he was in his cups." At his skeptical look she added with a dismissive laugh, "He was loud, certainly. He would roar at everyone, but I soon learned to simply disappear from sight until his sobriety was restored."

"And a very young girl was, I suspect, left to tidy up the disorganization he created. My heart goes out to that child."

"You refine too much on it, Meacham. Besides, all of that is well in the past."

"Not the responsibility." He rose, walked to the window, and stood looking out for some time without speaking. "I don't mean your father's responsibility. His illness makes his negligence irrelevant now. Nothing can be done about that. It is you I am concerned with, and you pose a very prickly problem for me."

"I cannot see how," she protested. "I am of age and

in a few months will have a perfectly acceptable independence with which to manage under any conditions you may impose on the estate. If I must leave Tarnlea, why, I shall settle in the village with Miss Script, or even make my home with Lady Nibthwaite, who has offered the dower house as my residence when my father dies. You needn't have the first thought as to my welfare."

He turned to face her and shook his head slightly. "My dear Drucilla, that is precisely my problem. Nothing concerns me more than your welfare because, you see, I have conceived an affection for you which I am not at all certain is reciprocated." He paused, then more diffidently added, "I find it impossible to make plans for the estate without knowing your feelings on the matter."

Drucilla sat, bemused, at the desk, her lips trembling slightly. In five paces he crossed the room and held out his hands to her across the small desk. Hesitantly, she placed hers in them and allowed him to draw her to her feet. For long moments they stood looking into each other's eyes as a smile, tremulous at first but growing stronger, curved Drucilla's mouth. Meacham raised her hands to his lips and kissed them one after the other.

"My hope," he said, "is that you will consent to marry me, my dear. Everything else is of little moment. We could live both here and at Meacham Court. Your father could stay here or come with us when we journeyed there. Miss Script could come with you, or go to one of my sister's homes. The only matter of any importance to me is whether you will have me."

Drucilla felt the ache that had been in her heart begin to fade. "You're certain that it is not pity you feel for me, sir? I should not at all like to accept an offer inspired by compassion."

His eyes danced. "Compassion? My dear Lady Bountiful, it is you who would be gracing *me* with your generosity of heart, your charming vivacity, your ..."

But deeds seemed more appropriate here than words, and Meacham moved quickly around the desk. Taking her unresisting body into his arms, he bent his dark head down to her upturned face. His kiss, tender at first, became very much in earnest, and at length Drucilla was forced to pull back to get a breath of air.

"I see," she said, with a shaky laugh. The blue eyes beamed up at him. "Then I shall most certainly have you, Meacham."

"And will you come home with me for Christmas, my love? My sisters will have the Court all festive with candles and holly, and filled with the laughter of their children. I could not possibly bring them home a present they would more delight in than you. Just say you will come and I will make arrangements for everything else."

"Of course I'll come." Drucilla raised her hand to stroke his beloved cheek. "I knew, from the moment I heard you were coming, that you would change my life—one way or another. I was more than a little afraid that it would not be in a pleasant way. Until I came to know you. And then I wondered if I should ever be the same if you disappeared from my life as quickly as you had entered it."

Meacham kissed the disordered blond curls that fell on her forehead, hugging her to him. "And I knew from the moment I saw you, Drucilla, that this—with a modicum of luck, and the holiday spirit—would be no ordinary Christmas."

A Mummers' Play

by Jo Beverley

London, December 1814

"My dear girl, it's far too dangerous."

"Nonsense," said Miss Justina Travers coolly. "And I do wish you'd stop referring to me as a girl, Charles. I'm twenty-three years old."

Lord Ormsbury's plain but honest face pinkened slightly. "That's not a terribly advanced age and"—he cleared his throat—"I do think of you as dear."

"How can you say that? You don't pay me a penny."

Though Justina spoke with carefully judged playfulness and softened the words with a smile, she wanted to scream.

Not Charles too.

She was so tired of besotted men. The fact that she still wore mourning three years after Simon's death should be warning enough. Perhaps she should have paid more attention to her older sister. Marina had warned, rather enviously, that black suited healthy blonds all too well.

Perhaps she should finally move into half-mourning, for grays and mauves had never become her. But she knew all her anxious friends and family would see it as a sign that she was finally "getting over it."

She wasn't.

She would never "get over" Simon's death, or not until those responsible were punished. Every last one.

Charles was studying her as if he would say more, but he took the hint and dropped the subject, moving away to busy himself with the wine tray.

Justina let out a breath of relief. She liked and respected her superior at the Home Department, and the amateur spy-catching work she did with him had become almost essential to her sanity, but if he embarrassed her with attentions she would have to cut the connection.

He came over to top up her wineglass, once more the efficient administrator. "You simply can't go poking around in the affairs of the duke."

"Even if he's a traitor?" Justina demanded, sipping the wine to humor him, though she rarely drank alcohol.

Ormsbury sat on the satin striped sofa opposite her chair and crossed one leg over the other. "I haven't failed to notice your obsession with this man, Justina. Thus far, it's been of little significance, but now . . ."

"But now he's a duke he's untouchable? Charles, that is horribly wrong."

"But realistic. What shred of evidence do you have?"

Justina looked down at the tawny wine made mysterious by crystal and firelight. "You know what I have."

"The fact that Lucky Jack Beaufort was the only survivor of the ambush in which your betrothed died," he said crisply. "I've humored you on that, but I've checked into the story and I assure you there's nothing in it." He leaned forward, and his tone gentled. "War isn't logical, Justina, and it certainly isn't fair. Some men are simply blessed by fate. Beaufort gained his nickname before that event."

She looked him in the eye. "Perhaps because he was working for the French all along."

"My dear girl . . . !" Then he caught himself. "Justina, you must see that this is an unbalanced obsession! There has *never* been the slightest evidence that Beaufort had irregular dealings. And you have looked, I know."

She felt herself coloring like a guilty child. She hadn't thought her actions so obvious. "I've never had the opportunity to search in a likely place. All you've ever let me do, Charles, is listen to gossip and search houses in which I was a guest. It would have been the sheerest luck to come across evidence in that way, but now—"

"But now he's a duke, he's even farther out of reach!" Then he flashed her a keen look. "Unless you've already wangled an invitation to Torlinghurst."

Justina put down her scarce-touched glass and rose to pace the room. "I could, of course. . . ."

"Then why not? You'd be safe enough as a guest, and able to poke around a bit."

She closed her eyes briefly. He was humoring her. She hated to be humored. "He'd recognize the name of Simon's promised bride. They were quite close."

"That would give you the greater entrée."

"But he would be bound to talk of him. . . ." Justina thought she had said it without great feeling, but then realized her hand had risen to cover the miniature she wore pinned on her bodice. She didn't need to open the locket to see the image. Blond hair, crooked smile, laughing eyes.

Simon.

Her heart and soul.

Dead.

Charles's tone gentled as he said, "Justina, my dear, it's been three years. Surely you can at least talk of it."

"Not with *him*! Not with the man who caused Simon's death."

She swung away to hide tears by staring at a lovely Raphael hanging on the wall, praying for the outward tranquility of that Madonna.

Revenge, they said, is a dish best eaten cold, and she had sheathed herself in ice in order to pursue her cause, not even permitting herself tears. Tears were weak, a sign of despair. She had chosen action instead, and resolved to destroy all those who had destroyed her hope of happiness.

Though her role had been minor, her work with Charles had helped bring down Napoleon, the man indirectly responsible for Simon's death. The Corsican Monster was now defeated and languishing on Elba, and Justina gained some satisfaction from that.

But nothing she had done had touched Lucky Jack Beaufort. He'd even made colonel and been mentioned in dispatches before his cousin had unexpectedly died, making him Duke of Cranmoore. How could fate be so unfair as to clear the wretch's way to such a title while Simon lay cold underground?

Or perhaps, she thought—and it almost seemed that the placid Madonna winked—fate had finally cleared the way to justice.

Yes.

With a tingle in her head that almost made her dizzy, she felt that Simon was guiding her, guiding her to Torlinghurst, guiding her to the evidence that would avenge him at last.

With a steadying breath she assumed the Madonna's tranquil smile and turned back to redirect the conversation. "As long as Beaufort stayed in the Peninsula he was out of my reach. If he'd returned as an ordinary man-about-town it would have been quite hard to search his possessions without being caught. But as the Duke of Cranmoore . . ."

". . . he's blasted untouchable!"

Justina's smile became genuine and she returned to sit in her chair. "No, Charles, you don't understand. As the duke, he's part of a community. I've visited Torlinghurst. It's a small town unto itself. Jack Beaufort's only been there a month and can't know everyone. With Christmas mere weeks away, the place will be filling with friends, relatives, and connections—all strangers to him. It's *easier* to slip into such a huge place than into a set of rooms on Clarges Street. No one will pay attention to one more person at Torlinghurst."

At last Charles showed guarded interest.

She pressed her advantage. "This idea came to me when Maplethorpe was wondering whether to go there this year for Christmas. He's a connection, but he doesn't know the new duke. Apparently just about all branches of the Beaufort family tree feel entitled to spend Christmas there. They always have."

Charles worried his lips with his thumbnail, which meant that at last he was seriously considering her plan. "But how will you get inside? You're not even a twig on the family tree, and you apparently don't want to go as Justina Travers. If you're thinking of passing as a servant, forget the notion. You exude breeding from every pore, and you're far too beautiful."

She didn't protest the assessment. Her fine-boned beauty brought her no joy these days so there was no vanity in acknowledging it. "There are pretty maids."

"Not for long."

"You cynic!" she said with a laugh, but then

shrugged. "In fact, I have no intention of trying to pass as a servant. It would not suit at all. Most servants never even enter the family's part of the house, and a lingering servant is always an object of suspicion. No, I intend to pass myself off as a well-born young lady of limited fortune, and thus ignorable by all. The servants will not question me, and the company will assume I'm one of them but beneath their notice. I will be able to search Torlinghurst at leisure."

The nail rubbed again at his lips. "Looking for what? If there was anything, he'll have destroyed it."

"It was you who taught me that villains keep dangerous mementos, Charles, and anyway, I doubt he's changed his spots. You know there are people conspiring to restore Napoleon. He'll be working with them."

Charles shook his head, but he did not argue that point. "I have one serious concern, Justina. In your previous exploits there has been virtually no risk. I've always seen to that."

"And I wish you hadn't!"

He ignored her protest. "Even if you'd been caught prying, your high birth would have made it a mere embarrassment. If anything worse had occurred, I would have admitted that you were working for the government. But in this case, it would be impossible. Impossible to admit that the government was investigating a *duke* on no evidence at all."

Justina reached to touch his hand. "Poor Charles. You're looking so flustered. So you're saying that if I do this, I do it alone?"

He covered her hand with his and squeezed. "I'll help as best I can, you know that. But yes, in the end you will be on your own."

It took only a moment to say, "So be it."

"Oh, my dear . . ." His pleasant, intelligent, honest

face was almost anguished. "If you do this and find nothing, will you put it all behind you?"

She wanted to drag her hand from his. She wanted to scream *no*! But in her heart Justina knew he was being reasonable. They were *all* being reasonable, all the family, all the friends, all the people who begged her to forget.

She met his anxious brown eyes and even squeezed his hand back a little. "If I have the opportunity to really search at Torlinghurst and find nothing, then yes, I will try to forget Jack Beaufort and move on with my life."

He smiled as if she'd given him a precious gift. "Then I'll help you all I can. What do you need?"

She gently freed her hand and rose, pulling on her black leather gloves. "Plans to Torlinghurst. It was built only fifty years ago. There must be architect's plans somewhere. I need to know exactly where all the private rooms are, and the location of side passages and servants' stairs."

He assisted her into her sable-lined black pelerine. "That should be possible."

She turned and bestowed her warmest smile on him. "Thank you, Charles."

He laughed dryly. "Turning me up sweet? I know your tricks. The main reason I'm not objecting to this, Justina, is that you'd do it anyway. You're too independent by far."

"You can hardly expect me to admit to that." She turned to the door and he opened it for her.

"There's one thing you haven't told me," he said.

"What?"

"How *do* you intend to get into Torlinghurst?"

"Oh," she said with a genuine, teasing smile, "I rather think I'll sneak in as Delilah."

* * *

Two weeks later, on Christmas Eve, Justina quietly merged with the group of mummers on their way up the drive to Torlinghurst. She'd been shadowing the Great Borbury group for the past two hours as they worked their way from village to village, manor to manor, gaining drink, pies, and pennies at each. She'd been smugly pleased when her assumption proved correct and two other groups merged with hers, all converging on the biggest of the big houses, Torlinghurst.

In a mixed group, no one would notice a stranger.

Now, the forty or so costumed mummers tramped cheerfully up the long drive in the moonlight, singing songs fueled by cider and wassail bowls. Justina joined in, keeping her voice pitched low, for all the mummers—even those in long wigs and dresses—were male.

"Here We Come a Wassailing . . ." was followed by "Good Master and Mistress . . ." which became tangled with "God Rest Ye Merry Gentlemen . . ." which then developed a few ribald verses that made her blush.

No one would notice her red face in the dark, but she made sure her coarse yarn wig hung forward.

Between the songs she listened to the chat, putting names to costumes. Lord Nelson and Lord Collingwood, both in knee breeches and braided jackets, were Giles and Jemmy. The serpent was Eli. The man in the horse's head was Fred. St. George, in bits of metal that were supposed to be armor, was actually called George. His dragon was Dobby. The maiden sacrificed to the dragon was Bert, the French whore was Brock.

It amused her that the innocent maiden and the whore looked identical—both wore a coarse yellow wig, bright red lips, and a gaudy shiny gown with a cushion shoved into the bodice to make a bosom of

truly amazing proportions. There were three other female characters—Good Queen Bess, Eve, and one she
thought was supposed to be Lady Hamilton—all looking much the same.

Which is why Justina was dressed that way, too.
She'd known how it would be, for these costumes were
traditional, often passed down from generation to generation. Samson and Delilah were part of the cast inherited from medieval mystery plays. There was one
Samson in the group. He was a huge man, probably a
blacksmith.

Underneath her gaudy costume, however, Justina
wore a different one, that of the poor dependent who
would be invisible in the crowded ducal establishment.

Suddenly the group let out a drunken cheer, and
Justina looked ahead to see Torlinghurst, glowing like
a huge faceted diamond, pale stone glimmering in the
moonlight and every window lit to celebrate Christmas
Eve. In some windows, tiny figures could be seen.

Which one of those people was her target? Which
one was Lucky Jack Beaufort, whose "luck" had finally brought him the grandest prize of all, the dukedom of Cranmoore?

Whose luck, she hoped, had finally run out.

Lucky Jack Beaufort was sitting in the grand salon
of Torlinghurst, thinking that clearly his luck had finally run out. What the devil was he doing here listening to some distant family connection caterwaul a
sentimental ballad while inadequately accompanied by
another distant connection on the harp?

Of course, as a blessing, the entertainment had si-
lenced his great-aunt Caroline. He'd never met the
woman until today, but she'd been lecturing him all

evening on the correct behavior required of the Duke of Cranmoore.

Resting his aching head on his hand, hoping the pose looked contemplative, Jack glanced around at the appalling collection of people who seemed to think they had a right to spend Christmas in his home.

Home! He almost laughed out loud. Whatever Torlinghurst might be, it was no person's home. It was a damned institution.

When he'd arrived here six weeks ago, abruptly and shockingly master of this domain, he'd thought it a dismal mausoleum with too many servants for the sparse collection of distant dependents and hangers-on. They, at least, had pretty much left him alone.

Then his mother and sister had arrived, reminding him why he'd chosen a profession that kept him away from England most of the time. But still, in such an enormous place it had been possible to avoid them. The duke was wisely provided with a vast private suite of rooms.

But then the Christmas crowd had begun to trickle in.

After witnessing a family of ten spilling into the hall, he'd cornered Rossiter, the elderly secretary he seemed to have inherited along with everything else. "Who the devil invited all these people?"

"Invitations are not required, your grace," said the thin, gray-haired man. "It is a tradition."

Jack stared at him. "You mean they just turn up, year after year?"

"Yes, your grace."

"Why?"

"They are all Beauforts, your grace, at least by connection."

"Good God!"

And so, day by day, Jack watched Torlinghurst fill with strangers until no peaceful corner remained except his private suite. He didn't feel able to hide there all the time and didn't even want to, for they were a ponderously decorated and gloomy set of rooms.

So, bowing to the inevitable, Jack moved among the crowds and made the acquaintance of his extended family, hoping against hope that some of them would prove entertaining. But the older people wanted to preach to him, and the young ones seemed insufferably callow. Those of the middle years talked of nothing but children, politics, and the price of corn.

He had survived, however, until tonight, when the whole lot of them decided they had been put on Earth to entertain one another. The past hours had been an endless amateur performance.

And worse was to come.

He'd just learned that some of his guests were rehearsing a play to be performed on Twelfth Night. He'd not even been aware that Torlinghurst had a theater. Now he knew it did, complete with proscenium arch, lighting, and seating for fifty.

Who in his right mind would construct such a torture chamber?

His damned cousin, that was who. The last duke had apparently so loved this Christmas gathering he'd developed it to this horrendous state.

Adora Beaufort-Chilworthy finished her screeching and simpering at him. He stirred himself to clap, being careful to show no particular enthusiasm.

It had quickly become obvious that all his more distantly related unmarried female guests knew exactly what they wanted for Christmas—him on his knees, offering hand and heart.

Or to be precise, his title and fortune. Any and all body parts were clearly irrelevant.

He'd become very adept at avoiding kissing boughs.

Now Priscilla Beaufort-Gore-Peebles rose with a superiority that reminded him forcibly of a camel, and progressed toward the pianoforte. . . .

But then, blessing of blessings, a raucous noise broke the genteel quiet. With any luck, Napoleon had escaped from Elba and invaded England!

"The mummers!" squealed one excitable girl and ran to a window. The younger members poured after, pushing and exclaiming.

Great-aunt Caroline sniffed. "Stone-drunk as usual."

"Sounds marvelous."

She stared at him. "If you think that noise sounds marvelous, no wonder you didn't appreciate dear Adora's performance."

Jack didn't explain his meaning. He had an excuse to escape and, like any experienced military man, took it. But at the door his way was blocked by his awe-inspiring butler, Youngblood, bearing a bowl of coins in front of his stately paunch.

"We pass round a collection plate?" Jack asked. "Things are looking up!"

Youngblood's full lips moved upward a fraction. "Your grace is pleased to joke. Ha. Ha. No, your grace, these are the sixpenny pieces for you to give to the mummers."

"I toss them into the crowd?"

"Not at all, your grace. That would encourage unruly behavior. You give one to each person along with a comment upon their singing or their costume."

On the floor below, the main doors opened and the rowdy singing abruptly grew in volume. "'Struth," muttered Jack. "A favorable comment, I suppose."

But suddenly fond memories assailed him, memories of his youthful days when the costumed mummers had been an exciting part of Christmas, especially if they acted out the story of George and the Dragon.

Since he clearly could not slip away, he threw off his bitter mood and grabbed the bowl. "Right. Everyone to the hall!" he declared in a voice that had carried over battlefields. "Let's greet the mummers properly."

He grinned at his scandalized great-aunt and his sour-faced mother, neither of whom wished to get close to the lower orders. "Come along, *everyone.* That's an order."

He'd tamed unruly battalions in his day and the tone still worked, even from behind a smile. The glittering company rose and followed him down the stairs to cram into the spacious hall.

Some of the older people looked decidedly mutinous, but if he was the blasted duke, for once they could do as he said. No matter how bucolic, this entertainment couldn't be worse than what he had endured thus far. The mummers—a motley crowd in ragbag costumes—stood ready to sing, though they looked startled at the crowd they'd drawn.

"Welcome!" Jack declared, acting to the full the part of the generous lord. "Let's hear your songs, my good men, and see your play, and you'll be well rewarded."

The group cheered—though a couple, he noted, were so drunk they were propped up by their fellows—and started into the traditional begging song, "Come gentlemen at Christmastide, give cheer to all mankind. . . ."

They sang raggedly to begin with, but soon settled into it, even managing a bit of harmony. Jack led the applause.

The mummers seemed to think they were done, but

as the largess didn't begin, they looked at each other, murmured for a moment, and started the wassail song. When they got to the line about pennies in bowls, quite a few bowls appeared as a broad hint.

"Excellent, excellent!" called Jack, applauding again. "But now, my good fellows, have pity on a poor soldier who's not spent a Christmas in England since he was a boy. Can you give me the play of George and the Dragon?"

The motley group shifted uneasily and he suspected that they were not actually in the habit of acting any kind of play. What had England come to? He was about to take pity on them and give their bounty anyway, when one George clanked forward. "By God, but I can play my part for a hero of the wars," he declared. "Indeed I can! Is there no dragon here to help me?"

After a moment, a man in a dragon head and long green cloak shuffled forward. "All right, all right. But be careful with that blinking sword, Georgie."

St. George waved the sword, which Jack noted did actually look real—no wonder the dragon was concerned—and declared, "I am George, great soldier of Rome and Christ." His accent was solid Gloucestershire. "I 'ave come to rescue the fair maiden, Melicent. . . ."

At that, he looked back at the group and repeated, *"The fair maiden, Melicent . . ."*

Yet more shuffling and murmuring, including a "He's stone-drunk," and "Not on your jolly life." Then a creature in a bright pink dress with a wig of long yellow yarn was ejected from the group.

The fair maiden Melicent ran to huddle behind the dragon, more in the manner of one seeking protection than one waiting to be saved, but it sufficed. St. George took up his part.

"I come," he yelled, so his voice bounced and echoed off marble pillars and gilded walls, "to rescue the fair maiden Melicent, cruelly given to the foul dragon to be its dinner."

The dragon got into the spirit of things and growled. It sounded more like a complaint of acute indigestion, but the younger members of the house party decided to support him with cheers.

"Odds on the dragon!" shouted one young spark. After a moment Jack found a name for him. Stephen, Viscount Leyland. Perhaps there was more to the jessamy than he'd thought.

"St. George always wins," the saint pointed out, somewhat aggrieved.

"My money's still on the dragon," replied Leyland. "I like the way he roars."

The dragon stood taller and roared again.

More cheers.

Jack laughed for the first time since coming to Torlinghurst. "My money's on St. George," he declared. "He handles his sword like a true hero!"

St. George stood taller and swung his sword, narrowly missing a horse nearby.

"Watch it!" squawked the horse.

"Well, keep out of the way!"

"I'm trying to blinking help. St. George 'ad to 'ave a blinking horse, didn't 'e?"

"Oh. All right then, Fred. But keep back."

St. George adjusted his helm, which tended to slide over his eyes, and turned to face the dragon again. "Give up that fair maiden, foul dragon, or I will kill you."

"Direct and to the point," declared Jack. "Good man!"

"Come on, dragon," called Leyland. "What say you to that?"

"I defy you!" declared the dragon. "This tasty wench is my dinner!" He hauled the maiden from behind him and pretended to eat her arm.

"Save me, oh sir knight!" the maiden screeched, clutching her wig.

"An excellent maiden!" called Jack. "A guinea for you, my friend, if your voice don't break before the end."

"Help, help!" screamed the maiden at an even higher pitch, clearly after the reward.

"Release her!" bellowed St. George.

"Not on your pipe and drums!" bellowed the dragon.

"Oh, my head," groaned Jack's mother from beside him.

Jack grinned. "Excellent speeches, my friends, but let's have some action."

Holding his helmet with one hand, St. George advanced, sword first. "Let her go."

The dragon clutched the maiden tight. "Go blow yerself!"

Jack's mother gasped.

St. George poked with the sword, but as the maiden now formed a shield, she shrieked, "Stop that!"

"Sorry, Melicent," said St. George and tried a poke from the side and made contact.

"All right, all right!" cried the dragon, flinging the maiden at the saint. "You're a blinking lunatic with that sword, Georgie!"

The maiden staggered, tripped on her long skirts, and fell at the saint's feet. Grinning, St. George put his foot on her and took a victory stance, sword high. "Thus prevail all righteous Englishmen!"

"Bravo! Bravo!" shouted Jack, applauding. "Thus

should every hero vanquish the women who seek to en-
tangle him!"

As the hall rang with cheers and applause, the
maiden pushed away the holy foot and scrambled up,
adjusting her costume and flashing Jack a surprisingly
angry look. He ignored it and gestured to the servants
to come forward with the punch and pies, then went
about putting silver sixpences into hands and bowls,
always commenting on their excellent costumes and
singing.

The spirit of Christmas did finally seem to be sparking in his soul.

When he looked for the maiden to give him the
promised guinea, however, the man had disappeared.
Clearly the poor fellow really had been embarrassed at
playing such a part.

Sad to have bad feelings on Christmas Eve, but Jack
held on to his lighter mood. Before the stultifying atmosphere could return, he gathered some of the younger people, including Leyland, and started a game of
hide-and-seek. Not only was it wild fun—which had
the added benefit of annoying Great-aunt Caroline and
his mother—but it gave him a chance after a while to
hide in a place where no one would dare to seek.

When he slipped into his private study, however, he
found a strange woman pulling a book off his shelves.

Justina hadn't expected to play such a prominent
part in the mummers' show, but it hadn't interfered
with her plan. She had still managed to slip away and
discard her costume to reveal her other one—a gray
round gown, some years out of date and faded, worn
over a prim white chemisette and under a sagging
brown knitted shawl.

Round wire-rimmed spectacles and a wilting cap

completed the appearance of Miss Esme Richardson, genteel young lady of reduced circumstances.

As she stuffed her Delilah costume into a large Chinese vase, however, Justina seethed at Lucky Jack Beaufort. Not only was the man a heartless traitor and murderer of his companions-in-arms, he was a buffoon and a misogynist! She could still see the glint of his white teeth as he cheered on St. George in his conquest of women.

How wickedly unfair that he should survive the war to enjoy glory and riches while other better men perished.

Hurrying along corridors toward his private rooms, she added to his list of sins. No doubt he'd been exploiting his dark curls and sculpted features all his life to use women, to conquer their virtue with not a moment's thought of the consequences. Doubtless abandoned Beaufort bastards littered Europe!

This fueled Justina's already fiery resolve. She could imagine what havoc such a wretch could create as an English duke. He must be stopped.

Once in his private suite, she set about a search that would leave no secret unexposed.

An hour later she rubbed dusty hands on her drab skirt and admitted that she had found nothing.

The enormous ornate desk was as good as unused, with neat stacks of unmarked paper beside undisturbed rows of pencils and pens. No pencil had so much as been blunted by use.

"Bone idle as well," she muttered.

But Justina wouldn't be so easily thwarted. The very blandness of everything showed she had not found Lucky Jack's real possessions. She'd set about a rigorous search for secret compartments, even crawling underneath the desk to tap for hollow spots.

Eventually, she emerged disheveled but no further forward.

Pushing her cap frill out of her eyes, she stared around the room. Where could the dratted man be hiding things?

Perhaps in his bedchamber? She opened an adjoining door to see a large tester bed with the handle of a warming pan poking out, and a nightshirt hanging on a rack close to the fire.

Two wardrobes and a set of dressing drawers offered many hiding places, but a bedchamber was open territory to servants, who had to clean all the corners and dig around in the drawers. He'd be a fool to hide his secrets there.

No, she thought, closing the door and turning back, it was much more likely that any incriminating material was hidden in the study where few would venture. In fact, it was probably hidden among the books.

She surveyed the tiers of shelves, almost overwhelmed by the task, but Charles had trained her well. Searches were not butterfly affairs—a peep here, a poke there. They were tedious and methodical. But in the end, painstaking precision brought results.

Making herself think of only one book at a time, Justina started at the glass-doored shelves to the right of the main door. She climbed the library steps, took down the first book on the top shelf, and riffled through the pages. Then she checked down the spine for inserts, and inspected the endpapers to see if they had been disturbed.

Nothing.

She replaced it and took the next.

She had worked her way down three shelves, remembering to check that the shelves themselves did not have false backs, and was standing on the carpet with a new book in her hand when Jack Beaufort walked into the room.

They stared at each other in shocked silence for a moment.

Then he snapped, "What the devil do you think you're doing, ma'am?" Anger scorched through it, but leashed in a way that alarmed her more than open rage would have.

Justina pushed the glasses back up her nose and tried to calm her frantic heart. "Oh, sir! My lord ... Your grace! What a fright you gave me."

And that was the honest truth.

From a distance, his height had not been so apparent, or his broad shoulders and shrewd, steady eyes. She was suddenly reminded that Jack Beaufort had served as a colonel and been decorated for it.

He was undoubtedly a very dangerous man.

Stepping closer, he said, "I'm likely to give you a worse fright. What business have you in here?"

He was so close that Justina had to tilt her head back to face him. Anger was emanating from him like heat, parching her mouth, causing sweat to slick her palms. . . .

She managed not to back away, but she had to escape those furious dark eyes. To save a scrap of honor, she told herself she was looking at the book in her hand, seeking an explanation for her intrusion. To her relief, she found it was a gazetteer. There could conceivably be a reason for someone to want such a reference book late at night.

"I . . . I was looking for some geographical information, your grace. For her ladyship . . ."

"What ladyship?" he demanded.

After a quick review of his family tree, she picked a

great-aunt of his who Maplethorpe said always attended this Christmas gathering. "Lady Dreckham."

"Great-aunt Caroline?" Something in his tone let her risk a peep at him. She was right, his anger was fading. "Do you have the misfortune to be that woman's companion?"

Justina looked down again, knowing how easily eyes revealed a lie. "Yes, your grace."

"Poor you." His tone was markedly more sympathetic. "She could have played the dragon's part in the mummers' play, couldn't she? Well," he added, with a startling touch to her bare hand, " 'tis the season for entertainments, it would seem. Let's pretend we're in a new play, one where a poor companion and a duke can meet as equals. Join me in some wine."

Alerted by touch and tone, Justina looked up to find that he really was smiling at her. It was not the wild smile he'd worn while cheering on St. George, but a charming one with a certain wistfulness behind it.

Now she did step back, away from both touch and smile, clutching the book to her chest like a shield. "Oh, I couldn't, your grace!"

"Scared?" He moved away, strolling lazily toward a tray holding decanters and glasses. "Yes, I'm a little drunk—I had to deaden my senses in some way—and I intend to become more so. But I've never been a bad drunk. I become a bit silly, and inclined to be indiscreet . . ." He stopped speaking to pour amber fluid into two glasses.

Justina, however, had the feeling that the action was the excuse for the pause rather than the reason for it. What in his words had so distracted him?

Her nerves were settling now he'd moved away, and so her wits were returning to their normal sharpness.

He'd accepted her story. First skirmish to her. And drink made him indiscreet, did it?

If Lucky Jack Beaufort was about to be indiscreet, Justina Travers would be here to witness it!

He turned, glasses in hand, and if he had been disturbed in some way he'd overcome it. "Because of the indiscretion, I haven't touched more than a sip of wine in three years. I'm making up for lost time. The freedom to get thoroughly foxed is the only advantage I've found in my change of circumstance."

With another disturbingly charming smile, he offered one glass to her.

Justina took it with what she hoped was an appropriate simper. If her imaginary Esme Richardson had actually found herself sharing wine with a duke late at night in his private apartments, she would certainly simper.

Miss Esme would probably run screaming from the room, but that didn't suit Justina's plans at all.

She sipped the wine and let out a genuine gasp. "Oh, my! What is it?"

"Port." That smile still lingered, muted in intensity but not in effect. "A new experience for you?"

"Yes, your grace." It wasn't a lie. "It tastes very strong."

"I suppose it is, but I assure you, on my honor, that one glass will not turn you into a wanton woman. Won't you be seated?"

A titter seemed to be in order, so Justina let one out as she perched on the edge of the seat of an upholstered chair by the fire.

He took the other chair with all the lazy elegance of a man in fine physical shape who was master of all around him.

Simon would be in equally fine shape but for him,

Justina reminded herself. She needed to prick her mind back to its target, for her image of Lucky Jack Beaufort did not accord with this pensive, friendly Duke of Cranmoore.

Downing half his glass in one gulp, he studied her with those shrewd, experienced eyes. "Now, my companion-in-mischief, what is your name?"

"Miss Esme Richardson, your grace."

"Esme." Perhaps there *was* a slight slur on it. The sooner he became indiscreetly drunk, the happier Justina would be. "A lovely name. You must have Scots blood."

"My mother, your grace." To be thorough, Justina had devised a complete life history for her character, but she hadn't expected to have to produce it in a situation like this.

"And where were you born?"

"Rugby, your grace."

He drained his glass. "Can I persuade you to not call me your grace?"

"What else am I to call you, your gr—"

Laughing at her slip, he said, "Cranmoore? No, too mannish, I see that." He slid a little further down in his seat. She did hope he wouldn't pass out without the indiscretion stage at all. "You could always call me Jack," he said wistfully. "No one does these days."

Simon had called him Jack in his letters. Jack was such fun. Jack was a knowing one. Jack was the best of all fellows.

"That would be most improper, your grace." Why the devil couldn't the man show his true stripes and be obnoxious? This bosky amiability made it hard to remember that he was her enemy.

"It's improper to be here drinking with me," he

pointed out. "Consider it a wild adventure, my dearest Esme, and go the whole way. Call me Jack."

Justina could find no way to refuse and stay, but it was only with great reluctance that she said, "Very well . . . Jack."

He graced her with a devilish and even more danger-ous smile, as if they were confidants engaged in mis-chief. "How very pleasant this is. Now, tell me what search for knowledge brought you here."

Justina realized she still clutched the gazetteer in one hand. She placed it on a tambour table by her chair and took another tiny sip of wine, trying to think of a location that would require research. "Lady Dreckham wished to know where Senegal is, your . . . Jack."

He blinked. "And where the devil is it?"

"On the coast of Africa."

"Why would she want to know a thing like that?" With audible hope, he added, "She isn't thinking of traveling, is she?"

Justina had to suppress a chuckle, which was alarm-ing. Humor had no place here! "I don't think so. I think it's more a case of good works."

"Poor bloody Africans. So, how long have you been her dogsbody?"

"A year."

"An age. Is this your first visit to Torlinghurst?"

"Yes."

He grinned. "You can't bear to call me Jack, can you? And since I won't let you call me your grace, you end up not calling me anything. Poor Esme, impris-oned in conformity."

Poor Justina was aware that if this man wasn't who he was, she would be sliding under the influence of his lazy charm like ice under warm water, and like such ice, melting.

She couldn't melt, though. If she thawed, then like a child's snow statue, she'd cease to exist entirely.

"I could call you sir," she said crisply.

"You're not one of my subalterns." Suddenly sober, he added, "But call me Colonel, if you want. I still probably respond to that in my sleep."

"No."

"Why not?" His eyes turned steady. The effect of drink on him was alarmingly mistlike, and easily dispelled.

Taking a sip of wine as distraction, she muttered, "I don't like to think of the war."

"Lose someone?"

This was dangerous ground, for if she said yes he'd want regiment and engagement. "No one in particular. It is just that so many promising lives were lost."

"True enough. Far too many. Far, far too many . . ." He tried to drink from his glass but found it empty, so pushed out of his chair to return to the decanters. Justina suspected that he, too, was seeking distraction. From what?

Grief?

Or guilt?

This time he brought the wine back with him, offering her more.

"No, thank you."

He sat, then filled his glass to the brim before placing the decanter by his elbow. After downing about half the wine, he said, "At least the slaughter's over. Tell me about your family."

So. He didn't want to talk about the war. Not surprising, if he had any conscience at all. But a guilty conscience didn't absolve him.

However, Justina obligingly related her fictitious story of a parson father with a large family, of her stint in a girls' school, followed by this post as companion to Lady Dreckham.

"And will you stay?" he asked, refilling his glass yet again. How much did he need to drink to become indiscreet? And how much to escape into insensibility?

"I suppose I must," she replied, assessing his state.

He looked back at her over the rim of his glass. "You don't seem the type for servitude, you know. I detect an adventurer beneath the mousy disguise."

For a moment she thought he'd caught her out, but then realized it was merely an honest observation. It showed again that alarming shrewdness, however. "I have little choice, your grace."

"Ah ha! You slipped up. I think I'll make you pay a forfeit for each 'your grace.' " He dug in his pocket, pulled out a sixpence, and placed it carefully on the table. "I'll mark each one with a coin."

"Nonsense." He was right. Drink turned him silly. It was time to pump him before he drained the decanter and fell asleep. "Now you should tell me about your family, Colonel."

Yes, Colonel suited him. He still had the physical and mental effectiveness of a good officer, even dressed in the height of fashion and blurred by drink. She had the strange thought that he, too, was in disguise.

Of course he was. Beneath it all he was a foul traitor.

"My family," he repeated. "As ordinary as yours, really. My father was the grandson of the third duke, so he had no title, but he married well. Which means, he married money. He kept busy and out of the house as a member of parliament, even a minister now and then. Not a bad fellow, but he died when I was twelve, which left me in the clutches of my mother."

"She was cruel?"

He laughed dryly. "Not unless it's cruel to bore someone to death. She's an amazingly stupid woman who loves to talk but has nothing to say that isn't petty or malicious. She could find a bad side to a haloed angel. Mostly I could avoid her, though, which is more than can be said for my poor sisters. No wonder they all married young. All except Mary, who's a hopeless case." He grimaced at her. "See what I mean about indiscretion? I'm sounding as malicious as she is, and boring you with personal matters, to boot."

"I'm not bored, Colonel." Justina wanted to keep him talking at all cost, but she wished he wouldn't go on about his family. She didn't want him to be a human being with feelings and flaws, parents and siblings. She needed to see him as a black-hearted monster cackling over his ill-gotten gains.

He toasted her. "How polite you are, Esme. Anyway," he continued contemplatively, "my childhood was pretty good. My brother and I had great fun in the schoolroom and then at Westminster, after which I went into the army and he went into the navy." He sipped from his glass. "He died without glory in a storm off Portsmouth four years ago."

For simple words, they carried a weight of stark grief that caught her breath. For a moment she wondered if this was his reason for sin, an excuse of sort. But no. Nothing could excuse treasonous murder, and why would the death of his brother turn him *toward* Napoleon?

"I'm sorry," was all she could say.

He shrugged. "That's war for you. Just one damned death after another, and most of them without glory." After draining his glass, he added, "*I* didn't die."

"That is clear." Since his wits were clearly now all

adrift, she pushed a little closer to matters that interested her. "You must have made good friends in the army."

"The best. They died, too. . . ."

But then he sat straighter and made a visible effort to rise up out of gloom. "Forgive me—this is no talk for Christmas."

He looked at his glass and seemed surprised to find it empty again. Refilling it, he said, "We had the strangest Christmases in the army, you know. One year, we had nothing to eat but onions and stale bread, and nothing to drink but water. Another, we spent in a Spanish estancia drinking wonderful wines and feasting on . . ."

Suckling pig, Justina could have completed. Her bitterness, her pain, her memories, all came rushing back. No wonder his careless words had been cut off. No wonder he was staring into space as if lost in dreams.

Or nightmares, more like.

She'd read and reread Simon's hilarious letter about that Christmas Eve three years ago, about the sudden abundance of food and wine, about the behavior of the demure ladies of the household, who proved not to be demure at all. One had ended up in Lucky Jack Beaufort's bed, and Justina had always wondered if perhaps one had ended up with Simon. She was a realist about these things.

In fact, she rather hoped one had, for that had been the last letter Simon had ever written to her. He'd died the next day, Christmas Day, in the ambush surely orchestrated by the only survivor, Lucky Jack Beaufort.

Lucky Jack sat before her now, staring into his wine as if it reflected his soul like a crystal ball. If only she could look into that glass and see what he saw.

She knew the official report by heart. The troop had

been caught in an impossible situation without cover, and picked off by musket fire. All except Lucky Jack. She'd assailed the Horse Guards with this fact, demanding that they court-martial the villain, but nothing had ever been done.

She stared at the wretch, graceful even in a sprawl, handsome even with disheveled black hair and drink-slack eyes, and wondered how he could bear to be alive when so surrounded by corpses. She tried to pick his secrets out of the shadowed line of his mouth, out of the shape of his strong hand around the glass, or the smudge of his shielded eyes.

She could not decipher him at all.

Suddenly, he looked up with a smile, but this time it was clearly an artificial one. "Most Christmases weren't one extreme or the other. I usually spent them in dreary billets eating salt cod and dreaming."

He'd slid away from that memory, but she'd get him back to it. She swore it.

"And what did you dream of?" she prompted.

"Oh, England. Goose and plum pudding, watching mummers' plays surrounded by friends and family . . . And now look at me."

"Eating goose and plum pudding, and watching mummers' plays surrounded by friends and family."

It was a mistake to speak so sharply, for he focused his eyes on her. "How can they be family if I don't know 'em? And what few friends survived the war are off with their own families, wise fellows."

As Simon would have been, you villain.

He relaxed again, resting his head back against the chair and staring at the ceiling. "When I thought of home, in fact, I thought of Northham. That was where I grew up. A decent, solid, red-brick house with just enough space for a family and just enough servants to cope. Not this,"—he waved a vague hand—"this monstrous pile."

"Torlinghurst is considered one of the finest homes in England."

He slanted his eyes down to look at her. "One of the finest houses, perhaps, though to call it less than a bloody palace is ridiculous. It's not a home."

Justina could tear her hair out. She was not at all interested in a discussion of English architecture. The only thing, however, was to keep him talking and hope she could steer him back to Spain and that ill-fated Christmas three years ago. "Yet people seem to be enjoying their visit here."

"Are they? How nice."

Some of her feelings escaped. "Your ennui and bitterness are absurd, your grace. You are the envy of England!"

Her unwise words cut through the alcoholic mist. He straightened slightly, snapping to alertness. "That's two, dear Esme,"—he placed a florin by the sixpence—"and people often envy foolishly."

He surged to his feet and paced the elegant room like a caged lion. "Consider, if you will, my excellent situation. Certainly I have money enough to indulge every whim, but unless I permit myself a total disregard of duty, I cannot do as I really wish—I cannot live in a simple home. I cannot seek a wife who would *want* to live in a simple home, for then she would be as miserable as I. Instead, I must seek a wife who thinks this place delightful, who thinks being a duchess desirable, and who is thus the direct opposite of the type of woman I admire!"

She stared at him and he suddenly stopped his pacing. "You probably think me mad."

"No," said Justina. "I understand."

And she did. Unwillingly, she was remembering some of Simon's letters, the ones in which he'd talked admiringly of Jack Beaufort. Jack was the best of fellows, brave, bright, and always lighthearted unless he got into his cups and began to talk of his position as heir to the Duke of Cranmoore. On that subject he soon became morose. Simon and the others had cheered him with the fact that his distant cousin, the duke, was young, healthy, and recently married, and so bound to provide little Beauforts to stand between Jack and his dire fate.

Because Justina had been obsessed with this man, she knew the rest. The duchess had proved to be a poor childbearer. She had suffered two miscarriages, then perished of the third. Before the duke could remarry, he had succumbed to a simple cold that settled in his chest and carried him off on the very day of Napoleon's abdication.

"Penny for your thoughts," Cranmoore prompted lazily. "Or am I just boring you to sleep?" He'd come to rest with one arm stretched along the marble mantelpiece, and the dancing flames illuminated a disturbingly fine length of leg and torso.

"You are giving me much to think on," Justina replied, wishing her thoughts were more disciplined. "You could almost be an object lesson to all those who lust after riches."

"Oh, I've nothing against the riches," he admitted with a quirky, endearing smile. "It's the trappings I mind. This is my house, or so they say, but if I try to change anything I am positively assaulted by the pain and anxiety of the staff." He picked up a bristol figurine and walked around to place it on the other end of the mantelpiece. "That will be back in its place by the time I wake up tomorrow."

Before she could comment, he went on. "And of course my mother seems to think Torlinghurst is a museum where everything should be preserved unchanged forever. She's a distant Beaufort, too, you know. She always wanted to end up here."

"Then perhaps your problem, your grace, is inbreeding."

After a startled moment, he laughed. "I knew you were no prim and proper miss! Miss Esme Richardson, you were sent to me by angels." But he tossed a ha-'penny with the other two coins.

Justina eyed those coins with some concern. They were evidence that his wits were still very much in place, and she had to wonder just what forfeit he intended to claim.

Then he was beside her with the decanter unstoppered. "A little more?"

Justina realized with alarm that her occasional sips had drained her glass. She let him fill it, but resolved not to drink any more. The faint effect of the wine had fueled her saucy tongue. Much more and it could be she who turned indiscreet.

And that could prove fatal. Literally so. She had no illusions about the lengths to which a man like Jack Beaufort might go to keep his secrets.

He looked down at her. "Will Lady Dreckham be looking for you? Frankly, I've no mind to cause a scandal."

Justina had to think quickly. "No. She was going to bed when she gave me the command."

"And how did you end up in here?"

"I thought this was the library."

Without warning, her chin was raised by a strong finger so she had to meet his steady eyes. "You're lying, my dear. The library is on another floor entirely."

A shiver ran through Justina. Despite the effects of wine, no one could doubt that this man had been an officer, and a capable one. She supposed effective officers had to learn to keep their wits about them, even when clouded by drink.

"But this place is so confusing. It's hard to remember even the floor one is on! Your grace," she added desperately, hoping it would send him off to add another coin to his hoard.

He grinned, clearly seeing straight through her ploy. "I'll mark that with another coin when we've sorted this out, my charming debtor. I want to know exactly what you're up to."

Though his tone was light, Justina shivered again. In her wildest dreams she had never expected an encounter such as this, never expected to fight a battle confused by such sensuous maleness.

She had to escape his touch!

The warmth of his finger on the sensitive skin beneath her chin was tearing her apart. No man had touched her so since Simon.

She had to escape his closeness.

She could even *smell* him. Nothing unpleasant, but *him.*

"Perhaps," he said softly, brushing her chin with his thumb, "you made no mistake. Perhaps you are just where you planned to be. Do you have someone primed to interrupt us?"

That snapped Justina out of her weak, muddled thoughts. He thought she was here to trap him into *marriage*? "Of course not," she declared, twitching her chin out of his control. "I merely mistook the rooms, your grace."

He moved away and tossed two more coins onto the

small table. "You must think the forfeit will be pleasant. A lifetime imprisonment here, perhaps?"

"Really!"

But he overrode her. "So, no accomplice. Perhaps you are relying simply on your charms. Let me guess how it was. You knew you would have no chance to be noticed out among the pretty young things with their simpering admiration and artistically exposed ankles. But here, you thought, in private, you might catch my eye. Congratulations, Esme." He gave her the accolade of a nod. "You have, in fact, caught my eye."

Justina was gaping at this interpretation. It was so far from reality that she had no idea how to react.

He moved closer, and again raised her face with his hand, raised it to study. "You are not bad looking, you know." His thumb came into play again, stroking across her chin. "Good bones. But even better strategy. Everyone knows that the way to attract a man is to listen attentively to his ramblings." He grinned. "You look astonished."

Furious was more like it. Furious at his appalling arrogance! Justina grasped his wrist to force his hand away, but her fingers didn't even meet around it and her push had no effect. "I came here looking for a *book*. I am not such a clever creature as you imagine."

"Not clever?" His thumb brushed her skin again. "I've learned that cleverness and good looks do not relate, Esme, but there is a look that goes with intelligence, and you have it. Don't try to act the simpering idiot. Please. At least be honest."

Justina pressed her head back, trying to escape him, to escape his words, his touch, but above all, the effect he was having upon her. "I tell you honestly that I have too much sense to want to marry Torlinghurst!"

His finger and disturbing thumb never lost contact

with her skin. "Fustian. It's a burden, but even I'd choose it over servitude to Great-aunt Caroline."

Desperate to be free, she shifted her grip to his thumb, remembering a trick Simon had taught her. . . .

Then froze and squinted down.

"I'm sorry," he said, suddenly passive in her hold. "Does it bother you?"

His index finger was missing, leaving an ugly knob of scar and bone. It must have been his middle finger that had raised her chin.

"No," she said, trapped, for how could she thrust him away now? "I thought you undamaged, though."

He removed his hand and returned to his chair. "Why make such an unlikely assumption?" With a slight smile he added, "You can count my other scars if you wish."

A new danger wove into the room, causing her heart to flutter. "I thought you promised not to be a bad drunk, your grace."

Without comment he added a golden guinea to the coins on the table. Though Justina told herself those coins could count for nothing, they sat there like warning signs.

"In what way am I being bad?" he asked. "Am I seizing you? Am I demanding anything of you? Yes, that was a slightly scandalous suggestion, Esme, but it was an offer, nothing more."

He filled his neglected glass with a remarkably steady hand and sipped from it. "You're probably going to be mightily offended, Miss Esme Richardson, but it's not unusual for a lonely spinster to simply want a night's comfort. In the true spirit of Christmas, I am offering it."

Justina froze, stunned by his casual words.

Then she wanted to throw her wine in his face. She

wanted to shatter the glass, even, and use it to ruin his handsome, decadent, tempting beauty. How had he sensed her loneliness? How had he guessed the number of nights she had lain awake wanting comfort?

He couldn't have.

He *couldn't* have!

Please God, he did not know the hollow, aching need that stirred within her now, summoned in some inexplicable way by him. Not a need of passion, but a need that sprang from memories of tender embraces and sweet kisses beneath the apple tree in her father's garden.

Simon's kisses, she reminded herself.

Simon.

Dead because of this man.

"I'm sorry," he said, his expression somber. "I see I *have* offended you. I will not mention it again. As for my war wounds," he continued lightly, "my hand is the most notable deformation. The finger was neatly shot off by a musket ball. I hardly even felt it at the time. Such a loss is minor enough compared to those suffered by others."

Justina grasped the opportunity to get back on course. "So you consider yourself lucky?"

He was about to drink from his glass, but halted in place like a statue. "Oh, no, Esme. I consider myself damned."

Her startled heart rattled off tempo for a moment. Now the moment had come, she almost didn't want to hear the words, but she gripped her hands tight on her own untouched glass and waited for his confession.

And waited.

And waited.

After what seemed an age, she moistened her lips

and prompted, "Why do you consider yourself damned, your grace?"

Like a clockwork model switched back into motion, he sipped from his glass, then shifted to produce another coin. But he did not merely place it with the rest, but deftly set it spinning. "I am damned," he said, studying the spinning coin, "because I seem condemned to live and live and live while those I care for fall in their blood all around me." The coin slowed, then wobbled down beside its fellows. He looked up, shadow-eyed. "Can you imagine living with so many ghosts?"

"No." *It is bad enough to live with one, and that not soured by guilt.* But she would not, could not, be sorry for him. He'd as good as admitted his sin. All she needed now was proof and retribution. "Are you saying you would rather be dead than Duke of Cranmoore?"

He laughed bitterly. "Oh, no doubt of it!"

But even as he opened his mouth to say more, the mantel clock chimed, ripping through the intimate moment. Distantly around the house, others joined the chorus, high and low, slow and merry, counting out the full twelve hours of midnight.

He smiled in a more conventional way and raised his glass. "Happy Christmas, Miss Richardson."

He was retreating, escaping, aided by those damned clocks. She crudely jerked him back. "But all those deaths in the war were not your fault, so why consider yourself worthy of damnation?"

"As Juvenal said, we can never escape the judgment of our own heart."

"And your heart condemns you?"

But now other bells began to ring—distant church bells from three parishes. He turned to listen. "Hark, the herald angels ... No, that's wrong." He rose and grabbed her left hand to pull her to her feet, pulled her so roughly that her wineglass was knocked from her hand to roll on the carpet. " 'Hence loathed melancholy, of Cerberus and blackest midnight born.' Though we have no mistletoe here, dear Esme, I feel we must kiss."

And he kissed her hotly, binding her to his body with strong arms so that, struggle as she might, she was helpless.

So she surrendered.

Even with an enemy, an hour of dim-lit, wine-fed intimacy has power to enchant, and Justina had not been kissed for many a long year. The port also weakened her, robbing her of the power to resist this man, who was not quite the monster of her dreams, though still her darkest enemy.

What did it mean, she wondered dazedly as his lips pleasured hers, to kiss the enemy?

Was this a Judas kiss?

Who was the Judas, though? He was surely a betrayer, but she would betray him to the gallows as soon as she could, despite the alarming sweetness of his mouth on hers, of his supportive arms, his strong body pressed to hers. . . .

He drew back smiling, dark dazed eyes absorbing her, admiring her as he stroked her cheek. . . .

His eyes widened, and he blinked as if trying to focus.

Then his smile vanished as he tore off her cap. "Justina Travers?"

Snatching her wits, Justina ripped free of his slackened hold and ran behind the desk, aware that her hair was escaping its loosened pins and tumbling down her back.

"What on earth . . . ?" It was clear he was still dazed
with drink, shock, and perhaps lust. "I'm sorry."

"Sorry?" Justina was judging the distance to the
door, and the angle of his interception.

"I had no idea you'd fallen on hard times, Miss
Travers. I understood you to be well provided for by
your family."

She relaxed a fraction. He thought her driven into
servitude under a false name? Such a strange notion
would not survive his return to sobriety, but it gave her
breathing space now.

"I don't know why you would take an interest in me,
your grace."

"Simon was like a second brother to me."

"And yet he died." She could not stop the bitter
words.

"Being my brother is no ticket to immortality. That
is proved."

He'd killed his brother too? His older brother, who
would have inherited . . . But no, his brother had died
in a storm. And he didn't want the dukedom. Unless he
was the greatest actor ever seen, Jack Beaufort didn't
want the Duchy of Cranmoore.

Slowly, like wounds tearing, a part of her was opening, letting in doubt that this man was quite the black-
hearted villain she had lived with through the years.

He admitted it, she reminded herself. He *admitted*
his guilt. He described himself as damned.

But he seems quite pleasant, and so sad. . . .

As Justina's convictions warred with the reality before her, she watched him warily.

He did not attack, however. Instead, he went to
throw up a long sashed window so the still-pealing
bells poured in on frosty air. Laughing voices told of
young people running outside to welcome Christmas.

They must have seen him, for they started to sing the mummers' wassail song beneath the window, calling up to him to throw them pennies.

He turned his back on them. "Justina, will you marry me?"

"What?" She really wished her voice hadn't squeaked like that, but he'd finally shocked her.

Surely no villain could ever smile so sweetly. "I can think of no better way to start this season of joy and hope than by playing St. George and rescuing you from the Great Dragon Caroline. Simon spoke of you a great deal, you know, and often showed us his miniature of you. I've been half in love with you for years."

It felt like a violation that he'd ogled that miniature, fellow to the one she wore now around her neck beneath her gown. The lockets had been gifts to each other upon their engagement, just before their last parting.

She'd wanted to marry immediately, but her parents had insisted that they wait. Simon hadn't pressed for it, though she knew he'd wanted the wedding, too.

When the news of his death arrived, her mother had remarked how fortunate it was that Justina was not left a widow, perhaps with a child. Justina had never quite forgiven her for that.

"Well, Justina?" he prompted. "Can you not answer me?"

"I couldn't consider it," she said coldly.

"Why not?" The impromptu beggars were still singing and with a distracted curse, he scooped up the coins on the table and tossed them out the window, calling, "Merry Christmas! Now, cut it!"

Then he slammed the sash on their laughter and thanks. "Can we think of that as throwing our problems out and starting afresh?"

"I doubt it," she whispered.

He went to throw extra logs to crackle on the fire, then turned to her, dusting his hands. "Let me at least make my offer in better form, my dear. I don't expect you to love me, but you seem to be a pleasant companion, and you'll make a good chatelaine of this place. I really cannot bear to think of you brought so low. Simon would have my hide."

The bells, the laughter, the frosty air blending with the roaring fire, all conspired to make Justina feel that she had lost touch with reality. "Simon is dead. The dead know the truth."

"Lucky corpses. Or perhaps not," he added with a sigh. "Truth is a harsh rider. But if Simon knows the truth, he'll know that my intent is nothing but to make reparation. He'll know that you've never broken faith with him, that you marry for convenience, and perhaps out of kindness since I've told you of my sorry state."

It was shockingly tempting to say yes.

"What do you mean," Justina demanded desperately, " 'truth is a harsh rider'?"

He came closer, to stand on the other side of the empty, sterile desk. "Do you not have truths you'd rather forget, or at least sugarcoat into something easier to swallow?"

Again she tried to pin him down. "Why did you say marriage to me would be reparation? For what sin?"

"For living."

Justina wanted to tear him apart with her bare hands and expose his dark secret. Oh, he was sorry. She sensed that. But he was damnably guilty as well.

This night, however, would be her only chance. Something—perhaps Christmas—had softened him, weakened him, but when morning came, Jack Beaufort would retreat out of reach and keep his guard high forevermore.

How, then, could she tear him apart?

Drink wasn't fully working. She suspected that sex might. Men, they said, went wild when with a woman, and lost all self-control. Hadn't Samson let Delilah cut his hair because of love and sex? Naked in bed, Jack Beaufort might lose his last restraints and become just as foolish.

Then she would destroy him, and perhaps at last be at peace.

But her own thoughts startled her. *Naked in bed* ... Could she really do such a thing, now, tonight, with a man who was as good as a stranger, even to win justice and peace?

She looked at her quarry with sex in mind, and swallowed nervously. He'd thought of himself as St. George opposing his great-aunt, the dragon, but Justina knew she was the hero here, and he the monster.

She just wished she felt heroic.

Had St. George quivered with terror when he'd first sighted the power and strength of his opponent?

Perhaps there were other ways, she thought frantically. There must be other ways. He had teetered on the brink of confession time and again as they spoke. More conversation was a great deal less daunting than naked intimacy.

Warily, she left the barrier of the desk and moved toward the warmth of the fire. "Tell me about Simon's death."

He turned to keep her in view. "You don't want to get into that on Christmas Day."

One hand on the cold marble mantel, she challenged his uneasy eyes. "Don't tell me what I want. You were the only survivor."

"Yes."

"So tell me what happened. I will never rest until I hear it from the only witness. You."

He rubbed his hands—one deformed—over his face. "Does it not occur to you that I might not want to speak of it?"

Oh, she'd go odds he didn't! She continued to look at him, so when he lowered the shield of his hands he saw only her. "You owe it to me."

She thought he'd protest that, but he sighed and surrendered. "Perhaps you're right." He gestured her back to her chair and took the other, but not before getting her a fresh glass and filling it, then refilling his own. "Where do you want me to start?"

She'd had an account of sorts from the colonel of the regiment, who'd had the facts, of course, from Jack Beaufort. She didn't expect this retelling to be any different, but she had to hear it from him. She hoped to pick up nuances that would fill in details.

"Why not start with that Christmas Eve at the estancia?"

He was studying her over the rim of his glass, puzzled, and perhaps wary. He must be confused by the change from Esme to Justina, from stranger to indirect acquaintance, from nervous spinster to interrogator.

She could sympathize. She was equally disturbed by the change from faceless monster to troubled man.

"I'm sorry I mentioned that dinner party earlier," he said, "I couldn't know it would upset you."

"It didn't upset me. I just want to hear about it all from the only person who can tell me the truth."

Though she watched intently, she detected no flinch at the word "truth."

Instead, he sighed. "Very well. If it's any consolation, it was an unexpectedly merry Christmas. Wellington had put the army in winter cantonments to rest. We'd had the rest, but supplies were thin and there were few luxuries. We didn't expect much better at Christmas. Anyway, by the time Christmas came we were stirring for the assault, which would start with the New Year. With that in mind, I was sent with a troop of men to investigate the Estancia Cabrera, estate of the Conde de Cabrera. Simon was my lieutenant."

He glanced at her as if he expected her to stop him, perhaps hoped that she would stop him. Justina sipped from her glass. "Go on."

Again he sighed. "I don't know how much you know of the situation then. The French were being beaten back and the Spanish were generally on our side, but the Cabrera family had always been suspect. Wellington had plenty of evidence of their support for France in the past, and their estate sat right on the preferred route to Ciudad Rodrigo. He wanted to know the state of affairs there. Whether the family was in residence. How many able-bodied men were around. If there was any sign of the French. We approached the estancia cautiously—it was close to the French lines—but found nothing suspicious. Eventually we left most of the troop in concealment and approached the house. Myself, Simon, and two troopers."

He was staring into space, now, looking into the past, perhaps reliving it. "It was a beautiful place even at that time of year—rich golden stone and fertile fields all around. The house was scarcely marked by the war, which was suspicious in itself, since the French armies generally left scars."

Just as you are suspiciously unmarked, Justina thought. But then she remembered that he was not totally unmarked and claimed to have other scars besides his hand.

He was alive, though.

He was also haunted by many ghosts.

Suddenly enough to startle her, she realized that her interest was no longer solely to reveal the truth and punish the traitor. She needed, quite desperately, to understand this man's secrets.

"Many of their servants had fled or been conscripted into armies," he said. "We certainly saw no young, healthy males. But the family was managing to keep in quite a good state with just women and older men. However, when we were admitted, we were told that the conde was absent and the condessa was ill, so the three daughters were the only ones available to handle our inquiries." He came back to the present and looked at her with a hint of humor. "Did Simon mention in his letter that they were three very pretty and seemingly very silly young women?"

"Yes," she said. "But how did you know about the letter?"

Humor died. "How could I not know? He wrote it that night, while ... Later ... later I saw to it that it was sent to you."

He'd sent it, that tragic, blessed letter? She didn't know whether to curse him or thank him. Had he read it first to check that nothing there incriminated him?

Oh, surely he had, damn him.

"Now, where was I?" he asked, returning to the past. "Ah, yes, the three pretty sisters. The war had assuredly been dull for them, when it wasn't being terrifying. The oldest was twenty-two and a widow, the younger two betrothed but unwed. They would all have been married and mothers in more normal times. They were clearly starved of company, especially male company. Since it was Christmas, they begged us to stay and eat the Christmas Eve feast with them, despite the disapproval of some elderly maids who were acting as duennas. There seemed no reason not to, and we could already smell the roasting pork. . . ."

He looked across at her, and though he still held his glass in his hand, he hadn't drunk from it for some time. "It was a misjudgment on my part, as was the amount of wine I drank and permitted the others to drink. As was," he added after a pause, "agreeing to comfort the eldest daughter through the night. It had been a long and dreary war, but that is no excuse."

"Did Simon . . . ?" Then she wished the question unasked.

"No. I told you, he spent the evening writing a letter to you, then slept the sleep of the virtuous. If the troopers visited the younger sisters, I am unaware of it. It seems unlikely. They were virgins, one assumes."

"I wish he had. Gone to bed with one of the ladies, I mean." Oh, God, why was she saying these things to this man, above all? She stared in horror at her glass, again half-empty. Perhaps she, too, was a foolish drunk.

"Perhaps you wish *you* had gone to bed with him," he said, understanding altogether too much. "But it would have distressed him in his final moments, you know, to have used you that way and had to leave you unwed."

The last thing she wanted was his awareness of her secret regrets. She firmly put her treacherous wine aside. "Was it true, what the colonel wrote, that Simon's last words were of me? That was not a polite fiction?"

"Of course not." As if discussing the weather, he said, "His precise words, if you want them, were 'Oh, God, Jack. She's going to be so unhappy. She takes things so hard. I wish . . .' " But then his composure broke and he looked at her with bitter memories in his eyes. "I honestly don't know what he wished done or undone, Justina, except that he did not want to die."

It was Justina who looked away, looked down, then covered her eyes with her hand. Jack must have a gift for mimicry, for it had been as if Simon were there speaking exactly as he would have said those words. . . .

And of course Simon would have known how harshly she would take his death. She had always been intense in her emotions, while he'd slid more lightly through life. They'd quarreled about it sometimes, she saying he was a careless wretch, he complaining that she had the makings of a worrywart.

If she could believe those words, and she did, Simon had not suspected Jack Beaufort of causing his death. Perhaps there was a blessing in that.

She took a deep breath and straightened to look at him again. "So, how did the ambush occur?"

He, too, had put aside his glass. Now he tented his hands and rested his chin on them. "We set out in the morning in pretty good order despite the festivities, collecting the rest of the men as we went. I'd decided that the conde had fled to join the retreating French, but I could see nothing at the estancia that would endanger the route to Ciudad Rodrigo. So, despite the pleas of my partner of the night, we went on with our mission."

Justina was tempted to say something tart about his remarkable attractions, but controlled herself and acted the lady.

"We were to go on to another estate nearby," he continued, "one solidly anti-French, to warn them to prepare supplies for the coming army. We had to go a little closer to the French lines, but we didn't expect trouble. The countryside was quiet. We thought that was because it was Christmas Day." He paused for a moment, then added, "The French were ready for us at just the right spot, a place with no concealment other than leafless bushes. They picked us off like straw targets."

For a moment she couldn't speak, then she said, "All except you."

"Lucky Jack," he admitted.

"A strange kind of luck. How did it come about that you were spared?"

She did not really expect an answer to that blunt question, but she got one, tossed out idly as if of no account.

"My sexual prowess," he said with a grimace. "Senorita Dona Maria Bianca was apparently so grateful for the comfort offered that she begged that I be spared."

"*What?* I never heard anything of that!"

He quirked a brow. "It is hardly the sort of detail a colonel would relate to a young lady. I shouldn't have spoken of it myself, but you seemed to want the whole story."

Justina tried to weigh his words, his tone, and the look in his eye. If there was any expression there, it was embarrassment, not guilt.

Surely that couldn't be the explanation for everything, however—that he had been spared because he was a good lover! No, there must be more to it than that.

"Why were you ambushed at all?" she demanded. "One small English troop was hardly worth the bother."

"Another detail that could not be told to you. As Wellington suspected, El Conde and his family were still on the side of the French. Seeing the way the war was running, however, they'd decided to move behind the French lines, but taking as much of their movable wealth as possible. We had the bad timing to arrive in the middle of the business and so had to be distracted by the pretty senoritas. Unfortunately our route on Christmas Day meant we would overtake the line of carts carrying the first of the goods. Dona Maria did try to detain us, but when she failed it was decided it would be simpler to dispose of us."

He studied her face and remarked, "War is like that, my dear. Few of the deaths make heroic sense."

Could she believe this story of petty matters? What of his talk of ghosts and damnation. No, this was just a clever tale honed by years of telling. She'd already detected a hole in it. "Why," she asked, "could I not be told about the conde's movements?"

He shrugged slightly. "The military like to keep secrets. Cabrera is a powerful man, and everyone knew that in time both the Spanish and the British would want his support."

She gripped the arms of her chair. In fact, she almost shot out of it. "*What?* Despite the murder of a whole troop of English soldiers, the British would deal with him again?"

"But the French slaughtered the troop, my dear. El Conde, of course, had no notion of the plan. He was properly horrified when he heard."

Justina had thought her rage was old, consisting mostly of bitter cinders and ash, but now it flamed anew. "And where is the Conde de Cabrera now?"

"Back on his lands in Spain."

Justina collapsed back, as confused as if she'd been blindfolded and spun around. If this story was true,

then this conde was her enemy and must not be allowed to enjoy his honors and his fine estate.

But this story couldn't be true, so Jack Beaufort
must still be her enemy.

And yet, so convincing was he that her original grief
and rage were collapsing into formless misery.

A touch of humor twitched his lips. "Simon always
said you were ferocious. Are you thinking of going
to Spain to denounce Cabrera and demand that he be
brought to justice?"

"Yes, if it is true."

"Oh, it's true. He is back on his estates already."

She had meant if Jack Beaufort's story was true.
Had he really misunderstood her, or was that more
sneaking cleverness?

"You are painting a picture of remarkable sophistry
and wickedness," she accused, but she knew that
Charles would have no difficulty with such a story.
Politics and war were a series of cynical accommodations.

In fact, she realized angrily, Charles had doubtless
heard this version of the story and not thought it proper
to pass it on to her.

Desperately seeking an anchor point in all this,
Justina grabbed onto her original suspicions and Jack
Beaufort's words. He couldn't evade the fact that he
had condemned himself. "Why did you describe yourself as damned rather than lucky?"

His eyes snapped to hers, and she saw guilt there. In
a bitter way it was a relief. It steadied her, caused her
mind to click together like a clever machine. Lucky
Jack was guilty, no matter what story he told.

"Well?" she asked, even though she knew the danger
of persistence. He must guess now that she suspected
him, that she would pursue him to hell and beyond.

When he rose and came to her, when he reached for her, she thought it might be to throttle her, but he simply pulled her to her feet. "Damned? Can you not imagine what it feels like to lose friend after friend, colleague after colleague, until you don't dare make friends or care for colleagues again? Is that not to be damned?"

If it was, she shared that hell, for after one loss she had not allowed herself to love again.

And he knew it. He tilted her chin and looked at her, looked, it seemed, deep into her soul. "Justina, you must put all this behind you. You have life and must live it to the full."

Oh, that would suit him, to have her forget. "I have a very full life."

"I don't think so."

He kissed her then, gently at first, giving her time and opportunity to resist if she wanted, but she didn't. They'd played out the first part of the battle with no resolution. He knew who she was, and probably suspected something of her intent. She knew he felt guilty, and even damned.

Now he was going to bring out his heavy guns and try to seduce her into forgetting her suspicions. Perhaps he even thought he could drive the memory of Simon from her heart.

With a start, she realized that even his strange proposal of marriage could be part of an underhanded scheme. A wife could not testify against her husband, so anything she learned here tonight could be rendered safe.

Very well, then. She could encourage his base lust, but turn the weapons against him. At some point he would lose control and then, like Delilah, she would shear him down to raw truth.

She framed his face, wider and heavier-boned than Simon's, dark-stubbled now as Simon's never was, but still almost as beautiful.

Devil beauty.

She kissed him back, opening her lips, teasing at him with her tongue. His eyes widened with surprise, then closed, almost as if in pain. But she had him in her power. She sensed it in the tension of his body and the change in his breathing.

She deepened the kiss, and never stopped kissing him as he swung her into his arms and carried her into his bedroom, kicking the door shut behind him.

He freed his mouth and smiled, a strangely tender, almost concerned smile that threatened to disturb her sense of purpose.

He was the dragon, she reminded herself. Or Samson. Or even Lucifer himself. She mustn't let herself think of him as a man.

As he slid her to her feet she closed her eyes and held onto her vision of wickedness cloaked in charm. It was supported by the expertise with which he unfastened buttons and peeled her gown down to pool around her feet on the carpet.

He's handled hundreds of women like this, Justina.

Bare fingers touched bare shoulders and she caught her breath, reminding herself that she must not succumb.

But then a silent stillness forced her to open her eyes. He was staring at the locket nestled between her breasts.

"May I?" he asked, sliding fingers down to touch it.

She wanted to refuse, but she nodded, and he flicked open the silver case.

"It's an excellent picture," he said gruffly, his expression satisfyingly full of guilt. She carefully didn't look at the picture herself.

"Does it bother you?" she asked. "I won't take it off."

If there *had* been dark guilt in his face, it disappeared. "No," he said, snapping the locket shut. "It doesn't bother me."

He turned her and unlaced her stays as deftly as any maid. Resisting an urge to cling to the locket, Justina studied a picture on the wall. It was a singularly unpleasant painting of dead pheasants, necks drooping over the edge of a table alongside the knife that would sever them.

It strengthened her. She was the knife, and soon he would feel it against his neck.

He slipped off her corset and tossed it aside, so she was only in her knee-length shift. When he turned her back, she was careful to look at his ruffled shirt, not his beguiling features.

"Nervous?" he asked softly.

"A little." It wasn't a lie.

He drew her into his arms. "Do you want to stop? We can. I'm offering a gift tonight, nothing more."

The sensation of being nearly naked in a man's strong arms was new to her. It alarmed her, but in ways she didn't entirely expect. "No. I don't want to stop." It was half-truth, half-lie.

Fingers threaded into her hair, moving there in a distressingly soothing gesture. "My offer of marriage still stands, Justina. I think perhaps you have not wed because you still love Simon, because you are too honest to offer a man half your heart." His other hand slid down her back to rest there, low and comforting. "I, above all men, can understand your feelings about that. I will be satisfied by half. By less." His hand slid around to raise her chin. "I will be grateful for whatever you can give me."

A cinder, she thought, trying to see the monster in his somber, gentle face. That's all that's left. A black, brittle, sharp-edged cinder.

But the cinder was suddenly trembling high in her chest, warming and glowing as if it still had life in it. "Are you doing this just for Simon, then?" she asked.

His soothing hand on her back paused. "In part. He would want you to be rescued."

"From your great-aunt, the dragon?"

"Not entirely. From this living death."

"Why?"

"He would have done as much for me."

And to her own astonishment, she smiled. "Made love to some chance-met sad woman? I do hope not."

He laughed then, joy sparking in his eyes, and picked her up to swing her around, to carry her, circling, to his huge bed, where he tucked her, dizzy, between the warm sheets.

Then he began to undress himself, folding his clothes with military precision and laying them neatly on a chair. He'd been an excellent soldier, they said, and well-loved by his men.

The men who had died, so many of them, under his leadership, while he lived on.

But that was the fate of an officer. Even Simon had spoken of it once or twice.

As her Sampson, her dragon, her devil undressed, she saw his scars. A long one ran down his upper arm, distorting the muscles there. A wide one—a burn perhaps—splashed across his thigh. Neither muted the power of his solid body. She knew the dark hair on legs, chest, and groin was nothing like Simon's would have been, had she ever seen it. She had never seen Simon's naked legs or chest.

Or his private parts.

The effect of a naked, muscular man was so unsettling to Justina's nerves that she fought back with a question. "What did Simon die of?"

He stopped halfway to the bed, unconcernedly naked, but frozen by her question. "Of bullet wounds."

"But where?"

"Justina, it won't help to know."

"I need to know. I need to know *everything.*"

It was a warning of sorts, though she didn't know why she felt compelled to give it. Perhaps because they were both finally running out of disguises and balanced on the razor edge of truth.

His hand tightened around the bedpost. "In the gut."

"Did he suffer?"

He released that white-knuckled grip. "Yes." But then he was in the bed and silencing her questions with kisses.

Then she discovered why Senorita Dona Maria Bianca had begged that he be spared, for Jack Beaufort knew how to touch a woman. He knew when to be strong and when to be gentle, and he gave his knowledge as a generous gift this Christmastide.

And Justina found it was a gift she could not spurn. Her long-neglected body responded to him as a parched man might respond to a fountain of sweet water.

She hardly noticed when he stripped away her last trivial disguise, her shift. She made no complaint when he pushed back the covers to absorb her with his all-too-perceptive eyes, for it let her study him in turn. When he ran his hand over her body, she moved toward it like metal to a lodestone and only wanted to touch him as he touched her.

She didn't, though. That would be too weakening. When his hands and mouth began again to play on her most sensitive spots, she sank into herself, observing with amazement the slow flowering of budding senses she had never known existed. . . .

But even as she inhaled at the wonder of her body, and reveled in its pleasuring, she fought to keep a part of her mind clear. She must not forget her purpose. If she understood this business between men and women at all, at some point he too would fall victim to sensation, and far more deeply than she.

When that happened, she would destroy him, despite this skillful pleasuring. She was more ruthless than Dona Maria.

She couldn't help hoping, however, that her buds would flower before that moment came.

Then she realized that flowering and clearheaded vengeance just might be incompatible.

Without conscious intent, she was sliding her hand over his body—hard muscle and bone under silken skin. Though she knew she should stop, she couldn't. What was worse, she longed to taste his salty sweat. She wriggled closer, then paused, tongue on skin, struggling to remember why she shouldn't entirely surrender. . . .

She did remember.

As his hand slid again between her welcoming thighs she gathered her wits and studied him, desperately seeking signs of his dissolution. She saw only dark-eyed attentiveness, as if she were a delightful book under study.

"Shouldn't you enter me now?" she asked, deliberately trying to break the spell.

His expression lightened to smiling. "Not yet. Not for a while yet. I'm enjoying this far too much." His eyes brightened with mischief and his fingers moved so that she gasped.

She seized his wrist. "Where is the pleasure for you?" Her small hand still didn't encircle him, however, and he twisted free without effort.

"It is pleasure to touch and taste you, Justina, and to see you move to my touch." Skillfully, he made her move again. "But the real joy is wakening you to this. Truly," he added with a grin, "it is better to give than to receive at Christmastide."

Afraid she'd grin back, Justina turned her head away, but he captured it and turned her back to face him as his fingers worked magic. "Look at me, Justina. Please."

Look at him.

Yes.

How could she tell when he was vulnerable if she did not watch him?

But in the end she did not watch him. Instead, she became lost in him, lost in those dark eyes that seemed to see within her and understand all the newfound mysteries.

With an artist's skill, he stripped away layer after layer of restraint, coaxing her past every hesitation, pushing her over each barrier, until the Justina entwined panting around him was a new creature entirely, a stranger to herself and to the world.

And then the world itself was gone.

And at the last moment, a tiny protesting part of her cried, *Oh, Simon, Simon, where are you in this?*

As Justina struggled to gather her wits, to focus and recall her purpose, he seized her wild hands, overwhelmed her trembling body, and slid slow and deep to burst her maidenhead.

She cried out, but more in shock at that unique sensation than in pain. As she tried to adjust to the stretched fullness, he moved in her, moved her around him, so that the disintegration threatened again.

She fought it, though. Now was his moment of weakness. This was the moment when she could rip his secrets from his soul.

What naïveté!

Jack Beaufort was certainly overwhelmed by sensation, but he was vulnerable to nothing but his own shattering lust.

When he rolled off her, he gathered her to him, looking at her again with those dangerous eyes. What he saw there killed his sated pleasure. "I'm sorry. Did I hurt you?"

She turned her head away. "Yes."

He stroked her soothingly. "It only hurts the once."

Justina stared at the dead pheasants, feeling as pathetic as they. It wasn't pain she spoke of. She had let him destroy her and gained *nothing*.

Not true, whispered a small voice. You have gained a new existence.

Not one I want! I have lost my armor. I have lost the battle and the war and am left naked.

"I wanted you to stop," she said, making herself rigid in his embrace.

After a moment, he freed her and turned onto his back. "Then it must have been too late, for I was not aware of it. I'm sorry. I can apologize all blasted night if you want, but it won't change anything."

"Just as you can't change the fact that Simon is dead."

He turned back to her with a frown. "What the devil has Simon to do with this?"

And Justina realized that she had, in a sense, won. A Pyrrhic victory, perhaps, but a victory all the same. They were both stripped down to raw truth. "You killed him," she said. "You caused his death. You betrayed him. And I came here to prove it."

She expected him to deny it, to throw up his guard again. She did not expect the naked shock and pain. "How did you know?"

Her heart almost stopped. Why had she not realized this moment would be so painful? "I just knew," she said, almost gently. "I have always known."

"The letter? There was something in the letter?"

"No. If there had been, I would have reported it to the authorities."

"Then how did you know?"

"You were just too lucky. You had to be a traitor."

He rolled over her then, pinning her down in the bed with his angry body. "A *traitor*? Is that what you think? Then why the devil were you so stupid as to come here tonight?"

She struggled fiercely, uselessly. "Because I could not live with you so fortunate!"

He captured her wrists in one strong hand and placed the other around her throat. "If I were a traitor, I'd strangle you now."

She swallowed, and felt his pressure there. "Then do it! Do it! I'd rather die than live like this!"

His hand jerked up to cover her mouth. "No. Never that! For Simon's sake, you will live, Justina. You will live as long as I can make you."

He made it sound like a curse out of hell.

They stared at one another, and Justina realized tears

were escaping to slither down her cheeks. She swallowed the rest of them. She did *not* cry.

But she certainly wasn't made of ice anymore. For good or ill she was thawed, softened, and opened to pain as subtle and complex as the pleasure he'd shown her.

Then she saw the tears in his eyes and knew that some of her pain was his.

Gently, he released her mouth.

She licked her lips. "What happened?"

He rolled out of the bed. Silently, he picked up a gray banjan that lay on the bench at the end of the bed and shrugged into it. Then he went to a wardrobe to fish out another, this time bright blue, and toss it to her. "Put that on and I'll tell you what you came here to learn."

She slid her arms into the soft wool robe, but stayed half under the bedcovers, watching him. Her Delilah plot had worked after all. Samson was shorn, and he was going to tell her all.

The only reason she didn't stop him was because she sensed that he needed to.

He sat on a chair some distance from the bed, once more lounging back, but this time, she thought, more with weary despair than ease. "I told you I become indiscreet when drunk," he said. "Then I went on to prove it. After that night in the estancia, I touched no more than a sip of wine for the rest of the war."

"You're trying to tell me you let something slip because you were drunk?"

"Drunk and in bed with a beautiful woman. A fatal combination, as you can see."

"And did you give up women, too?" she asked tartly.

His reply surprised her. "Yes, I gave up women, too. I'm sorry if I was out of practice."

"How would I know?" Horribly off balance, she hit out. "You were going to tell me how you killed Simon."

He didn't so much as flinch. "Yes, I was, wasn't I? I don't know if I can make it dramatic enough for you, though."

He met her eyes calmly. "It is simply as I said. I was indiscreet. I assumed Maria Bianca was as silly as she appeared to be and let her tease our next day's route out of me. She was very clever, actually. She pretended to beg for escort to her cousin's home, which led me in the end to explain that we were going nowhere near the place. In the course of which I told her where we *were* going."

His eyes were still steady. "The rest is as I told you. When she knew our route, she knew that our march would overtake the carts carrying the Cabrera wealth. To her credit, Maria Bianca did her damnedest to get us to stay for Christmas Day, but when I insisted on going on, we were doomed. Except me, of course, Maria Bianca's all too skillful lover."

He was right. It wasn't dramatic enough for her. She stared at him, wanting to believe that there was more, but saw, at last, the naked truth.

She put her elbows on her knees and sank her head in her hands. "But why call yourself damned? It was a mistake. A mistake anyone could make!"

She looked up to see him shrug. "It's the consequences that matter. My carelessness killed them all. If I'd died there, I'd have just felt stupid. But I was condemned to live, and live, and live."

"I'd think war gave many chances to die, if that was what you truly sought."

His lips twisted. "How true. But I'm Lucky Jack. A hail of bullets would take everyone but me. One horse threw me just before a cannonball would have shattered my head. A dense fog once stopped my entire regiment from finding one of the bloodiest engagements of the war. Sometimes I thought Simon was watching over me just to get his own back."

"If Simon was watching over you, it was because he cared."

As soon as Justina said it, she knew it was true. Simon had never been one for revenge, and would be the last person to hold a grudge over a mistake. If the dead could watch over those left back on earth, Simon must have been tearing his hair out for three years as his closest friend tried to kill himself and his beloved sealed herself in ice and pursued revenge.

Oh, Simon. I'm so sorry.

"So," Jack said, "now you have it all, though I doubt it will do you much good. In the heat of the war that story might have got me court-martialed. In peacetime, and with my exalted rank and list of war achievements, no one will act on it."

Justina rested her head in her hands again, trying to think, trying to sort logic from emotion, right from wrong. In the end she realized she couldn't hate anyone for such a small mistake, even one that had led to tragedy.

But what did that leave for her? She was thoroughly melted now, and as she'd feared, the Justina Travers she knew simply did not exist. That woman had dedicated three years to a pointless crusade; she had shaped herself into a weapon of destruction, armed to fight an enemy who had turned out to be rags and straw.

Simon, Simon. Why did you do this?

For she had no doubt that he had. She remembered

that dizzy spell back in Charles's office, when she'd felt guided to Torlinghurst. But she'd not been brought here for revenge. Simon had guided her here this Christmastide to learn this truth so that she could put all this behind her, pick up her life again, and live it to the full.

She looked at Jack. "I feel lost. I don't exist."

He rose slowly and came over to the bed. She saw his deformed but beautiful hand and experienced an insight. Or perhaps it was a message from beyond death.

"One musket ball got you."

He followed her gaze down to his hand. "In the ambush, yes. How did you know?"

"I guessed. You tried to save him."

"Of course. I tried to save them all." He took a deep breath. "I saw the flash of the musket and put out my hand to stop the ball. It was instinctive but futile. It went through and into him. I stood there begging them to shoot me. . . ."

He was lost again in the past—how much time did he spend back there, begging for death?—but then he shook his head and reached out to gently touch her cheek. "Put it behind you, Justina. Please. It's what he'd want. I remember talking once to a Portuguese priest who'd traveled in the East. He told me that there they believe that too much grief ties the dead to us and stops them from moving on. I think it's time for us both to let Simon go. Can we try?"

He held out that injured hand and she put hers into it.

He drew her out of the bed and to the window. Clear in the midnight-blue sky shone the Christmas star. "I would consider myself lucky for the first time in years," he said, "if you would stay with me and help me make something of this strange new life."

She turned to look at him. "Why?"

"Perhaps because you are the one person with whom I can be myself. I'm so tired of disguises. If I have to play the duke, I'd like to be able to retreat to these rooms now and then and just be Jack."

"Simon loved you."

He understood her. "Yes, I want to marry you for his sake, too. He can't like seeing you in servitude to the dragon."

Justina chuckled, and it was like the cracking of a shell. "Haven't you realized that was a fabrication? Your great-aunt doesn't know I exist."

He stared at her. "Disguises indeed! How did you get into Torlinghurst, then?"

"I came with the mummers."

Now he was smiling as if it were a newfound skill for him, too. "The fair maiden Melicent!"

"Yes, though I thought of myself as Delilah."

The smile didn't fade. "A role you play very well."

"I don't think so. You still have your hair and your eyes, your grace."

"You're just lucky that I don't have any coins in the pocket of this robe," he said with a wicked twinkle.

The ability to tease was as weak as the ability to walk might be to an invalid. But there was hope that it might grow stronger in time.

"What forfeit were you planning to inflict?" she asked.

"You'll have to wait and see. Perhaps it depends on your answer to my proposal."

Justina realized she hadn't said whether she would marry him or not. Moreover, she didn't know.

She turned to look at the shining star. "I wonder what Melicent thought when the dragon was dead and she realized she was supposed to bind herself to George for the rest of her life."

He rested a hand on the nape of her neck and rubbed her there. It was a touch that offered strength and caring all her life long. "Perhaps she saw that George needed her, and that was why he'd braved the dragon in the first place."

"The George downstairs thought he'd conquered his maiden."

He turned her gently to him, his hands on her shoulders. "This George has no such illusions. You have conquered me. But as I told you, I was slain years ago. I would listen to Simon speaking of his Justina, and look at your picture, and wonder why Lucky Jack was not nearly as lucky as he. In fact," he said, releasing her, "it seems wrong for me even to hope . . ."

She caught his hand, his scarred hand. "No. It isn't wrong. If you are tired of disguises, then so am I. Who else can I be honest with but you?" She searched his eyes. "You will not mind me speaking of him?"

"Never."

She chose her next words with care. "You understand that I might never feel for you as I still do for him?"

"Yes." His look was direct and undefended. "I never want to drive Simon out of your heart. But I don't think he would mind if we shared the space there one day. We shared many another billet."

Justina echoed his wistful smile, holding the miniature in her hand. "No, he wouldn't mind." She looked out again at the peaceful estate lit by the moon and starlight, considering it all. "I think perhaps this is Simon's Christmas gift to us. The traditional one of peace and joy. I have the peace already. It is strange to my heart, but very sweet. Even the dreadful conde can enjoy his estate, for I'll wound myself no more with hate. And I can believe in the possibility of joy, here, with you."

"And so can I." He put his arm around her as they looked out at the star. "Go in peace, Simon."

"Amen," said Justina, though with the tiniest ache in her heart. She knew it came from a healing wound, however, not a festering one. She turned to smile at the man beside her. "And I will marry you, your grace of Cranmoore, and do my best to make you think of yourself as Lucky Jack every day of your life."

She saw tears start in his eyes before he gathered her into his arms with a strength that almost crushed her. "Thank God. Thank God. And thank you, Simon. No man has ever received a Christmas gift as precious as this."

The Surprise Party

by Mary Balogh

It was snowing halfheartedly. Not enough to make a picturesque scene of the garden below the nursery window. Not even enough to whiten the ground. Only enough to dust the edges of the lawns with white powder and to blow in thin white streaks across the path. Only enough to make the sky heavy and leaden so that it seemed more like early evening than midafternoon.

It was not exactly the type of Christmas scene one dreamed of. But then Christmas was still three days away. Perhaps it would snow properly before then.

"Enough to build a snowman with," Rupert Parr said, frowning speculatively up at the sky through the window.

"Enough to make snow angels with," Patricia Parr, his sister, added, contemplating rather glumly the few thin flakes that were drifting slowly downward.

Caroline Parr was kneeling on the floor, her elbows on the window ledge, her chin in her hands, gazing outward. "Will Christmas come soon, Rupert?" she asked wistfully. "Will it snow?"

She remembered Christmas last year, when there had been goose and plum pudding to eat. But it had not been quite the happy day she had been led to expect. Nurse had been cross and Rupert and Patricia had been peevish. It had not snowed—Caroline could not really remember what snow was like. And Mama and Papa had not come home. They had had to go to an unexpected but very important meeting, Nurse had explained to Rupert, and would come home as soon as they could. They sent presents which arrived a week late.

"Tell me about Christmas," Caroline said now, addressing herself to her eight-year-old brother, whom she considered omniscient, though she did not turn her gaze from the outside world. "Tell me about snow."

But it was their nurse who answered. Caroline loved Nurse dearly, but she had been cross and sharptongued lately—even worse than she had been last Christmas.

"There will be no talk of Christmas this year," she said firmly. "And no talk of snowmen and snow angels either, Master Rupert and Miss Patricia. The two of you are old enough to know better. For shame, filling Miss Caroline's head with ideas that are not proper. There will be other years and other Christmases to enjoy."

"I beg your pardon, Nurse," Rupert said in the voice that always made Caroline want to hold his hand and rub her cheek against his arm for reassurance. It was his grown-up voice, not his real voice.

"You must understand, Master Rupert . . . ," Nurse said.

But Caroline stopped listening and watched the snow snakes slithering diagonally across the path, all going the same way. She watched for one going the other way, but there were none. They were all fleeing from a fierce dragon, she decided. The dragon was holding a beautiful princess captive. It was a bad dragon. Soon one of the snow snakes would turn back to fight the dragon and rescue the maiden and become a great hero. He would marry her and they would live happily ever after. She watched intently for the hero snake to slither back across the path, into the teeth of the wind.

She only half heard Nurse, who was reminding Rupert and Patricia that with Mama and Papa so recently passed on—Caroline sometimes wondered where it was they had passed on to, but when she had asked, Nurse had said it was heaven with angels singing around the throne of God and she was not to ask so many questions—they must not even think about presents or mince pies or caroling or anything else that would make them forget they were in mourning.

Patricia hated her black dresses, but Nurse would not let her wear anything else. Caroline did not mind hers. She never minded what Nurse put on her provided she was warm and comfortable.

"What is to become of us?" Rupert was asking Nurse behind Caroline's back. He was still using his grown-up voice. "Everything will be taken away, will it not? And the house sold. To pay Papa's debts. And you will not be able to stay with us because there will be no money to pay you. We will be sent to the orphanage, Nurse, will we not? I don't mind. I will look after Patricia and Caroline until they are grown up and married. I will go out and seek my fortune."

"And I will come with you, Rupert," Patricia said eagerly. "We will leave Caroline in the orphanage because she is too little and come back for her when we have made our fortune. I am seven. I can cook for you and mend for you."

"Don't talk silly," Nurse said sharply. "You will frighten Miss Caroline. Of course you will not be sent to the orphanage. Your aunt or your uncle will come for you and give you all a home. They were notified. They will come for you any day. Now, I want you two to get out your books and read. Come, Miss Caroline." Her voice softened somewhat. "Come and sit on Nurse's lap, dearie, and I will read you a story."

Caroline did as she was told and listened to the story of a little girl to whom very good things happened because she was always a very good little girl. But Caroline would have preferred to stay at the window, weaving stories about the snow snakes and the hidden dragon and the beautiful princess. Or she would have preferred hearing from Rupert about Christmas or about snow.

She wondered why they wore black and why there was to be no Christmas and no snowmen or snow angels and why they must go to the orphanage just because Mama and Papa had passed on. Mama and Papa had never come home anyway. She could not remember them much more clearly than she could remember snow.

Who were her aunt and uncle? she wondered, pillowing her head on Nurse's ample bosom and yawning loudly. She could not remember them either. Why were they coming?

Lady Carlyle moved her head closer to the carriage window and peered anxiously up at the sky. Snow had been threatening for the past few hours. Was it about to fall in earnest? She shivered despite the fact that she was dressed warmly and her legs were covered with a heavy rug and the brick at her feet was still almost warm, even though it was two hours since they had stopped at an inn for luncheon and had it heated again.

She hoped that at least she would reach her destination before it snowed. Not that she was traveling toward it with any great eagerness. She had never been

very close to Adrian. She had been even less so in recent years. His children were strangers to her. *All* children were strangers to her. She had never had a child
of her own despite seven years of marriage before her
widowhood began two years ago. Not that there had
been many opportunities . . .

Her lips thinned for a moment and she buried her
hands deeper inside her muff.

She had no idea what she was going to do with three
young children. The time had been when she had
wanted a family of her own, but the desire had died
during the first year of her marriage, and now she was
quite content with her childless state. And with her
widowhood. She liked being alone and independent.
She liked being one of London's most respected hostesses. She enjoyed the knowledge that invitations to
her weekly drawing rooms were coveted among members of both the *ton* and the intelligentsia. She did not
even mind the occasional label of bluestocking.

What, in heaven's name, was she going to do with
three children? She could not possibly have them live
with her. They would turn her home and her life upside
down. They would drive her insane. She had earned
her present very pleasant and peaceful life through
seven years of a dull marriage.

Adrian and Marjorie had led lives of selfish irresponsibility—and that was an understatement. They
had lived almost all their married life in London,
spending lavishly on expensive lodgings and fashionable clothes and costly jewels and amusing themselves
by gambling away money they did not have. Even
without the gambling they would have always been
deeply in debt. Adrian's small fortune and the property
he had inherited from their father had been gone within
the first year. But the most selfish thing they had ever

done was to bring three children into the world, only to neglect them almost totally. They had died, the two of them, in a gamehell brawl. Lady Carlyle suspected that their deaths might have been arranged by the money-lenders to whom they were helplessly indebted.

She felt a flash of the old anger against them, even though one was not supposed to harbor negative feelings against the dead. How dared they live so carelessly when they had had children to care for. And how dared they leave the responsibility of those children to her. Her anger was irritated by an accompanying guilt. She had been unable to grieve deeply for the death of her only brother. And she was unable to feel much sympathy for his innocent children who had been left behind. She was too aware of the fact that they had complicated her life, and selfishly—perhaps she was not so unlike Adrian after all—she did not want it complicated. And she resented the guilt that the knowledge brought with it.

Poor children. They were her nieces and nephew. But she could feel no kinship, no love for them. She had never seen them. She and Adrian had been estranged since soon after his marriage.

And why should *she* be the one on whom the children were to be foisted? Marjorie had had a brother—Viscount Morsey. He was a wealthy and influential man. He had more than one home. It would be easy enough for him to take the children and never really feel the burden of having them. But she would wager a fortune that he would ignore any appeal that had been made to him.

Her lips compressed again. Yes, it would be just like him to do that, to assume that someone else would look after them. He was an arrogant, cynical, hard-hearted man. She had learned that years ago. For years now she had avoided him, an easy enough task even though they were both frequently in London. He seemed just as eager to avoid her.

Well, she would see to it that he did not shirk all responsibility for the children. She would confront him. She would demand that he do his part.

But it was her Christmas that was going to be ruined, not his. She always enjoyed Christmas in town and its busy round of social pleasures. The chances were slim that she would be back in town in time for any of the celebrations. Especially if it snowed in earnest. Perhaps she would be incarcerated in the country for a week or more. She could think of no worse fate.

Yes, she could—incarceration in the country for a week or more *with three children, aged eight, seven, and four.* The very real possibility was unthinkable.

What on earth would she do with them? Apart from going insane?

For the last several miles the carriage had been stopping and starting as her coachman asked directions. But finally, it seemed, they had arrived. Lady Carlyle peered out of the window and grimaced. Adrian had bought this cottage with a night's winnings soon after losing his own property, her girlhood home. She had never seen the cottage before. It was no mansion. It was no hovel, either, but it had seen better days. There was an air of shabby gentility about it and to the garden before it. Clearly no more winnings had ever been spent on the upkeep of the property or on the hiring of servants to care for it.

She drew a deep breath. "Well, this is it, Netty," she said to her maid, who was beginning to stir from a lengthy nap in the far corner of the carriage. "A Christmas to remember."

But her carriage had not stopped at the garden gate,

she realized suddenly, but some distance to one side of it. When she pressed the side of her face to the window and peered ahead, she could see the reason. Another carriage was blocking the way, and someone was descending from it—a tall, well-formed gentleman, whose already broad shoulders were made more so by the many capes of his fashionable greatcoat and whose hat hid thick hair of a rich brown, she knew though she could not at present see it. And whose handsome face was marred by its usual arrogant expression.

Now her day, her *Christmas*, was complete, she thought irritably as he turned to look at her carriage. She drew her head away from the window in some haste. She would not have him believe that she craned her neck merely to catch a glimpse of *him*.

A moment later the door opened.

"Ah," Viscount Morsey said in the well-remembered voice she hated. He always sounded almost too bored to draw breath. "I see that I would have lost my wager had I been unwise enough to make it with anyone. You came."

He had felt grief at the news. Perhaps not as intense a grief as one would expect to feel for a sister who had died violently before reaching the age of thirty, but grief nevertheless. His grief had stemmed from his memories of her as a child and young girl. Before she had met and become besotted with Adrian Parr. Before she had defied him and married the wastrel. Before love, or whatever it was she felt for him, had made her so blindly devoted to him that she followed him through all the follies of his short life. Before she had given birth to children she neither wanted nor cared for.

Perhaps his grief lacked intensity because she had

become a person he disliked, a person he had turned his back upon years ago after discovering that the money she had begged from him to feed her children with had all been gambled away.

And it was all his fault. Unwilling guilt had weighed heavily on him after her death. If it were not for him and his early infatuation with a woman he now hated, Marjorie would never have met Parr. But he had shaken off the guilt. She had always been a silly, weak girl and difficult to handle. Perhaps she would have met Parr anyway or someone just like him. She had been immune to advice and even to commands. She had eloped with Adrian Parr when her brother had withheld his consent to the marriage.

Well, it was all history now. Though not quite all of it. There were the three children. The viscount had seen the boy as a baby. He had not seen either of the girls. But they existed, the three of them—a millstone about his neck. He knew nothing about children. He did not *want* to know anything about children. He had no wish to get himself involved with these three. But they were his nephew and nieces and he was their closest relative, with the exception of Lady Carlyle, their paternal aunt.

His nostrils flared at the very thought of the woman. Fortune hunter. Imposter—setting herself up as one of London's most fashionable hostesses after scheming and elbowing her way to the top. Bluestocking. His lips formed into an unbecoming sneer.

No, he certainly could not expect that Lady Carlyle would have the maternal instincts to cause her to rush to the assistance of three orphaned children. He would wager against it, in fact.

Christmas, of course, had been ruined. There was the necessity, for very decency's sake, of putting on

mourning and of curtailing his social involvements.
But he might have accepted the invitation to spend the
holidays on Hinckley's estate. There was to be conge-
nial company there, including Hinckley's daughter. . . .

But no. He was doomed to spend Christmas trying to
settle the future for three children who were strangers
to him. And from the look of the weather as his carriage drove closer to the cottage where they lived, he
might well be trapped there with them for a number of
days. What a delightful prospect!

What the devil would he do with three children?

He frowned at the cottage when his carriage finally
stopped outside its gate. It was small enough, though
larger than he might have expected, considering the
fact that Parr and Marjorie between them had wasted
both his property and small fortune and her considerable dowry and had got themselves deeply and irrevocably into debt. But it was a shabby enough place.
Gloomy. Depressing.

He felt rather sorry for the children. He wondered
how deeply they mourned. Marjorie and Parr had been
their parents, after all.

He became aware as he jumped down from his carriage that another was drawing up behind it. And a
glance in its direction revealed the face of Lady
Carlyle pressed to the glass, peering out at him. She
withdrew her face hastily enough. Of course. It would
be far beneath her dignity to give the impression that
she was in any way interested in him.

He was annoyed. She had proved him wrong and he
hated to be wrong. He would hate to think that she had
an ounce of compassion for children in her soul. And
the thought flashed through his mind that they would
be at the house together. With Christmas approaching.
And with a snowstorm imminent.

Bloody hell! He allowed his mind the luxury of the expletive.

Sometimes he hated the constraints placed upon him by the fact that he was a gentleman. He would have liked to ignore her presence and stride up the path to the cottage door alone. But he was a gentleman. He strode toward her carriage instead and opened the door. But he could not deny himself altogether the indulgence of bad temper.

"Ah," he said, looking into her beautiful, cold, arrogant face, so at variance with the vivid red hair visible beneath the brim of her bonnet. "I see that I would have lost my wager had I been unwise enough to make it with anyone. You came."

Her lovely wide mouth became a thin lin and her jaw became so hard that he imagined her teeth must be just about cracking from the force with which they were pressed together.

"I came, *my lord*," she said, her voice every bit as icy as the day, "because in my wildest imaginings I did not believe that you would. It seems that we can both occasionally be wrong."

He did not like having to look up at her. Yet there was no sign of her coachman approaching to put down the steps for her to descend.

"Allow me, ma'am," he said, and he leaned inside the carriage, pushed aside the blanket that covered her legs, set his hands at her waist, and swung her down to the roadway to stand in front of him. That was better. The top of her head barely reached his chin. Her waist, he noticed belatedly, was as small now as it had ever been. And she still wore the same perfume she had used to wear, a subtle scent that teased rather than assaulted the nostrils.

"Thank you," she said with curt sarcasm, "for awaiting my permission, my lord. Your hands?"

He removed them and pursed his lips.

"Ma'am." He bowed with exaggerated courtesy and contemplated pleasurable ways of curbing her sharp tongue. "Will you take my arm so that we may approach the house in seemly fashion to meet our nephew and nieces?" He waited for her answer.

"Thank you." She elevated her chin and her nose—though both of necessity moved together, she succeeded in making it appear to be two quite separate motions. She set her arm lightly along his as if he were about to lead her into a dance and so saved herself from the appearance of having been bested.

They proceeded through the gate and up the path in stiff silence.

What a Christmas it was shaping up to be, Viscount Morsey thought. A shabby country cottage, an unwelcome snowstorm, three young children, a cold, haughty woman. Good God, what a Christmas!

He wondered by what madness he had once imagined he loved the woman. And he wondered for what unknown good deed the powers above had rewarded him by saving him from marrying her.

Two carriages. Not one, but two. They had all felt an almost sickening excitement at the sight of one drawing up outside the gate, especially since it was far grander than any carriage they had ever seen before. But when the second appeared behind it, they were saucer-eyed and ecstatic. Except that they were not allowed to enjoy the sight for long. Nurse whisked them away from the window and was soon scrubbing their faces with painful haste and changing the girls' aprons for newer and cleaner ones.

It seemed that their aunt and uncle had arrived.

Rupert and Patricia, instantly alert, wanted to rush downstairs to meet the visitors. But Nurse said that neither the excitement nor the eagerness to leave the nursery was seemly. They must wait quietly where they were until their aunt and uncle had recovered from their journey and chose to call on them or summon them. And they must be on their best behavior.

Children should be seen and not heard. Children should speak only when spoken to. Caroline recited the rules in her head, though they were unnecessary. She was glad they had not been allowed to run downstairs. She hoped her uncle and aunt would take a long time recovering from their journeys. She hoped she would remain unspoken to even after they had.

They came very soon. Nurse had said that they would want to wash and change and have a cup of tea, but Nurse must have been mistaken. Caroline tried to hide behind her when they came into the nursery, but she was pushed firmly forward after Nurse had curtsied deeply, and so Caroline clung to her brother's sleeve instead and stood half behind him, peeping around his arm.

"Rupert," her uncle said. "Patricia. Caroline." He looked at them each in turn and inclined his head to them. Caroline ducked right behind Rupert when it came her turn. Her uncle was a stern-looking man and very tall. She thought he was taller than Papa had been, though she could not remember Papa very clearly. Papa had never bowed to her. She liked being bowed to. Princesses were always bowed to.

"Hello, children." Her aunt smiled at each of them in turn. She was a very pretty lady. She had hair like Patricia's. Caroline had heard the servants say that Patricia's quick temper came from having red hair.

Though Caroline had not noticed that Patricia was bad-tempered. She wondered if her aunt was. Her aunt, she noticed, would like to hide behind her uncle's sleeve as Caroline was hiding behind Rupert's. Her aunt was feeling shy.

"Good afternoon, sir. Good afternoon, ma'am." Rupert was bowing, taking Caroline's hand forward with him. He was using his grown-up voice.

"Good afternoon, Uncle. Good afternoon, Aunt." Patricia's curtsy was one of the best she had ever accomplished. She did not lift her skirt too high or topple sideways. Nurse would be pleased.

There was a slight pause and Caroline realized that it was her turn. Her thumb wandered toward her mouth, but she caught herself in time and lowered it firmly. Thumb-sucking was for babies. She moved in against Rupert's back for reassurance and fixed the one eye that was not hidden against his sleeve on her aunt.

"There are snow snakes," she said.

At first she thought she had said the wrong thing. Rupert and Patricia shuffled uncomfortably, and her aunt and uncle looked at her as if they did not understand. They were *both* looking at her.

"Are there?" her aunt asked at last. "Where?"

"Out there." Caroline motioned with her free arm to the window, though she did not turn her head. "On the path. They are all going the same way."

"Caroline!" Patricia's voice was agonized.

"Caroline has an imagination, ma'am," Rupert said, rushing to her defense. "She is only four. She will grow out of it. Did you have a pleasant journey?"

"Thank you, yes," their aunt said.

But their uncle was talking at the same time. "Perhaps you would be good enough to show us, Caroline," he was saying. And he had stepped forward and was stretching out a hand for hers.

Caroline looked all the way up into his face. He was not smiling and he still looked stern. But there was something in his eyes, something that took away some of her terror. But she had been talking to her aunt, and she had not intended to show them the snow snakes. She had merely been making conversation. Nurse always said that ladies—and gentlemen—had to learn to make conversation. She reached out a hand tentatively and set it in her uncle's large one. She left the sanctuary of Rupert's back and led the way to the window. Her aunt came too.

"There," Caroline said, pointing downward. The snakes were still there, but there were more of them now and they were moving faster. She could not see them too clearly herself, though, because she was not kneeling down and leaning across the window seat.

And then her uncle set his hands at her waist and lifted her up to stand on the seat. He kept his hands where they were so that she would feel safe. Caroline did not like to tell him that it was forbidden to stand on the window seat. She waited for Nurse to scold him, but she did not do so. Perhaps Nurse was being polite to guests.

"They do indeed look like snakes," her uncle admitted.

"And they really are all going the same way," her aunt said. "It is because of the wind, you know. They are not as strong as the wind and must go wherever it decides to blow them."

Caroline was encouraged to say more. People usually called her silly when she said such things. These days she usually kept them to herself.

"One is going to go back the other way soon," she

said. "A hero snake. A prince. He is going to rescue the princess."

"Ah," her uncle said. "Of course. Hero princes always rescue princesses."

"And marry them and live happily ever after," her aunt added.

"Miss Caroline is given to flights of fancy, my lord and my lady," Nurse said quickly, her voice breathless and flustered. "If the children are a trouble to you . . ."

"They are not," Caroline's uncle said. "They are our kin, Mrs. Chambers."

"Perhaps you would care to take the opportunity to go down to the kitchen for a cup of tea, Mrs. Chambers," her aunt added.

"The fierce dragon has taken her captive," Caroline said. It was getting dark. It did not look as if the hero were going to slither back across the path today. Perhaps tomorrow. The princess would have to spend another night in captivity.

"Dragons have a tendency to do that," her uncle said.

"I do believe it is starting to snow in earnest," her aunt said. She did not sound too happy about it.

"We are not to build snowmen," Rupert said. He was talking in his own voice again. His own voice, but sad.

"Or to make snow angels," Patricia said. She sounded sad too.

Caroline remembered last year and the dreams that had not come true. They were not going to come true this year either. "Or to have Christmas," she said, forgetting about her snow snakes and staring into the gloom of the road beyond the gate. "*Is* there Christmas? Or is it just a story?"

"We are in mourning," Rupert said. He had changed voices again.

"Our mama and papa have passed on," Patricia said, "and we must wear black out of respect for them."

There was a silence.

Caroline turned on the window seat and looked into her uncle's face. It was not so far above her own now. He looked a little bit like a prince himself, only old, of course. She liked his eyes. They stopped her from feeling frightened of him. And she liked his embroidered waistcoat. Her eyes were drawn to the gleaming black button visible above his coat. She reached out a finger and touched it. It was smooth and ridged where the pattern was.

"*Is* there Christmas?" she asked him. She suddenly felt very sad, expecting that he would say no, just as Nurse always said that there were no fairy godmothers and no elves at the bottom of the garden. And no dragons with captive princesses. She wanted desperately for there to be Christmas.

His eyes—they were blue, like Rupert's—changed and became quite noticeably kind. "Yes, there is Christmas," he said. "There is always Christmas, every year."

"But not this year," Rupert said. He remembered his manners. "Sir."

"And there is a story too," their aunt said. "A wonderful story that comes true every year."

"Except this year," Patricia said.

"Mama and Papa passed on to heaven," Caroline told her uncle, in case he had not heard Patricia or did not know the completion of their story. "They are with angels. And there is a throne."

"Yes." Her uncle did something unexpected. He slid one arm down from her waist to the back of her knees and the other up about her back, and he lifted her into his arms. She was looking down at her aunt and at

Rupert and Patricia. She liked being up there. She felt
safe. And she liked the way he smelled. It was all
snuffy and leathery and soapy. She set one arm about
his neck.

"Are we going to the orphanage, Uncle?" Patricia
asked.

"No," their uncle said.

"No," their aunt said at the same moment.

"Why did Mama and Papa pass on?" Caroline asked
her uncle.

His arms tightened about her, but he did not answer
her question.

"Oh, dear," her aunt said, and Caroline could tell
that she was pretending to be cheerful when she did
not feel cheerful. "I think we had better ring for tea."

The tiresome butler—or, rather, the servant who performed the functions of butler, footman, groom, and
probably gardener too—had placed them at opposite
ends of a rather long dining table. He—Viscount
Morsey—was at the head, of course. She was at the
foot. She had thought of asking for a dinner tray to be
sent to her room, but she would not give him the satisfaction of believing that he had driven her into hiding.

She looked down the table at him while the servant
was ladling out her soup. "They will not be sent to an
orphanage, of course," she said. "But I cannot be expected to be solely responsible for their care. I live in
town, and neither the place nor my home is adapted to
the upbringing of young children. You, on the other
hand, have three homes, two of them in the country.
You would not be inconvenienced by them at all."

"Except that I am a single man," he said. "Children
need a mother's care."

"And a father's," she added, bristling.

"Girls need a mother figure on whom to pattern their ways," he said, spreading his napkin rather ostentatiously on his lap and picking up his soup spoon. He had changed into evening clothes grand enough for a court appearance—black, of course, she noticed, and wondered if he had dressed so immaculately in mockery of her. But then he had always dressed well and still did, if the occasional glimpses she had of him in town were anything to judge by. And he was handsomer now than he had been. . . . Well, perhaps not. But his good looks irritated her.

"And boys need a father figure for the same reason," she said. "This family includes both genders, my lord."

"Perhaps," he said, his empty spoon suspended halfway between his mouth and his dish, "you would suggest that we split the family, my lady? You take the girls and I take the boy?"

"Absolutely not," she said tartly. "Did you not see how the little one depends upon her elder brother and how protective he is of both sisters? They must remain together."

"At one of my country houses," he said, setting his spoon down altogether and gazing down the table at her with half-closed eyes. The bored look. The look she had found irresistible as a girl. To say that she had been head over ears for him was to understate the case. Foolish girl.

"They will not be an inconvenience to either of us there," she said.

She cursed him silently for not making an immediate reply. Silence stretched and her words—her callous, heartless words—seemed to echo and reecho about the walls of the large and gloomy dining room. How could she have spoken them? Worse, how could she have meant them?

"Just as they were no inconvenience here to Marjorie and your brother," he said at last.

She felt her cheeks grow hot and made matters worse. "Do not pretend that you want them any more than I do," she said. "Both our lives are set on a course of childlessness."

"Not really," he said, nodding to the butler to remove his dish and bring on the next course. "I am a viscount, heir to an earl's title, and this year I reached that dreaded landmark for a single man of title and property, my thirtieth birthday. I will doubtless do my duty and marry and set up my nursery within the next few years."

She felt her blush deepen. They had once intended to set it up together. Four children, they had both agreed. They would do it in good order, he had said laughingly. Boy, girl, boy, girl—the perfect family.

"Why did you never have children?" he asked.

She looked up at him, shocked. "My lord?" she said.

"I have often wondered," he said. "You married him eagerly enough, less than a month after you ended our betrothal, as I recall."

She drew breath slowly. "My marriage and my childlessness are none of your concern, *my lord*," she said. "None whatsoever." She had had no children because after the first month of her marriage Carlyle had made it clear to her that he far preferred his men friends to her, and guessing at his meaning, she had kept her bedchamber door locked against him ever after. He had married her for respectability, she suspected—a suitable fate, perhaps, when she had married him for escape.

"No. My apologies." He glanced toward the window, across which the curtains had not yet been drawn. "This is the most damnable time for a snowstorm. We are going to be trapped here together for days, Ursula. And with three children. Over Christmas. Can you imagine a worse nightmare?"

"No," she said curtly. "Not even if you gave me an hour to think about it. And I would be obliged if you watched your language in my presence, my lord. And I have not granted you permission—lately—to use my given name."

"Lady Carlyle, ma'am," he said—there was as much frost in his voice as there was snow outside, "do accept my humble apologies."

She tackled the veal course with as much appetite as if she had already eaten twelve hearty courses.

"They have to wear black," he said, "for parents they rarely saw. And they must behave as if they are in deepest mourning." He sounded faintly angry.

"They will not be allowed to play in the snow tomorrow," she said, "though there will undoubtedly be plenty of it out there to tempt them. No snowmen and no snow angels. Or snowball fights. Or sliding on the paths. Or shrieking for the mere fun of it."

"And no Christmas," he said. "No decorations, no presents, no goose or any of the trimmings, no caroling. Just perhaps a sedate attendance at a Christmas church service."

"The little one asked if there is such a thing as Christmas," she said. "She is four years old. Surely she can remember Christmas from last year, even if not from the year before." She had been disturbed by the question. She faced its full implications now. She looked up at him, her eyes troubled. "Have they never had a proper Christmas, Timothy? Were Marjorie and Adrian never here with them? Not even at Christmas?"

She realized too late that she had used his name and hoped he had not noticed.

"Christmas is a time adults are often most reluctant to give to anyone but themselves," he said.

His words stung as she remembered her own peevish irritation in the carriage earlier.

"Myself included, *my lady*," he said, with such emphasis on the last words that she knew he had noticed her slip of the tongue.

"It is criminal," she said at last. "If you and I miss Christmas, we merely miss a few parties. If children miss Christmas, they miss one of the magic elements of childhood. Have Marjorie and Adrian deprived these children of it in the past? Are they to deprive them again this year because they have died? Is it fair to make children mourn?"

"For two people they scarcely knew?" He was not eating his pudding. He was leaning back in his chair and turning his spoon over and over on the cloth with one hand. "Is the making of snowmen and snow angels disrespectful to the dead?"

"Who makes the rules by which these children live?" she asked.

"Their nurse?" he said. "A competent, affectionate, unimaginative woman, by my judgment."

"In charge of at least one child of superb imagination," she said, thinking with unexpected fondness of the snow snakes and the snake prince and the dragon and princess. "Should it not be you or I making the rules?"

He pursed his lips and looked at her from those maddeningly drooping lids. "You want to give them Christmas?" he asked. "Do you know how, Urs—, my lady?"

She thought. "It has been a long time," she said.

"But I can remember. I can remember the magic and perhaps what caused it. And you?"

He too thought for a while. "Yule logs," he said. "Holly, ivy, mistletoe. Stirring the pudding. Wrapping gifts. Unwrapping them. Singing carols."

"And the Christmas story," she said.

"Ah, yes." He laughed softly. "Sometimes one almost forgets. So we are to break all the rules and sacrifice our own comfort and time in order to give our nephew and nieces a Christmas to remember—before they are incarcerated on one of my country estates. Snow is always an extra bonus at Christmas, of course. Are you prepared to acquire red and tingling fingers and toes—and nose, my lady, in the cause of entertaining three children neither of us really cares a damn about?"

"Mind your language," she said sharply, glaring at him. "And it is not true." Her eyes wavered from his when she remembered that it was perfectly true, as she would realize when she had got past this madness of wanting to give them something they had never had. "It is not true. I felt something in the nursery earlier. Rupert is trying to be the man of the family. He is trying to be brave. And Patricia is trying to be worthy of him. The little one is simply adorable. Patricia has my red hair. Rupert has your blue eyes. Caroline is quite herself. They might almost be—"

"Ours?" His eyebrows had shot up and his eyes had opened wide to reveal the full extent of their blueness. "Hardly, my dear ma'am. We have never bedded down together, even once, though we came close on that one occasion in Vauxhall when your mama allowed us to slip free of her chaperonage for almost a whole blissful hour."

He had kissed her hotly, with opened mouth and

probing tongue. His hands had wandered all over her—on top of her clothing—as had hers over him. She had been pressed, and had pressed herself, hard enough against him and had known enough about life even then to realize how aroused he was and how easy and pleasurable it would be to couple there on the darkened path beyond the main thoroughfare. She was still not sure which of them had ensured that it had not happened.

It was a memory she did not care to take out of the recesses of her brain with any great regularity.

"It is just like you," she said, "to have the vulgarity to remind me of that indiscretion."

"Is it?" he said. "Am I vulgar, ma'am? I suppose that to a bluestocking like yourself most activities that are not of the intellect appear vulgar."

"Touché!" she exclaimed, slapping down her napkin on the table and rising to her feet. "I shall leave you to your port, my lord."

"On the contrary, ma'am," he said, getting up too and coming toward her in order to offer his arm. "We will adjourn to the drawing room in order to plan the Christmas we are going to give the children who could not possibly be of our own bodies. Do you suppose we can remain civil to each other long enough to make it happen?"

"I always know how to be civil, my lord," she said.

"Except," he said, "when you are ending a betrothal."

"I believe your memory is at fault, my lord," she said. "I believe the ending of our betrothal was at least mutually agreed upon. I believe I was accused of being mercenary and conniving. Not quite the words of a man who valued his betrothal."

"And I was cold and tightfisted and hard-hearted,"

he said. "Not quite the type of accolade a man expects of his betrothed."

"You were quite right," she said. "This is a *damnable* situation we find ourselves in. I cannot imagine anyone in whose company I would less like to spend a few days. Even the devil himself would be preferable." It was his nearness, the firmness of his arm muscles beneath her hand, the heat of his body, the smell of him, all so strangely familiar, that was doing it. She hated his nearness. She hated the thought that they must live in the same house for an indeterminate number of days, and *sleep* in the same house.

Perhaps, she thought, one could hate so intensely only someone one had once loved with an equal intensity. It was not a comforting thought.

"The question is," he said, seating her in the drawing room and standing before her, his hands clasped at his back, "can we put aside this mutual antipathy for each other, my lady, in order to bring a little happiness into the lives of innocent children. I can. Can you?"

"Yes," she snapped at him. "Yes, I can. But we must find something a little less personal on which to converse, my lord. Shall we begin with the weather?"

"It seems a topic on which there is much to be said at the moment," he said, seating himself opposite her, taking a snuffbox out of his pocket, and flicking it open with his thumb in a well-remembered gesture.

This was certainly not going to be easy.

He stood at the window of his bedchamber, drumming his fingers on the sill and staring outward. It was as he had expected, only perhaps worse. The light of morning hurt his eyes, though the sky was still full of heavy clouds and there was not the glimmering of a sign of the sun. It was still snowing, in fact. His eyes

hurt because there was nothing outside except whiteness. Nothing. Even the fence posts were laden with
snow, and the branches of the trees. It was impossible
to know where the lawn ended and the path began or
where the road began and ended. The gate was hardly
visible. It would be next to impossible to open it. At a
guess he would say that at least a foot of snow had
fallen during the night.

Wonderful! All his predictions had come true. They
were well and truly marooned in this house for days.
For Christmas. He and Lady Carlyle and the three children. And he would not even have the dubious comfort
of shutting himself in his room or in the bookless library downstairs with the few books he had brought
with him and a decanter of brandy. Just last evening he
had agreed to break all the rules of decency and propriety in order to allow the children to enjoy Christmas.
He had not changed his mind, but he was realizing this
morning that giving three young children a Christmas
was going to involve some considerable exertion on
his part.

He could not expect *Lady Carlyle* to put herself out.
It had not escaped his notice that she had avoided answering his question about her willingness to expose
her fingers and toes and nose to the cold of the outdoors. Doubtless she would remain indoors, smiling
encouragement through the windows. Perhaps even
that would be too far from the fire for her.

He scowled and his fingers drummed harder. He
should have let her know that he was coming down
here himself. She could have stayed in London. But,
damn it, that would not have been fair. It was as much
her responsibility as his to arrange for the future of
their orphaned nephew and nieces. More hers than
his—she was a woman, after all, and children were a

woman's domain. Though he had the grace to admit—irritably—to himself that there was little justice in that argument either.

But he wished she had stayed away or that she had given him notice of her intention to come here so that *he* could have stayed away. It was not a large cottage. Their bedchambers were next to each other. He turned his head to glance at the wall between his chamber and hers. He had looked at the wall several times during a restless and almost sleepless night. He had even found himself idly calculating how many feet there must be between his bed and hers.

And he had found himself remembering unwillingly the lithe, vividly beautiful, smiling, intelligent, witty girl she had been during her first season. And his own deep infatuation with her. And hers with him. They had been betrothed after two months, even though she was from an untitled family and had almost nothing for a dowry. For a month after that they had planned and dreamed and loved—innocently. The only real embrace they had shared was that one at Vauxhall.

He had known many restless, almost sleepless nights in those days.

And then her brother, whose unsavory reputation he had ignored because he loved her, had started paying attention to his sister, who at the age of seventeen had not even been brought out yet. And the two of them, who had been meeting behind his back, had soon declared their intention of marrying. They had driven Ursula and him apart. They had quarreled bitterly, each defending a brother or sister that each cast off just a short while later. But not soon enough to save their own betrothal.

The viscount drummed his fingers faster yet. He had had a narrow escape. Before he had been able to gather together the shreds of his pride in order to go to her and apologize and patch things up, she had announced her betrothal to Carlyle and had married him almost immediately after. Such had been the depth of her feelings for him.

He turned resolutely from the window and crossed the room to the door. He did not normally go without breakfast, but he did not feel like any this morning. He did not feel like being sociable or a prey to her sharp tongue. Not that she was likely to be up yet. Most ladies of his acquaintance, and even more so those who were not ladies, did not emerge from their boudoirs until close to noon. But he was not willing to take the risk. He turned his steps in the direction of the nursery. At least taking the children outside would give him a chance to escape from her altogether for a few hours.

He turned the handle of the door quietly and opened the door slowly. Perhaps even the children were not up yet. But they were, and predictably they were clustered in front of the window with their nurse. No—their nurse was not slender. Neither did she have red hair.

Damnation! His mind reached for—and found—a few far more satisfactory words with which to describe his feelings as he stepped into the room and closed the door behind him. The children's nurse was curtsying deeply somewhere off to his right. He turned his head and nodded to her before giving his attention to the group by the window.

"Good morning, sir."

"Good morning, Uncle."

A frosty inclination of a proud head.

Big brown eyes staring silently upward from beneath soft brown curls.

The way I spent my Christmas, he thought ruefully,

returning the greetings and strolling across the room toward them.

"An empty, white world," he said, looking out over their heads. "I believe your snow snakes have been buried, Caroline."

She shook her head and pointed. When he looked down, he could see that sure enough, there were snakes—far longer ones—blowing across the top of the snow cover.

"Ah," he said.

"They are going to the ice palace," the child said. "Where the prince lives."

"I see. They are going to tell him so that he can go and rescue the princess," he said. He had almost forgotten the magic wonderland of a child's imagination, the world in which anything could be something else and nothing was impossible. He felt a sudden and quite unexpected wave of nostalgia.

"Patricia is going to paint, sir," Rupert said. "She is a good painter. I am going to practice my penmanship. I make too many blots when I write and my letters are different sizes."

"But he tries, Uncle," Patricia said. "And he is getting better."

The viscount looked down at them, at the brave little eight-year-old boy who was trying valiantly to be a man and to ignore the snow beyond the window, and at the loyal little seven-year-old redhead, who would defend her brother in any way she could from an uncle's possible wrath over a blot or a malformed letter.

Something that felt very like his heart turned inside him.

His eyes met Lady Carlyle's and held them. She looked steadily back.

"I left it for you," she said. "Men are generally the rule-makers."

He looked down at the upturned faces of his nephew and nieces, faces without any hope, but with only a quiet acceptance of the way things were and must be.

He clasped his hands at his back. "Do painting and penmanship sound more inviting than going outside into the snow to play and build snowmen and make snow angels and throw snowballs?" he asked. "If they do, we will forget about going outside. But I for one will be sorry."

The little one gazed up at him without a noticeable change of expression. An almost painful hope came alive in the eyes of the other two.

"My lord—" The nurse sounded almost panic-stricken.

He turned to look at her, his eyebrows raised. He shamelessly used his haughtiest, most aristocratic manner. "Yes, Mrs. Chambers?"

"My lord," she said. "The vicar. The Misses Hickman-Pugh. There would be a scandal."

He would have verbally consigned the vicar and the Misses Hickman-Pugh, whoever they were, to the devil, but he remembered the presence of the children and the two reprimands for his language he had received the evening before. "We will use the back garden so that no one will see and be scandalized, Mrs. Chambers," he said. "If, that is"—he turned back to the children—"anyone wishes to accompany me outside. If not, I shall stay inside too. It is no fun playing in the snow alone."

"I'll come, sir," Rupert said hastily. "If it is not improper and disrespectful to Mama and Papa."

"It is not, sweetheart," Lady Carlyle said quietly.

Lord Morsey's eyes flew to hers. She had called him

that—twice—during the month of their betrothal. But she was smiling down at their nephew, something like tenderness in her eyes.

"I'll come too." Hope sounded almost like agony in Patricia's voice. "May we, Nurse? Please, please?"

"With respect to Mrs. Chambers, Patricia," Lady Carlyle said firmly, "it must be said that your uncle Timothy now stands in place of your papa, since your papa is—has passed on. If Uncle Timothy says you may play outside in the snow, then you may do so."

"Oh," Patricia said, her eyes widening with longing.

"I am going to make a snowman eight feet tall," Rupert cried, his eyes beginning to sparkle, his voice sounding like an exuberant child's. "And six feet broad."

Someone was patting one leg of the viscount's pantaloons, just above the knee. Big brown eyes were gazing up at him. "Are you our Uncle Timothy?" Caroline asked.

"The one and only." He smiled at her. "And this is your Aunt Ursula." He realized that the children had not even known their names. He should not have turned his back completely on Marjorie, he realized. He should have tolerated her, and the intolerable Parr, if only for the sake of the children. Children needed uncles and aunts. And cousins. He thought briefly of the four cousins—two boys and two girls—he and Ursula might have been able to present them with by now.

"Nurse will bundle you all up warmly," he said. "We will meet downstairs in ten minutes' time. Are you coming too, Caroline?"

She nodded. Her face was still tilted up sharply to him. How could any parents with three such children look for treasure elsewhere? he wondered, setting a hand lightly on her soft curls.

"Can Aunt Ursula come too?" she asked him.

"I believe your aunt would prefer the comfort of the indoors," he said. "Grown ladies usually do."

"What?" He heard the indignation in Lady Carlyle's voice before he looked up to see her nostrils flaring, her eyes flashing, and her hair glowing—he could remember teasing her that her hair seemed to take on more vivid color when she was angry about something. "I have never heard anything more ridiculous in my life. I am to be denied the fun of romping outdoors after a rare snowstorm merely because I am a grown lady and ladies usually are milksops? *This* one is not, my lord." She turned in the direction of the door. "I shall see you all downstairs, suitably attired for the outdoors, in *nine* minutes." The door closed none too gently behind her.

"I think Aunt Ursula wants to go out to play," Caroline whispered.

The other two children whooped and squealed and snorted with glee at the idea of a grown lady wanting to go out to play, and Caroline giggled at the reaction her words had provoked. It was the first time the three of them had really looked or sounded like children since his arrival, Viscount Morsey thought.

"She was bristling like a hedgehog when I suggested she might want to stay indoors, was she not?" he said. "Grown ladies have to be handled with kid gloves, you know."

His words threw the children into spasms of renewed hilarity.

Viscount Morsey, deliberately avoiding looking at their nurse and her reaction, smirked and left the room.

* * *

It was wonderful. It was the most wonderful time she had ever had in her life. There was no doubt about it in Caroline's mind. There was nothing else to compare to it—even the picnic the Misses Hickman-Pugh had taken them on last summer when they had got to ride in a landau and when she had got to hold Miss Olga Hickman-Pugh's parasol and even to twirl it above her head until Miss Iola Hickman-Pugh had remarked that she might break it and Miss Olga had taken it back and kissed her on the cheek and called her a dear child.

Even that had not been *nearly* as wonderful as the morning playing in the snow turned out to be.

It started disastrously. Or what seemed to be disastrously. Caroline ran out the back door after Rupert into the deep white snow, skidded before she had taken three steps, and landed flat on her back. She did not hurt herself—there was too much snow and she was wearing too many clothes. But there was the shock of falling so suddenly and the coldness of snow under her collar and up her cuffs and on her cheeks and in her mouth. And there was the humiliation. Everyone laughed.

Caroline might have cried, though she rarely did so. But no sooner had she fallen and everyone had started laughing than Uncle Timothy skidded quite clumsily and bellowed quite deafeningly and landed with a great thud on his back and roared with fury when the laughter was suddenly turned on him. Until Rupert took a step closer to see if Uncle Timothy was really hurt and their uncle caught him by his ankle and tumbled him down too. And when Patricia ran to help *him* up, Uncle Timothy reached up with both hands to catch her by the waist and roll her in the snow.

And then they were all laughing, Caroline too. Except for Aunt Ursula, who stood with her hands on her hips and told them that she had never in her life seen four people make such spectacles of themselves. But Caroline noticed that her eyes were twinkling as she said it, so she did not mean it. And then Uncle Timothy stretched out one long leg and hooked his boot around one of her ankles, and she toppled down too.

And they all laughed again. Aunt Ursula too this time. Though she threatened to get Uncle Timothy back. And she did too. After they had all got up and brushed themselves off and were wading away into the garden to find a good spot for building snowmen, Aunt Ursula lagged behind with Caroline, stooped down to pick up a handful of snow, molded it into a ball, winked at Caroline, and hurled it at Uncle Timothy's back. It hit him on the neck, where the snow was bound to drip down inside his collar.

Caroline giggled. She giggled even harder when Uncle Timothy whirled around and, faster than anyone could blink, formed a ball of snow of his own and threw it right into Aunt Ursula's face. Which meant, of course, that Aunt Ursula had to get him back again. Soon there were snowballs zooming through the air, even though Uncle Timothy was roaring out that it was unfair they were all throwing theirs at him.

"Children know how to defend a lady's honor," Aunt Ursula yelled back at him. "And this lady knows how to defend her own, my dear lord."

But Caroline knew that it was all in fun. That was what made it so wonderful. And Uncle Timothy only threw the littlest snowballs at her. He hit her every time until she was so helpless with giggles that she could not throw back.

They finally made the snowmen. Or rather, Rupert and Uncle Timothy made a snowman, fat and round and tall. Caroline preferred to make a dragon and Aunt Ursula and Patricia helped her, even though Aunt Ursula at first declared that she had no idea what a dragon looked like or how they were to build one. Rupert said the dragon they built looked like a tired cow, but Uncle Timothy disagreed and said that their dragon definitely looked the type to run off with a beautiful princess. And then he disappeared into the house and came back with carrots and a few pieces of coal. He had left Cook with her jaw hanging, he told them, but no self-respecting snowman or snow dragon was complete without a nose and eyes and a few buttons.

"Does a dragon have a nose?" he asked Aunt Ursula after he had finished with Rupert's fat man. He was holding the remaining carrot in his hand.

"Without a doubt," Aunt Ursula said. "But not buttons, I suppose. Does our dragon have buttons, Caroline?"

"He has fangs," Caroline said. And she was allowed to put on the carrot fangs before they all stood back and laughed at their creations. Caroline thought that her dragon looked too lovable to kidnap a princess, but she did not say so. She did not want to hurt Aunt Ursula's feelings or Patricia's. She loved her dragon.

"And now Patricia's snow angels," Aunt Ursula said. "Unless everyone's fingers and toes are ready to fall off and everyone would prefer to go inside by the fire to drink chocolate."

"Coward," Uncle Timothy said, which was a rude thing to say, but Caroline could tell that he was only teasing. "Shall we let Aunt Ursula go inside for her chocolate, children? Ladies are such delicate creatures, you know."

Aunt Ursula was the first to make a snow angel.

Uncle Timothy and Rupert did not make any at first. They merely watched.

"What is the matter?" Aunt Ursula asked. "Is the snow too cold for you, my lord?"

"Snow angels always look distinctly feminine," Uncle Timothy said. "I do believe making them is beneath our dignity, is it not, Rupert? Of course, we could make Lucifer angels. What do you say, my lad?"

Lucifer angels did not look very different from real snow angels to Caroline, except that they were made with a great deal less care so that snow went flying and blurred some of the outlines.

"Now," Uncle Timothy said at last, slapping snow off his greatcoat, "what was it someone said a while ago about chocolate and a nice warm fire?"

Caroline realized suddenly how cold she was. And how tired she was. She yawned without putting a hand over her mouth or silencing the sound. Nurse would have reproved her if she had seen and heard. Aunt Ursula merely smiled and stooped down to pick her up.

"Tired, sweetheart?" she asked. "We have played hard. We will have you warm and dry in no time at all."

But Uncle Timothy was there beside them before Caroline could snuggle her head against Aunt Ursula's shoulder. "Here," he said, "I will take her. She is too heavy for you."

He reached out his arms and set them about Caroline, but before he lifted her against him and right inside his greatcoat where she could feel his warmth and smell that pleasant snuffy smell again, he looked into Aunt Ursula's face and she looked back. They must have been cross-eyed, they were so close, Caroline thought. She did not know why they stared at each other so quietly or why both their arms went stiff about her. They did not say anything or smile or laugh. Caroline yawned once more.

And then she was up high once more with Uncle Timothy and feeling thoroughly safe again. And warmer. And they were going inside for cups of chocolate.

It was wonderful. It was the most wonderful time in all her life.

She was feeling decidedly uncomfortable. Because she was feeling altogether too cozy and comfortable. A bewildering paradox.

It was time to dress for dinner, but she had not made a move yet. Neither had he. And she felt the treacherous desire to prolong the moment and either be late for dinner—something she was never ill-bred enough to be—or else go down without changing, something she had never done, even when dining alone in her own home.

She was sitting in a deep chair in the nursery on one side of the fire, Caroline cuddled in her lap. *He* was sitting in a matching chair at the other side of the fire, his arm about the waist of Patricia, who was sitting on the arm beside him, and his free hand on Rupert's head as the boy sat on the floor in front of him, leaning back against his legs.

It was an unbearably domestic scene.

They had started as two groups. She was to read Caroline a story. The other children were talking to Timothy—to Lord Morsey—about anything and everything. But she had discovered that the only available books contained moral and dull tales intended for the improvement of children's minds. And so she had closed the books and told a story instead—a story she had not realized was in her, all about wizards and witches and enchanted, animated forests and the inevitable prince and princess.

Before she was very far into it, she was aware of silence at the other side of the fireplace and realized that she had an audience of three children. Before she had finished, a few glances across to the other chair revealed that the man too was listening, his head back against the chair, his lazy eyes fixed on her.

It might have been their own home, she thought treacherously, and their own nursery. These might have been their own children and this might have been a regular daily ritual. He might have been her husband. Her companion. Her lover. When he had touched her outdoors earlier, his one arm coming about Caroline pushing beneath her own, his other arm brushing across her breasts, and when he had turned his head to look at her, his face a mere few inches from her own . . . No!

"And so," she said, "they lived happily ever after."

Caroline sighed with contentment.

"That was the most beautiful story I have ever heard," Patricia said with a matching sigh.

"I liked the part where the tree reached down its branches and caught the wizard and tangled him up forever," Rupert said.

Viscount Morsey looked sleepy. And hopelessly attractive. Damn him! She was glad he had used the word the evening before. Just thinking it was a great relief to the feelings. And then he yawned. Perhaps, she thought, he had some reason for being tired. When she had returned to the nursery after an afternoon rest—an unaccustomed thing with her, necessitated by the morning of vigorous outdoor play—he had been down on all fours, an imitation horse being ridden by his two nieces. He had even been whinnying.

She felt frightened suddenly. She had come down here to make some rational decisions about the future of her brother's children, to take them back to London with her until some more satisfactory arrangement could be made. She had not expected Lord Morsey to come, but when she had seen his carriage and then him, she had expected that they would coolly and sensibly arrange things between them. She had hoped that he could be persuaded to house the children in one of his country homes and that her own responsibility to them would be reduced to some monetary assistance and the occasional visit.

She had certainly not expected this. Even when they had decided last evening to give the children a real Christmas despite the fact that they were all in mourning, she had not expected this sense of personal involvement, this sense of—of *family*. She was feeling almost maternal. She had thought such feelings long dead. She would not have expected that she could feel fond of children, at least not to the extent of doing things with them.

What could be more tedious than having to spend time with children? Or so she would have thought yesterday. And would think tomorrow, she thought firmly. Was she forgetting the thoroughly satisfactory life she had made for herself in London?

"Tomorrow is Christmas Eve," Viscount Morsey said.

"What is Christmas Eve?" Caroline asked.

"It is the day before Christmas, silly," Rupert said. "The day after tomorrow is Christmas. But there is to be no Christmas this year. Nurse said so. It would be disrespectful to Mama and Papa."

The lazy contentment of the moment had been shattered. Rupert leaned forward, away from the viscount's legs and hand. Patricia sat more upright on the arm of the chair, her shoulders hunched. Caroline was silent and big-eyed.

"There is always Christmas," Lady Carlyle said quietly. "It is the birthday of Jesus. Do you know the story?"

"He was born in a manger," Patricia said.

"In Bethlehem," Rupert added. "Nurse told us."

"There was a star," Caroline whispered.

Her aunt hugged her more tightly. "I will tell you the story again, tomorrow," she said.

"And tomorrow," Viscount Morsey said, "we will go out and gather what greenery we can find in the snow to decorate the house. And your Aunt Ursula will talk to the cook about cooking a goose and baking mince pies. We will sing carols and go to church in the evening if you can all stay awake long enough. It would be disrespectful not to celebrate the birthday of Jesus."

"And presents?" Patricia's voice was almost a wail.

"Presents?" Caroline echoed her sister on a mere breath of sound.

"Of course there will be no presents," Rupert said, using the elder brother voice he tended to use when he was not forgetting himself and being the child he really was. "Nurse said so. Besides, presents come from Mama and Papa, and they have passed on."

"I think Mama and Papa would want you to be happy on Christmas Day," their uncle said. "And since they can no longer give you presents themselves, I believe they would be happy if someone else did instead. Perhaps someone else will. Shall we enjoy Christmas Eve tomorrow and hope that there will be presents on Christmas Day?"

None of the children said anything. They merely stared at him. Lady Carlyle found herself swallowing hard more than once. They were children—innocent, vulnerable children, totally at the mercy of people and circumstances beyond their own control. And yet she had resented their existence when word came of the death of her brother. She had resented her own responsibility for them. She had hoped that they would conveniently be sent far away from London, where she would not have to concern herself with them beyond a courtesy visit once or twice a year. She still wished it. She did not want anything to change her life. She liked her life the way it was.

He must have brought presents too, she thought. Otherwise he would not be raising the children's hopes like this. He had talked of setting up his nursery within the next few years. Was it just a duty thing with him, the desire to have an heir to succeed him? Did he still *want* children? But if so, why had he waited nine years since their betrothal ended? Was this what he was going to be like with his own children?

She felt slightly sick at the thought. Who would share them with him? Who would lie with him and take his seed? Who would bear them for him? *Them?* Would there be four, two boys and two girls? Would he sit thus in the nursery with his own children and their mother?

She swallowed again and heard a gurgle in her throat that drew Caroline's eyes. She smiled. "It is time for your Aunt Ursula to change for dinner," she said. "And it is almost your bedtime."

The child scrambled off her lap.

"When Mama was home once," Patricia said, "she came to our rooms and tucked us in and kissed us good night. I remember. I'll always remember. Caroline was only a baby. She would not remember. Mama was pretty."

Yes, she had been. Marjorie had been exceedingly pretty. Adrian, who had probably never spared a single thought to marriage, took one look at Timothy's young sister and decided to pay her serious court. Or he learned of her large dowry and laid siege to her person in order to acquire it for himself. Which had it been? Lady Carlyle had never been sure. She still was not. For years she had not given him the benefit of the doubt on even one count.

"After dinner," she said, "I shall come up and tuck you in and kiss you good night. May I?"

Patricia smiled eagerly at her. Rupert looked slightly wistful. Caroline gazed up at her and clung to a fistful of her skirt.

"And I shall come too," Viscount Morsey said, "to make sure that no corner of the blankets has been left hanging. We must be tidy about such things."

Rupert chuckled and the girls turned their smiles on him. Caroline giggled in the totally gleeful way that had quite turned Lady Carlyle's heart over the first time she heard it outside.

Lord Morsey was on his feet too. "My lady?" he said, offering his arm. "Allow me to escort you to your dressing room."

She wished it could have been avoided. She hated having to touch him. She had been wise to stay as far away from him as possible for so many years. Her heart had been at peace for many of those years. She wanted it to remain so.

He bowed formally when they were outside her door, and released her arm. He moved on to his own room next door without a word.

She wished his room did not have to be so close to her own. She had imagined the night before that she had heard his every movement in bed. And in her imagination she had pictured him there, warm, asleep, tousled. Male.

She closed her eyes briefly and entered her dressing room. She was going to be very late for dinner if she did not hurry.

They had scraped through dinner with the sort of conversation that was second nature to them both. They had both contrived to settle their eyes on the silver bowl of fruit in the center of the table when good manners dictated that they lift their eyes from their plates. Doubtless she had been as thankful as he that the table was rather long and that the butler had placed them at either end of it.

She looked incredibly beautiful. Black was unbecoming on most women, sapping them of color and youth and character. With her red hair and the heightened color that several hours in the outdoors had brought, her black gown looked spectacular. She still had the figure and complexion of a girl, but age had added dignity and beauty.

They had gone up to the children afterward. She had gone into the girls' room while he had gone to bid Rupert good night. Rupert had been crying and had dived beneath the bedclothes when he saw his uncle coming. He did not know what was to become of them. He still thought they would be sent to an orphanage. He did not know how he was to make his fortune in order to provide for his sisters.

Lord Morsey had had to resist the urge to take the child into his arms. It would have been the wrong thing to do. He had sat on the edge of his bed instead and agreed that they had a mutual problem, since they were the two men of the family. He could no longer provide for *his* sister, he had explained, but he could provide

for her children and would do so for a time since he
was a man already and already had a fortune. Perhaps
Rupert could do his part by loving his sisters now, by
learning his lessons well so that he could grow into an
educated and informed gentleman, and by doing his
part to settle his sisters well in life when they had all
grown up.

Rupert had dried his tears and they had shaken
hands on their gentlemen's agreement. One thing was
clear, Lord Morsey had thought as he went to the girls'
room. He was not going to be able to abandon the children on one of his estates with only a competent nurse
for company. Had he really ever intended any such
thing?

"In tears," he had muttered to Lady Carlyle, mo-
tioning with his head in the direction of Rupert's room.
"Uncertainty about how he is to provide for his sisters.
Treat him like a man."

"In tears," she had murmured in reply, her eyes indicating Patricia in bed behind her. "Realizing that
Marjorie is never coming back." She had hurried from
the room.

The little one had been gazing up at him with her
huge eyes. Patricia had been lying with closed eyes
and composed face.

"Good night, Caroline," he had said softly, leaning
over her and touching the back of one finger to her
soft, plump cheek. Who knew what went on in the
mind of a shy, imaginative infant? "You are going to
be safe forever and ever. Uncle Timothy and Aunt Ursula are going to see that you are always safe."

She had not smiled or answered. She had yawned
hugely.

Patricia had not moved or opened her eyes when he

turned to her. He guessed that Lady Carlyle must have said something to comfort her.

"Your mama was the prettiest little thing when she was your age," he had said. "She had Caroline's hair and your face. She was my sister just as you and Caroline are Rupert's. I loved her dearly."

Her eyelids fluttered and lifted. "Aunt Ursula said that Papa took one look at her and fell in love with her," she had said.

Or with her dowry. But who was he to know what had motivated Adrian Parr's determined courtship of a giddy seventeen-year-old?

He had smiled. "I remember a time . . ." He had told her childhood memories he had forgotten himself until he started to talk.

And now they were sitting in the drawing room, he and Lady Carlyle, sipping tea and making conversation again like two civilized strangers. Except that the silences between topics were lengthening. Yet from the look on her face, he guessed that she was unaware of any awkwardness.

"What is it?" he asked when she looked up at him with vacant eyes after one such silence.

Her eyes focused on him. "Nothing," she said.

He should have left it at that. He did not want any part of her life. Not now. Not when it had taken so many years to purge her from his own.

"It seems to be a night for sadness," he said. "My guess is that we gave the children a happy day and released them from the deadness within that has been instilled in them over years of instruction on propriety. Tears at the end of what was to be a day of enjoyment. Did we do the wrong thing, do you suppose?"

He thought she was not going to answer. She stared away from him, across the room. "No," she said at last.

"No. They had parents, however little they saw of them. They were an anchor, a source of security. If the loss of those things is left dormant inside them, it might do them irreparable harm. I think the tears were necessary. And perhaps healing. We can only hope so."

"I will take them," he said abruptly, surprising himself. "You need not worry about having your way of life upset or about unwelcome demands being made on your time or your resources. I will have them to live with me, wherever I am."

"Oh, no, you will not." Her eyes flashed at him and her hair glowed. He would swear it glowed brighter. "They are my nephew and nieces as well as yours, I would remind you, my lord. *I* will have them to live with *me*. You may visit them occasionally. And my resources are quite adequate to the raising of three children. I am a wealthy woman now, if you did not know it."

"Hm." He leaned back in his chair and regarded her angry face. "Perhaps we will have to allow our lawyers to handle this matter, Ursula. But we will not wrangle over the children. They are people, not property."

"Precisely," she said, but the anger died from her eyes and she visibly relaxed. Her eyes became vacant once more.

"What is it?" he asked again softly.

Her eyes came to his and lingered there. "I have been so judgmental," she said. "I have allowed myself to stifle love in order to do what was right and proper."

His heart jumped uncomfortably until she continued. "He gambled away my childhood home," she said. "I felt as if part of my identity had gone, my roots. I could not forgive him. And then he would come asking for things, begging loans. Always *loans*. And he ruined my life." She bit her lip and closed her eyes, perhaps realizing what she had admitted. "He was always weak and wayward and careless and selfish. But I used to love him. He was my only brother. And maybe I was wrong about one thing at least. Maybe he loved her. Do you think he did?"

"I have pondered the same question," he said. "When I discovered that the money I had given Marjorie to feed the children—there were only two then—had been squandered across a gaming table, I told her never to come back. I told her my doors would be closed to her forever after and that any letters she sent would be returned unread. It was no idle threat. And they deserved such treatment from both of us— perhaps. But she was my only sister. I taught her to ride and to swim and to climb trees. As a very young child she had a giggle like Caroline's. Did he marry her for her dowry? I thought so at the time, as did you, though you would not admit as much to me. Or did he love her? They were utterly selfish and they neglected their children. But perhaps they loved each other. They were always together, even at the end."

"I wish," she said, "that I could go back and tell him that there would be no more money but that my door would always be open to both of them for friendship and comfort and love. I wish I had known their children from the start."

"We cannot go back," he said.

"No."

He was aware that she was crying only when she got sharply to her feet and turned in the direction of the door. But taking that direction would have brought her past his chair. She turned jerkily instead to stand facing the fire.

"Oh." She laughed shakily. "I must have got something in my eye." She dabbed at it—and the other one—with her handkerchief.

He got to his feet and took the few steps that separated them. He set his hands on her shoulders from behind. "I think you were right, Ursula," he said. "I think the sadness of the evening has come from the happiness of the day. By deliberately stopping ourselves from mourning them in the conventional way today, we have realized their absence. And we have remembered that they were persons and that they touched our lives and that they gave life to those three children upstairs. Selfish and irresponsible as they were, it is right that they should be mourned fully at last. You need not be ashamed of your tears."

He expected that she would turn into his arms. And if she had done so, he would have held her there and comforted both her and himself. But he was glad when she did not. He did not want her in his arms. He did not want them to share grief that closely, that intimately. He felt her bringing herself gradually under control.

"You are right," she said at last. "Thank you."

But he could not quite leave it at that. His emotions had been rubbed raw. And she had once meant a great deal to him. All the world.

"Why did you not wait for me to come back to you, Ursula?" he asked. "You knew I would have come. Why did you not come back to me?"

She spun around, her eyes wide and watery and rather red. "Wait?" Her voice was incredulous. "You would have come back? You expected me . . . ? I would have spat in your face."

"It was a love match with Carlyle, then?" he asked. It had seemed incredible, but he had always wondered.

Not that he had ever really wanted to know the answer. Not until recently. It could no longer hurt now.

"Of course it was a love match," she said, but her eyes slipped slightly lower than his. "Of course. What did you think?"

"And it was a good marriage?" he asked. Carlyle had moved in different circles from his own. He had never liked the man—perhaps because he was Ursula's husband. He could not put a finger to any other reason for the antipathy he had felt for a man who had appeared to be perfectly amiable.

"Yes, it was a good marriage," she said. "It was very good. The best. It was wonderful. It was the best thing I ever did."

Her eyes were haunted. Because Carlyle had died and the wonderful marriage was at an end? Or because she was lying? If it had been so wonderful, would she not have told him to mind his own business?

"Not that my marriage is any of your concern," she added.

"No," he said. "Since it is not also my marriage, it is none of my concern. I must be thankful for that at least. Two more days and then, weather permitting, we can think of leaving here. I will take the children and you can return to the life you enjoy so well. Can we remain civil for two days, do you suppose? I think we have done rather well today."

"I have never found civility difficult," she said stiffly. "And they will be returning with *me*. You may arrange for your lawyer to call upon mine in London, my lord. But I warn you of a stiff battle ahead."

"On which amiable note I shall offer you my arm, my lady, and escort you to your room," he said. "I would hate for us to prolong the evening only to find that we spoil the day by quarreling."

"An admirable idea," she said, taking his arm almost vengefully and fairly marching in the direction of the door.

The trouble with Ursula, he thought ruefully, was that she was always temptingly desirable when she was angry. Yet somehow he was going to have to get himself a good night's sleep in a bed that must be only a few feet from her own. It was a good thing, at least, that there was a thick wall between those two beds.

A very good thing.

They left the baby sleeping in his cot in the nursery. Nurse was going to look after him, in case he woke up and cried while they were gone. They would not be gone long. It was important that they be back soon so that he would see that he had a mama and a papa and a brother and two sisters and so that he could know that they would never be gone from him for long. Especially Mama and Papa. They would always be there for him when he went to sleep and when he woke up. They would always make snow dragons with him and laugh with him and keep him warm inside their greatcoats and tell him they would keep him safe forever and ever.

And she would tell him the same things. She was his elder sister and she would look after him. He would never have to wake up, as she had sometimes done, to wonder where Mama and Papa were. They would be there, in the house. The baby had red hair, like Patricia's, and blue eyes, like Rupert's. His hair curled like her own. And he sucked his thumb. That was not a bad thing to do. She knew it brought him comfort. When he was older, she would explain to him that only babies sucked their thumbs and he would stop. But now he was a baby.

His name was Jesus.

They were going to get a surprise party ready for him. That was what they were doing now. That was why they had had to leave him sleeping in the nursery. It was to be tomorrow, a birthday party, though he was a very tiny little baby.

Christmas Day was his birthday.

She was riding up on top of the world, far above Rupert and Patricia and even Aunt Ursula. She was riding on Uncle Timothy's shoulder, her arm firmly about his head. She was pushing his hat so far forward that he laughed and told the others to lead him by the hand because he was a blind man.

And then they came to the holly bushes, and she was set down with the others while Uncle Timothy cut some bunches of it for them to take back to the house for the party. Only the holly leaves were sharp—she should have warned him but did not think of it until it was too late—and he yelled out that he had pricked his finger and might well bleed to death. He put his finger in his mouth and sucked on it after pulling off his glove. Aunt Ursula told him not to be so foolish, that he was frightening Caroline. But she was wrong. Caroline knew that he was only pretending.

And then they trudged over to the evergreens and Uncle Timothy cut down some of the smaller boughs that they could carry back with them.

"Not too many," he said, "or we will destroy the trees—or else make them look so lopsided that someone will take pity on them and chop them down."

Rupert, with spread arms and bent back and crossed eyes and lolling tongue, became a lopsided tree and staggered about as someone tried to chop him down. Nurse would have told him sharply to mind his behavior and to act his age. But Uncle Timothy chuckled and

Patricia became another lopsided tree. Caroline tried it too. It was fun. It was even more fun when Uncle Timothy joined in and actually toppled over into the snow as he was felled.

"Really," Aunt Ursula said, her hands on her hips, "I have never witnessed such undignified behavior in my life."

But there was something in her face that Uncle Timothy must have seen too. "You cannot scold and laugh at the same time, my lady," he said. "The effect of the scolding is immediately nullified."

And so Aunt Ursula laughed and said she had some strange, strange relatives and they must get it from *his* side of the family. Uncle Timothy said that it was fortunate, then, that everything had not come from *her* side, and for a moment Caroline was puzzled. There was something behind the words and the laughter that she did not quite understand. But it passed almost before she could think it. Aunt Ursula threw a snowball that knocked his hat sideways, and the fight was on again. Only this time they did not throw snowballs at Uncle Timothy but jumped on him while he was still on the ground—all except Aunt Ursula—and tried to roll him in the snow.

They all got rolled in the snow instead. Caroline giggled so hard that she thought she was not going to be able to catch her breath.

"Enough," Aunt Ursula said at last. "You are the unruliest child of the lot, Timothy."

Uncle Timothy turned his back on her as he slapped snow off himself and pulled a face at them so that they giggled all the harder.

And then he thought of mistletoe. Christmas would just not be Christmas without mistletoe, he declared, and so they went tramping off to find some, leaving the holly and the fir boughs on the ground to be picked up later. But mistletoe was not easy to find. It did not grow by itself, like holly and fir trees. Caroline grew anxious and took Aunt Ursula's hand when it was offered. They *must* find some if it was so essential for Christmas. The party tomorrow must be perfect.

But all was well. Aunt Ursula herself spotted some on two old oak trees that grew side by side, and Uncle Timothy and Rupert climbed up—Caroline had to hide her face against Aunt Ursula's cloak for fear they would fall—in order to gather some. It was a relief when they were down again, but they had the precious mistletoe with them, so the baby's birthday party would not be ruined after all.

Uncle Timothy looked at her and grinned. "The trouble is," he said, "that not all mistletoe is Christmas mistletoe. I will have to try it out to see if it works."

She felt instant anxiety again. If this was not Christmas mistletoe, where were they to find some that was? Uncle Timothy stooped down on his haunches, raised his arm above her head with some of the mistletoe in it, and kissed her lips. Caroline gazed at him. His nose against her cheek had been cold.

"Yes," he said. "It works perfectly."

Caroline breathed a sigh of relief.

"Of course," he said, turning his smile on Patricia, "it is as well to be quite sure. A man has to be able to kiss ladies beneath the mistletoe, you see. Let me see if it works with Patricia too."

It did. It really was Christmas mistletoe, then. But perhaps they should be quite, quite sure. She tugged on Uncle Timothy's greatcoat and tipped her head right back so that she could gaze up at him.

"Try it on Aunt Ursula," she whispered.

She should have kept quiet. She could see from the

expression on his face as he looked back down at her that he did not want to try it on Aunt Ursula, and she could see when she looked across at her aunt that Aunt Ursula was looking quite dismayed. And if it had worked on both her and Patricia, it must be Christmas mistletoe.

"A good idea," Uncle Timothy said. "One must be thorough about such important matters."

Aunt Ursula had backed up against one of the trees, her hands behind her on the trunk. Caroline had the impression that she would have liked to press right through the tree, but it could not be done. Uncle Timothy stepped up close to her, raised the mistletoe, and kissed her. He took rather longer doing it than he had done with her and Patricia, and when he had finished he did not immediately move back or say anything. Neither did Aunt Ursula. They stared into each other's eyes, and Caroline started to worry again. Maybe the mistletoe did not work after all and they would have to keep hunting. But Uncle Timothy turned and grinned when first Rupert and then Patricia snickered and giggled.

"Well," he said, "that settles that. It certainly does work. There is no doubt about it—this is Christmas mistletoe."

But his voice was breathless and Aunt Ursula's lips were trembling and she looked as if she might burst into tears at any moment. There was something Caroline did not understand, but it was not a *bad* thing, she was sure. And the mistletoe had worked.

They started back for the house then, carrying as much of their decorations as they could. Uncle Timothy was going to come back for the rest. They were going to decorate the drawing room. All of them, Caroline too. Aunt Ursula said they would pick her up so that she could help deck the mantel and the pictures with holly. They did not tell her, as Nurse often did, that she was too little and would be in the way and that it would be quicker to do things while she stood back and watched.

She thought her Aunt Ursula and Uncle Timothy were the most wonderful people in the world. She loved them.

She was glad they were the baby's mama and papa. She was glad they were *her* mama and papa and Rupert's and Patricia's. She was glad they were one family and would all live together forever and ever.

"Amen," she whispered.

She was searching for sanity. Only two days ago she had been traveling down from London and she had been entirely herself. She had been confident and contented—except that she had had a problem to deal with. She had known who she was and she had been happy with the way her life was developing. Two days ago she had lived her life according to reason rather than feelings. Living on one's emotions was a dreadful way to live. She had stopped living that way years before and she had been happier for it.

Two days ago she had stepped out of her carriage and found herself in a different world. Perhaps in a different universe. She was no longer certain of anything and her mind was in too much of a turmoil for her to be contented. She was no longer sure that her former life—former! As if it were all years or eons ago—was not dull and barren. In this world, in this universe, she was living very much on her emotions, and there was something dreadfully unsettling about it. And something rather wonderful too. She had discovered that she liked children after all. She had discovered that she *loved* these three children. She could not bear the thought of being separated from them again after Christmas, and yet she was sure that *he* would fight her for them.

She would fight him tooth and nail.

She had been so sure that no man could ever arouse her feelings again, so sure that she could never desire a man again. And she had liked it that way. Life had been peaceful for a number of years, especially since Carlyle's death.

But *he* had kissed her beneath the mistletoe outdoors in full view of the children, and even this new universe had tipped upside down. Throughout the walk home and the couple of hours they had spent decorating the drawing room and the extra couple of hours it had taken to fashion and paint a large wooden star to hang beside the mistletoe in front of the fire because Caroline had asked about a star with an irresistibly wistful look in her eyes—throughout all that, she had been intensely aware of him, of his attractiveness, of his maleness. And her body was reacting to him in a way it had not really reacted since Vauxhall. Even on her wedding night it had not reacted so.

She wanted him. She wanted to feel his mouth on hers again. She wanted to feel his body against her own. She wanted his hands on her. She wanted him inside her body. She wanted him there even though her only experiences with intimacy—during the first month of her marriage—had been disappointing at best, distasteful at worst.

She wanted him. But she could not want him. When she was back, in her own world—within the next few days—she would no longer want him. Her life would return to normal.

But she wanted babies of her own. Her body ached

for the experience of motherhood as it had not for almost nine years. But she was seven-and-twenty already. It was too late. She would never be a mother.

She wanted *his* child. He would make such a wonderful father.

And so she searched for sanity as they set out for church during the evening. They walked, since the distance was not great and the snow was still deep. Rupert and Patricia held her hands while Caroline rode in Timothy's arms, his greatcoat wrapped about her for extra warmth.

If she did not hold very firmly to sanity, she thought as they took their seats in a pew close to the front and admired the Nativity scene set up before the altar and listened to the bells ringing from the bell tower—if she did not keep very firm touch with reality, she was going to start imagining that they really were a family. Caroline had been transferred to her lap. Patricia was at one side of her; Rupert was at one side of Timothy. But they were next to each other, their shoulders almost touching. She could feel his body heat. She could smell the snuff he used and the soap.

Christmas had always been an enjoyable time because it was a time of heightened social activities and extra feasting. Church attendance had always been pleasant because everyone who had stayed in town was there, most of them at the same church, and they always lingered to talk afterward. She had always enjoyed the holiday.

She had never realized fully until now that it was a holiday for families. That it was about birth and parenthood and love. And about hope and commitment. She realized it tonight.

And sanity disappeared without a trace.

By the time the service ended, Caroline was asleep against her bosom, her mouth slack about the thumb she had sucked, and Patricia was sleeping against her arm. Rupert was leaning against Timothy's, but he was awake and sat up valiantly.

"Can you carry her?" Timothy asked, turning his head, only inches away from her own, and nodding down at Caroline. "I'll take Patricia."

And so they walked home side by side, each carrying a child, while Rupert trudged along between them, firmly denying that he was tired. And they carried the girls up to the nursery, and she stayed to help their nurse undress them and put them to bed. She kissed them and smiled tenderly at them, even though they were both more than half-asleep.

"Good night, Aunt Ursula," Patricia murmured.

"The party is tomorrow?" Caroline asked sleepily. She yawned. "The baby will be surprised. Won't he, Mama?"

She touched the backs of her fingers to the child's hair and wondered what dreamland she was in. Something ached in the back of her throat.

"Wonderfully surprised," she said before going into Rupert's room to wish him a good night and to assure him in answer to his question that yes, she really believed there might be presents in the morning for his sisters. And maybe for him too.

She met Timothy in the hall outside the bedrooms and took his offered arm. But he led her toward the stairs instead of to her room, late as the hour was.

"Christmas punch," he said, "before we retire for the night."

She allowed him to lead her downward without protest. But there was a decision to make, she sensed.

Soon. Sanity or madness. She tried to tell herself to be strong and to remain sane.

But she wanted to be mad. Mad now and ever after.

She had hurt him badly once. Very badly. He had even wondered for a while if he would survive, though he had realized even at the time that the thought was rather ridiculous. One did not die of a broken heart. And the fault had been in large measure his. He had lashed out at her when Marjorie had eloped with her brother with accusations that could almost make his hair stand on end in retrospect.

The difference was that with him it had been merely temper. With her it had been actual dislike and indifference. She had turned to another man as if their relationship had never been and had married him and presumably lived happily with him for seven years.

He did not care to recall the pain she had left him in. It was a pain he had vowed would never be repeated. He would never allow himself to love again.

Just two days ago the mere sight of her had irritated him. He had wanted nothing to do with her. And the two days had progressed anything but smoothly. They had been civil to each other for the sake of the children, but hostility had poked through the thin veneer of civility on occasion.

He must keep his lips firmly buttoned up until they could get away from each other within the next couple of days. He would be able to see things clearly enough once he was back in his own world—with the children. There was no way on this earth she was going to take the children away from him.

He loved them.

Why the devil had he brought her downstairs for punch, he asked himself, when it was after midnight and he did not wish to be alone with her? He retrieved his arm when they entered the drawing room, forgot all about the punch, which was warm and inviting in a bowl on the sideboard, and crossed the room to stand unconsciously beneath the mistletoe—and the Christmas star—and rest an elbow on the mantel. He stared into the flames of the fire.

"They need parents, Ursula," he heard himself say. "Not a mother. Not a father. Both. Parents. Plural."

"Yes," she said softly from somewhere behind him.

And he knew that he had stepped irrevocably into the unknown.

"You and me," he said.

"Yes."

His hand opened and closed against the mantel. "Not for a few months with one and then a few with the other," he said. "With both of us in one house all the time."

"Yes."

What the devil was he saying? What the devil was he doing? But whatever it was, it was too late now to go back. He could think of nothing more to say except the final words. The final question.

But they hated each other, did they not?

He turned his head and looked at her. She was standing in the middle of the room, her arms at her sides. Her face was pale. Her eyes looked haunted.

"Ursula," he asked her, "why did you marry him?"

"I don't know." He watched her swallow. "There was scandal. There might well have been ostracism. You were gone. There was so much pain. And he asked me. It—it seemed like a good idea."

"Poor devil," he said, though he could still feel nothing but intense dislike for her late husband.

"I believe he used me too," she said. "We deserved

each other. It was not—well, not really a marriage. Not after the first few weeks. There were no children. There was not really"—she flushed—"not really the possibility."

In seven years Carlyle had bedded her for only the first few weeks? *Why?*

"We rubbed along well enough together," she said. "We both had what we wanted out of the marriage, I believe."

"What was it you wanted?" he asked her.

"Peace," she said. "I wanted to stop feeling. Feelings hurt. Love hurts."

"Yes," he said.

Her eyes were filled with pain suddenly. "You said you would have come back," she said. "Would you?"

"Of course I would have come back," he said. "I loved you. I suffered hell on your wedding night."

"Ah." She covered her face with her hands.

"Did you really believe it was all over?" he asked her.

"Yes." Her voice was dull and low against her hands.

"What were your feelings?" He had picked up her agony.

"I did not want to live," she said. "I did not know how I was to drag myself through another fifty years or so of living."

There was a long silence, which he had no idea how to break. She stood where she was and kept her hands over her face.

"Ursula," he said at last and waited for her to look up at him with suffering eyes. He reached out his free arm. "Come here."

She came slowly and did not stop until her body rested against his own and her face was nestled in the

folds of his neckcloth. He felt her draw in a deep
breath and let it out slowly through her mouth. He
closed his arms about her.

"If we do what you suggest for the children," she
said, "it will be just for their sakes. Will it not?"

He understood the uncertainty behind the question,
the need for reassurance. The need for him to say the
hardest three words in the language to string together.
Though he had had no problem with them once.

"The children are more important than you or I," he
said. "Their need for love and security and parents to
lean on is almost a tangible thing. We can supply that
need, and we must."

"Yes," she said.

He lowered his head to rub his cheek across her hair.
It was as soft and silky as he remembered it.

"They will be our family," she said. "Almost as we
planned it. But—"

"But?" he said when she did not continue.

Her hands clutched the lapels of his coat. Tightly.

"I wish I had waited for you to come," she said. "I
wish I had known that you would come. We might
have loved and had a family of your own. It is too late
now."

"Too late?" He took her by the upper arms and
moved her back far enough that he could look down
into her face. "How old are you, Ursula? Seven-and-
twenty? Eight-and-twenty?"

"Seven," she said.

"I was unaware," he said, "that a woman's fertile
years are over so soon. And I have not noticed any tendency to impotence in myself even though I have
passed my thirtieth birthday."

She blushed and her hands reached for the top button of his waistcoat. Just like Caroline. Her eyes watched her hands.

He lowered his head close to hers. "Maybe we should try," he murmured to her, "and find out if even at our advanced ages we can produce a child of our own. Shall we?"

She bit her lower lip.

"Or children," he said. "Shall we be really clever and try to produce two? Or four? Boy, girl—"

"—boy, girl," she finished for him and laughed softly, though her eyes and her hands were still on his button.

"Don't twist too hard," he said. "My valet will be inordinately cross if I take a waistcoat upstairs with me minus one button."

Her hands stilled and she set her forehead against them.

"Timothy," she said, "these two days have been the happiest of my life."

He listened to her in some surprise. But she was right. They had been the happiest of his too. And that included all of the three months between his first meeting with her and the breaking of their betrothal.

"And of mine," he said. There was a short pause. "Shall I say it first?"

"Yes, please," she said. "I will feel foolish if I say it first and it turns out that you were not about to say that at all."

"But it is all right for me to make an idiot of myself," he said. He rubbed his chin across the top of her head. "I love you, Ursula."

"I love you, Timothy," she said so quickly that they finished almost together.

"Will you marry me?" he asked. "Do you want it on one knee?"

"No," she said. "How foolish. And yes. No for the bended knee, that is, and yes for marrying you. Will we regret it, do you suppose? When Christmas is over and we are back home and all this is a memory?"

"The children will not be gone when Christmas is over," he said. "And my love will not be gone. Or yours. It never did die, did it, just as mine did not."

"No." She sighed and lifted her face at last to look at him. Oh, so close. "It never did. The only way I could deal with it was to kill all feeling in myself. And convince myself that what I felt—or did not feel—was peace and contentment. I never stopped loving you. I never will."

He swallowed. If this was unreality, he never wanted the real world back. He closed the gap of a few inches between their mouths.

They moaned in unison and then had to pull back in order to laugh together. And to gaze into each other's eyes.

And to return to the serious business of embracing.

A long time later he raised his head and sighed. "I believe we had better go up to bed," he said. "Separately, though doing so may well kill me and you too if I am reading the signs correctly. But it would be in bad taste to take to the floor here—a notion that has crossed both our minds during the past several minutes. And in bad taste to share the same bed in our nephew and nieces' house. Can you wait until our wedding night?"

"How long?" she asked.

"Approximately twenty-four hours after the soonest moment we can return to London," he said.

"Will you spring your horses?" she asked.

"Actually," he said, "I am going to get them to spread their wings."

He touched noses with her and they both laughed at the absurdity.

"We will make love for the first time on our wedding night," he said. "Sleep now and for the next few nights while you can. I shall be keeping you busy once we are married."

"Will you?" She buried her face against his neckcloth briefly once more. "How wonderful that sounds. Promise?"

He chuckled and hugged her tightly to him before releasing her and offering his arm.

"Propriety, my lady," he said. "Propriety."

"Yes, my lord," she said meekly, laying her arm along the top of his.

They walked upstairs in silence. He kissed her outside the door to her room and reluctantly stepped away from her. Her eyes were shining so with love that for a moment he felt weak-kneed.

"Happy Christmas, Timothy," she said.

"Happy Christmas, Ursula," he said, making her a half bow. "The mistletoe works quite superbly, by the way."

"Sweetheart."

"My love."

They laughed quietly. Their laughter sounded little different from the children's giggles earlier in the day. They were being childish. It felt wonderful. He blew her a kiss. She blew one right back.

He opened his own door and stepped inside.

"Enough," he said.

"Agreed."

She closed her door before he did.

Nurse had helped them dress and had brushed her curls and was combing Patricia's hair more carefully.

She was telling Patricia not to squirm, but she was saying it in her kind voice. Patricia was too excited to sit still. Caroline was excited too, but she could keep excitement deep inside herself so that people would not call her silly.

And then Rupert came into their room. He was dressed and washed and combed and he was bursting with excitement too. He was usually not allowed to come into the girls' room. It was not proper, Nurse always said. But nothing was said today. Nurse even smiled at him as she bade him good morning.

"Do you think, Rupert?" Patricia asked him, her eyes meeting his in the mirror. "Do you think?"

"I am not sure," Rupert said. He switched to his man's voice. "I do not care as long as Caroline gets at least one. And I hope there is one for you too, Patricia."

"Oh, but I do not want one unless there is one for you," she said. "Caroline is the important one. She is only four."

Caroline knew they were talking about presents. But she did not really care if there were none. It was not her birthday, after all, but the baby's. And they had decorated the drawing room downstairs for him as a surprise. They were going to take him down there afterward and they were all going to wish him a happy birthday. And they were all going to kiss him and coo over him. She was going to spin the Christmas star for him to look up at. And Mama and Papa were going to be there, and he was going to feel safe.

She was going to feel safe. She already did. Papa had said he would keep her safe forever and ever. But the baby had not heard him.

"Aunt Ursula said she was almost sure there would be," Rupert said. His voice was his own again, and it was trembling so that Caroline knew that he very badly wanted for there to be presents. "For all of us."

"Oh," Patricia said on a sigh. "Do you think, Rupert? Do you think she is always right?"

"I think maybe she always is," Rupert said carefully.

And then the door opened again and Aunt Ursula and Uncle Timothy were there, hand in hand and smiling. Nurse left the room quietly.

"I think," Aunt Ursula said after they had all exchanged greetings, "you had better all come down to the drawing room. There are some strange parcels down there. And each of your names seems to be on more than one."

Patricia shrieked.

Rupert jumped up and down three times on the spot.

"Of course, if no one is interested . . ." Uncle Timothy said. He was grinning.

Rupert and Patricia collided in the doorway and disappeared from sight. Aunt Ursula laughed.

"Come, sweetheart," she said and reached out a hand to Caroline.

But Caroline hung back. "I have to go to the nursery," she said. "You go on and I will come after."

Both Aunt Ursula and Uncle Timothy looked closely at her. They were still holding hands, Caroline noticed. It looked nice.

"Very well," Uncle Timothy said. "We will hold back the troops downstairs until you come."

And so Caroline went to the nursery and tiptoed inside and leaned over the cot. The baby was looking up at her, his little fists waving in the air. She smiled at him and lifted him carefully into her arms. She carried him all the way downstairs, her arms held out carefully in front of her. She took the stairs slowly, one at a time, so that she would not trip and fall. They had left the door of the drawing room open for her.

"Here she is," Uncle Timothy said. He was standing by the fire, under the mistletoe. Aunt Ursula was beside him.

"Caroline. Look." Patricia's voice was still almost a shriek.

"Presents," Rupert cried in his dearest boy's voice. "For all of us, Caroline."

But Caroline stepped carefully into the room and looked neither to the right nor to the left.

"What is it?" Aunt Ursula asked gently.

"You have hurt your hands?" Uncle Timothy asked, a look of concern on his face.

"I have brought the baby," Caroline said.

"The baby." Aunt Ursula looked as if she did not understand. She glanced at Uncle Timothy and he glanced at her.

"It is his birthday party," Caroline said. "We decorated the room for him. Look, he is awake. He wants Mama."

"Mama?" Uncle Timothy looked puzzled for a moment longer, but only for a moment. Caroline could see that he understood then as she had known he would. And Aunt Ursula too. She leaned down and stretched out her arms.

"You had better hand him to me, then," she said. "My, what a beautiful baby." She took the baby carefully into her own arms and smiled down at him and rocked him. "Look at him, Timothy."

"He does not know that he has a mama and papa and that he will be kept safe forever and ever," Caroline explained. "But now he will know."

She was surprised when she saw that Aunt Ursula

was crying and that Uncle Timothy was blinking his eyes. But they were not sad tears. She could feel that.

"Yes, now he will know," Uncle Timothy said. "He will know that he has a mama and papa and a home where they will always be with him until he is a man. And that they will love him every day of his life. And his brother and his sisters too. His mama and papa are going to be married and live together always so that his family can always be together."

"We are really going to live with you?" Rupert said. "Always? There is *really* to be no orphanage?"

"We are going to be with you and play with you every day?" Patricia asked.

Aunt Ursula nodded and smiled. She would have wiped her tears away, Caroline knew, if she had not been holding the baby.

"What is the baby's name?" Patricia asked politely.

"Why, Jesus, of course," Aunt Ursula said before Caroline could open her mouth to speak.

"Under the Bethlehem star," Uncle Timothy said, glancing up, "where one would expect to find him."

"Caroline has such an imagination," Rupert said fondly but apologetically. "She will grow out of it."

"I hope not," Aunt Ursula said with a smile.

"And since this baby is too small to open presents or even appreciate them," Uncle Timothy said, "how about you children opening your parcels instead?"

Rupert and Patricia darted over to the window ledge and the parcels with whoops of delight. Caroline waited a few moments to watch Uncle Timothy smile into Aunt Ursula's eyes and lean carefully across the baby to kiss her on the lips.